Her Last Promise

Kathryn Hughes is the internationally bestselling author of *The Letter, The Secret, The Key* and *Her Last Promise*.

Her novels have been translated into 28 languages.

Kathryn lives with her husband near Manchester and has a son and a daughter.

Visit www.kathrynhughesauthor.com to find out more about Kathryn, follow her on Twitter @KHughesAuthor or find her on Facebook at www.facebook.com/KHughesAuthor.

By Kathryn Hughes

The Letter
The Secret
The Key
Her Last Promise

Praise for

THE KEY

'A wonderful, enthralling story; one that I didn't want to end' Lesley Pearse

'A heartbreakingly powerful read' *Sun*

'Un-put-downable with a twisting plot' *My Weekly*

'A fabulous read' *Woman's Weekly*

'A must-have' *Sunday Express*

'Impeccably researched' *Daily Mail*

'An intriguing and emotional tale with some surprising twists that will keep the reader absorbed throughout. Another winner' *People's Friend*

'Shocking, stirring' *Woman*

'A very atmospheric, heartbreaking and intriguing read that will shock and surprise you' *Alba in Bookland*

Praise for

THE SECRET

'An emotional and intriguing read . . . Keeps you guessing right to the end' *People's Friend*

'Gripping' *Good Housekeeping*

'Heart-warming and optimistic' *Jen Med's Book Reviews*

'A gripping and moving family drama that will tug at the reader's heart' *Writing* magazine

'A moving, emotional tale which will bring tears to your eyes and also a smile, this is a perfect Sunday afternoon read. Loved every bit of it!' *Peterborough Telegraph*

'Pulled me in right from the first page . . . I really enjoyed this book' *Rea's Book Reviews*

'I so thoroughly enjoyed this book, it was filled with all kinds of mystery, family secrets, [and] characters that really stood out' *Read Along With Sue*

'One that you just HAVE to finish' *Hollie in Wanderlust*

Praise for

THE LETTER

'A wonderful, uplifting story' Lesley Pearse

'Autumnal Sunday afternoons were invented to read heart-tugging novels like this' *Red*

'This moving love story had everyone talking . . . Get set to be hooked' *Look*

'A beautiful story . . . I didn't want to put it down' *Reviewed by Fran*

'A moving story of love, loss and hope' *Bella*

'You will find it hard to put down. I cried buckets of tears reading it' *Books With Wine And Chocolate*

'Beautifully written and incredibly poignant. You cannot fail to fall for this story' *The Last Word Book Reviews*

'The story kept me gripped . . . A breath of fresh air, and just what I needed after a long day in the office' *Here.You.Me*

Her Last Promise

Kathryn Hughes

REVIEW

First published in 2019
by HEADLINE REVIEW
An imprint of HEADLINE PUBLISHING GROUP

Cataloguing in Publication Data is available from the British Library

ISBN 978 1 4722 6593 7

Butterfly motif © Vladimirkarp/Shutterstock
Cross image © MicroOne/Shutterstock

Typeset in Garamond MT by Palimpsest Book Production Ltd,
Falkirk, Stirlingshire

Printed and bound in Great Britain by Clays Ltd, Elcograf S.p.A.

MIX
Paper from
responsible sources
FSC® C104740

HEADLINE PUBLISHING GROUP
An Hachette UK Company
Carmelite House
50 Victoria Embankment
London EC4Y 0DZ

www.headline.co.uk
www.hachette.co.uk

For Rob

For everything you've done for me and for everything you're going to do.

I've watched you now a full half-hour;
Self-poised upon that yellow flower
And, little Butterfly! indeed
I know not if you sleep or feed
How motionless! – not frozen seas
More motionless! and then
What joy awaits you, when the breeze
Hath found you out among the trees,
And calls you forth again!
From 'To a Butterfly' by William Wordsworth

Donde una puerta se cierra, otra se abre.
'Where a door is closed, another is opened.'
From *Don Quixote* by Miguel de Cervantes

1

2018

It all began in the November. I can clearly recall the heavy charcoal skies and the mist which hovered two feet above the lawn. The damp smell of rotting leaves mixed with old bonfire smoke. The whole garden seemed to carry the weight of a burden. I'm not even sure why the weather's relevant but lots of stories seem to begin with it. Perhaps I'm trying too hard. Perhaps I should have started with the letter instead. After all, it's where the story really begins. It was the catalyst for everything that came after.

I dropped the letter onto the kitchen table and flicked on the kettle. I knew I needed the fortification of caffeine before I would have the strength to open it. My appetite had vanished but in another attempt at procrastination, I pushed some bread into the toaster and stared at the letter again. My name and address were type-written and the envelope was a rich cream colour and luxuriously thick. I might have known. The sender had deemed the contents so important that I'd had to sign for it. I propped it up against the bread bin and pulled down my 'World's Best Mum' mug. I popped a tea bag into the mug and picked up the letter again, fanning myself with it. I was deliberately putting off opening it because I knew that when I did, my life would never be the same again.

I left the unopened letter on the table and took my mug of tea over to the window, prolonging the state of blissful ignorance for as long as possible. I stared out over the garden to the shade of the horse chestnut tree where Dylan's red and yellow toy car was still parked. A layer of green algae covered the roof, which was no surprise as he hasn't driven it for years. His turtle-shaped sandpit was still embedded in the lawn, the grass underneath long dead. His whole childhood stretched out before me and I remembered fondly the little tea parties he used to hold for his teddy bears in the Wendy house when he thought I wasn't looking. He calls it the shed now and denies ever having owned a tea set but it's safely wrapped in tissue paper and stored in the attic ready for my grandchildren. I thought of him all alone in his room at university, poring over his books, rubbing his eyes with tiredness, his stomach rumbling with hunger as he wondered where his next meal was coming from. On the day Ralph and I dropped him off, I'd carried a box full of pans and cooking implements into the kitchen he was to share with his fellow students. There was no room in the fridge for the fruit and vegetables I had brought as it was already full of the essentials – lager, vodka and a token bag of lettuce. I'd had a feeling all the years of nurturing were going to be undone in one term. There would be nobody who cared if he got his five-a-day, ensured he drank enough water or rationed his Percy Pig habit. And I was right, for in reality he lives on a steady stream of Domino's, Dairylea Dunkers and whichever lager is on offer in Tesco. He assures me that during the first term 'nobody' does any work. No wonder the NHS is in such a state.

I swilled my cup under the tap and wandered upstairs to Dylan's bedroom. The walls were bare, peppered only with the greasy stains from the BluTack he used on his posters. I slumped down on his bed and smoothed out his Manchester City duvet cover. His life can be measured in duvet covers. His first one was pale blue with little rabbits and ducks on. Then we had Teletubbies, Bob the Builder, a slightly worrying Barbie phase, Thunderbirds and then finally this one. He didn't take it to university though. He had insisted on a plain 'grown-up' one and I'd realised then that his childhood was well and truly over.

He's studying medicine at Newcastle and I could not be more proud of him. He's worked so hard for it and considering his father left us when Dylan went into Lower Sixth, it's nothing short of a miracle. It's one of the many things I cannot forgive Ralph for, but when your secretary is seven months pregnant with your twins what can you do? I felt the familiar bitterness begin to creep in. Ralph and I tried for years to have another baby but it just wasn't to be. I think I coped with the disappointment quite well. I threw all my energies into bringing up Dylan and Ralph threw all his into shagging his secretary. There has been a long line of secretaries over the years, culminating in Susie, the mother of his twin girls. I'm sure he loves them but it amuses me no end to see him struggling to cope with the demands of two toddlers and a young wife whose IQ is not much higher than theirs. Naturally, Susie has had to give up work and his current secretary sports a blue rinse and wears tweed skirts. I can't help thinking Susie must have had a hand in her successor's selection process. Ralph is fifty-five now, the same age as me. He should be enjoying a more leisurely pace. A couple of golf trips a year with the boys, a nice flash sports car, time to relax in the evenings with a good wine and a box-set. Instead of which, he has to go on holidays dictated by the availability of a kids' club and drives a huge family bus, the only vehicle capable of transporting all the paraphernalia that accompanies his new family wherever they go. As for relaxing evenings, they are consigned to distant memory. The twins are particularly demanding at bedtime, I believe. He spends the entire evening carting one or both of them up and down the stairs, offering more and more extravagant bribes as the evening wears on. Still, you reap what you sow, I suppose.

I'd known the letter was coming since the day Ralph walked out but I just couldn't bring myself to open it. It sounds pathetic now but I knew I wouldn't be able to read the words which would officially herald the end of my marriage. I closed the door on Dylan's room and headed downstairs, suddenly eager to get it over with. I picked up the letter and ran my finger under the flap. The paper inside was the same rich cream colour as the envelope. I pulled my glasses down from the top of my head and began to read. 'Dear Mrs Richards . . .' By the time I'd finished, my legs would hardly hold me up. The letter wasn't from Ralph's solicitors at all.

2

1978

Violet Dobbs studied her reflection in the cracked mirror over the kitchen sink. The scraps of their evening meal were still evident in the bowl full of cold water; swollen crusts of bread, floating peas, a slick of margarine on the surface. She upended the bowl, poured the greasy water away then scooped the resulting mulch out of the plughole. Drying her hands on the tea towel, she returned to the mirror. Using both middle fingers she smoothed out the skin between her eyebrows, erasing the two vertical lines that seemed to have appeared overnight. She really must stop frowning so much. She glanced over her shoulder to where Tara lay huddled under the heavy bedclothes, her teeth chattering dramatically. Lacy patterns of ice had already begun to form on the inside of the window pane.

Violet instinctively frowned, then reminded herself of the promise she'd made only a few seconds ago. 'You alright there, Baby Girl?'

'No, I'm not. Do we have to go tonight, Mum? It's bloody freezing.'

'Language, Tara.' She applied a dash of red lipstick and pressed her lips together. 'Yes, *I* do have to go tonight because we need the money.' Turning towards her daughter, she softened her tone. 'Look, I know you don't like coming with me but I don't know what else to do. Unless you'd rather stay here?'

Tara hugged the hot-water bottle to her chest. 'No! I can't stay here on my own, not with *him* downstairs.' She pulled the rough grey army blanket up to her chin as though this would afford her some protection.

'Tara, love, even if he does come knocking, you don't have to let him in.'

'But he's the landlord, Mum, he has a key. I can't stop him.'

Violet shook her head. 'It's not right, I'm sure there must be laws against that sort of thing. He may own the place, but it's our home. We pay the rent.' Violet noticed her daughter's raised eyebrows. 'Don't look at me like that, Tara. We pay the rent when we can afford to.' She peered into the mirror again, rubbing the red lipstick off her teeth with her finger. 'Anyway, that's why I'm doing it tonight.' She pirouetted on the spot. 'How do I look?'

'Beautiful, as I'm sure you're well aware.'

'Oh, I don't know about that. Look at these lines on me forehead.'

'Oh, yeah right. I wish I looked as hideous as you.'

Violet plonked herself down on the bed and touched her daughter's freezing cheek. 'You've no idea, have you, love?' She pointed to her own face. 'Look at the amount of slap I have to put on. But you, you're gorgeous from the minute you wake you up until the minute your head hits the pillow again. You don't need anything to enhance your youthful beauty.'

Tara folded her arms and frowned. 'You're just saying that. I'm nowhere near as pretty as you.'

'You'll grow to love yourself in time, Tara. Don't be so quick to grow up. All that's ahead of you.' Violet sucked her cheeks in. 'Do you think I had these cheekbones when I was fourteen? You think I had this hourglass figure when I was still at school?' She shook her head. 'No, straight up and down I was, boys never looked once, let alone twice at me.'

'Come off it, Mum! You were pregnant with me at fourteen!'

Violet averted her gaze and looked down at the bed. 'Ah . . . yes . . . well, that was . . . different.'

Tara picked at the candlewick bedspread, pulling out a tuft of thread. 'Where is he now?'

'I haven't a clue where your dad is, Tara, love. You know this already. His parents moved to Mongolia and he had no choice but to go with them.' Violet clapped her hands, then rubbed them together, indicating the conversation was over.

Tara did not pick up on the body language. 'Do you think he would've stayed if he'd known about me though?'

'I'm sure he would. Young as we were, we were still

very much in love.' She tucked a stray strand of hair round her daughter's ear and smiled. 'We're alright though, aren't we, Tara? I do me best. You're everything to me, love, don't you forget it.'

The banging on the door startled them both. 'Open up, it's Colin.'

'Oh, for God's sake,' Violet whispered under her breath. She winked at Tara. 'Erm . . . Colin who?'

'Don't play games, Violet. Your rent's due.'

'I know it is and you'll get it next week.'

'Next week's too late. I've warned you about this before, now you've left me no choice.' The bunch of keys rattled in his fist.

'He's coming in, Mum,' Tara whispered, clinging to her mother's arm.

Violet rose from the bed and planted her hands on her hips. 'Well he doesn't scare me.'

Colin flung the door open and barged into the room, his hairy stomach bulging through his string vest. 'You're four weeks in arrears, Violet. Time's up.'

Violet spoke in a soft voice, one that was better suited to trying to calm a fractious toddler. 'Come on now, Colin, can't we come to some arrangement?' She gestured to the threadbare armchair, the fabric stained with the grease of a previous tenant's Brylcreem. 'Sit down, let's talk about this.' She nodded towards Tara. 'Fetch Mr Simpson a glass of whisky, will you?'

He lowered himself into the chair and accepted the

drink. 'I've got bills to pay too, you know. This isn't a hostel for the homeless.'

'I know, I know,' placated Violet. 'And I can see you're a reasonable man.' She pulled up a chair next to him and ran a finger along his forearm, tracing the outline of his faded tattoo. 'Me and Tara though, we're good tenants, aren't we? Or would you prefer someone who had all-night parties? Imagine all that punk rock booming through the rafters, you tossing and turning, trying to get to sleep. Or what if you had tenants who turned this place into a drugs den? What then, eh? Place stinking of weed. Drug dealers banging on the door at all hours. Is that really what you want?' She squeezed his bicep and smiled. 'My word, Colin, have you been at those weights again?'

He downed his whisky and stood up. 'Nice try, Violet.' He slammed the glass down on the draining board. 'Payment in full by eight o'clock or else you're out on your ear.'

Violet glanced at the clock on the wall. 'But it's half seven now.'

He shrugged his hairy shoulders. 'Not my problem.'

Violet closed the door behind him. 'Bloody great ape.' She shuddered. 'Ugh, poor Mrs Simpson having to share a bed with that Neanderthal.'

'What will we do, Mum?' asked Tara. 'He said eight o'clock.'

Violet reached for her Afghan coat. 'Oh, it's all hot air,

Tara. Take no notice, he just likes to throw his considerable weight about.'

She wrapped a feather boa round her neck and picked up her handbag. 'Come on, Baby Girl. It's you and me against the world. We'll show 'em.'

3

Larry Valentine had left nothing to chance. Everything had to be perfect for tonight, everything from the lightness of the mushroom vol-au-vents to the quality of the champagne. Larry wasn't exactly a connoisseur of champagne, preferring instead a smooth single malt, but he knew his brother would be impressed by the extravagance of a vintage bottle of Taittinger. He picked up the crystal tumbler, tossed in a couple of ice cubes and poured himself a little sharpener. He grimaced at the first taste of the sour whisky, then chugged back the remainder in one go, making his eyes water and his nose fizz. He breathed in deeply for two counts, then out again, his lips pursed, his knuckles turning white as he gripped the back of the chair. Thinking about Martin always made his heart race faster than was good for him. He spread out the newspaper again and studied the grainy black and white image. Martin beamed into the camera as his young bride clung onto his arm, staring with undisguised adoration at her new husband. He ran his finger over Carol's face, searching for any signs that this might be an act and that she actually regretted her decision to marry his brother and not him.

Naturally, he'd not received an invitation to their wedding. He hadn't needed one. He'd simply slipped into the back of the church after Carol and her posse of taffeta-clad bridesmaids had shuffled down the aisle in a sea of pink froth. He saw the look on his brother's face as he turned around for his first glimpse of his bride, a face that radiated pure joy and, if Larry wasn't mistaken, more than a hint of smugness. Larry had had to close his eyes and concentrate on his breathing again, his fists clenched into two tight balls of steel.

When the vicar had asked if anybody knew of any lawful impediment as to why these two should not be joined in holy matrimony, Larry had bitten his lip so hard, the metallic tang of blood filled his mouth. He sneaked out of the church whilst the happy couple were in the vestry signing the register. He'd had no intention of offering his congratulations.

He pulled the net curtain to one side and stared down the street. He'd left the gates open so that Carol wouldn't have to get out and press the buzzer. There was mizzle in the air which played havoc with her smooth blonde tresses. He'd always been thoughtful like that, always put Carol's needs before his own. There was nothing he wouldn't have done for her.

The crunch of tyres on gravel alerted him to their arrival. He ventured towards the front door, stopping to stare at himself for a second in the hall mirror. He licked his middle finger and smoothed out his eyebrows before splashing on some more cologne even though the last dousing still clung to his skin. He undid one more button on his starched white shirt, swept his fringe back from his face and opened the door. He stared at Martin, sitting in the driver's seat, removing his leather driving gloves with the help of his teeth. The passenger door opened and Carol's elegantly shod foot emerged, her slim ankles looking as fragile as a thoroughbred's. She was the first to speak. 'Larry, how are you?' She glanced up at the house and pursed her lips as though about to whistle, but no sound came. 'Wow, it's quite a place you've got here.'

Larry felt his hands shaking and dug them into his trouser pockets. He wasn't exactly sure of the protocol expected in this situation. It wasn't every day you welcomed your brother and the girl he stole from you back into the fold. He leaned forward and gave Carol a brief kiss on the cheek, the scent of the Pond's face cream she meticulously applied transporting him back in time. 'Hello, Carol.' He held her gaze, determined not to look away even though it was painful to stare into her eyes and not see her love for him reflected back. 'Please come in.' He clutched at the handkerchief in his pocket, hoping it would absorb the moisture from his palm, before extending his hand to his brother. 'Martin.'

They followed Larry into the kitchen, Martin with his arm protectively slung over his wife's shoulders, leaving Larry in no doubt that she belonged to him now.

Dispensing with small talk, Martin launched into his opening gambit. 'Why did you ask us here, Larry?'

'Why did you accept, Martin?'

Carol looked from one brother to the other, her eyes already wide with anticipation of another argument. 'Boys, please, we don't want any trouble.'

Martin looked around the cavernous kitchen, all oranges, yellows and browns, contrasting with the shiny white units. 'Your pools numbers come up, did they?'

Larry snorted. 'It's called hard work, Martin, something you're a stranger to.'

Carol slammed her bag down on the counter top. 'Seriously, I'll storm out if you're going to carry on like this.' She looked at the fridge. 'Have you got anything cold to drink, Larry?' She glared at her husband. 'Preferably alcoholic.'

Larry opened the fridge and lifted out the Taittinger. He picked at the gold foil, removed the wire cage and eased his thumbs under the cork.

'Flash git,' muttered Martin.

The froth spurted out of the bottle and ran down the side. 'Don't waste it,' squealed Carol, thrusting her glass towards Larry.

He looked pointedly at Martin. 'Plenty more where that came from.'

Martin accepted a glass and proposed a toast. 'To the winners and the losers.' He smiled and looked at Carol. 'And to love.' He kissed her on the lips, lingering a little longer than was acceptable in company. He reached into his jacket pocket and pulled out his cigarettes, flipping open the lid and popping one between his lips in one practised move.

'Not in here if you don't mind, Martin. If you want to smoke, you'll have to go out into the garden. There's a bench out there down by the pond.'

'It's February, Larry, I didn't come here to sit in your garden freezing me nuts off in the dark.'

'Put the fags away then.'

Carol took a sip of her champagne. 'It's nice of you to ask us, Larry. And this place,' she swept her arm around the kitchen, 'it's magnificent.'

Martin scoffed. 'It's why he asked us here, you daft bint. To show you what you've missed out on, what you could've had if you'd stayed with him. He's so bloody transparent.'

'Is that right, Larry?'

'Let him think what he likes, Carol. I thought it was time we buried the hatchet. No point in holding on to all that resentment.' He picked up the bottle of champagne. 'Top-up?'

He poured some more into Carol's glass and sneaked a look at Martin. Damn right it was why he had asked them here. And judging by the look on Martin's face, the visit was going to be much more fun than Larry could have hoped for.

4

A blue haze of smoke hung in the air. The lights had been turned down and as Violet looked out over the audience, the burning ends of dozens of cigarettes danced like fireflies in the gloom. She waited in the wings as the compère finished telling his latest round of filthy jokes, which she didn't find in the slightest bit funny. Working men's clubs were hardly the most salubrious of venues, but the audience was appreciative, the money wasn't bad and the tips jar was pleasingly heavy at the end of the night. Tara stood by her side, picking her way through a bag of chips and curry sauce. Violet wafted her hand. 'For crying out loud, Tara, I'm going to go out there stinking of the Taj Mahal Curry House.'

Tara laughed. 'Good luck, Mum, I think you're on.'

The compère was shouting into his microphone. 'And now, back by popular demand, your favourite and mine, the sumptuous, delectable Miss Violet Skye.' He dragged her name out in the same way wrestlers were announced into the ring then raised his arm theatrically, beckoning Violet onto the stage. With an appreciative wave to the audience, she sashayed forth, her fishtail dress gliding across the wooden stage, picking up all kinds of dust and detritus. 'Thank you, Dean.'

He kissed her on the cheek and cupped his hand around her left buttock, giving it a firm squeeze. 'There you go, gorgeous, they're all yours.'

The crowd of lecherous, beer-swilling blokes rose to their feet, cheering, clapping, some of them practically salivating. She pasted on a smile, her cheeks aching as she waited for the noise to die down. Although it barely covered the bills there were worse ways to earn a living. She let the feather boa slide to the floor and nodded towards the sound guy.

Forty-five minutes later, after a standing ovation, pierced with the inevitable wolf whistles, she picked up the feather boa and hurried back to what was laughingly called her dressing room. It was more of a disused broom cupboard with a mirror propped up on a woodworm-infested trestle table and a shade-less single light bulb dangling from the ceiling. Tara was waiting for her, perched on the table, munching her way through a quarter of cola cubes.

Violet tutted. 'You'll have no teeth left, young lady.'

Tara ignored the remark. 'How did it go?'

'OK, I suppose. I just grin and bear it. It's to be endured rather than enjoyed but it all helps to keep the wolf from the door, or in our case, Mr Simpson.'

Tara shuffled off the table and handed her mother a note.

Violet frowned. 'What's this?'

'Telephone number of a bloke who wants you to call him. It's about a gig at The Amethyst Lounge.'

Violet grabbed her daughter's arm. 'Don't mess with me, our Tara. Are you serious?'

'Yes, Mum, I'm serious. You think I go around making stuff up now?'

Violet studied the note. 'The Amethyst Lounge. *The* Amethyst Lounge?'

'I dunno, do I? Why don't you call him and find out?'

'Don't worry, I will.' Violet clutched the note to her chest and gazed up at the ceiling where the cobwebs sagged with the weight of the dust. 'The Amethyst Lounge, Tara. They have glass in the windows and plush carpet on the floor, everything's crimson and gold. No sticky lino in there. And the audience probably don't throw things either. And I bet the money's better than this god-forsaken place.'

'Go and ring him then,' urged Tara. 'There's a payphone out in the hall.'

Violet patted herself down. 'Have you got tuppence for the phone, love?'

It was gone midnight by the time they arrived back at their digs. Arm in arm, they laughed together as they walked along the dimly lit street, the ice-cold air numbing their faces. 'Everything's going to be alright now, Tara, I just know it. I've waited for this opportunity all my life.

A gig at The Amethyst Lounge. It's the answer to all our problems.'

'Steady on, Mum. It's hardly the London Palladium.'

'But who knows where it will end? Bruce Forsyth's played there, Gene Pitney, Dusty Springfield. You've got to think big, Tara. I've done my time singing at the working men's clubs and the afternoon tea dances at church halls, now it's time for me to shine.' She flung her arms out wide and spun around a lamppost, throwing her head back as she sang out loud.

'Sshh, Mum, you'll wake everybody up.'

'Well they should be grateful that they heard a free performance from the talented Miss Violet Skye. They'll be able to tell their grandkids about it one day.'

Tara stopped walking and stared ahead. 'Mum.'

'What is it, love?'

She pointed along the pavement. 'What's that up there, outside our house?'

Violet squinted in the gloom. 'Looks like somebody lying in a heap. Probably some tramp passed out from drinking too much meths.' She linked her arm through Tara's. 'That's all we need. Come on, let's see if we can help him.'

They approached with caution, Violet keeping a protective arm across her daughter's chest. They crept up to the pile and Violet prodded it with her toe. 'Oh, it's not a person at all. It's a sack of something or other.' She bent down and gingerly opened the top, which had been tied with a piece of frayed string. She carefully put her hand inside and pulled out a cheesecloth shirt, holding it aloft between her thumb and forefinger.

Tara knelt down next to her mother. 'That's my best shirt, that is.'

Violet frowned and then, as the realisation began to dawn, rummaged more urgently through the rest of the clothes in the sack. 'The bastard,' she whispered. She straightened up and raised her fist up to the window. 'You won't get away with this, Colin.' She drew deep calming breaths, the chilly air making her lungs ache. 'Do you hear me, you despicable excuse for a human being? How can you sleep at night, knowing you've turfed a mother and daughter onto the streets?' She picked up the sack and heaved it over her shoulder. 'Well, it's your loss, Colin.' She raised her voice further, her vocal cords straining as she screamed into the still night air. 'I'm going places, I am, places you could only ever dream of. So, you can keep your disgusting little hovel and I hope you rot in hell.'

She grabbed hold of Tara's wrist as Colin thrust open his window and called down to her. 'Oi, Violet, you forgot this.' He reached down and brought up a bucket. Before Violet could react, he upended the pail and a torrent of ice-cold water rained down on her head. Shocked into silence, Violet could only open and close her mouth, a volcanic fury waiting to erupt just as soon as she could find her voice.

5

2018

Even after two years apart my default setting was still to turn to Ralph. He often worked from home in the mornings to allow madam to get her nails done or go for a skinny latte with her giggling friends. He picked up on the second ring. 'Ralph Richards.'

'Ralph, it's me.'

There was only a slight pause. 'Morning, Tara, what can I do for you?'

I stiffened at his business-like tone. We've been married for twenty-three years, we have a child together. 'I've received this really strange letter – from a solicitor.'

'It's nothing to do with me.' A piercing scream rang out in the background and I had to hold the phone away from my ear. Clearly one of the twins was having a tantrum. Ralph made a vain attempt to cover the mouthpiece but I could still hear him. 'Will you shut the fuck up? I'm on the phone here.'

I was genuinely shocked. 'Ralph,' I said. 'I know they can be little monsters but you really shouldn't swear at them like that.'

He seemed distracted. 'What? Oh no, the twins are at nursery. That was Susie. You were saying something about a letter?'

I was momentarily thrown off-guard by the chaos of his domestic situation, trying not to enjoy every moment of it. Nope, he's made his bed . . .

'A recorded delivery letter came this morning. I thought it was from . . .' I stopped myself, not wishing to give him any ideas. We may have sorted out the finances and be officially separated but we're still married and I didn't want him pinning that dreaded 'divorcee' tag on me just yet. 'It's from a solicitor's down in London, Irwin Fortis.'

'Never heard of them.'

'They want me to travel down in person and bring my ID and whatnot. They said they were following a specific set of instructions and wouldn't elaborate.'

I could hear him scratching at the stubble on his chin. 'How very mysterious. Will you go?'

'I'm not sure I have a choice.'

'What do you want me to do?'

It was a fair question and one I couldn't really answer. 'Nothing, Ralph. I just wanted to tell someone, that's all.'

It took me all day to pluck up the courage to ring Irwin Fortis. They were no more forthcoming on the phone than they were in the letter but at least I had an appointment for the following week. After booking the first off-peak train from Manchester Piccadilly to Euston, I jumped in my car and drove the familiar route to the hospice.

I parked up in the surprisingly empty car park, the familiar sense of trepidation making my stomach roil. St Jude's Hospice is a wonderful place, staffed by absolute angels, to whom myself and countless other people will be eternally grateful. St Jude though? The Patron Saint of Lost Causes. I know it's a hospice but something a little more optimistic wouldn't hurt, surely.

Nan's room had a window looking out over the pretty courtyard and her bed had been thoughtfully positioned to take full advantage of the view. She was fast asleep, her mouth hanging open, dried spittle caked in the corners. She looked peaceful, pain-free and I hesitated to wake her. Sleep was the only respite she got from the pain these days. It had all begun with the coughing but Nan hadn't paid much attention to it. In fact, with her sixty-a-day habit, she hardly noticed it. Even when the cough became productive, often streaked with blood, she still didn't say anything. It was only when she finally told me she'd been having chest pains for over a year that I whisked her to the doctor, but it was too late by then. The tumour is now so advanced that palliative care is the only option. At ninety-one, she's had a good innings but she's gone way beyond knocking at death's door; she has one foot over the threshold. I'm no stranger to loss, but the thought of her no longer being around crushes me. Next to our Dylan, she's the most treasured person in my life.

I took hold of her hand, the silvery skin stretched over mountainous blue veins. 'Nan,' I whispered. 'It's me, Tara.'

Her eyelids flickered open. 'My beautiful girl.'

I reached for the control which operated her back rest and with a soft whirr she rose up before me, her smile growing wider with every degree.

'How are you?' she asked and then without waiting for an answer, 'How's our Dylan?'

'Still loving it. He's definitely embraced the student lifestyle. He's not picked up a Geordie accent yet though.'

'I know, he rang me last week. Had a right good old natter, we did. He's a good lad, Tara.'

I nodded. 'He thinks the world of you, Nan.' My throat began to ache. 'We both do,' I managed.

I turned away and busied myself straightening the already-neat pile of magazines on the bedside table, not trusting myself to speak.

A week later, I elbowed my way onto the train at Piccadilly, my bag bulging with all the essentials I would need for the journey – newspaper, book, iPod and headphones, ham sandwiches. I was actually looking forward to just sitting back for a couple of hours and indulging in the things I always felt guilty about doing at home. I work two days a week on reception at the medical centre and as far as I'm concerned, I've earned the right to do whatever I like for the other three. It just doesn't feel right though and I can't sit in front of daytime television for more than half an hour before I get twitchy. It's even worse when Moira, my cleaner, comes in. It was Ralph's idea to hire her all those years ago. He thought it would give me more precious bonding time with Dylan and in a way, he was right, but there are only so many Thomas the Tank Engine books you can read before scouring the bath seems like a preferable way to pass the time. I don't really need Moira's domestic help anymore, as the two people who made the most mess in our house no longer live here, but the truth is she needs the money and I like her company. She knew about my meeting in London. She was convinced that some long-forgotten relative had died and left me a fortune. Goodness knows how she came to that conclusion. She knows my background as well as anybody.

I found my seat on the train and politely asked the great lummox who was sitting in it to move. The display above quite clearly stated the seat was reserved so I'm not sure why he had to tut so much and make an over-blown display of heaving down his bag from the rack. I settled myself into the seat, grateful that he had at least warmed it for me. I spread out my things on the table and relished the thought of the next couple of hours' peace, hoping I wouldn't be joined by someone who wanted to rabbit for the whole journey. Alas, I'd only got to page three of the paper before a rotund balding chap arrived by my side. He reached up to the bag rack, his armpits already stained a dark shade of blue. We hadn't even pulled out of the station and yet this guy was perspiring for Britain. 'Morning,' he said, plonking himself down opposite me. 'Going all the way to London?' Oh, dear God! A talker.

'Mmm . . .' I mumbled, fervently hoping he'd change at Crewe.

'Me too,' he smiled.

I smiled back. 'Lovely.' Then I reached for my noise-cancelling headphones.

I could feel the river running down my back as I sat in the plush reception area at Irwin Fortis. It was a brisk autumn day but they'd over-compensated with the heating and the result was verging on tropical. I instantly regretted wearing my grey blouse. I picked up one of the magazines from the coffee table and wafted it in front of my face, then, taking a tissue from my sleeve, I surreptitiously dabbed at my shiny forehead. The receptionist noticed and smiled. 'It is a bit warm in here, isn't it?' A bit warm! She'd got no idea. She must have only been in her twenties and was wearing a polo neck, something I haven't been able to wear for the past five years.

A door opened and a young man in a trendy electric-blue suit stepped forward, extending his hand. 'Mrs

Richards, sorry to keep you. I'm Jamie. Please come this way.'

I followed him into the lift and we rode the sixteen floors whilst making excruciating small talk. There were mirrors on three sides and I caught a glimpse of my reflection from several angles, none of them particularly flattering. An image of Susie, Ralph's young girlfriend, flashed up and for one fleeting, shallow moment, I could understand why he left me.

Jamie opened the door to his office and indicated the way forward. 'After you.'

My eyes were immediately drawn to the massive window, the London skyline resplendent even though it was partially shrouded by mist. Jamie pulled out a chair for me, then took up his position behind the vast mahogany desk. He didn't look much older than our Dylan so I assumed he must be some kind of intern and I noticed his hands were shaking. He clasped them together and rested them on the desk. 'So, have you brought your documents?'

The small talk was over. I leaned down, pulled the envelope out of my handbag and passed it over the desk. Jamie slid out my birth certificate, driving licence and passport. He opened the passport at the photograph page and studied my face. It was all I could do to stop myself squirming in the chair. I could almost read his mind, as he raised his eyebrows and looked at me, then back to the photograph. 'I've had a stressful couple of years,' I offered. 'My husband left me and then . . .'

Jamie held up his palm. 'No need to explain, Mrs Richards.'

He lifted the lid on the printer beside his computer and slid in my birth certificate. 'I just need to make copies for our files.' I nodded my acceptance then wondered briefly if I was just about to become the victim of an elaborate identity theft.

Jamie clapped his hands. 'Right, that's all the formalities out of the way.' He opened a buff file and pulled out a copy of the letter his firm had sent to me. 'I expect you're wondering what all this is about.' He looked through the notes in the file, following every word with his finger, like a five-year-old learning to read. 'OK,' he said finally. 'It appears somebody has been looking for you for a very long time, since 1981, in fact.'

My immediate thought was someone was coming after me for money. The heat rose under my collar. 'Oh,' was all I could manage.

Jamie reached across his desk and picked up a little box I'd not noticed until then. 'Here.'

My fingers were trembling so much it was difficult to prise the lid off. Underneath some black tissue paper was a business card. 'Loxton's Safe Deposit Box Company'. Frowning, I looked up at Jamie, who nodded at the box. I put the business card down and pulled out some more tissue paper. Resting on the bottom of the box was a small silver key. I held it up to the light, turning it in my fingers before clumsily dropping it onto the wooden desk. Jamie picked it up and stated the obvious. 'It's the key to a safe deposit box.'

'So I gathered, but what's in it?'

Jamie shrugged. 'I don't know. But whatever it is has been waiting for you for thirty-seven years.'

6

1978, San Sedeza, Spain

The day began as it always did. At the first hint of the sun appearing over the horizon Leonardo was jolted from his sleep by the cockerel calling to his counterpart at the farm across the valley. Not the melodious *cock-a-doodle-doo* as depicted in children's story books, but a strangulated screech which sounded like the poor bird was being throttled. The other hens scratched and clucked in the barn below, their quiet conversation almost lulling him back to sleep. He heard the clanking of the handle on the barn door as it was heaved open. Quiet footsteps followed and he smiled to himself as he lay back with his hands tucked behind his head, staring at the rafters.

The small high-pitched voice carried up the steps. 'Leo?'

'Mmm . . . who's that down there then?' he teased.

'It's me. Mama says it's time to get up.'

'Aah, just five more minutes, Little One.'

He heard his younger brother start to climb the ladder, taking his time, making sure he held on tightly just as Leo had shown him. His head appeared as he reached the top step, the indignation written into his dark eyes. 'Leo, I keep telling you I'm not little anymore. I'm nearly eight.'

'You're not nearly eight, you're barely seven and a half, Mateo.' Leo held his arms out wide. 'Come here, my *camarada*, you know you'll always be my Little One.'

Leo had already turned sixteen when his mother Marissa announced that she needed a hysterectomy. She had had what she called 'women's problems' ever since giving birth to Leo when she was only a teenager herself. Although Leo had long since accepted the fact he would never have a sibling, on the day Marissa was admitted to hospital for the operation, his last flicker of hope was extinguished. As his mother was prepared for surgery, Leo and his father, Felipe waited in the corridor. His parents had been together since they were twelve years old and Felipe had buffed the tiles to a shine as he paced up and down the corridor, his features creased with worry. When the doctor emerged from Marissa's room, his face was difficult to read but the first nugget of dread settled itself into Leo's stomach. Something was evidently not right. The doctor addressed his father first. 'Señor Perez.' He placed a firm hand on Felipe's shoulder. 'I'm afraid it's not possible for us to perform the surgery today.'

'Why?' asked Felipe. 'She has worked herself up to this for weeks and now you are telling me that . . .'

The doctor's face cracked with a broad smile. 'Señor

Perez, we will not be performing the surgery because your wife is pregnant.'

Leo clutched his father's arm as Felipe swayed on the spot. 'My *mama* is going to have a baby?'

'Yes,' the doctor confirmed. 'And we estimate she's about six months along.'

Felipe found his voice. 'You mean she's going to have a baby in three months' time?'

'There or thereabouts, yes. Would you like to go in and see her?'

'Did you hear that, Leo? You're going to have a baby brother.'

'Or a sister, Papa.'

Felipe shook his head. 'No, it's a boy. God has sent us a miracle.' He clasped his hands to his chest and mouthed a silent prayer.

The baby was born three months later, a boy just as Felipe had predicted. Marissa's face was used to smiling, the crow's feet around her eyes testament to that, but when Leo entered her hospital room later that afternoon and saw her cradling his baby brother, he thought he had never seen her looking so happy or so radiant.

She tilted the infant towards him. 'Say hello to Mateo.'

'The name means Gift from God,' Felipe interjected.

Leo was instantly smitten. The baby's eyes were closed but his little mouth moved as though he was trying to talk. 'Can I hold him?'

Marissa passed the bundle over. As Leo gazed at the

baby's face he knew in that moment that he would be the best brother anybody had ever had. He would teach him how to ride, he would pick him up when he fell, he would protect him from anything and everything that threatened to harm him and above all else he would love him.

'*Hola*, Little One,' he'd whispered.

Mateo scrambled off the top rung of the ladder and flung himself onto Leo's bed.

'Mama says you have to take me to the horse sale.'

Leo rubbed his chin theatrically. 'Well now, let me see. Does Mama say you've been a good boy?'

Mateo's eyes were wide and serious. He nodded furiously. 'The best.'

'In that case, you'd better scuttle off and tell Mama to make my coffee. I'll see you in the kitchen.'

'Thanks, Leo, I love you.'

Mateo jumped off the bed and began to climb backwards down the ladder, his tongue sticking out of the side of his mouth in concentration. Leo waited until he heard the barn door close then pulled the sheets over his head and closed his eyes, hoping for just ten more minutes' precious sleep.

Although it was still cold, Leo loved this time of the year. February came with the glorious anticipation of the spring and summer ahead. His mother would be busy washing sheets, beating rugs and sweeping out the stone floors of the six guest bedrooms, shaking off the remnants of winter and coaxing a freshness back into the old farmhouse. His father would be tending to repairs in the stables, fixing broken hinges, leaking gutters and warped doors. It was left to Leo to prepare the horses for the season ahead, improve their fitness and make sure the tack still fitted comfortably. He'd kept their hooves trimmed over the winter but they would all need to be shod before the season began.

He swung his legs out of bed and groped around on the floor for the jeans he had cast off the night before. He pulled on his leather boots and slung his shirt over his bare shoulders. His breath visible in the still morning air, he ran across the yard and into the farmhouse.

'Aah, *buenos dias*, *hijo*,' greeted his mother as he walked into the kitchen. She placed a cup of strong coffee in his hands.

'Morning, Mama,' he said, kissing her on the cheek. She smelled of lemon and garlic and lavender. All the things that reminded Leo of home. She'd already scraped her jet-black hair into a tight bun which pulled at the skin around her eyes. She blew out her cheeks as she carried a large pot of boiling water from the stove, looking as though she'd done a day's work already.

'Let me take that, Mama,' Leo said. 'You sit down and drink your coffee.'

She slumped gratefully into a chair, her ample frame

spilling over the sides. 'Ah, *gracias,* Leo. Now, you know you're taking Mateo to the sale today?'

'Yes, Mama, he's already been to see me this morning.'

'He's excited, Leo, but you take good care of him, you hear me?'

Glancing at the ceiling, Leo suppressed a smile. 'What's going to happen to him at a horse sale?'

Marissa tutted. 'You never know, Leo, all those beasts with their gnashing teeth and flashing hooves.'

'You let your imagination wander far too much, Mama.'

He walked over to the window. Mateo was in the yard tying up his own caramel-coloured pony. The little boy put his arms around Lala's neck, repeatedly kissing her soft coat. The pony nuzzled in his pocket for a mint. In one slick move, Mateo vaulted onto the pony's back and continued to caress her mane. Leo nodded his approval. 'He's certainly following in Papa's and my footsteps.'

Marissa heaved herself up and joined her son at the window. 'Mmm . . . didn't stand a chance, did he? He was hardly going to take up the flamenco.'

Leo downed his coffee. 'Right, I'll just get myself cleaned up and then we'll be off.'

Marissa prodded at the hard muscles on his stomach. 'Do you have to wander around half-naked? You can't be doing that once the guests arrive, you know?' She forked her fingers through his hair. 'And this is too long, Leo.'

He glanced at himself in the mirror over the fireplace. 'I like it, Mama.' He winked at her. 'And so does Gabriela.'

In the village of San Sedeza, the main square was reluctantly coming to life, taking its time, easing itself into the day. Half-timbered houses leaned over cobbled streets, shutters were being opened, pavements sluiced down, trestle tables loaded with plump fruit and vegetables, their bright colours contrasting with the bleached white of the plaza. The climb to the top of the walled hill-top village was short but could be challengingly steep, especially to the elderly and visitors not used to the summer heat or altitude. Leo took Mateo's hand as they entered the warm maltiness of the *panadería,* only slightly out of breath.

'Are you going to ask her to be your girlfriend?' Mateo asked.

'What? Who?'

Mateo giggled. 'You know who, Leo. Gabriela.'

Leo squeezed his brother's hand. 'Shush now, she'll hear you.'

'I don't know why you're taking so long about it, Leo.'

Gabriela finished laying out the *pan blanco* on the wooden shelves and smiled at the brothers. 'You pair are up bright and early.' She wrapped two of the loaves in tissue paper for them.

'We're going to the horse sale,' Mateo beamed. 'We're getting a new horse.'

'Oh, well isn't that lovely?'

'I want a Palomino, a girl one, so she can be friends with Lala.'

Leo ruffled the boy's hair. 'We're not choosing paint, Mateo. The colour doesn't matter. It has to have the right temperament. Some of our guests don't know how to ride, remember.'

Gabriela laughed, throwing her head back and patting her chest, just as she always did when she found something even faintly amusing. Her mahogany hair was tied up, not severely like his mother's, but loosely so that wispy bits still hung around her face. She'd probably been up for several hours already and yet her olive skin bore no trace of fatigue and her chocolate-coloured eyes were still bright and not ringed with the tiredness one might expect from someone who had barely slept the night before. Her generous mouth was set into a permanent smile and by any standards, she was effortlessly beautiful.

'Leo!'

He shook his head. 'What, Mateo?'

'I said, when are you going to ask Gabriela to go out with you? I think you should ask her before someone else does.'

'Ah, Mateo,' said Gabriela, coming round to their side of the counter. 'I'm saving myself for you.' She pinched his cheek. 'You hurry up and get big now.' She popped a couple of warm *churros* into a paper bag and pressed it into Mateo's hands. 'Enjoy, Little One.'

She smiled at Leo. 'Have a good day, *chicos*.'

Out in the plaza, Leo turned to Mateo. 'What did you have to say that for?'

'You needed a push. Mama told me to say it.' Mateo pulled a long *churro* from the bag.

Leo rubbed his face vigorously. 'For the love of God. Can't I sort out my own love life without interference from my mother and brother?'

Mateo smiled, his lips coated with sugar. 'You'll be twenty-five this year, Leo, so I think the answer is no.'

In spite of his annoyance, Leo laughed. 'And I suppose you got that from Mama too.'

He turned back towards the *panadería*. Gabriela was outside now, winding the striped canopy over the front of the shop. She stopped and wiped her hand across her forehead. She noticed Leo staring, dipped her head and offered him a coy smile.

The sun had risen above the mountains in the distance, casting an apricot glow which warmed the fields. The overnight rain had dampened down the dust and rows upon rows of horses stood in makeshift stalls, ready to be paraded into the ring. Mateo wriggled in his seat next to Leo, bombarding him with questions.

'Why is that horse pawing at the ground, Leo?'

'She's impatient, Mateo. She wants someone to buy her so she can go home.'

'Can we buy her, Leo?'

'No, Mateo, she's too big and too expensive.'

Leo's mind was elsewhere. 'Do you think she'd say yes, Mateo?'

'Do I think who would say yes to what?'

'Gabriela. Do you think she'd say yes, if I asked her out?'

Mateo folded his arms and shook his head, a stance he had obviously adopted from their mother. 'Mama says you two need your heads banging together.' He frowned and chewed on his thumb nail, obviously mulling it over. 'I don't know how that would help though. Surely it would hurt and then you'd both have a headache and then you probably wouldn't feel like going out anyway.'

Leo laughed. 'You're not wrong there, Little One.'

The shadows had lengthened, and Mateo's eyes were heavy by the time Leo finally found a horse that was the right size and appeared to have the ideal temperament to carry inexperienced holidaymakers who had a habit of pulling too sharply on the reins or else just sat in the saddle like a sack of potatoes.

'What shall we call her?' asked Mateo, suppressing a yawn.

'She's already got a name. It's Armonia.'

'That's a pretty name for a pretty pink horse.'

'She's a strawberry roan, Mateo. Come on, are you ready to go? We need to load her into the box. Here, you can take her.' He passed Armonia's lead rein to Mateo, the little boy's chest inflating with pride at the trust Leo had placed in him.

The pens were being taken down as the brothers made their way to the field where the horse box was parked. Mateo pointed to a pen which had been left erected under the inadequate shade of a leafless tree. 'What's wrong with that horse, Leo? He looks sad.'

The black horse stood in the middle of the pen, his head hanging down, his front leg joined to his back leg by a length of thick rope.

'Why has that horse got his legs tied up, Leo? I don't like it.'

'It's called hobbling, Mateo. I don't like it either but there's probably a good reason for it. Come on, let's go and take a look.'

The old man lay in a chair beside the pen, his cap pulled down over his face, a cigarette smouldering between his fingers. 'Erm, excuse me,' said Leo. 'Is this horse for sale?'

The man jumped and lost his balance, his arms flailing as he tried to recover himself. 'Do you mind?' he growled. 'You almost frightened me to death.'

'This horse,' persisted Leo. 'Is he for sale?'

'*Sí*, but as usual nobody wants to buy.'

Mateo stood in front of him and placed his hands on his hips, his face screwed up with fury. 'Why is he tied up like that? It's cruel.' He jabbed his finger in the old man's direction. 'You are a very cruel man.'

The man narrowed his eyes as he took a long drag of his cigarette. 'He's wild, young man. You no like to see him without the hobbles.'

Leo climbed over the metal fence and advanced slowly towards the horse. The animal lifted his head as he heard Leo approaching, the whites of his eyes showing and his nostrils flaring. He bobbed his head up and down and pawed at the dust with his free foot.

'There, there, boy, it's OK. Shush . . . no need to be frightened.'

He ran his hand down the horse's hobbled foreleg. The rope around his fetlock was too tight and had cut into the flesh, leaving a livid open wound.

Leo smoothed the horse's neck, the black coat slick with sweat. He looked around the pen. 'Where's his water?'

The old man scoffed. 'No water. He kick it over.' He stood up and leaned against the railing.

Leo swallowed down his rising anger. 'How much?'

The man shrugged and turned down his mouth. 'About a bucketful.'

'No, how much do you want for the horse?'

'You want to buy him?'

'Depends how much.'

'He's a thoroughbred, a stallion, he can have many sons.'

Leo could feel the horse's flesh quivering under his touch but his breathing had steadied and he seemed calmer.

'You good with horses then?'

Leo nodded. 'Been around them all my life.'

'You can have him for thirty thousand pesetas.'

Mateo tugged on Leo's arm. 'Please, Leo, we can't leave him here with this nasty man.'

'Why so cheap?' asked Leo. 'He's a thoroughbred stallion you say. He's worth more than that surely.'

The old man grinned, his lack of teeth enhancing his manic expression. 'I told you, he's wild, untrainable. I'm just being honest with you and you should be thankful for that.'

Leo looked at the horse again. He didn't look wild, in fact he looked broken, as though the spirit had been beaten out of him.

'Please, Leo,' implored Mateo, tears streaked into the dust on his face. 'We can't leave him.'

Leo held out his hand to the old man. 'Twenty-five thousand and you've got a deal.'

The old man spat into his own palm, then clasped Leo's hand. 'He's all yours. But don't say I didn't warn you.'

Leo bent his head and breathed into the horse's nose. The horse pricked his ears and returned a warm breath of his own. 'What his name?' asked Leo.

'Diablo.'

Leo didn't flinch.

Diablo. The devil.

7

1978

Violet trembled beneath the Afghan coat, its wet fibres now stinking like an ageing Labrador. Her teeth chattered together and her lips had turned an alarming shade of blue. Tara wrapped a comforting arm around her mother. 'Come on, we need to keep moving.'

Violet shuffled forward dragging the sack of clothes along the pavement, the tight dress only allowing her to take tiny steps. 'I can't believe he did that,' she said for the umpteenth time. 'There was just no need, it's so vindictive.'

'Yes, Mum, you said, but it's done now and we need to concentrate on finding somewhere to stay, unless you want to bed down in the underpass with the other down-and-outs.'

Violet rubbed at her panda eyes, the mascara now smudged half-way down her cheek. 'I'm fed up, our Tara. As soon as something good happens, then something bad comes along to cancel it out. It's as though I'm not allowed to be happy.'

'Mum! Stop that now. I'm supposed to be the whiny little brat here, not you.'

Violet managed a smile. 'How did you turn out to be such a good kid, with a disastrous mother like me, eh?'

'Yes, it's a mystery alright.' Tara paused. 'Perhaps it's time to go back home. You know, to your mum and dad's.'

Violet stopped so suddenly, she inadvertently yanked at Tara's arm. 'No, Tara, you know that's not possible.'

'Anything's possible, Mum. We could . . .'

'I said no, Tara. Now just drop it.'

They walked on in silence; the streets were deserted save for a scabby dog that was playing with a tin can down a back alley. 'What a racket,' Violet mumbled. They came to the outskirts of the town, to the familiar parade of shops, most with their metal shutters down and strewn with graffiti. A blue light was on in the hardware store though, one of those lights that was meant to kill flies or something. It gave the interior of the store an ethereal glow. Violet stared at their reflections in the shop window. 'Look at the state of us, Tara. Imagine going on stage at The Amethyst Lounge looking like this.' She picked up the hem of her fishtail dress. 'It's ruined, it is.'

Tara ignored her mother. 'Seen this?' She pointed to the postcard in the window. 'Room to Rent – Enquire Within'.

Violet scoffed. 'I'm not living above a bloody hardware store. I can't go on stage stinking of paraffin and moth-balls.'

Tara glared at her mother. 'I think this is one of those beggars—choosers situations, don't you, Mum?' Without bothering to wait for an answer, she banged on the glass door, causing the 'Closed' sign to swing back and forth on its hook.

'What're you doing, Tara? It's gone one o'clock in the morning.'

'Mum,' Tara sighed. 'I'm cold, I'm tired and I'm hungry; not to mention fed up. I'm sick of traipsing the streets like a couple of whores . . .'

'Tara! Don't be so crude.' Violet leaned against the shop window and closed her eyes, the exhaustion suddenly overwhelming.

Tara peered through the door, leaving a nose print on the glass. 'Eh, up, someone's coming.'

She cleared her throat and stood a little straighter as they listened to the bolts being slid back. The door opened and the sound of a bell cut through the stillness. The elderly gentleman had found time to slip on his tartan dressing gown but his teeth were probably still in a glass beside his bed. He squinted at them through his thick-framed glasses. 'It's gone one o'clock in the morning.'

Violet tugged at her daughter's arm. 'That's exactly what I just said. I'm so sorry to wake you, Mr . . . err . . . ?'

'Bickerstaffe,' he supplied. He looked Violet up and down. 'What happened to you?'

'It's a long story, Mr Bickerstaffe and I really do apologise for waking you. We'll be on our way just . . .'

'We're desperate,' interrupted Tara, her voice cracking. 'Please, can you help us?'

Violet pursed her lips and stared at Tara before turning back to Mr Bickerstaffe. 'Well, we're not exactly desperate, I mean . . .'

'Stop it, Mum,' Tara snapped. 'We need his help, stop being so proud.'

Violet let the sack drop to the floor and ran her hands through her soaking wet hair. She swallowed hard and lifted her chin, adopting the clipped vowels of a television presenter. 'We'd like to enquire about the room you have to rent.'

Mr Bickerstaffe looked from one to the other, before opening the door a little further. 'Why don't you come in and have a look then?'

They followed him through the shop, careful not to trip over the various assortments of brushes, baskets, tins of paint and boxes of rags and chamois leathers. 'You've got a heck of a lot of stock, Mr Bickerstaffe,' said Violet, squeezing through the narrow aisle.

'Aye, mind how you go.'

They climbed the steep wooden staircase to the first floor and waited patiently whilst the old man tried half a dozen keys before finding the one that would open the door. 'After you, miss.'

Violet and Tara stepped into the room as Mr Bickerstaffe flicked on the light. The iron-framed double bed took up most of the space. There was a cracked washstand in one corner and a single wardrobe in the other. The orange glow from the street lamp outside shone through the thin floral curtain, which appeared to have suffered an attack of moths. The cast-iron Victorian fireplace was now home to a two-bar electric heater. The smell was not unpleasant, if one was partial to the smell of sweet stale biscuits. Violet gripped her daughter's hand. 'It's . . . err . . . very . . . erm . . .'

'We'll take it, Mr Bickerstaffe,' said Tara. She glanced at her mother's face, where despair and sadness dragged down her features. 'It's perfect, thank you.'

Mr Bickerstaffe clapped his gnarled hands together. 'Really? Oh, well I'm pleased, I really am. It'll be nice to have some company and a young 'un about the place again.'

Violet tried to smile but knew the resulting grimace would not be enough to convince Mr Bickerstaffe that she was completely happy with the situation. 'The bathroom?'

'Aye, it's across the landing. We'll have to share it, mind, but I'm not in there much. I have my bath on a Friday night between seven and half past. Kitchen's at the back. It's cosy enough, not a bad size, but again we'll have to share it.' He shuffled out of the room. 'I'll leave you to get settled in, give us a shout if you need anything.' He stopped and turned. 'The rent's eight pounds a week, not including the lecky, but I'll let you pay me a month in arrears.'

'We don't need your charity,' said Violet. 'We can . . .'

Tara moved to stand in front of her mother, cutting her off. 'Thanks, Mr Bickerstaffe, we appreciate that.'

He nodded. 'Aye, well, there's just one more thing. Please call me Alf.'

They cuddled together under the icy sheets, Violet's hair wrapped up in a towel, Tara swathed in her big Arran jumper. 'He's seems nice, doesn't he, Mum? Better than bloody Colin anyway.'

Violet's eyes were closed. 'Language, Tara,' she mumbled, her voice thick with sleep, but her mind alert to the utter mess their lives had become.

'Mum?'

'Lord above, Tara! What is it now?'

'I've had an idea.'

'Go on then, let's hear it.'

Tara propped herself up onto her elbow. 'Why don't we try and ask my grandparents for help?'

Violet's eyes flicked open. 'Not this again, I've already told you . . .'

'No, not *your* mum and dad, my other grandparents.'

'Tara, even if I knew where they were, they'd have no money to help us, and we're strangers to them, don't forget. Your dad didn't even tell his parents I was pregnant.'

'They could be really wealthy by now though. If he's been trapping fur in Mongolia for the past fourteen years, then he must have earned a bob or two.'

Violet almost laughed. *Trapping fur in Mongolia.* How on earth had she come up with that one? Still, as long as it spared Tara the truth, she would have to go along with it.

8

As Larry had predicted, his brother had been unable to withstand the temptation of the tobacco. 'Where did you put my coat, Larry?'

'It's in the cloakroom, I'll fetch it for you.'

Martin nodded at Carol. 'You hear that? It's in the cloakroom. I remember when we were kids and we'd just hang our coats on the banister. Now *he* has a special room for them.'

'Stop it, Martin. Larry's been good enough to invite us over, the least you can do is stop sniping. Go on, go and smoke yourself to death in the garden.'

Larry stiffened at the exchange. Surely Martin wouldn't take this kind of abuse in his stride, but his brother shrugged on his sheepskin coat, walked over to his bride and kissed her on the check. 'Sorry, love, you're right, as always. I'll be back in a jiffy.'

When he'd left the room, Larry sat down on the settee next to Carol, their thighs touching. It was barely noticeable but she definitely shuffled away an inch or two.

'I miss you, Carol.'

She gave a nervous laugh and glanced towards the door. 'Don't be saying daft things like that, Larry.'

'It's not daft, it's true. I never stop thinking about you.'

'Oh, Larry.' She picked up his hand and rested it loosely in her own lap. 'We've been through all this and I can't keep apologising. I fell in love with Martin and there's nothing I can do about that. It happens to people all the time. It wasn't that I didn't love you but I love him more.'

Larry winced. 'Ooh, that's a dagger to the heart, that is.'

'I'm just being honest, Larry. I don't regret my decision to leave you for Martin.' She reached for her glass. 'Of course, I regret all the hurt I caused you and I regret that I drove a wedge between you and your only brother, but I'll never regret marrying Martin.' She shrugged. 'I'm sorry.'

Larry stood up and wandered over to the mantelpiece, keeping his back to her as he spoke. 'I came to your wedding, you know.'

'What?'

He heard her get up and pad across the carpet. 'What on earth for?'

He turned to face her. 'I suppose I just wanted to see if you would go through with it. I slipped in quietly at the back, like Dustin Hoffman in *The Graduate*.'

Carol ran her finger round the rim of her glass. 'I love that film.'

He smiled. 'I know you do.'

'It's time for you to find your own happy ending now, Larry. There's someone special waiting for you out there, I just know it. And whoever she is had better deserve you.' She stumbled over the Persian rug, jerking her glass and spilling champagne down the front of her blouse. Larry reached out to steady her. 'Careful.'

She dabbed at the stain with her handkerchief. 'It's OK, I don't think it's ruined.'

'No, I meant be careful of the rug, two grand that cost.'

She laughed and flicked her hair over her shoulders, a habit she'd had for years. 'Two grand? You can buy a new car for that.'

'It's antique.'

'Bloody hell, Larry. You've come a long way. Two grand on a rug that's not even new.'

'Its value goes up, not down. Unless of course some-body chucks champagne all over it.'

Carol smiled and reached for his face, stopping just before her fingers connected with his cheek. 'Oh, Larry, I really hope you find someone soon.' She cast her hand around the room. 'I don't like to think of you rattling round here on your own. How many bedrooms did you say you have?'

'Six.'

'Wow, six?'

She turned and ran her hand along the back of the

cream leather sofa. She picked up the furry purple cushion and bashed it into shape, before clutching it to her chest and burying her nose in the fur. 'It's all fabulous, Larry, but you can't tempt me back with material things. You of all people should know that I'm just not that shallow. I love Martin and I know that's painful for you to hear but I made my choice.'

He looked down at his feet, her words affecting him more deeply than he cared to show. He might have known Carol wouldn't be swayed by this ostentatious showing-off, but it would annoy Martin no end and the fact that Larry had appeared to have made something of himself would gnaw away at his brother until all that remained would be a bitter empty shell. He managed a smile. 'I know I've lost you, Carol.' He held his palms up in defeat. 'I know you love Martin, but it's too painful for me to witness. You'll always be my one true love. I'm sorry, but I just can't imagine being happy with anyone else.' He reached for her hand. '*Tis better to have loved and lost than never to have loved at all.*' She didn't reply but as her eyes glistened, a single tear escaped which he gently caressed away with his thumb. She tilted her face up to his, their mouths only inches apart. He could feel her warm breath on his lips. The tender moment was savaged by Martin returning from the garden.

'Bloody hell, Larry,' he yelled. 'I leave you alone for five minutes and here you are quoting Shakespeare to my wife.'

Carol swivelled round. 'Stop shouting, Martin, you're showing yourself up. Larry and I were just talking.'

Martin strode into the room, flecks of soil from his shoes sprinkling the cream shag pile. He positioned himself between them and stared up at Larry. 'Well, what do you have to say for yourself?'

Larry calmly reached for his glass, swirled the contents around, then took a sip. 'It was Tennyson, Martin, not Shakespeare.'

9

They drove home to San Sedeza along lanes that were unkempt, littered with rubble and full of potholes. Fearing he would spook the horses in the trailer behind, Leo kept a slow, steady pace, his foot barely touching the accelerator. Mateo slept in the seat beside him, his head lolling forward every now and then, momentarily jolting him awake. Diablo had moved quietly and without fuss into the trailer and stood patiently alongside Armonia, who had proven the more difficult horse to load. Perhaps the old man had exaggerated Diablo's manic tendencies. Maybe Leo had got himself a bargain.

His father was in the yard when they returned. Leo jumped out of the truck and called to him. 'Papa, come and see what we've got.'

Mateo woke, scrambled down from the cab and ran over to his father. He tugged excitedly on his arm. 'Papi, we've got two horses, a pink one and a big black one who the man said was mean but he isn't. It was the man who was mean because he had him tied up and he didn't give him any water and . . .'

Felipe patted his younger son's head. 'Whoa, slow down,

Mateo.' He called to Leo for clarification. 'What's all this?'

Leo had pulled down the back of the trailer. 'I couldn't leave him, Papa.'

Felipe frowned when he saw Diablo. 'He's hobbled?'

Leo nodded. 'I decided to leave him like that for the journey, just in case.' He handed his father a halter. 'Can you take the mare?'

Felipe nodded his approval. 'She's a fine specimen, *hijo*.'

Armonia allowed herself to be led into the paddock, her ears pricked to the sights and sounds of her new home. Released from her halter, she flicked her tail, gave a little buck then cantered around the field, whinnying to the other horses in the distance.

Marissa came out of the farmhouse, clutching a feather duster, her cheeks flushed. 'At last, you come home. Where is my little boy?'

'I'm here, Mama.' Mateo ran to her and she scooped him up, squeezing him to her chest.

He kicked his legs. 'I can't breathe, Mama.'

She let him slide to the ground as Leo led Diablo out of the trailer, the horse hesitant, his hobbled gait unnatural.

Marissa stared, her mouth open. 'What is that?' she managed eventually.

'He's our new horse, Mama. Leo saved him. The man who had him was cruel.' Mateo pointed to Diablo's bloodied fetlock. 'Look at his poorly leg. The man did that to him.'

Marissa took a step back. 'I don't like the look of him. He has the evil look in his eye.'

'No, Mama, don't say that. Nobody else wanted him.'

'And you wonder why?'

Felipe slung his arm over his wife's shoulder. 'Leo knows what he's doing, Marissa. I've taught him well. You worry too much.'

She flicked the feather duster into his face. 'It's my job to worry.' She called to Mateo. 'Come in the kitchen and get washed before supper.'

'Aww, Mama, I want to help Leo. How will I ever learn?'

'There's plenty of time for that but right now you have to learn to be a good boy and do as your *mama* says. Come, come.'

'Go with Mama,' Leo said. 'It's better that I see to Diablo on my own at first, just whilst he's getting used to his new surroundings.'

'Diablo? What is this madness?' Marissa shouted. 'You bring a horse named after the devil into my home?' She crossed herself and looked skywards. '*Santa Maria, madre de Dios.*' She took the grumbling Mateo by the wrist and led him into the kitchen, all the while shaking her head.

Dusk had already fallen as Leo tended to Diablo. The cold began to nip at his ears and nose. Leo pulled his hat down and adjusted the scarf so that it covered his mouth. The horse was tethered to a post in the yard, munching contentedly on the hay net. Leo stroked his velvet muzzle and pulled gently on his ears. He traced his finger over the white star between his eyes then ran his hand along the horse's flank; Diablo's coat shone like polished ebony. He seemed calm, docile even, and Leo silently congratulated himself on his ability to spot a good horse when he saw one.

'*Buenas tardes,* Leonardo.'

He looked up to see Gabriela sashaying into the yard, a crocheted shawl around her shoulders to ward off the evening chill. He instinctively smoothed his hair. 'Gabriela, what're you doing here?'

'Ha, charming as always.' She carried a wicker basket in the crook of her elbow. 'Your *mama* invited me for supper.' She indicated the basket. 'I've brought dessert.' She peeled back the tea cloth. 'The last pomegranates of the season.'

It appeared his mother had taken the matter into her own hands.

'I've got to tend to this one.' He nodded at Diablo. 'See his foot? Been tied up and the rope has cut into his skin. I'm just going to hose the leg and then apply some honey. It'll help to heal it.'

'The poor thing. Can I do anything?'

'You can come and talk to him, keep him calm, if you like.'

Gabriela laughed, the sound delicate, like the tinkling of fine china. 'Talk to a horse? You are funny, Leo.'

He reached for her hand. 'Come here and stroke his

nose then.' He guided her hand under Diablo's mouth and she giggled as his whiskers tickled her palm.

'What's he called, Leo?'

'Diablo.'

She whipped her hand away as though she had been bitten and took a step backwards. 'Oh no, Leo, you must change it.'

'You're as bad as my mother. It's unlucky to change a horse's name.' He turned the hose on and let the cool water run down the horse's leg. 'There's no such thing as a bad horse, Gabriela, only bad owners. And this one's had his fair share of those, but he's home now, all that's in the past.' He turned off the water and nuzzled Diablo's neck. 'You're a fine horse, Diablo, and nobody is going to hurt you anymore.'

After supper, Gabriela and Leo retired to his loft bedroom over the barn. A few winters back, he and his father had converted it into a rustic but comfortable living space, thus affording Leo some privacy, which he had taken full advantage of. The floorboards were bare and there were too many cobwebs lurking in the corners but it was his space and he only had to share it with the mice.

Gabriela sat on the bed and bounced up and down, testing the springs. 'This is lovely, Leo, very homely. I bet you've brought a few girls up here, haven't you?'

The mischievous glint in her eye confused him and he decided to ignore the question. 'I like to be close to the horses.' He flicked on a bedside lamp and saw then that she was smiling, a crooked smile that seemed to hint at something else.

'Leo, I've been thinking about what Mateo said this morning.'

He pretended he had forgotten. 'What was that then?'

She pinched him playfully on the arm. 'You know what, Leo. About you asking me out.'

'Oh, that. Just ignore him, he's only a little kid, he doesn't know what he's saying.'

'Do you ever think about it? Asking me out, I mean.'

He sat down next to her on the bed and fell silent as he pulled off his boots. No greater chance than this would ever present itself. He reached for her cheek, then stopped before making contact. It was too soon for such a bold move. 'I rarely think about anything else, Gabriela.'

'Then what's stopping you, Leo?'

'I think . . . how can I say this . . . I think you deserve more than I can give you. You deserve someone who can provide you with a better life. A life where you don't have to rise in the middle of the night to bake bread, a life which takes you away from here, a chance to flourish in the city perhaps, see the world, experience things that living here we can only dream of.'

'But I don't want all that, Leo. I love the *panadería*. My family has made the bread for this village for five generations. And I love *you* too, Leo.' She reached for his face and unlike him a moment ago, she had the courage to make contact with his shadowed cheek.

'You're so young, Gabriela. Perhaps you don't know what you're missing out on yet.' He removed her hand from his cheek but held onto it, lacing his fingers through hers. 'I'm older than you, more . . . um . . . experienced . . .'

'I don't care that I am not the first girl to lie down with you in this bed. I only care that I am the last one.'

She scooped his dark fringe off his face and leaned towards him, the sweet scent of the pomegranates lingering on her breath. With one hand, she began to unbutton his shirt. He gently took hold of her wrist. 'There's no rush, Gabriela.'

'But Leo, I've loved you for most of my life. We've grown up together, shared memories, childish secrets. You carried my books home from school, remember? I've watched you grow into a man . . . a beautiful man, caring and passionate, a man who has so much love to give. I've seen the way you are with Mateo, with the horses. It's wonderful.' She cast her arm around the loft. 'It's time to settle down, Leo. The time for frivolous conquests is over. You could search for another twenty-five years, but you'll never find anybody who will love you as much as the girl sitting on this bed right now.'

'Time to settle down? You've been talking to my *mama*.'

He seemed to be surrounded by women who thought they knew what was best for him. Maybe the time had come to stop fighting it and accept that this village was his home and always would be. Sometimes he did wonder what the rest of the world had to offer but he knew deep down that he would never leave this place. He'd travelled to Madrid once and had almost suffocated in the heat and the squash of people. There didn't seem to be enough air for everyone. It had been exciting for a weekend but he couldn't wait to return to the golden fields and comforting smells of home. If he could bottle the smell of horse sweat, manure and hay, he would surely make his fortune. There wasn't an animal in this world that smelled as good as a horse. He'd had his fair share of the girls, more than his fair share if truth be told. During the holiday season, he could take his pick from a different girl every week, each one of them eager to succumb to the wily charms of the exotic horseman, whose expert hands could calm the most nervous filly. But he'd never been in love. Until now.

'Leo?'

He closed his hands around her cheeks and leaned in, allowing one hand to slide round the back of her neck, pulling her closer. He could feel her warm breath as his lips met hers; her soft mouth was everything he had ever imagined. She pressed herself close to him as his hands searched under her dress. Then he stopped. 'Wait, Gabriela. I want to do things right this time. I want to slow down, I want to treat you with the respect you deserve.' He cleared his throat. 'Gabriela Cruz, would you do me the honour of accompanying me to dinner tomorrow night?'

She stood up and smoothed down her dress. She had

the ample figure of someone who had grown up in a *panadería* and the carb-laden diet had produced some generous curves.

'Leonardo Perez, I would be delighted to accept your kind invitation.'

'In that case, it's a date. I'll . . .'

He stopped at the sound of a horse whinnying. Not the contented snicker a horse gave when he was greeting another but an angry, guttural roar, followed by the sound of the stable door splintering.

Leo was on his feet instantly, grappling for his boots. 'Diablo.'

He shimmied down the ladder, not bothering with the rungs, and sprinted into the yard. Despite the gloom he could see Diablo was standing square, his chest heaving and his nostrils flared to reveal an angry red lining. White foam speckled his muzzle and his eyes were wide and manic. 'Easy there, boy. It's OK. Did something spook you?' Leo moved closer, his upturned palm stretched out so that Diablo could sniff it. He heard Gabriela gasp behind him but he didn't dare turn round. No sudden movements, just gentle coaxing and soothing words as he approached the terrified horse. He had almost managed to grab the halter when Diablo reared up onto his hind legs, his silver shoes flashing before Leo's eyes. Gabriela screamed as he leaped back out of harm's way but he was too slow and Diablo lurched towards him, knocking him to the ground. He landed hard on his back and felt the breath leave his body on impact. Groaning, he managed to roll onto his side and then up onto his knees. He felt like he was breathing through a straw. 'Where . . . where did he go?' he gasped.

Gabriela was beside him. 'He ran out of the yard and jumped the fence. '*Dios mio*, are you alright, Leo?' She rubbed his back as the farmhouse door opened and Marissa and Felipe ran into the yard.

'Leo,' Marissa screamed. 'Are you hurt?'

'Just . . . just winded, Mama.'

She hurried over and dropped to her knees. 'I knew that horse was trouble but would you listen?'

'Not now, Mama.' He reached for his father. 'Help me up, will you, Papa.'

Felipe hoisted him to his feet. 'He won't go far, Leo, I'm sure. He's just enjoying the freedom. Probably never had the chance to express himself so freely, that's all.'

'Mmm . . .' muttered Marissa. 'I'd like to get my hands on him and express *myself*.'

Leo smiled. He knew his mother wouldn't go within an arm's length of the beast.

'Leo, come into the kitchen and get yourself cleaned up. I'm just going to check on Mateo. I don't know how he can have slept through all this commotion.'

'Yes, Mama.'

Leo dusted off his shirt and stretched his back, pulling his shoulder blades together to squeeze out the stiffness. He would need a torch, a lead rein and a bucket of feed, for no way would he leave Diablo to his own devices. He had seen fear in the horse's eyes, not malice.

Gabriela came up behind him. 'I'm going home now, Leo.' She stood on tiptoe and kissed his cheek. 'I hope you find the horse.'

'Gabriela, I . . .' He stopped as his mother's scream echoed round the yard. She had gathered up her skirts and was now standing in the doorway, the warm glow from the fire in the grate enhancing her silhouette.

'Mateo's gone,' she yelled. 'My baby boy has gone.'

10

It was Gabriela who found him. He would never have thought her usually delicate voice would be capable of producing such an ear-splitting scream. 'Leeoooo!' She almost choked on the elongated vowels.

Leo was in the hay barn, lifting up horse blankets and heaving over bales. Mateo often liked to curl up with the cats, and his favourite smoky-grey one had just produced another litter of kittens. He ran into the yard, colliding with Gabriela. 'He . . . he's in the stable,' she gasped. 'I don't think he's breathing, Leo.'

Brushing her aside, he rushed into Diablo's stable. Mateo was lying amongst the straw, his dark hair plastered with blood, a gash across the bridge of his nose. His eyes were closed, his arm bent under his body, the unnatural angle confirming it was surely broken. Leo knelt beside him and pressed his fingers to the boy's neck. 'Thank God. He's alive.' He turned to Gabriela, who stood behind him, the silver cross she wore round her neck pressed to her lips. 'Go and get Mama and Papa, they went down to check the pond.'

Leo hovered over Mateo's body, hardly daring to touch

him. 'Mateo, can you hear me?' He gingerly stroked his brother's brow, then leaned down and kissed him in the same spot. 'Mateo, please.'

He took off his shirt and laid it across his brother's battered body. Mateo was breathing and that was all that mattered in this moment. He noticed the chunks of apple in the straw, bruised and turning brown. He shook his head. 'Ah, Little One, did you come to feed Diablo?'

His mother appeared at the door, wispy strands of sweat-soaked hair across her face. 'Oh, Mateo, my baby.' Marissa crouched beside her younger son, pushing Leo out of the way. 'Is he alive?' She worked her hands underneath his limp body, trying to lift him out of the straw and into the safety of her lap.

'Yes, Mama, he's alive.'

Mateo lay across his mother's knees, his arm hanging grotesquely by his side. 'I think his arm is broken, Mama.'

Felipe stood over his wife, his hands on her shoulders as he tried to keep his voice steady. 'I'm going for the doctor, Marissa. Keep him warm.'

Gabriela whipped off her shawl. 'Here, cover him with this.'

Marissa wiped away her tears with the back of her hand. Her tone was measured but Leo did not miss the angry undercurrent. 'Go after that devil horse, Leo. You make sure you find him and when you do, you take your father's pistol and you shoot him right here.' She pointed to the middle of her own forehead. 'Do you hear me, Leo? That horse does not come back to this yard.'

Leo struggled to his feet, his back still aching from his earlier fall. 'I'm really sorry, Mama.'

He brushed past Gabriela in the doorway, crossed the yard and entered the warm kitchen, where the remains of their evening meal were still scattered on the table. He picked up the bottle of Calvados and took a long slug, the warm liquor making his eyes water. He pulled down the lid of the old wooden bureau and found the tiny brass key nestled beneath a pile of old bills. He stared at the key as it lay in his palm. Despite its small size, it felt heavy in his hand, as though it carried the weight of what he had to do. He climbed the stairs to his parents' bedroom and from underneath the huge cast-iron bed pulled out the locked rosewood box in which his father kept his gun.

He had been walking for hours and now, over in the east, the sky had begun to redden. His worn leather riding boots, which had fitted him perfectly for years, had started to rub his toes and he was finding it harder to ignore each agonising step. He stopped by the creek, threw his bag onto the grass and removed his boots. The ice-cold water in the stream temporarily deadened the pain. He took a hunk of bread from his bag but it was already a day old and rock hard. He tossed it into the river for the fish. There had been no sign of Diablo. Last night, the horse had clattered out of the yard and jumped the fence into the paddock, and his hoofprints had been lost amongst the others. He could have gone in any direction, but Leo guessed that he would have maintained the same trajectory and just kept going, free of his shackles at last, flying over any obstacles in his way. Leo hadn't intended to come this far – if he had, he would have come on horseback – but he needed to walk, to clear his head, think about what he had to do. He lay back on the grass, using his bag as a makeshift pillow. Tiredness pulled at his eyelids and he reluctantly closed them. He would allow himself five minutes' rest before continuing his quest.

He was tugged from his sleep an hour later. The air was still and there wasn't a single sound. No birdsong, no rustling of the grass, no rumble of distant farm machinery. He knew he'd been woken not by noise but by the warmth of the sun on his face. He propped himself up onto his elbows and squinted at the heavy sky, the clouds dark and threatening. He touched his cheek, frowning. There was no warmth to the day at all. He heard it then, it was so close. A gentle snicker, then a warm breath. He turned to see Diablo standing right beside him, his head hanging so low his muzzle almost touched the ground. 'Diablo?' Leo shook the stiffness out of his legs and stood up, wincing as his bare feet found the sharp stubble. 'Hello, boy. Where've you been?'

Without taking his eyes off the horse, Leo picked up his bag and removed the halter and lead rein. He advanced towards Diablo with his arm outstretched, prepared for the horse to bolt at any moment. Diablo lifted his head and tossed his mane but beyond that he didn't move. Leo hardly dared to breathe as he touched Diablo's muzzle. He held his palm still and let the horse sniff him. With his other hand he reached up and tickled behind his ear, the fur there as soft as a puppy's. Murmuring platitudes and comforting words, he managed to ease the halter over the horse's head and attach the lead. It was only then that he allowed himself to breathe. 'Good boy, Diablo.' Leo pulled on the rope, and Diablo followed him to the nearest tree, where Leo secured the rope with a double knot.

He stepped back and took a long look at the horse. His flanks were mud-caked and there was white foam around his mouth. He'd also lost a front shoe and his damaged fetlock had been bleeding again. It could have been a lot worse. 'Are you thirsty, boy?'

He took his canteen of water and squeezed some into his palm as Diablo gently sucked on his hand.

'Oh, Diablo, what have you done?'

He thought about his little brother, lying in the straw, surrounded by dung and little pieces of apple. He remembered the splintered stable door, and the way Diablo had reared up and knocked him to the ground. But most of all he remembered his mother's anguished cries as she cradled her younger son, fearing his life had already ebbed away. Leo wiped his hands down his jeans and backed away without taking his eyes off Diablo's face, he felt around in his backpack and when his hands fell on solid cold metal he could look at the horse no more. He closed his eyes and pulled out the gun.

He'd witnessed his father do it many times before. There was certainly no pleasure to be gained from the actual act, but afterwards as the horse lay still, its once-tight muscles relaxed and its eyes half-closed, free from whatever pain had made its last few weeks miserable, there was a sense of calm relief. Deep sadness too, but no regret. All the horses at the Perez family farm had a good life but more importantly they also had a good death.

Diablo stood still, only the muscles on his flank moving, twitching away the biting insects. Leo tucked the gun into his waistband and removed his shirt. He stroked Diablo's neck, his soothing tones belying his inner turmoil. 'I'm sorry, boy. Whatever life is waiting for you after this one, I hope it's one you deserve. You're not evil, you've just been around evil people, that's all. Once it's over, you'll be free. You'll never again have to suffer the pain and indignity of being shackled. You'll be free to fly, Diablo. Free to be the magnificent horse you were always meant to be.'

He finished tying his shirt around the horse's head. There was no way he wanted Diablo to see what he was about to do. He pulled the gun from his waistband and took two steps back. Death would be instant. Diablo's legs would buckle but Leo had no way of knowing which way he would fall.

Leo raised his arm and closed one eye. Still Diablo did not move. He kept his head still, as though he wanted to make the hideous task as easy as possible for Leo.

Leo's arm ached, his bicep quivering, his palm moist. He closed his eyes and squeezed the trigger gently to the point where he felt resistance. He heard the crack as the bullet left the chamber and felt the kick reverberate down his arm as he altered his aim and sent the bullet into the sky. He couldn't do it, he wasn't capable. If his life depended on it, he couldn't take the life of an innocent horse who had done nothing wrong. He dropped the gun and rushed forward, whipping the shirt off Diablo's head. Whether the horse had been startled by the gunfire, Leo could not tell. He hadn't made a sound.

'Diablo, can you ever forgive me, boy? I wasn't thinking straight. My mind was full of Mateo, but I know this is not what he would want either.'

He untied the lead rein and led the horse to the edge of the stream. Diablo dipped his head and drank thirstily as Leo pulled his shirt back on and stuffed the gun into his backpack.

'Come on,' he said, when the horse finally lifted his head, the water dripping off his muzzle. 'We're going home.'

It was late afternoon when Leo rode Diablo into the yard. After several hours of hobbling through the pain of his blistered toes, Leo had admitted defeat. He'd led the horse alongside a low stone wall and gingerly climbed onto his back. Diablo had tossed his head in the air and danced on the spot but had soon settled under Leo's expert guidance. It was as though an understanding had passed between them and without complaint, the horse dutifully carried home the man who had spared his life.

After turning Diablo out into the small paddock closest to the farmhouse, Leo hurried into the kitchen. All was quiet, the fire in the grate reduced to greying embers, the shutters firmly closed.

'*Hola?* Anybody home?'

With some trepidation he began to climb the stairs, unable to shake the image of his little brother's tiny body lying in a heap of urine-soaked straw. He opened Mateo's bedroom door. He was sitting up in bed, a book about training horses propped up in his lap.

'Little One.' Leo rushed to his brother's side. 'How are you?' He smelled of sleep and antiseptic.

Mateo pouted and rubbed at the bandage wrapped round his head. 'The doctor says I have to stay in bed and rest, but I'm OK, so I don't think that doctor knows best. Did you find Diablo?'

'Yes, I did. He'd gone a long way but he's alright.'

'It wasn't his fault,' insisted Mateo. 'I went into his stable to give him some apples but I dropped them on the floor and startled him. He started kicking and rearing but it was only because he was frightened and felt trapped.'

Leo nodded at the sling. 'What about your arm though? And your nose?' The cut there now sported a bloody crust.

'Dis . . . dislocated. It's a bit sore but I've got some tablets for the pain and it's not dislocated anymore because the man at the hospital put it back where it should be. My nose is fine. Only hurts when I do this.' He wrinkled his nose to demonstrate.

Leo winced. 'You're such a brave boy, Little One.'

Mateo frowned. 'If I've told you once, Leo . . .'

'Yes, yes, sorry. I think you're a big boy now . . . a big brave boy.' He stopped and lowered his voice. 'Where's Mama?'

'I'm here, Leo.'

Marissa stood in the doorway and jerked her head backwards, indicating he should follow her.

'I'll be back in a while, Mateo.'

Out on the landing, Marissa pushed Leo into the master bedroom and closed the door. 'You took your father's gun?'

'Yes, Mama, I did, but . . .'

'Did you find the horse?'

Leo nodded.

'And did you shoot him like I told you?'

He took hold of his mother's hands and squeezed them, trying to make her understand. 'I'm sorry, Mama, I couldn't do it.'

The breath seemed to leave her body all at once. Her

shoulders sagged and her head fell forward. When she looked up, tears had swelled in her eyes. 'Thank God, Leo.'

'But you said . . .'

She pressed her finger to his lips. 'I know what I said, but that was in anger. I was worried about Mateo. I thought he might die, Leo. I thought I might lose my baby boy.'

He took her in his arms, revelling in the reassuring bulk of her. 'It was an accident, Mama and I'm truly sorry.'

'So am I,' she sniffed. She placed her hands around Leo's face. 'I was terrified when I saw you'd taken the gun. I was wrong to ask you to do that and Mateo would never have forgiven me either. Where is he now?'

'Diablo? I've turned him out into the paddock.'

Marissa nodded. 'Take me to see him, will you?'

'Are you sure?'

'Yes.'

He held Marissa's hand as they approached the paddock. The clouds had reshuffled, allowing the sun to highlight Diablo's glossy coat. Leo clicked his tongue and Diablo twitched his ears but kept his head down, nibbling on the stubby grass.

'Here, boy,' called Leo.

'Why isn't he coming?'

'He will, Mama.'

'Diablo, here, boy.'

This time the horse took notice and ambled in Leo's direction. His mother withdrew her hand and crossed herself. 'Is he going to charge?'

Leo laughed. 'He's not a bull, Mama.'

Diablo stopped at the fence and snorted. Marissa took a startled step backwards. 'Why did he do that?'

'It's just his greeting. Honestly, Mama, you've lived around horses all your married life. I don't know why you're so nervous.' He stroked Diablo's long face, his fingers resting on the point between the horse's eyes, the white star, the place where he had intended the bullet to land.

He shook his head to dislodge the memory. He would only look forward from now on.

11

2018

Out on the street, I fumbled in my bag for my phone and automatically rang Ralph's office. The receptionist informed me he was working from home again and offered to put me through to his blue-rinsed secretary but I declined the offer on account she scares me. I called his mobile but it went straight to voicemail and I struggled to find the words to sum up what I had to tell him. 'Erm, Ralph, look, something's . . . oh never mind.' I rang his landline and predictably Susie answered. 'Is Ralph there?' There was no need for pleasantries, we both know we can't stand the sight of each other.

'He's taken Lily and Jasmine to Baby Aerobics.'

Several thoughts clamoured for my attention. What's he doing pratting around with the twins in the middle of a work day? Why did he never find the time to do anything with Dylan when he was that age? And what the hell is Baby Aerobics? I ended the call without bothering to say goodbye.

Next, I rang Dylan but his phone went to voicemail

too. I tried not to get too irritated because he only ever switches his phone off when he's in a lecture. Nan's mobile phone also went to voicemail but this wasn't unusual as it takes her so long to find the correct button to press to answer it. A double-decker bus hissed past, its exhaust spewing out an obnoxious cloud of smoke. Its brakes squealed as it came to a halt at the bus stop and disgorged its weary-looking passengers. It was no good, I couldn't talk out on the street. There was a wine bar type thing over the road. I found a table in the corner and ordered a glass of the house white. I dialled another number and mercifully Moira picked up on the first ring.

'Moira, thank God.'

There was immediate panic in her voice. 'Tara! What's up?'

My mind went blank and I struggled to know where to start. 'I'm in London.'

'I know, you told me.'

Of course I did. I tell her everything. 'That letter . . . well it turns out somebody's left me a key to a safe deposit box.'

'What? Who?'

'I don't know yet. All the answers lie in that box.'

'And probably more questions too.'

I love Moira. She's so down-to-earth and very wise. She's wasted scrubbing loos and ironing shirts for a living.

I tapped Loxton's business card on the table. 'I've got

an appointment with the safe deposit box company this afternoon.'

I was booked on the first off-peak train home so I'd got the time, but I had hoped to spend the afternoon on Oxford Street.

'Right,' said Moira and I could hear her clattering about in the kitchen. The woman never stopped. 'Ring me as soon as you come out. I'm dying to know what's in it.'

I promised to do just that as I caught the barman's eye and pointed to my empty glass. He got the message and trundled over with a refill. I spread out the little tube map that Jamie had given me and tried to memorise the route to Loxton's. I was determined not to have to ask someone and get labelled a clueless northern country bumpkin.

It wasn't too bad as it turned out. Four stops on the Bakerloo line and as long as I was heading south, there wouldn't be a problem. I tried Ralph's phone again but it still went to voicemail. Baby Aerobics must be a serious business, I thought.

The tube was fairly quiet and I managed to find a seat easily. A combination of tiredness and two large glasses of wine had made my eyes heavy. I dared to close them, but there was no danger of me falling asleep and missing my stop – I was far too agitated for that. Thirty-seven years since something had been placed in that box for me. I did a quick calculation. In 1981, I was eighteen. I was pleased the wine hadn't addled my brain too much even though I've always had the mental arithmetic skills of a professional darts player. I was living with my grandmother in 1981 and we came to London that year to watch Lady Di marry Prince Charles. With the help of Nan's tenacity and sharp elbows, we'd secured a spot outside St Paul's where we waited for hours with only a mound of egg sandwiches and a packet of mint Club biscuits to sustain us. Each time Nan lifted the lid on the Tupperware box, the sweaty sandwiches released their obnoxious odour to the groans of our fellow Royal watchers. When the soon-to-be Princess climbed out of the glass coach there was a collective gasp and my Nan's voice rang out above all others. 'Ooh, looks like she forgot to iron the dress.' Poor Lady Di. A creased wedding dress would turn out to be the least of her worries.

Loxton's was a plain-looking building with none of the shiny brass plaques and gilt-edged revolving doors that Irwin Fortis possessed. No pretence, just functional. There were more formalities to go through and out came my passport again. I was shown into a room with just a table and a chair; there wasn't even a window. Ten minutes went by before the door opened and in came a young woman in a tight pencil skirt and vertiginous heels. Her red satin blouse strained against her marshmallow bosom, acres of creamy flesh on show. She was wearing a long silver pendant but whatever was on the end of it was trapped in her cleavage. She placed the metal box on the table. 'I'll leave you to it.' She pointed to a buzzer by the door. 'Just press that when you've finished.' I heard a click as she closed the door. I was sure she'd just locked me in.

I turned my attention to the box. It was hard to calculate the dimensions but let's say it was much smaller than your average shoe box. My clumsy fingers fiddled with the key and after thirty-seven years I expected a minor battle, but no, the key turned effortlessly. All I had left to do was to lift the lid. I could hear Moira telling me to pull myself together and get on with it.

I saw it straight away. I recognised it without even lifting it out of the box. I clamped my hand over my mouth to stifle a scream and stood up so suddenly that the chair fell backwards. Hands on hips, I turned away and took huge gulps of the stale air. There was no one to hear me but I said it anyway. 'How is this possible?'

12

1978

'Tonight's the big night then, is it?' Alf reached for his pipe and crammed in some more tobacco. They had polished off their egg and chips, wiped round the plates with half a crust each and Tara was now struggling to open a rusty can of pineapple chunks for afters. 'How long have you had this can, Alf? Since the War? The first one?'

'It'll be fine, love. Stuff keeps for ever in tins. I say, your mum must be very talented to be invited to The Amethyst Lounge.'

'Oh, she is,' beamed Tara. 'She's going to be a big star one day.' She gestured around the cluttered kitchen. 'Soon we'll be able to afford a place of our own and then we can say goodbye to this . . . this . . .' She floundered, realising she was on the brink of hurting Alf's feelings. She passed him a bowl of pineapple and slumped in the armchair opposite his, stretching out her legs so that her toes were almost touching the grille on the electric fire.

Alf smiled. 'It's alright, love, I know it's not exactly home for you. You deserve better but it's my pleasure to have you here whilst you wait for your luck to change.'

'Don't get me wrong, Alf, we're happy here. The last few weeks have been the safest I've felt for ages. I don't mind me mum going out to work and leaving me here with you.'

He reached across and patted her knee. 'Company for each other, aren't we?' He pulled out his handkerchief and gave his glasses a cursory polish, before reaching up to take a framed photograph off the mantelpiece. He passed it over to Tara. 'That's our Judith.'

Tara stared at the young woman in her gown and mortarboard, clutching a rolled-up piece of paper secured with a red ribbon. Her eyes bored into the camera lens; her chin tilted upwards, something resembling a smirk playing on her lips. She did not look like a person you could warm to. 'You must be very proud, Alf.'

'Aye, I am, love. Worked hard she has, sacrificed a husband and kids for her career. Me and Ethel would've liked grandkids but you can't be selfish, can you?'

Tara shook her head. 'No, I suppose you can't. Where does she live?'

'Down in that there London, got a lovely flat, although she calls it an apartment, or summat, overlooking t'Thames.'

'What does she do down there?'

Alf sat up a little straighter, his chest inflating. 'She's

84

a political advisor. Very demanding it is. She works for the Tories, often has meetings with that Mrs Thatcher.' He curled his lip and shuddered.

'Not a fan, Alf?'

He shook his head. 'Nah. You can't have a woman *in charge* of the party. It's alright for the likes of our Judith working behind the scenes.' He clenched his fist and punched the air. 'But it takes a man to lead.'

'Don't let me mum hear you talking like that. She reckons Maggie should be the next prime minister.'

Alf guffawed so forcefully he dislodged his false teeth. He pushed them back in with his thumbs. 'Eee, I've 'eard it all now. Never going to 'appen, love. I'll plait fog if it does.'

'D'yer see much of her? Judith, I mean, not Mrs T.'

Alf shrugged. 'Well, she's very busy, you know. She gets up here when she can, stays for a cuppa if she's got time, and we speak on the phone every so often.'

'Doesn't sound like much.'

'Aye, well, I try not to make too many demands on her. I'm alright 'ere on me own. I've got me customers so it's not like I don't see anybody. Some old folks can go weeks without talking to another soul, so I count me blessings.' His face brightened a little. 'And now I've got you and your mum.'

Right on cue, the kitchen door creaked open and Violet entered the room, the sequins on her short red dress sparkling, her cherry lips sporting a wide smile. 'Ta-da!'

she exclaimed, throwing her arms in the air and tilting her hips.

Alf shuffled round in his chair. 'Violet Dobbs, you're a sight for sore eyes alright.'

'Skye, Alf. Skye with an "e" on the end. When I'm dressed in this clobber you have to use my stage name.'

'Violet Skye,' repeated Alf. 'It suits you, does that.'

'Mmm . . . I've been using it since I was five years old. I entered a talent contest at Butlin's in Skegness and when the Red Coat asked for my name, he said, "Dobbs! A pretty little thing like you can't go on stage with a stubby name like Dobbs." I was in the wings already so had to think of something quickly and it's the first thing that popped into my head. I loved it though. I wanted to change my name by one of those deed whatsits but I wasn't allowed.' She turned to her daughter. 'Tara, can you fix this blinkin' eyelash for me? It keeps fallin' off.'

Violet sat in the chair vacated by her daughter and drummed her fingers impatiently as Tara hovered over her, pressing the eyelash down onto her lid. 'Don't smudge me eyeliner, will you?'

'Do you want me to do it or not, Mum?'

'Sorry, love. I just want everything to be perfect for tonight.'

Tara straightened up. 'And it will be.'

'You look beautiful,' said Alf. 'You put me in mind of a young Vivien Leigh.'

'Really? What a lovely thing to say, Alf.' Violet stood

up, blinking furiously to test the strength of the fixed eyelash. 'Thanks, Tara. Now pass us me coat off that hook.'

Alf held out his hand. 'Help me up, will you, Tara?'

She hoisted him out of his seat and watched him shuffle over to the cupboard in the corner. 'You can't go out in that old thing, Violet. This is The Amethyst Lounge we're talking about, not the old Labour club.' He pulled out a three-quarter-length fur coat in shimmering tones of walnut brown and beige. 'I want you to wear this.'

Violet stepped forward and stroked the fur. 'Is it real?'

'Aye, mink, it is. Belonged to my Ethel and before that to her mam.'

Violet shook her head. 'Oh, I couldn't possibly wear this, but thanks anyway.'

Alf was insistent, thrusting the coat towards her. 'Take it, Violet. It's no use to anybody just hanging there in that cupboard. It deserves to be worn.'

'Take it, Mum,' urged Tara.

'Oh, I don't know, I've always had a go at folk who wear real fur. It's cruel, isn't it?'

'Vicious buggers they are,' stated Alf.

'Who are? The people who wear fur?' asked Violet.

'Nah, not them. I'm talking about mink. Spiteful little blighters. Bite your finger off soon as look at yer.'

'Doesn't mean we have to strip the fur off their backs though, does it?'

Tara held the coat up to her cheek. 'It's so soft, Mum, and so elegant, and the mink's long dead now. What harm could it do?'

Violet looked from Tara to Alf, their expectant faces waiting for her answer. 'Well, if you're sure, Alf. I'll look after it, I promise.' She kissed him on the cheek. 'Wish me luck.'

Violet stared into the mirror in her dressing room, the harsh lights showing no forgiveness. She took out her compact and blotted her forehead and nose. A loud rap on the door startled her. 'Who is it?'

A man stuck his head through the gap. 'Ian Cherry, *Evening News.*'

'*Evening News*? I've not got time to read the paper. I'm due on stage.'

He laughed and took a step closer. 'I'm not selling it, you daft bat. I want to do an interview. You've seen my column in the paper? Ian Cherry, Man About Town?'

'You want to do an interview with me?'

He glanced around the dressing room. 'Well there's nobody else here.' He took out his shorthand notebook and pencil and pulled up a chair. 'Don't look so worried, I've interviewed the best of them, you know. It probably won't be much but I'll squeeze you in.'

The velvet curtain had come down on the first half and Violet was on next. She peered through the curtain and gazed at all the people clustered round their little tables. Waiters and waitresses zoomed in and out, trays held aloft on one palm, expertly dispatching frothy pints without appearing to spill a drop. There was so much laughter and merriment in the room, the mixed audience seemingly intent on just having a good time. She drew a deep breath and peeled her tongue from the roof of her mouth. She could barely find enough moisture to speak, let alone sing. She was grateful for the high neckline on her sequinned shift dress because she knew for sure that her chest would be flushed a livid shade of scarlet. Her clammy palms had trouble finding purchase on the microphone and she looked round for something to wipe them on.

'Two minutes to curtain up, Miss Skye.' The stage manager glanced down at his clipboard. 'You ready?'

Violet nodded. 'I think so. Do you have a towel, my hands seem to be a little . . . well, you know?'

He whipped a handkerchief out of his pocket. 'Here, keep it.' He squeezed her forearm and winked. 'Break a leg.'

She could hear the compère on the other side of the curtain telling the audience about a bright young star whose pitch-perfect voice would thrill and mesmerise in equal measure. Never before had such mellifluous tones graced the stage at The Amethyst Lounge. Violet was wondering who on earth he was talking about when she heard him ask the audience to give a huge warm welcome to Miss Violet Skye. The velvet curtain began to rise, agonisingly slowly at first, until all at once there she was in the full glow of the spotlight, the microphone clutched to her chest, the politely clapping audience full of expectation.

Now more than ever before she had to give the performance of her life.

The twenty-minute set flew by in a blur and by the time Violet took her final bow, the audience was on its feet demanding an encore.

'Thank you very much, you're very kind.' She nodded to the people closest to her, just yards from her feet. 'Thank you.' To shouts of *More, more,* she swayed gently, the relief making her light-headed and giddy. She focused on the huge glitter ball in the centre of the room, until she felt the reassuring hand of the compère as he guided her into the wings.

Later, perched on a bar stool at the back of the theatre, she sipped her drink, reliving the glorious memory of her twenty minutes in the spotlight. Never before had she received so much adulation. She could hardly wait to tell Tara.

'This one taken?'

Violet lifted her eyes and stared at him. The first things she noticed were his bushy sideburns and a chunky gold incisor. 'Erm . . . no, it's not.' She gestured to the stool. 'Please have it.'

He eased himself on to the stool. 'Can I get you another?'

She glanced at the empty glass and, not wishing to appear rude, reluctantly accepted. 'Thank you. A Snowball, please.'

He clicked his fingers at the bartender. 'A Snowball and a Grasshopper when you're ready, pal.'

He took out his packet of cigarettes. 'Want one?'

Violet wafted them away. 'No, thanks, I don't smoke.'

'Aah, of course, not good for the voice.' He lit up one for himself and blew out a perfect smoke ring. 'You were sensational by the way.' His eyelids were heavy and he had a daft grin on his face.

'You really think so?'

He leaned over and whispered in her ear. 'Utterly captivating.'

She shuddered as his hot breath condensed in her ear. 'I . . . err . . .' she floundered.

The barman pushed their drinks over the bar. 'Shall I put them on your tab, Stu?'

He nodded and raised his glass, the smell of the *crème de menthe* mingling with his Brut aftershave. 'Cheers.'

'Cheers,' echoed Violet. 'And thank you . . . erm . . . Stu.'

They clinked their glasses together and each took a sip. Stu slid off his stool and manoeuvred it closer to Violet, so their knees were now touching. Violet regarded his greasy hair, the black curly tendrils reaching the top of his collar. The light bounced off his gold tooth. All he needed was an eye-patch to complete the washed-up pirate look.

'This your first time here then?' He swayed back and forth on the stool and Violet resisted the instinct to grab him to stop him falling off.

She nodded. 'First time here but I've been singing for years on the club circuit, the back-street club circuit that is, nothing like this place.' She popped the cocktail cherry into her mouth as Stu downed his drink.

He wiped his hand across his lips. 'Another?'

Without waiting for an answer he held two fingers up to the barman. 'Same again.'

'Oh, I'm not sure,' protested Violet. 'I need to be getting back to my daughter.'

'You have a baby?'

'Well, no, not a baby, she's fourteen.'

'Never! Never in a million years do you have a fourteen-year-old kid. I mean you can't be much more than that yourself.'

Violet laughed. 'You're obviously not looking closely enough. I'm almost thirty.'

He leaned forward, scrutinising her face, his cigarette-infused breath making her turn away and pick up her drink again. He pointed his finger at her chest, his words beginning to slur. 'You . . . you are an exqu . . . an exquis . . . a ravishing-looking creature.' He placed his palms on her thighs and began to inch them forward.

'Remove your hands at once, please.'

Stu looked perplexed. 'Why? You're obviously gagging for it. Letting me buy you drinks, leading me on.' He left his hands where they were and leaned in towards her face, his mouth open, his wet lips resembling two fat slugs.

Before Violet could react, somebody clamped their hands onto Stu's shoulders and dragged him backwards. 'I think it's time you left, sonny.' He hauled Stu off the stool and threw him to the ground, pinning him there with a foot to the chest. 'I suggest you apologise to the young lady and then get the hell out of here before my temper runs out.'

Stu scrambled to his feet and dusted himself down. He glared at his assailant with as much menace as he could muster before turning to Violet to deliver his venomous parting shot. 'Prick tease.'

The whole episode had lasted less than sixty seconds, but Violet's hand shook as she picked up her glass. 'My God, I thought this was a classy place.'

'Are you OK? Let me get you another.' He called to the barman. 'Two brandies over here when you're ready, mate.'

'I'm fine, thanks to you. What a creep he was.'

He held out his hand. 'Larry Valentine. Pleased to meet you.'

She took his hand, noticing the neatly clipped finger-nails. A diamond signet ring sparkled on his little finger. 'Violet Dobbs.'

He gestured to the stool opposite. 'May I?' He held his palms aloft. 'I promise I won't grope you.'

Violet managed to laugh. 'Yes, please have a seat.'

He shrugged off his camel coat and laid it over the back of the stool. 'I was just on my way home when I saw you might be in a spot of bother.'

'Well, I would have handled it differently. If you hadn't intervened he would've been dripping in advocaat by now.'

'Good job I stepped in then. Waste of a drink that would've been.' He took a swig of his brandy. 'I thought you were brilliant tonight by the way. Best singer they've had here in ages.'

'It's kind of you to say that.'

'It's true. I'm not in the habit of saying things I don't mean.'

Violet took a surreptitious glance at her watch, all of a sudden not wanting the evening to end, but conscious that Tara would be waiting.

Larry noticed her looking. 'Do you have to be somewhere?'

'I do really. I need to get home to my daughter. She'll be dying to know how tonight went and I don't want to miss the last bus.'

'The last bus? Don't tell me you came on the bus looking like that.'

She glanced down at her sequinned dress. 'I had a big coat on too.'

Larry rubbed his chin, his narrowed eyes fixed on hers. 'Tell you what, stay for a bit longer and I'll run you home. What do you say?'

'Well, I wouldn't want to put you to any trouble.'

He raised his glass and winked at her. 'Oh, I think we've had all the trouble we can handle tonight.'

The pot-holed car park was badly lit and Violet had to pick her way carefully along the uneven Tarmac. She stumbled over a rogue stone and would have crashed to the ground had Larry not grabbed her elbow and hauled her up. 'You really are my knight in shining armour tonight.' She cringed inwardly at the cliché and wished she hadn't sounded so much like the proverbial damsel in distress.

'This is a beautiful coat,' he said, running his fingers down the sleeve. 'Is it real?'

'Yes, but it's not mine. I borrowed it from a . . . erm . . . friend.'

Larry gave a low whistle. 'Must be a very good friend indeed.' He stopped outside a metallic-blue sports car and slipped his key into the door. Violet stared at the long sleek bonnet, the tinted windows and the sparkling chrome wire wheels. 'It's a beauty.'

'*She*,' he corrected. '*She's* a beauty.'

Violet resisted the urge to roll her eyes. Why did blokes always have to use the female pronoun on inanimate objects such as cars?

He opened the passenger door, allowing her to slide as gracefully as she could into the low bucket seat, the red leather freezing cold on her bare legs. He jogged round to the driver's side and climbed in beside her. 'Where to?'

Violet conjured up an image of their digs: the garish wallpaper, the dark green paintwork which had peeled in places to reveal the hideous sickly-pink colour underneath. Friday was the day when Alf washed his clothes in the kitchen sink, then ran them through the mangle before letting them steam in front of the electric fire. She'd mentioned buying a twin-tub but he wouldn't hear of it. His Ethel had had no need for fancy gadgets and neither did he. There was no way Violet could invite Larry in to that mess. 'You can just drop me at the end of Stockport Road.'

Larry took a sideways glance at her. 'You sure? I don't like to leave a lady to walk around after dark.'

'I'll be fine.' Violet dismissed his concern with a flick of her hand. 'I can look after myself, and besides, Tara will probably still be awake and I don't want to have to face a million questions about you at this time of night.'

'Well, I'm not happy about it but if you insist.'

They drove on in silence and she noticed how his hands continually caressed the thin steering wheel, stroking it as though it were a treasured pet. She looked at his profile, his thick sandy-coloured hair framing his face like a helmet. He reminded her of Steve McQueen; the same piercing blue eyes and permanently worried expression. She studied his watch – a Rolex – but whether it was genuine or one he had picked up from the market she couldn't tell. There again, a man who drove an E-Type

Jag was hardly likely to wear a knock-off watch. On his other wrist was a thick gold bracelet, which matched the chain around his neck. She wasn't a fan of jewellery on men but Larry somehow carried it off.

He applied the brake and brought the car to a gentle halt. 'Is this close enough?'

She nodded. 'My . . . erm flat is just up there.' She reached for the door handle but Larry had already jumped out and run round to her side. He opened the door and offered her his hand. 'Thank you,' she said, climbing out of the car. He brought her hand up to his mouth and pressed it to his lips.

'I'd like to see you again.'

She tried to keep the excitement from her voice, instead opting for a cool tone just the right side of aloof. 'Well, I'll have to check my diary.'

He smiled as he held onto her hand. 'Dinner, tomorrow night. I'll pick you up at seven.'

There was no uplift in his voice at the end of the sentence. It was not meant as a question. How arrogant could he get, just assuming she would be free.

'Perfect, I'll see you then,' she found herself answering. She pointed to the pavement. 'I'll be waiting right here.'

She removed her heels before climbing up the steep wooden staircase. God only knew how Alf managed to navigate these stairs. She hauled herself up by the handrail, careful to avoid the second-to-last step, which always produced a particularly ear-splitting creak. She eased open their bedroom door and crept in. 'Tara,' she whispered. 'Are you still awake?'

'No,' came the muffled reply. 'I'm asleep.'

Violet eased under the covers and snuggled up against her daughter. 'Sorry I'm so late, Tara.' She stroked the back of her head, her thoughts again turning to Larry. Never before had a man of his means showed any interest in her. Most of them just wanted a good time, out for anything they could get, just like that letch in The Amethyst Lounge earlier. But Larry was different. Polite and respectful, good company and, judging by the look of things, not short of a bob or two. She leaned over and kissed her daughter's cheek. 'Everything's going to be alright now, Baby Girl.'

13

2018

It had gone ten o'clock by the time I arrived home. The house wasn't in darkness as I expected though. The hall light was on and the lounge curtains had been drawn. Moira, bless her, always thought of everything. I hadn't rung to tell her what was in the box because I'd needed time to process it myself. I was grateful that she'd taken it upon herself to be there for me. 'I'm back,' I announced unnecessarily as I opened the door. I could smell the wood burner in the kitchen.

I took the time to notice the hall floor had been mopped, the solid oak restored to its showroom glory. There was a jug of freesias on the hall table. Moira was so much more than my cleaner.

I was beginning to feel a little lighter but as soon as I opened the door to the kitchen my shoulders sagged and my mood instantly darkened. 'Ralph! What the hell are you doing here?'

He stood up to greet me, holding his arms out. I side-stepped the impending embrace and pushed past him.

'You left a garbled message on my voicemail and then Susie said you rang the house so I knew it must be important.' He gave a little chuckle, although I failed to see anything remotely amusing. I caught a whiff of his aftershave, once so familiar I had stopped noticing it. The perfect blend of sandalwood and cloves immediately transported me back to happier times. An unexpected and unwelcome wave of sadness overwhelmed me.

'Oh, Ralphie. Why did you have to ruin everything?'

I hadn't called him Ralphie since the day he walked out. He seemed taken aback for a second but offered no answer. I wasn't expecting one. I dumped my bag on the worktop. 'And that key I gave you is for emergencies only.'

'I thought it sounded urgent.' He opened the door of the wood burner and chucked another log on.

'Make yourself at home, Ralph.' He could not have failed to notice the sarcastic edge to my voice and yet he responded with a suggestion that we have a nightcap.

I nodded meekly as though I didn't have a choice and watched as he went to the cabinet and lifted out the glasses and Jack Daniel's. Even though it was the middle of winter he was in his beige chinos, crisp white shirt, a powder-blue cashmere sweater draped casually over his shoulders. His face was still tanned from a recent holiday to the Canaries. His dark hair was greying at the temples but this only added to his good looks. I remembered my own dishevelled state and ran my fingers through my hair, trying to coax it back to life.

'You still haven't said why you called.'

The truth is I didn't want to tell him anymore. It had nothing to do with him, he wasn't around back then and I knew he'd only start telling me what to do. I regretted involving him but old habits die hard as they say.

'It doesn't matter now, Ralph.' I took a slug of my drink as I settled into my chair by the wood burner. 'Why don't you start by telling me why you really came round?'

Instead of taking the chair opposite, he sat on the arm of mine. 'It's peaceful here.' He gazed down into my face and for the first time I noticed how tired he looked. Baby Aerobics was obviously more demanding than it sounded.

'You don't know how lucky you are, Tara. Having this place to yourself, nobody else to think about. You can come and go as you please, watch what you want on the television . . .'

I jumped up so quickly, my drink sloshed down the front of my blouse. 'Ralph, you're a clueless twit sometimes.' The conversation was in danger of heading the way all our conversations went and I didn't have the mental energy to cope with all the accusations, recriminations, blame and a competition as to who had the shittiest life. 'Will you stop feeling sorry for yourself? You've got two lovely daughters, a trophy girlfriend who thinks the world of you for some unfathomable reason

101

and a son who still loves and respects you in spite of the fact you tore our family apart.'

He bowed his head and stared into his empty glass, nodding slowly. 'I know and you're right.'

I hefted him up by his elbow. 'You need to go now, Ralph. Go on, get back to your bedtime stories.' I bundled him out of the front door and watched as he climbed into his car. He gave me a little wave as he pulled away and I was annoyed at the pang of pity I felt for him.

Back in the warmth of my kitchen I pulled the little package from Loxton's out of my handbag. I glanced at the clock on the wall. There was only one person I wanted to talk to at that moment but it was too late. Forty years too late.

14

1978

Tara heaved her school bag onto her shoulder, hooked the wicker cookery basket into the crook of her elbow and with her free hand picked up her PE bag. 'The person who came up with my timetable should be lined up against the wall and shot.'

'Tara,' admonished Violet. 'Don't say things like that.'

'Maths, geography, biology, home economics and PE all on the same day? I need a pack mule to get this lot into school.'

Violet kissed her daughter on the cheek and handed her a lunch box. 'Don't forget this.'

Tara stuffed it on top of her games kit. 'Right.' She nodded at the cookery basket. 'Don't forget it's quiche for tea. Tell Alf there'll be enough for him too. We can open a tin of baked beans to go with it.'

'Ooh, I don't know,' said Violet. 'Eggs and beans? Alf's insides won't know whether they're coming or going.'

Tara had a slightly longer walk to school than she'd had when they lived in Colin's hovel, but it was a small price to pay. Nonetheless, her arms had all but seized up by the time she arrived at the school gates. As usual, a cluster of boys hung around the entrance, smoking and generally trying to look cool. Some girls fell for this. Lisa Cooper for starters. There she was hanging on to the arm of that Tom Marshall. Tom didn't bother with his school blazer, preferring instead his denim jacket. Tara wondered how on earth he got away with it. Unless of course the teachers were as smitten as the rest of her classmates. He stood with his back to the wall, one foot up behind him, flicking ash onto the ground.

'Hi, Tara,' smiled Lisa, stroking Tom's arm. 'You OK? You're looking a bit crimson. Your face is all . . . you know . . . shiny.'

Tara hurried on, keeping her big shiny head down. 'Fine, thank you.' *You absolute total bitch.*

There was no doubt Lisa was pretty but when you used your entire pocket money to fuel your Superdrug habit, then there really was no excuse to go out looking like . . . like . . . well, Tara.

Being two years her senior already gave Tom the edge and made him more attractive than the boys in her year, who were mostly clowns. They were taught separately, boys and girls, with just a communal playing field dividing the two schools. Once a week though, they would come together for combined studies, giving the girls a chance to have a bash, literally, at woodwork and the boys to try their hand at sewing a patchwork quilt.

Tara hated going over to the boys' side. It smelt stale and stuffy, of unwashed clothes, like some great big charity shop. Violet had a theory of why this was. The girls all wore skirts, which allowed the air to circulate. The boys on the other hand all wore trousers, which meant their nether regions were never afforded the luxury of fresh air and so became sweaty. Tara would rather not think about a boy's nether regions, sweaty or otherwise. She sat down at her desk, lifted the lid and pulled out her pencil case. Double maths to start the week. She laid out her protractor and ruler and began to sharpen her pencils whilst she and the rest of the class waited for the form teacher.

'Oi, you.'

Tara looked up. 'Me?'

Lisa Cooper stood in front of the desk, her hands on her hips, chewing gum without bothering to close her mouth. 'You stay away.' The rest of the class had fallen ominously silent.

'From you? With pleasure.' Tara carried on with her pencils.

Lisa slammed her palm down on the desk. 'Not from me, you idiot. From Tom Marshall.'

'Stay away from Tom Marshall? I doubt he even knows I exist.'

'Really,' said Lisa, dragging out the word. 'Then how come he was asking about you?'

In spite of herself, Tara felt the blood rise in her

cheeks. 'I . . . I don't know. Um . . . what did he want to know?'

'Never you mind.' Lisa took a step backwards, the smirk on her lips an indication of what was to come. 'I set him straight. Told him how you don't even have a proper house and have to live above an ironmonger's and that your mother's a stripper.'

Tara stared down at the desk, running her fingers over the years of graffiti. She took a deep breath and slowly stood up, enunciating her words. 'My mother is not a stripper. She's a singer.'

Lisa tossed her head. 'Hah, that's not what my dad says.'

'And how would he know?'

'He saw her down The Acres of Flesh in town.'

Damn. This was true. Violet had performed at the seedy strip club but she'd only been able to stomach it once and she had certainly not taken her clothes off. She'd been hired to warm up the crowd by singing a few numbers and she was back home before nine.

'Goes there a lot, does he? Your dad, I mean. Likes looking at other women, does he?'

Lisa didn't miss a beat. 'Well at least I have a dad.'

Lisa's smirk vanished as Tara lurched over the desk and grabbed a handful of her hair, yanking it upwards. Tara's other hand whipped across Lisa's cheek, making a perfect connection, which produced a most satisfying slap. Lisa screamed just as the form teacher came through the door,

106

clutching the register. 'Tara Dobbs! Headmaster's office. Now!'

Tara stood on the gritty floor behind Alf's counter. Saturday was her favourite day of the week, and rather than go into town with her friends shopping for make-up or records, she revelled in helping out Alf and his customers. She advised on paint colours, took charge of the deliveries and counted out the screws and nails which Alf sold by the half dozen. Four weeks had now passed since her mother had met Larry Valentine, and together with more gigs at The Amethyst Lounge, this had served to make Violet more contented, bordering on happy even. Violet had told her all about Larry's house, a huge detached thing in an affluent suburb Tara had only ever seen pictures of in *Cheshire Life*. Apparently, it had a huge corner bath in green (although her mother said Larry called it *avocado*), which doubled up as a Jacuzzi, with taps which were actually gold-plated. Of the six bedrooms, four of them had their own little bathrooms attached, which Larry called by some French word her mother couldn't remember. The master bedroom had a four-poster bed swathed with pink silk drapes and piled high with satin cushions. Tara hadn't liked to probe how her mother knew anything about the master bedroom and its range of luxury bedding. She pushed the image out of her mind and stared out of the window at the fine smattering of snow that had come down during the night. 'Bloody ridiculous weather for April this is.'

Alf wandered in from the back. 'It's nothing is that. I lived through the winter of '47. Twenty-foot snow drifts there were. Stockpiles of coal froze solid, couldn't be moved at all. Power stations had to shut down and spuds froze in the ground. Couldn't get them up without a pneumatic drill.' In spite of the hardships he was describing, Alf had a melancholy smile on his face as was often the case whenever he reminisced. 'My Ethel knitted me a Fair Isle jumper, with a polo neck. Took her weeks, but I swear you'll not find anything warmer. I've still got it all these years later.' He looked up towards the ceiling. 'I can still smell you on it, Ethel.' He pulled on his brown overall. 'Anyway, I've got a new lad starting today.'

'What for, Alf? We don't need anybody else.'

'Thought we could do with a bit of muscle around here, to help with all the heavy lifting and that. Might even expand into doing deliveries. You've got to keep up with the competition, haven't you?'

Tara glanced at the clock. 'Well, he's late so that's not a good start.'

The shop bell rang and they both looked over at the door.

'Morning, lad,' greeted Alf. 'Come on in, will you, say hello to Tara.'

Tara's mouth hung open in what was no doubt a most unattractive way. 'Hello, Tom.'

Alf raised his eyebrows. 'Oh, do you two know each other?'

Tom smiled and took a step forward. 'We've never been formally introduced.' He offered his hand. 'Tom Marshall, pleased to meet you.' He sounded so grown-up.

Tara shook his hand, trying to sound casual. 'Yeah, I've seen you around.'

'First things first then,' said Alf. 'Tara, lass, show Tom where the kettle is.'

She pointed to the door leading to the hallway. 'It's down there.'

Alf nudged her. 'Go after him then and make me one whilst you're at it.'

Tara followed Tom into the back kitchen, unable to take her eyes off his slim hips. He wore a washed-out Stranglers t-shirt, with a full list of their 1977 tour dates listed on the back, and his denim flares were frayed at the bottom from the constant contact with the ground. He wore his dark, wavy hair rebelliously long and he had a habit of scooping it out of his eyes with his hand or with a quick shake of his head. She caught a whiff of his Hai Karate aftershave.

'What are you doing here, Tom? I mean why are you working here, at Alf's?'

'I came in one night after school and asked if he needed anybody to help out on Saturdays. He said he did and here I am.'

'Does Lisa know?'

'Lisa? What the hell has it got to do with her where I work?' He seemed genuinely puzzled.

'You knew I worked here though.' She cast her eyes skywards. 'Well, live here actually. Up there.'

'I did know,' Tom confessed. 'I thought it would be a laugh, us working together.'

'You hardly know me.'

'That, I was hoping to rectify.'

Tara refused to let herself get carried away. 'But why?'

'I like you, OK? You're funny.'

Tara rubbed at her temples, trying to erase the unwelcome thought now clamouring for attention. 'You . . . um . . . well, you wouldn't be doing this to get back at Lisa, would you?'

Tom laughed. 'See, you're funny.'

She looked him up and down. 'But you're so . . . you know . . .' She stopped as Alf wandered in from the shop.

'I thought you two had got lost or summat,' Alf said. 'What's keeping you?'

'I was wondering if you wanted to go to the ice rink tonight,' said Tom.

Tara looked up. 'Me?'

Tom nodded towards Alf. 'Well I wasn't asking him.'

Instinctively, Tara's fingers flew to the huge spot on her chin. 'Tonight? Bloody hell, you don't hang about, do you?' She mentally ran through her sparse wardrobe, wondering if she would have time to nip out and buy a new top. 'Hmm . . . I suppose I could.'

'Oh, don't put yourself out,' Tom said, folding his arms, the trace of a smile on his lips.

'She'll be there,' said Alf. 'I'll make sure of it. Violet's no doubt off out somewhere with that Larry fella so it'll be nice to 'ave the place to meself for once.'

With every fibre, Tara wanted to accept, but ice-skating? Images of Bambi came to mind, sprawled on the ice, legs akimbo, all dignity out the window. She looked at Tom's expectant face, his smooth skin not yet ravaged by a razor. 'Go on then,' she said. 'Thanks.'

A couple of hours passed before Tara had the chance to bound up the stairs. She burst into their bedroom with such gusto that the door crashed against the wall, startling Violet, who was absorbed in the latest Jackie Collins. 'Flamin' Nora, Tara, there'd better be a fire.'

'Mum,' Tara panted. 'You'll never guess what.'

Violet laid down her book. 'In that case, you'd better tell me then.'

'Tom's asked me out! Tonight. To the ice rink.'

'Who's Tom when he's at home?'

'You know, that one from school. He's a couple of years above me. He's gorgeous, looks like David Essex. Alf's only gone and taken him on in the shop.'

'I don't remember you mentioning him before.'

'That because he's out of my league but by some

miracle he's asked me out to the ice rink . . . tonight.' She stopped and ran her hands through her hair. 'Oh my God, you don't think he's doing this for a bet, do you?'

'No, Tara. I can't imagine anyone would be so cruel, but in any case you're a beautiful young lady and any lad would be proud to be seen with you on his arm.'

'You're only saying that because you're my mum. It doesn't count.' She moved over to the mirror and peered at her reflection. 'Look at this.' She pointed to the spot on her chin. 'How can I go out on my first date with this thing? It's huge.'

Violet rose from her seat and took a closer look. 'Tara, there's nothing there, stop worrying.'

'Nothing there? A blind man on a galloping horse would notice it.' Tara returned to the mirror. 'Looks like it's about to erupt like bloody Vesuvius.'

'No need to swear, Tara.'

Tara ran her fingers through her mousy-brown hair. 'And what am I going to do with this? It's so bloody flat, it needs more . . . more . . . oomph. Do you think I've got time to do a demi-wave before tonight?'

'Stop panicking, love. I'll help you and by the time I've finished you'll be able to give that Farah Fawcett a run for her money.' Violet stood and reached for her vanity case, opening the lid and rooting inside. She took out several items and laid them out on the bed as though she were a surgeon preparing to carry out an operation.

She tapped her lips. 'Hmm . . . I think I have everything I need here. What time can you get away from the shop?'

Tara shrugged. 'Dunno. How long will you need?'

Violet studied her daughter's face, running a finger along one of Tara's eyebrows.

Tara registered her frown. 'What is it, Mum?'

'I think you're perfect just as you are, but if it's what you want then I'll see if I can work a little magic.'

'Yes please, Mum, but I hope you've got a wand.'

Violet laughed. 'There'll be no need for that but we need to get to work. Go downstairs and tell Alf he'll have to manage without you.'

Tara nibbled on her thumb nail and glanced at the clock on the mantelpiece. 'Is that the right time, Mum? You did remember to wind it up, didn't you?'

'Yes, Tara, stop fretting. He's only five minutes late.'

'I think I'll go downstairs and wait in the shop.'

'You'll do no such thing. Alf'll let him in and he can jolly well make the effort to come up here.'

'Mum, don't say anything embarrassing, will you?'

Violet tutted. 'Me? As if.'

'What if he tries to kiss me? What do I do? I mean where does everything go? What do you do with your tongue, should I close my eyes? Oh, God, I feel sick.'

Violet took both her daughter's hands in hers. 'Oh, my Baby Girl, you're over-thinking things. Just relax and

113

everything will be perfect. He probably won't try to kiss you on a first date anyway.'

Tara headed for the door. 'I'm just nipping to the loo again. And please stop calling me Baby Girl.'

She stared at her reflection in the speckled bathroom mirror, hardly recognising the face she saw. Her mother had done a thorough job alright. She'd sent Tara to the chemist for a little sachet of toner, which had resulted in her hair losing its mousy look. It now radiated a hint of chestnut and shone like a new conker. Violet had used her sponge rollers to give it some volume, blow-dried the sides so that they flicked out, then applied a cloud of hair lacquer to ensure that not even a force ten gale would shift it. Her eyebrows had been given a thorough plucking, Violet telling her to stop being such a baby when she complained about the agony. The concealer had done an admirable job of disguising the spot and the blusher her mother had applied had actually given her a hint of cheekbones. A double coating of mascara and a slick of Vaseline to the lips completed the transformation. She smiled to herself. The whole effect had taken hours but the end result meant that Tara looked like a natural beauty and not one who had to rely on cosmetics before stepping out of the door. Her mother really had worked a miracle.

There was a tap on the door. 'Tara, love, Tom's here.'

She gripped the edge of the sink and took a long breath. 'Coming.'

*

Saturday nights at the ice rink were always manic and as Tara watched the throngs speeding past, their blades flicking up pieces of ice, she wondered what on earth she'd let herself in for. Tom sat beside her lacing up his boots. 'Have you been here a lot then?'

He straightened up, his hair falling round his face. He tucked it behind his ears. 'A few times.'

She stood up tentatively, her feet wobbling on the thin blades. 'Blimey, I feel about ten feet tall.'

She extended her arms in an effort to balance herself and took her first faltering step. 'I can't do it, Tom.'

'Course you can,' he laughed. 'It's so much easier once you're on the ice.'

'Hmm . . . I'll be the judge of that.'

He pointed to her denim flares. 'You might want to tuck those into your socks. If you get the blade caught in the hem, then you'll come a right cropper.'

He held onto her elbow as he guided her to the gap in the partition which surrounded the rink. He hopped onto the ice and skated backwards for a few steps before extending both arms towards her. 'Come on, grab my hands.'

With legs as shaky as a newborn foal, she reached out for Tom and he pulled her onto the ice. 'There you are, I told you it was easy.'

Tom held onto her hand as they moved away, side-by-side, staying close to the edge so she could grab the handrail if she needed to. Her legs were rigid and her back was already aching.

'Try to relax a bit and stand up straight.'

She lifted her gaze and saw the way ahead blocked by a family of five all holding hands. 'Ooh, no, look.'

'It's alright,' reassured Tom.

A steward sped past them, shouting to the family. 'Oi, can't you lot read? No skating in chains, break it up.'

Tom turned to Tara, smiling. 'See? Everything's under control.'

They had completed a few circuits, Tara gaining confidence with each lap, when a klaxon sounded. 'Bloody hell, what on earth's that for?'

'We'll have to get off, it's time for the ice dancing.'

'Oh dear, I was just getting going.'

'It's only for about twenty minutes, we can grab a hot chocolate from the vending machine if you want.'

The lights were dimmed and a kaleidoscope of colours was projected onto the ice as the dancers took up position. Tom and Tara watched from the sides, clutching their plastic cups of watery hot chocolate. She was mesmerised by the graceful way the couples moved, perfectly in sync with each other, making it seem effortless.

'Hiya, Tom.' A young girl stood in front of them. She wore a short, ballerina-type skirt teamed with American-tan tights. Her boots were white, indicating that they were her own and not the uncomfortable rented ones like Tara's. Her hair was scraped back into a tight bun, her eyelids sparkling with metallic blue eyeshadow. 'Wanna dance?'

Tom looked at Tara. 'This is Melanie.'

'Mel, actually. You don't mind if I borrow him, do you?'

Tom raised his eyebrows. 'I won't if you don't want me to.'

Tara looked at the other couples on the ice, their bodies pressed up against each other. Damn right she didn't want him to. 'It's OK,' she replied eventually. 'I'll be fine here watching.'

As Tom and Mel stepped on to the ice, the music slowed and he took her in his arms, his eyes locking with hers as they moved off. Judging by the way he spun her round and then lifted her onto his shoulder, he had been here more than just a few times. Mel was so pretty, so dainty and graceful that Tara had the sudden urge to get up and leave. She couldn't compete with someone like that. She felt frumpy in her faded flares, even though she had daringly teamed them with one of her mother's blouses which she'd tied at the waist, leaving a strip of flesh on show round her midriff. She tugged at the blouse and tried to pull it down, suddenly feeling foolish. She wished she'd never agreed to come.

Tom and Mel arrived breathless by her side, Mel's face flushed and dewy with perspiration. She stood on tiptoe and gave him an affectionate peck on the cheek. 'Thanks, Tom.'

'Any time.' He kissed her on the temple, causing Tara to avert her eyes. 'See ya, Mel,'

Tom plonked himself down next to Tara, his chest heaving. 'Phew, I'm knackered. It's hard work that.'

'She . . . erm . . . she seems nice.'

'Mel? Oh yes, she's a lovely girl. Very sweet.'

'Pretty too.'

Tom shrugged. 'I suppose she is. Never really thought about it.'

'Oh, come off it, Tom. I saw the way you gazed at her. Why did you go off with her when you came here with me?'

'I didn't "go off" with her as you put it. I asked you if you minded and you said you didn't.'

Tara's voice rose a level. 'Well, I didn't mean it.'

He frowned at her. 'Are you . . . are you jealous, Tara?'

She had never hated herself more. How could she tell him that all she had wanted to do was rip off Mel's stupid tutu, and pull out her immaculate bun? 'No, I'm not jealous.'

He nudged her on the arm, smiling. 'Yes, you are.'

'No, I'm not,' she insisted. 'You can dance with anybody you want to.'

'Tara, look at me.' He took hold of her chin and she grimaced as his thumb touched the big spot there. She willed him to remove his hand. 'I don't fancy Mel, alright?'

'Why wouldn't you? She's gorgeous and she clearly adores you.'

He let go of her chin and laughed. 'I'll tell you why I don't fancy her, shall I?'

'It's none of my business, Tom.'

'I don't fancy Mel because she's my flippin' cousin.'

118

Tara closed her eyes and bowed her head, not wishing Tom to see her crimson face. She had behaved like the silly schoolgirl she was. She wasn't mature enough to go out with boys. She forced herself to look at him. 'I'm sorry, Tom. It's just that when you and her . . .'

He leaned in closer and for one terrifying second she thought he was going to kiss her but instead he touched his finger to her lips. 'Stop talking,' he whispered.

At Tara's insistence, Tom had hopped off the bus at the stop before hers. It was only ten thirty, her stop was virtually outside Alf's and she'd wanted to avoid an awkward goodbye, wondering whether she was supposed to invite Tom in for a cuppa and if she did, would he expect more than a mug of PG Tips? She crept through the deserted shop and upstairs to the kitchen where a sliver of light shone under the closed door. Alf was by the fire, his trouser legs rolled up, his bare feet resting in the hearth. 'Eee, the wanderer returns.' He nodded at the chair opposite. 'Come and tell me all about it then.'

'I'm an idiot, Alf,' she said, collapsing into the chair. 'Such a bloody idiot.'

'Hey, stop that talk, lass. Tell me what's happened.'

'Well, Tom's never going to want to see me again, that's for sure. I don't blame him either. Is Mum back yet? I need to talk to her.'

'Erm, no, love, she rang earlier. She's stopping at Larry's tonight.'

'Oh charming! I thought she'd want to hear all about my evening. That Larry's got her right where he wants her.'

'She said to call her when you got home. I've written t'number on t'pad.'

Tara scowled. 'Sod that, she can wait. She can't be that bothered.'

'Now, now, don't be like that. Your mum deserves a life too and she'll be worried about you. She's waiting up for your call.'

Tara smiled inwardly at the thought of Larry trying to coax Violet to bed, her mother insisting on waiting until she had rung. She rose from the chair and moved over to the sink. 'Fancy a brew, Alf?'

'Erm . . . your mum?'

'Yeah, yeah, I'll ring her in a bit. There's no rush, is there?' She filled the kettle. 'Any of that Battenberg left?'

Before Alf could reply, the phone in the hall rang. Tara carried on slicing the cake. Alf placed his hands on the arm of the chair ready to heave himself up.

'Ignore it,' said Tara, spooning the leaves into the teapot.

'You go then. It'll probably be your mum anyway.'

She sighed and screwed the lid back on the tea caddy, slamming it down on the shelf a little harder than she had meant to. 'Alright then,' she said, heading out to the hall.

She returned a minute later. 'Couldn't wait to get off the phone, could she? I could hear him too, he was right there breathing down her neck. She was giggling like a schoolgirl. I hate him.'

'You've never met him, Tara. Don't be so quick to judge.'

'Yeah, well . . . apparently he wants to meet me, or rather Mum wants him to meet me. Doubt he feels the same way. We're going round for Sunday lunch next week. You an' all.'

'Me?' Alf chuckled. 'Eee, I can't imagine why he wants to meet me.'

'Tough,' Tara declared. 'If I've got to go then so do you.'

They sipped their tea in silence, Tara reliving the excruciating way she had behaved earlier, accusing Tom of fancying his own cousin. It was truly cringe-worthy.

'What's up?' asked Alf.

'Nowt.'

'Oh, you just groaned, that's all.'

'Oh, did I? I was just thinking about something.' She looked at his bone-white feet, the blue veins clearly visible beneath the thin skin. She seized on the chance to change the subject. 'Why've you got your socks off, Alf?'

He looked at his feet in surprise, as though he had forgotten the reason. 'I think I was trying to cut me toe nails but I couldn't reach.'

'Would you like me to help you?'

'You'd do that for me?'

She looked at his nails, thick and yellowing. She'd seen

shorter talons on a bird of prey. It was a wonder he could get his shoes on. 'Where're your nail scissors?'

He reached down by the side of his chair and passed them over to her.

'Those are the kitchen scissors, Alf! Me mum cuts the rind off the bacon with those things.'

Alf looked a little perplexed. 'What's your point, Tara?'

She wrinkled her nose. 'Well, it . . . it's unhygienic, isn't it? I'll just run and get ours.'

She returned a few minutes later and knelt down in front of Alf, placing one of his feet in her lap. In spite of everything, she smiled to herself. She'd had such high hopes for this evening and sitting on the kitchen floor cutting the toe nails of a near-octogenarian was not how she had hoped the evening would pan out. She squeezed the scissors using both hands, her face turning red with the effort. 'It's no good, Alf,' she puffed. 'They're too hard. We'll have to soak them. Have you got a bowl?'

'Aye, there's the washing-up bowl in the sink.'

'Seriously? The bowl where we wash the pots? The same pots that we eat off?'

He nodded. 'That's the one.'

Tara scrambled to her feet and began to fill the bowl. 'Go on then, but for God's sake, don't let on to Mum about this.'

After Tara had successfully trimmed all Alf's toe nails, she collected up the clippings and dropped them into the sink, before turning on the tap to blast them down the plughole. She clapped her hands together. 'All done, Alf.'

'Thanks, petal. You're a good kid, you are.' He looked down at his lap. 'I can't imagine our Judith doing that for me.' He dug his hand into his pocket and brought out a pound note. 'Here.'

Tara held her hands up. 'I don't want paying, Alf.'

He thrust it towards her. 'I insist. I know you're saving up for summat special for your mum's birthday. Put it towards that.'

Tara reached out and took the crumpled note. 'It's too much, Alf.' She looked at his smiling face. It would be gracious to just accept and acknowledge that the pleasure Alf derived from giving her the money was greater than hers was to receive it. She leaned forward and kissed him on the forehead. 'Thanks, Alf.'

Tara was still in bed when Violet returned the next morning. She shook her daughter's shoulder. 'Hey, sleepy head, wake up. I'm dying to hear all about it.'

Tara stirred and squinted at the clock. 'There's not much to tell.' She closed her eyes again and pulled the blanket up tight beneath her chin. 'I'm going back to sleep.'

'No, Tara, don't do that, I've got some exciting news.' She peeled off the bedcovers. 'Wake up, Tara.'

Tara yanked the covers back.

'You're not getting married, are you?'

'What? No, of course not, don't be silly.' Violet paused, noticing her daughter's expression, her eyebrows drawn together. 'Would that be such a terrible thing?'

'Yes, it would! You hardly know him.'

'There's something there though, Tara. An intimacy I've never had with anyone before.'

'Not even with my dad?'

Violet resisted the urge to scoff and, not trusting her voice, merely shook her head.

'What's the big news then?'

Violet clapped her hands together, squealing in delight. 'Larry's taking us on holiday.'

'Us?'

'Yes, Tara, you and me. We're going to the continent.'

'The continent? What continent?'

'I don't know, Tara. We're going in the car, we're going to get on the ferry and then we'll be in France, I suppose. How exciting is that, eh?'

'We don't have passports.'

'Then we'll have to get them. Work with me here, Tara. We're going on holiday abroad for the first time and all you want to do is throw up obstacles. You'll love Larry when you get to meet him next week, I promise.'

'What about Alf?'

'What about him?'

'He'll be here on his own.'

Violet stood up, throwing her hands in the air. 'There you go again. What's the matter with you? Alf was fine on his own before we came along, he'll survive for a few weeks.' She turned to the door. 'I'm going to make some breakfast and then you can tell me all about your evening. Do you want a bacon butty?'

Tara nodded. 'OK then.' She remembered the kitchen scissors, probably still lying in the hearth. 'But don't cut the rind off mine.'

15

Diablo stood patiently whilst Leo tightened the girth, only giving a slight flick of his head in protest. The pre-dawn air was still and thick with the promise of warm sunshine. Mateo finished brushing Lala's flaxen tail. 'Why can't I come with you, Leo?'

Leo crouched down so his face was level with his brother's. 'It's too far, Little One. Lala wouldn't be able to keep up and you can't go all that way on one of the big horses.'

'But . . .'

'Shush, Mateo, listen.' He stood up and pulled his little brother to one side. 'There's something else.' He snapped a look towards the farmhouse. He could see his *mama* through the window, singing to herself as she scrubbed away at the breakfast pots in the sink. 'Can you keep a secret?'

Reaching into his saddle bag he pulled out a small package. He opened the lid and held it out to Mateo.

'What's that?'

Leo lowered his voice. 'I'm going to ask Gabriela to marry me.' He took out the ring and let it rest on his palm. 'It belonged to our *abuela*. Mama gave it to me some time ago.'

Mateo picked up the ring and turned it over in his fingers. 'It . . . it's lovely, Leo. Gabriela will love it.' He passed the ring back to Leo, balled his little hands into fists, then ran into the barn. In his haste, he clattered into a metal pail of water, sending the contents sloshing over the yard.

'Hey, Mateo, wait. 'What's the matter?'

Mateo sat on a bale of hay and scooped up a nearby cat, burying his nose in the soft fur. His dark eyes sparkled with unshed tears. His voice sounded small, almost petulant. 'I don't want you to marry Gabriela.'

Leo sat down beside him. 'Why not? You like her, don't you? I seem to remember it was only a couple of months ago that you were encouraging me to ask her out. What's changed, Mateo?'

Mateo swallowed his tears. 'I don't want you to leave, Leo.'

'Leave? I'm not going anywhere. Why would you think that?'

The cat struggled in Mateo's arms and he released his grip. 'You'll go and live with her in the *panadería*, won't you?'

Leo pulled Mateo onto his knee. 'What nonsense you talk. Of course I won't.' He flicked Mateo under his chin. 'As if I'd leave my little *camarada*. Gabriela will come and live here with us. She can help Mama with the guests.'

Mateo brightened, his eyes losing their wounded look. 'Do you promise?'

Leo made the sign of a cross on his chest. 'I promise.'

'In that case, I hope she says yes. I like her, Leo. And she's very pretty.'

Leo gazed up at the rafters, his heart lurching as he thought of Gabriela. He'd wasted enough time already, even though he would never admit this to his *mama*. 'Me too, Mateo. Now run up that ladder and look under my bed. I've got a present for you.'

Mateo wrapped his arms around his brother's neck. 'I love you, Leo.'

Leo watched Mateo climb the ladder, listening as he scrabbled around on the wooden floor above. He drew a long piece of straw from a bale and slipped it between his teeth. He'd been too nervous to eat breakfast, and now he fidgeted with the ring, turning it over and over until his fumbling fingers lost their grip and it clattered to the ground.

'Leo, I've found it,' sang Mateo from above.

Leo was on his hands and knees scratching round for the ring. He retrieved it and stuffed it into the pocket of his jeans. 'What do you think, Mateo?'

'It's nice but I've already got a fishing net.'

'It's not a fishing net, Mateo.' Leo held up his hands. 'Throw it to me and I'll show you. Come back down, carefully now.' Leo caught the net, then waited at the bottom of the ladder for Mateo.

'It's a butterfly net,' he said, as Mateo jumped off the last rung. 'I'm going to show you how to catch butterflies and learn to recognise all the different ones. Would you like that?'

Mateo nodded, his bright eyes wide and eager. 'Butterfly hunting? Yes, I would, Leo. Can I keep them?'

'No, that wouldn't be fair. You can keep them for a little while but then you must let them go. You can keep a journal of all the ones you've caught, maybe draw a sketch of them, but they deserve to be free, free to spread their wings and bring joy to other people as well.'

Mateo fingered the netting. 'Where did you get it?'

'I made it just for you, Mateo. Now come on, let's get you cleaned up. Gabriela will be here soon and you can show it to her.'

They had been climbing for almost three hours and Diablo's sides heaved with the effort as they emerged from the cool forested hills into the blinding sunlight. The sun's rays had grown stronger and now they coloured the landscape, highlighting the ochre lime-stone cliffs rising either side of the emerald river below. Diablo tossed his mane and flicked his tail to rid himself of the flies, his gait bouncy and alert but never threatening.

'You've worked a miracle with that horse,' said Gabriela. She sat astride the more placid Armonia, the reins loose as she held onto the front of the saddle.

Leo patted Diablo's neck. 'Horses need kindness and patience not brutality. I always knew he wasn't bad.'

They rode side by side along the top of the gorge, a vertiginous drop to the winding river far below. Peregrine falcons and griffon vultures glided on the thermals above them, occasionally swooping to land on a poor unfortunate vole or mouse.

'It's glorious up here, Leo. Thank you for bringing me.'

'I wanted us to have a special day out before the guests start arriving. There's not much time for anything once they're here.' He reached behind and patted the saddle bag, swallowing hard as he felt the bulk of the little box.

'You're unusually quiet, Leo. Is anything the matter?'

How could he tell her that this day would live in his memory for the rest of his life? Hers too, if all went according to plan. He reached over and took her hand. 'I'm fine, Gabriela.' An overnight shower had doused the pine trees and their mood-elevating freshness filled the air. 'Everything's just perfect.'

She returned his smile. 'I'm getting hungry, Leo. Shall we stop for an early lunch?'

Food was the last thing on his mind. His stomach felt as though he'd swallowed an inflated balloon. 'Why not?'

They chose a spot beneath an almond tree, its green velvet hulls beginning to swell with the promise of the sweet nut inside. After dismounting, Leo secured the horses' reins to a nearby tree. Both dipped their heads and began to nibble at the new grass.

'This is special, Leo. It's wonderful to have time to ourselves for once.' She spread out the picnic rug. 'Come and sit down.' She unwrapped a packet of greaseproof paper and pulled out a fresh *pan blanco*, a hunk of cheese and a little pot of quince jam. Leo paced the bridle path, chewing on his thumb nail, the words circling in his head. He'd over-rehearsed, he knew that now. Everything was going to come out in a jumble and he would ruin the best moment of his life.

'Leo!'

He turned around, startled. 'Yes?'

'I said come and sit down. Honestly, I don't know what's wrong with you today. You're so jumpy.' She patted the rug. 'Come here and have something to eat.'

He sat down beside her and took a slug of water from his canteen. He could use something stronger.

As though reading his mind, Gabriela produced a bottle of rosé and poured out two small paper cups.

'To us,' she toasted. She kissed him on the mouth, pausing briefly before making contact. He closed his eyes and felt the merest brush of her lips before she pulled away again.

He fought the urge to grab her and press his mouth to hers. 'Gabriela, I . . .'

'Shush, Leo.' She broke off a small piece of *manchego* and pulled back the orange rind. She held the cheese up to Leo's face. 'Open.'

He dutifully obeyed and she popped the cheese into

131

his mouth, leaving her finger resting on his lips for longer than was necessary. She gazed at him from under her long lashes, the powdery scent of her perfume mingling with the smell of the saddle soap on her thighs. He inwardly marvelled at the power she exerted over him. At this moment, she could have asked him to do anything and he would have acquiesced.

It took a couple of cups of wine to settle his nerves. Enough to make him relax a little but not too much that he wouldn't be able to remember every last detail later. 'It's so peaceful here, Gabriela. It's as though we're the only two people in the whole wide world.' He finished his custard pastry and flicked the crumbs off his jeans.

'Look at you, Leo, you've got custard on your cheek.' She delicately scooped it off with her forefinger, her touch excruciatingly tender, her eyes locked on his as she opened her mouth and licked off the custard.

Leo could stand it no more. He rolled her onto her back, revelling in the comforting folds of her soft body. 'Oh Gabriela, marry me.' He kissed her face, her neck, her chest, any bare flesh he could find.

She propped herself up on her elbows. 'What did you just say?'

He laughed as the relief took hold. After all that preparation, all that rehearsing, the words had just come out exactly as they should have done. In the right moment, with feeling, with passion and with absolute conviction, even though it may have sounded more like a command than a question. 'What I meant was, Gabriela, I love you, will you marry me?'

She pulled him to her and whispered into his ear, her hot breath made him shiver. 'Yes, Leo, I will.'

16

As she lay in his arms, her eyes closed, a contented smile on her lips, Leo traced his finger across her forehead, thinking about what they'd just done. He'd slept with girls before, plenty of them, but it was the first time he'd ever made love. He understood the difference now. He could see those dalliances for the vacuous acts they were, devoid of any feelings. 'Any regrets, Gabriela?'

She sat up, sighing as she fastened the buttons on her shirt. 'Leo, it was everything I'd ever dreamed of, more in fact.' She looked down the deserted path. 'But what if someone saw us?'

He smoothed her hair, then wound a strand of it between his fingers. 'There's no one around for miles.' He nodded towards the horses. 'And they're oblivious.'

'This is the happiest day of my life, Leo.'

'And that is exactly how I wanted you to feel.'

He stood up and stretched his legs. 'Wait here for a minute.'

He approached Diablo and took the box out of the saddlebag, stopping to give the horse a gentle pull on his ears. 'She said yes,' he whispered.

He returned to Gabriela and dropped to one knee. 'Leo?'

He opened the box and held it out to her. 'It was my grandmother's.'

'Oh, Leo, it's beautiful.' She took the ring and slipped it onto her finger. The tiny diamond sparkled under the sun. 'And it fits perfectly.'

She began to kiss him again, weaving her hands into his hair, her body pressed close to his. 'Leo . . . I love . . .' She stopped and looked in the direction of the rustling sound close by. 'What was that?'

Both horses looked up and stared along the path where the vegetation thickened. 'It'll be an ibex or a mountain goat or something,' said Leo. 'Nothing to worry about. Now, where were we?'

The sound came again, closer this time. Something was shuffling along the dusty track. Leo placed a protective arm in front of Gabriela. 'Shush, don't make a sound.' He spoke slowly and calmly. 'Just back away and wrap up the food. Put it in the bag and hang it from the tree, as high as you can.'

'Why, Leo, what is it?' Her excitement of a moment ago had been replaced by apprehension.

'It might be a wild boar after the food.'

'Are they dangerous?'

'Don't worry, Gabriela, I'm here and I won't let anything happen to you.'

She packed up the remnants of their picnic as Leo

stood guard, hands on his hips, ready to . . . ready to do what? Even he couldn't take on a wild boar, or worse, a wild boar with young to protect. A tense moment passed before a figure swathed in white, from his hood-covered head to his sandal-clad toes, emerged from the bushes, his face puce and shimmering with sweat.

'*Buenos dias*,' he panted. 'Forgive me if I startled you. I heard voices and I need help.'

He pulled out his flask, removed the cap and tipped it upside down. 'I've nothing left . . . and . . . I need . . . something to drink.' He clutched at his throat as if to further demonstrate his need.

'Of course,' said Gabriela. She passed over their canteen of water and he gave a slight bow before taking a couple of mouthfuls.

'Please, have as much as you need.'

He shook his head. 'That will be plenty.' He handed back the canteen. '*Gracias.*'

Leo regarded the young monk; his heavy white robes were hardly suitable for hiking in the heat and his thin-soled sandals were wholly inadequate for this terrain.

'Are you hungry?' Gabriela asked. Without waiting for his answer, she turned to Leo. 'Get that bag out of the tree and bring over some bread and cheese, will you?'

She addressed the monk again. 'Can you tell us your name?'

'Brother Florian.' He accepted a hunk of bread from Leo. 'Although that's not the name I was baptised with.

I chose it when I entered the monastery because Saint Florian is the patron saint of Austria, where my mother was born

'How far have you come today then?' asked Gabriela, slicing some cheese.

'From Monasterio de Justina.'

Leo took a step backwards. He knew about the community of cloistered monks who inhabited the crumbling monastery perched high on the cliffs above the river. He'd never met one though or been anywhere near the monastery for that matter. A hermitic existence, deprived of family, friends and all contact with the outside world, was just too horrific to even think about. He couldn't imagine a more suffocating existence. 'Have you escaped then?'

'It's not a prison. I'm there because I want to be. I'm there to atone for my sins.'

'Good Heavens!' exclaimed Leo. 'What did you do?'

Br Florian took a cup of water from Gabriela. 'We're all sinners . . . um . . . Leo, is it?'

Leo nodded although he was not prepared for an impromptu modern-day sermon on the mount.

'In God's eyes,' continued Br Florian, 'we're all sinners but a monk dedicates his life to worship and prayer. He eschews the outside world for all its worthlessness.'

'But you could pray anywhere. You don't have to give up your life to do it.'

'I'll admit the ascetic life is not for everyone, Leo. It

137

is a calling. We abandon ourselves to God and trust Him to lead us along paths we do not know.'

'He didn't do a very good job of leading you along this particular path.'

'Leo,' hissed Gabriela. 'What's wrong with you?'

Br Florian gave a good-natured laugh. 'Who knows what God has in store for us? This meeting may yet prove to be serendipitous. It might be part of God's plan.' He looked from Leo to Gabriela. 'For all of us.'

Leo steered the conversation away from divine intervention. 'How far have you actually walked then?'

Br Florian ran a hand over his smooth head and squinted at the sun. 'I'd estimate I've been walking for around three hours.'

'Three hours!' said Gabriela. 'You seem to be wholly unprepared if you don't mind me saying so.'

'I guess I got carried away. Once a week we're permitted to take a walk, either alone or in a group. I always go alone.'

His shaven head made it difficult to tell for certain, but Leo estimated they were of similar age. He couldn't imagine squandering his life sequestered away with only male company and no contact with family. 'Well, we've kept you long enough . . .'

Gabriela glared at Leo. 'There's no rush. Tell me, Br Florian, how long have you been a monk?'

'Been there since I was eighteen, so ten years.'

'You mean to say you've wasted the best years of your life?' said Leo.

'Not wasted, Leo. I've enhanced those years beyond measure. Before I went to Justina's, I was lost. I'd dabbled in drugs, drank too much and had many . . . um . . . women if you understand what I mean.' He nodded an apology to the blushing Gabriela. ' I was unfulfilled. There was no joy. I needed to turn towards God.'

Leo kicked at the stones beneath his feet. 'Couldn't you have just gone to church once a week like the rest of us?'

'Repentance is more than just feeling sorry for your sins and asking for forgiveness, Leo. You have to deny yourself, be prepared to say goodbye to your sinful self and be born again to live in Christ.'

He lifted his hood over his head then gave a slight bow. 'I will bid you farewell now and thank you for the water. God bless you both.'

They watched him walk away, his white robe trailing in the dust.

Leo took hold of Gabriela's waist. 'I thought he'd never leave.' He kissed her on the mouth but her lips were tight and tense. 'What's wrong?'

She pushed him away gently and stared after Br Florian. 'Do you think he's going to be alright?'

Leo pointed at the sky. 'I should think so. He's got Him up there looking out for him.'

'I can't imagine a life like that, can you, Leo?'

'It's his choice, nobody's forcing him to do it.'

'But what if that's the only way to get to Heaven? You

139

heard him, Leo, we're all sinners, what if we haven't done enough to convince God we're sorry? After what we've just done on that rug, we could be damned to Hell for eternity. Why would God let us in, when people like Br Florian have dedicated their whole lives to Him?' She leaned her head against his chest. 'I'm scared, Leo.'

He stroked her hair, wondering how on earth they'd managed to go from passionately consummating their engagement to talk of eternal damnation in the space of half an hour or so.

'Gabriela, you have absolutely no need to worry. You're the sweetest, kindest girl who ever graced this planet. Look how you cared for that monk, insisting on giving him food and water. I'm the one who should be worried about getting into Heaven. I couldn't wait to get rid of him. God's not going to take kindly to that.'

Gabriela was not convinced. 'I think I'm going to go to confession tomorrow. Shall we go together?'

Leo didn't think they'd anything to confess but he pulled her close and kissed the top of her head. 'If that's what you want.'

17

Dusk was falling as they arrived back home, grubby, bone-tired, every muscle aching. Leo untacked the two horses, brushed their flattened coats where their saddles had been, then turned them out into the paddock. Free of his saddle at last, steam rose from Diablo's back as he cantered freely around the field before dipping his head into the trough and taking a long drink.

Gabriela stretched her arms over her head, suppressing a yawn. 'I don't know where he gets his energy from.'

Leo rested a saddle over the fence. 'Come on, let's go and tell Mama and Papa the good news.'

'Do you think they'll be happy, Leo?' She twisted the ring on her finger.

'My *mama* has had you picked out as a potential daughter-in-law since you were five years old.'

Felipe was dozing in the chair when they walked into the kitchen. Marissa put her finger to her lips. 'Shush, let him sleep. He's been pruning the olive trees. Back-breaking work it is. He's worn out. Did you have a good day?'

Leo squeezed Gabriela's hand. 'Show her.'

Gabriela held up her hand and wiggled her fingers, the

diamond ring catching the light from the chunky candle on the table.

'*Oh, Dios mio!*' Marissa exclaimed. 'It is a miracle.' She grabbed her husband's shoulder. 'Felipe, wake up, there is to be a celebration. Quickly, go and bring some cava from the cellar.'

Felipe rubbed his eyes and tried to speak. '*Silencio, esposa,*' he managed, as he rubbed his temples. 'Now, what is this you are talking about?'

'Gabriela and I are engaged, Papa.' Leo held Gabriela's hand out towards his father to show him the proof.

Felipe took hold of her fingers and squinted at the ring, nodding slowly before speaking again. 'Congratulations, *hijo*, Gabriela. You make your *mama* and me very happy.' He stood and kissed Gabriela on both cheeks before slapping Leo on the back.

Marissa banged four glasses onto the table. 'Cava, Felipe. Now!' she commanded.

Felipe jerked his thumb in the direction of his wife. 'This is what you have to look forward to, Leo.'

Mateo appeared in the doorway, his eyes heavy and his hair ruffled. He clutched a pad to his chest. 'I've been drawing butterflies, Leo.'

'Let me see, Little One.'

Mateo passed the pad over to Leo. 'Are they any good?'

Leo looked at the rudimentary sketches. 'They show much promise, Mateo. Why don't we go butterfly hunting tomorrow?'

'I'd like that.' Mateo turned to go back upstairs then changed his mind. 'Did she say yes, Leo?'

Gabriela laughed, the delicate sound bouncing off the stone walls of the farmhouse. 'Yes, I did. You think I'd say no to having you as a little brother?'

Marissa sat at the table, her pen poised over her writing pad. Opposite, Felipe poured his wife a second cava, then raised his eyebrows at Leo and Gabriela. Clasping hands under the table, they both nodded their acceptance.

'Right,' said Marissa. 'We need to start making the plans. Gabriela, expect me at the *panadería* tomorrow to speak with your mother.' She glanced at the clock over the fire grate. 'It is not too late, is it? You're not too tired?' She rocked back in her chair, laughing. 'Of course it's not too late. I expect you'll be much too excited to sleep anyway. It's not every day you get engaged to the most handsome, eligible bachelor in the village, no?' She pinched her son on his cheek, as though he was an impudent child. 'You take care of her, you hear me? You will walk her home later, make sure she gets home safe.'

Leo shuffled in his seat. 'Um . . . I thought Gabriela could stay with me tonight, Mama. That's alright, isn't it?'

The swift cuff around his head gave him the answer. 'You show some respect towards your intended, Leo. Gabriela is not one of your, how do you say, notches on the bedpost. She wants to save herself for the marriage, don't you, Gabriela?'

Lest her voice betray her guilt, Gabriela merely nodded. In a clear attempt to steer the conversation away from pre-marital relations, she changed the subject. 'We met one of the monks from Monasterio de Justina today. He was awfully nice, wasn't he, Leo?'

'Mmm . . . he was a bit odd if you ask me. It's not natural hiding yourself away like that. What does it achieve?'

Leo was rewarded with another cuff from his mother. 'Everlasting life at the right hand of God, that's what. Down here his sins are forgiven, up there he's guaranteed a home in Heaven.' She shook her head. 'What is so hard to understand about that, Leo? These monks spend their lives praying for all our sins, even yours. You should be thankful to them.'

'He was ever so handsome,' said Gabriela. 'Young too, not how you would imagine a monk to look.'

Leo pointedly withdrew his hand. He knew Gabriela had been quite taken with Br Florian. 'He wasn't that good-looking, Mama. He'd shaved all his hair off for a start and you need a good-shaped head for that.'

'Mmm . . .' mused Gabriela. 'The trouble is you don't really know what shape your skull is until you've shaved all your hair off and by then it's too late.'

Felipe ran his hands through his own thick hair. 'You wouldn't catch me doing that.'

Marissa tapped her pen on her notebook. 'Can we stop all this talk about misshapen heads and concentrate on this wedding?' She looked at Gabriela. 'I'm thinking autumn would be best. It's April now, so that gives us . . .' she counted off her fingers, '. . . say six months. October? All our guests will have left and the weather will still be mild. What do you say? Shall I write that down?'

'I'll have to check with my *mama*, Señora Perez.'

Marissa snorted. 'What is this Señora Perez nonsense? You call me Mama Marissa now, *si*?'

Leo stared out of the window to the paddock beyond. Under the crepuscular sky, he could make out the silhouettes of Diablo and Armonia nibbling each other's necks. He thought back to the pitiful creature Diablo had been when he'd first encountered him. Malnourished, bad-tempered and dead behind the eyes. The young horse had come a long way in two months, his contentment evident in the way he handled and the way he interacted with the other horses. There was no more gnashing of teeth and flailing hooves. No need to enter his stable with trepidation, fully prepared for an onslaught of equine fury.

'Leo?' Gabriela touched his arm. 'Where were you?'

'Oh, sorry. I was just looking at the horses. I think Diablo has found his soul-mate.' He leaned across and kissed her on the cheek. 'Just like I have.'

Mateo skipped into the meadow, his butterfly net slung over one shoulder. Leo trailed behind, his mind still in the dark confines of the confessional box. He'd kept his promise to Gabriela and accompanied her to church that morning but as he squashed himself into the tiny booth, the velvet curtain separating him from the priest, he wondered why he was bothering. He didn't feel in the slightest bit remorseful about what had happened between him and Gabriela on that picnic rug. If pre-marital relations were the passport to Hell, then Leo already had a first-class ticket. He watched as Mateo swung his net across a bush with all the grace of a farmer spreading muck. 'Not like that, Mateo,' he called. 'Wait for me, I'll show you.'

He caught up with his brother and took the net. 'You need to be gentle; you don't want to hurt the butterfly but you do need to be quick. Watch me.'

A cabbage white landed on a nearby thistle and folded its wings. Leo put his finger to his lips and in one swift, elegant movement closed the net over the butterfly. Mateo held up the jar and Leo eased it in. 'Pop the lid on, Mateo, and we can have a closer look.'

'It's a bit boring,' declared Mateo. 'Can't we find a more interesting one?'

'You think this one is just plain white? Look closer, and you'll see it has a black dot on either wing.'

Mateo wrinkled his nose, obviously not convinced. He unscrewed the lid and tipped it over a bush. The grateful butterfly took flight, then settled on a stalk of wild thyme, apparently none the worse for its ordeal. The next capture seemed to satisfy Mateo. Leo held up the jar and peered at the frantic butterfly inside. 'It's a swallowtail, Mateo. Look at those two red dots at the base of its wings and the little forks below. Like a swallow's tail, see?'

Mateo pulled out his sketchbook. 'Can I draw it, Leo?'

'Put the jar in the shade then and don't take too long about it.'

Leo lay down on the grass, his hands clasped behind his head, musing over how uncomplicated his life was. There was joy to be found in the most mundane of pastimes. He could revel for hours in the sheer tranquillity of his surroundings, never tiring of the riotous splendour of the coloured hills in the distance or simply sitting under the shade of a fig tree, the rim of his hat pulled low over his eyes as he dozed off his midday meal. Life was good. He thought of Gabriela. And it was only going to get better.

18

Violet stood at the sink, peeling potatoes. She gazed out over Larry's back garden, where the daffodils were past their best but still providing a flash of colour. A stepping-stone path led to a small pond which was filled with water lilies and Koi carp. 'Do you do all this yourself, Larry, or do you have a gardener?'

He approached her from behind and moved her hair to one side before kissing her neck.

She shivered and turned around, allowing Larry to kiss her lips instead. 'Come back to bed, Violet.'

'No, I can't.' She swiped him playfully on the arm. 'I've got too much to do. They'll be here soon and I have to get these spuds in.'

'I know, you're right, but you're just so damn irresistible, Violet.' He drew her fingers to his lips, kissing each one. 'You shouldn't be peeling potatoes with these hands. They're far too delicate.' He picked up the potato peeler. 'Here, let me.'

Violet unfastened her pinny. 'Well, I don't need asking twice. I'll lay the table instead.'

She never tired of wandering round Larry's house, marvelling at the sheer grandeur of it all. The rooms were vast, with high ceilings, ornate cornices and plush carpets which were so thick she left footprints behind. She stood in the dining room, surveying the table. The mahogany was so highly polished she could see her reflection in it. The table could seat twelve so the four of them would look a bit ridiculous all clustered at one end, but this was an occasion that didn't warrant eating in the kitchen. She opened the drawer of the sideboard and took out the silver place mats and napkin rings. Napkin rings! She'd had no idea what they were for until Larry had told her. He really was in a different league and she couldn't wait to introduce him to Tara.

Violet had never met anybody like Larry. It wasn't just that he was attractive physically; for there could be no doubt that he turned heads. She had become used to other women staring at him adoringly whilst giving her daggers as she held onto his arm, trying to keep the smug expression off her face. He was generous too and whilst he could afford to be, it didn't always follow that someone with as much money as he had was willing to splash the cash. On their first few dates, Violet had been careful to pay her way, not wanting to be labelled a gold-digger. She might be down on her luck, but she still had her pride. She'd grown tired of the battle though and now allowed Larry to pay, reluctantly accepting that she couldn't afford to keep up with his champagne lifestyle on her Babycham income.

She finished laying out the silver cutlery and crystal

wine glasses and stood back to admire the table. She glanced over to the sideboard at the candelabra with its five red candles, wondering if it would be over the top to put it on the table. Larry popped his head round the door. 'Potatoes are all peeled. Care for an aperitif, my darling?'

'Cinzano, please.'

'I'll have it made in a jiffy, then you can put your feet up and leave everything to me.'

Violet smiled at his retreating figure, his aftershave lingering in the air. She could hear him singing to himself in the kitchen and the clink of ice as he tossed it into her glass. She couldn't recall a time when she had been this happy. She looked at her watch and followed Larry out to the kitchen. Tara would be here soon and she was going to love Larry as much as she did.

Tara banged on the bathroom door. 'Alf, what *is* taking you so long?'

'I'll be with you in a second.'

Tara could hear him fumbling with the lock before he inched the door open. 'Good God, Alf! What have you done?' His face was dotted with pieces of blood-stained toilet paper.

'Cut meself shaving. Blade must be blunt.'

'Oh, bloody hell, Alf. What're we going to do with you, eh?'

'It'll stop in a minute. Now, where's me shirt?'

'Hanging on the back of the door. I've ironed it for you.'

She steered him through to the kitchen and took the shirt down. 'Hurry up, Alf. The bus comes at twenty past.'

She watched as he did up his buttons, his chunky arthritic fingers making the job a lot harder than it needed to be. 'Where's your tie?'

Alf frowned. 'I've only got me funeral tie. Shall I wear that?'

'You've got that other one, the orange and brown striped one, wear that.'

He shook his head. 'No good, love, I spilt egg down it t'other day.'

'Alf,' cried Tara, not bothering to hide her exasperation. 'I'll sponge it off, where is it?'

'Linen basket.' He finished tucking his shirt in. 'It seems an awful lot of bother to go to just for Sunday lunch.'

Tara grabbed the tie from beneath the mound of clothes. 'I agree, but Mum said we had to dress up. Best bib and tucker she said. Apparently, it's what they do round where he lives.' She scraped at the dried-on egg with her fingernails then gave it quick wipe with the dishcloth. 'Do you want me to tie it for you?'

He raised his bushy eyebrows. 'Can girls tie ties?'

'I wear one for school, don't I?' She turned up Alf's collar, wrapped the tie around his neck and began to fold one end over the other, not wishing to admit that it was indeed a lot more difficult to do on someone else. She

151

patted his chest. 'That'll do, now come on, we need to be quick.'

Alf picked up his flat cap and walking stick. 'Sorry, love. I don't do *quick*.'

Tara glanced down at the *A–Z*. 'It's next on the left.'

She linked her arm through Alf's and propelled him along the pavement. As they turned into Larry's road, Alf gave a long, low whistle. 'Blimey, it's like summat out of *Upstairs Downstairs*. I wonder if he has servants.'

Tara stared at the blossom-lined avenue, the pavement carpeted with little pink petals. 'Number 40, we want.'

They stopped outside a gated entrance, two stone lions standing guard either side. Tara pressed the button and her mother's voice floated over the intercom. 'Hiya, love, come in.' She heard a buzzing sound and the gates opened. She glanced at Alf. 'Flippin' 'eck, Alf. He's got magic gates an' all.'

Violet was standing on the step, bouncing on the balls of her feet. Larry stood next to her, his arm slung over her shoulder. There was no doubt they were an attractive couple. They looked like they belonged on the cover of a knitting pattern.

'It's lovely to see you again,' said Violet, clapping her hands together.

'Mum, you only saw me yesterday.' Tara rolled her eyes at Alf.

'Larry,' Violet said. 'This is our Tara.'

Larry stepped forward and half-bowed as he held out his hand. 'It's nice to meet you at last, Tara. I see you've inherited your mother's good looks.'

Tara felt her cheeks redden, her words coming out in a jumble. 'Erm . . . ta . . . nice . . . to have . . . I mean nice to meet you as well.'

'And this is Alf,' Violet said. 'Our saviour. I don't know what we'd have done without him.'

Larry grasped Alf's hand. 'I've heard a lot about you, sir.'

'Well, come in then,' said Violet, ushering them into the hall. 'Shall I take your jacket, Alf?'

They trooped after Larry as he made his way into the conservatory. Everywhere there were plants, huge rubber plants in pots, ferns dangling from the ceiling in macramé holders, a row of cacti on the windowsill. Larry gestured to the rattan peacock chair in the corner. 'Have a seat, Tara, and allow me to fix you a drink. Cinzano and lemonade is it, like your mother?'

Tara glanced at Violet who gave an almost imperceptible shake of her head. 'I'm only fourteen, Larry.'

'Oh, sorry, of course.' He looked at Violet. 'A weak one wouldn't hurt though, would it, Violet?'

Tara waited for her mother to answer, willing her to agree. If there was one thing that would make this afternoon more bearable it was alcohol.

'Go on then, just a splash, as it's a special occasion.'

Tara couldn't see anything special in the occasion but

153

if it meant she got to have a proper drink then she'd go along with it. She watched Larry as he poured in the Cinzano under the close observation of Violet. As soon as Violet turned her back, he added another slug and winked at Tara. He lifted the lid on a plastic pineapple and brought out a chunk of ice, before topping up her glass with lemonade. 'There you are, Tara, cheers.' He handed a glass of foaming beer to Alf. 'It's lovely to have you both here.'

Larry and Violet settled themselves on the two-seater sofa opposite, their upper arms touching, Larry's hand resting on Violet's knee. Tara looked over at Alf seated on a chair in the corner, watching as he raised his pint glass to his lips, his hand shaking with the effort.

'Well, this is nice,' announced Violet, breaking the long silence. 'Isn't it, Tara? What do you think of Larry's house?'

Tara glanced down at the glass-topped coffee table, the acidic orange shag pile visible beneath. 'It's alright, yeah.'

Violet laughed. 'Alright? What are you like, Tara? It's beautiful. I'll give you a guided tour later.'

She turned to Larry. 'Tell our Tara about our trip to the continent.'

Larry leaned forward, placing his elbows on his knees, his face animated. 'Oh, it's going to be fantastic. We'll drive down to Dover, take it nice and easy, find a nice country pub for a spot of lunch and then we'll get the car ferry over to Calais. From then on, the world, or

154

Europe at least, really is our oyster.' He looked at Violet. 'You can choose, darling, we can go anywhere you want to. There're vineyards, forests, mountains, beaches, medieval villages, whatever you fancy.'

Violet clapped her hands together. 'I can't wait, Larry.' She leaned over and kissed his cheek. 'Thank you so much.'

He ran his finger down the side of her face. 'The pleasure is all mine.' They locked gazes for so long that Tara was forced to dramatically clear her throat. 'I hear they're thinking of building a tunnel under the English Channel. Mr Long, our geography teacher, reckons it'll happen.'

'Nah, can't see it myself,' said Larry. 'Too bloody expensive. What do you think, Alf?'

Alf shook his head. 'No, we're an island, we are. We'll have rats coming through bringing rabies and whatnot. We can't have that. What's wrong with the car ferry or that hover thing?'

Violet steered the conversation away from rabies and rats. 'How was Tom yesterday, Tara?'

'Fine, no mention of another date but he was his usual self, cheerful and playing pranks on me and what have you. Just like I was his little sister.'

'Nonsense,' Violet dismissed. 'Thinks the world of you that lad. Anyway, you could always ask him out.'

Tara stood up. 'You're mad, Mother. Now where's the loo? Upstairs?'

Violet beamed with what looked like pride but surely

couldn't be as they were only talking about toilets. 'There's one in the hall,' she replied, with more than a hint of excitement. 'You don't have to go upstairs. Can you believe it?'

'Mmm . . . truly radical.' Tara glanced over at Alf who did his best to stifle a giggle.

The downstairs loo turned out to be more of a cupboard under the stairs. There was just a sickly pink sink with gold taps and a vanity unit underneath. And yet another plant hanging from the ceiling.

A bar of her mother's favourite pink Camay soap lay in a dish beside the taps. Tara lathered up her hands, rinsed them under the scalding hot water and looked round for a towel. There was an empty towel ring but nothing with which to dry her hands. 'Damn,' she muttered, wiping them down her skirt. She hesitated at the door. Perhaps there was a towel in the drawer below the sink. Feeling like a cat burglar, she eased open the drawer and looked inside. There was a pile of fluffy white guest towels, each adorned with a strip of frilly lace and satin rosebuds, no doubt geared to match the wallpaper. Larry was certainly in touch with his feminine side. She pulled out the top towel, dried her hands and placed it over the towel ring. She was about to close the drawer when she noticed the gilt-edged photo frame sticking out from beneath the towel at the bottom of the pile. Careful not to disturb anything she eased the picture out and held it up. With its pure white background and carefully positioned subjects, the photo had obviously been taken in a studio. The woman was dressed casually in a pale blue shirtwaister which showed off her tanned legs. Her face was turned away from the camera and towards the little blonde girl who sat beside her, laughing into the camera lens. Even though Tara was only looking at the woman's profile she could tell there was deep affection between the two of them. It was indeed a touching photo of a mother and her daughter. So why was it buried beneath a pile of towels in Larry's downstairs toilet?

19

Alf perched on his stool behind the counter, issuing orders. 'Tom, lad, take them trays of bedding plants outside, will you, and arrange them on the upturned fruit boxes, stagger them like, so that it makes a nice display. Tara, you make a pyramid out of these pots of paint for the window display.'

Tom winked at Tara. 'Yes, boss.' He stamped his feet together and gave a salute.

Alf hurled over a wet cloth which caught Tom square in the face. 'Cheeky beggar.'

A week had slipped by since the lunch and even though Larry had been nothing but charming and clearly adored her mother, Tara could not shake the feeling that something was not quite right.

She picked up the first pot of paint and placed it on the window sill, then another, until she had a row of ten. The next row contained eight pots, then six and so on until she had to stand on tiptoe to place the last one on top. Frowning in concentration, she jumped a mile when Tom grabbed her waist from behind. 'Tom, what're you playing at?'

'Sorry, I couldn't resist, you seemed miles away.'

'I was. I've got a lot on my mind.'

'Revision?'

'No, nothing to do with bloody exams, you fool.' She stopped and looked around for Alf. 'Where is he?'

Tom nodded towards the back. 'Gone to answer the phone, why?'

'Can you keep a secret?' Tara whispered. 'I mean it, you can't tell anybody.'

'Why, what is it?'

Tara shook her head. 'No, you have to promise first, cross your heart.'

Tom laughed. 'What are you . . . six?'

She thumped him on the arm. 'Do you want to know or not?'

'Alright then,' he relented. 'Cross my heart and hope to die, stick a needle in my eye.'

Tara lowered her voice as she heard Alf shuffling back into the shop. 'Meet me at the café in the bus depot after work, say five-thirty.' She turned to Alf. 'What're you grinning at?'

'That was our Judith on t'phone. She's coming to visit tomorrow.' He reached for his jacket off the back of the door. 'I'll have to get summat in, you two mind the shop, will yer?'

Tara sat fidgeting with her glass of milk as she waited for Tom, running her finger round the rim of the glass.

Even with the warmth of the spring day, the paraffin heater was blazing away in the corner, the diesel fumes from the buses outside adding to the stuffiness of the busy café. She waved at Tom as he came in, his face breaking into a broad smile as though he hadn't seen her for weeks. He plonked himself down in the chair opposite, speaking in hushed tones. 'I don't think I was followed.'

Tara laughed. 'You daft apeth. I just didn't want loads of questions from Mum and Alf, that's all. They're bound to think we're on another date.'

'We could be.'

She swallowed the flutter of excitement. 'Could we?'

He shrugged. 'Do you want to?'

'Do you?'

He reached across the table and took both her hands in his. 'Yes, I do. Now can we stop all this dilly-dallying and just admit that we would both like to go out on another date?'

'OK, I'd like that.'

'Well, I'm glad that's sorted. Now, what's all this about a secret?'

Tara puffed out her cheeks as she pondered where to begin. 'You know me mum's . . . erm . . . boyfriend?'

'Larry? Yes, you might've mentioned him once or twice.'

'Well, we went round to his gaff last week for the formal introduction. He lives in this massive house in Hale.'

'Nice.'

'I don't trust him, Tom. You should see the place; no way is it a bachelor pad. There're plants everywhere, frilly towels, the lot. Even satin cushions on his bed. It's just not a bloke's taste.'

'Perhaps he had help from one of them interior designers. He's rich, isn't he? That's what they all do. They don't wander into Alf's for a couple of tins of paint. They have people for that sort of thing.'

She reached down for her handbag. 'There's something else.' She took out the framed photo and laid it on the table between them.'

'What's this?'

'I found it at Larry's in the downstairs toilet, buried beneath a pile of towels.'

'And you stole it?'

'Borrowed,' she emphasised. 'What's he gonna do? I'm sure he was hiding it, so he can hardly ask me about it, can he? Besides, even if he knows it's missing, he doesn't know I was the one who took it. It could have been Mum or even Alf.'

Tom studied the photograph. 'You think this is his wife and kid, do you?'

'I think it could be.'

'Well, maybe they're not together anymore and this is just a painful reminder, so he keeps it hidden.'

'He told Mum he's never been married and doesn't have any kids. Why would he lie about that?'

When Tom didn't answer she pressed on with her

theory. 'I think he is married and I think she still lives there and he's just using my mum. You know, having his cake and eating it.'

'But your mum stays there sometimes, doesn't she? I'm sure his wife would have something to say about that.'

Tara rubbed her hands over her face. 'There's something else.'

'Go on.'

'Over the fireplace in the big lounge is this huge blank space, no pictures, nothing.'

'So?'

'It looks odd, all that bare space. Anyway, on one of my visits to the loo, I took a closer look. There's a faint black mark, sort of rectangle-shaped.' She rocked back in her chair, folding her arms in triumph.

'Erm . . . I'm not with you, Tara.'

'Don't you see, there's usually a picture hanging there. A picture of Larry's wife probably, her and their sprog.'

'Bloody hell, Tara, you thought of joining Charlie's Angels?'

'There's more. I had a peek upstairs when they were all knocking back the old vino. One of the rooms is all decked out for a little kid.' She prodded the photo on the table. 'A little kid like this one. Sindy dolls, a massive Palomino rockin' horse thing, hair bobbles on the dressing table.'

'But surely your mum must've seen this room too.

162

Hiding a couple of pictures is one thing, but a whole room?'

Tara wrinkled her nose. 'I know, that bit doesn't make any sense.'

'None of it makes sense, Tara. Isn't Larry taking you on holiday soon? How could he do that if he was still married?' He touched her lightly on the back of her hand. 'Do you think you're just looking for problems because you don't like the fact Violet's spending so much time with him? Perhaps you feel a bit left out.'

For the past fourteen years it had just been the two of them. Violet had had boyfriends before but never anything serious. Having to share her mother was new territory for Tara and she had to admit that she was finding it all a bit weird. But her mother was blind where Larry was concerned and Tara had to trust her own instincts. She looked at Tom. 'Maybe, you're right, but I have to find out for sure. I'm going to ask Mum.'

20

She'd promised to help Alf get ready for the 'Royal visit' as he called it. Everything had to be perfect for Judith, nothing was to be left to chance. Tara was sure there'd been military campaigns waged with less planning. To her credit, Violet was mucking in too. Larry had suggested driving out to the countryside with a picnic basket as the weather was so unseasonably warm, but for once he'd had to take a back seat. Tara watched as Violet weighed out the flour, her tongue sticking out of the side of her mouth as she placed the tiny weights on one side of the scales, delicately adjusting them until they balanced.

'What're you making, Mum?'

'Victoria sponge, although God knows what it'll be like. I told Alf they sold Victoria sponge at the Happy Shopper but he was having none of it.' She turned and looked at Tara, a smudge of flour across her top lip. 'It has to be home-made for our Judith.' She looked out of the window. 'And to think I could be laid out on a rug by the side of the river sipping champagne and nibbling on strawberries.'

'Do you love Larry, Mum?'

Violet tipped the flour into a bowl before answering. She wiped her hands on her apron and joined Tara at the table. 'Yes, I think I do.' She cupped her hands around Tara's face. 'But not as much as I love you, Baby Girl. You'll always be number one in my life so don't you forget that. Larry's kind to me, so generous and although I don't like relying on a man, it does feel good not to have to worry about where the next meal's coming from for a change.' She paused, taking the time to let her words sink in. 'What's the matter? Don't you like Larry?'

It seemed like the right time to take the plunge. 'He's alright I suppose, but how much do you know about him?'

'Enough.'

'Mum, I'm not proud of myself and please understand that I was only looking out for you . . .'

Violet backed away. 'What've you done, Tara?'

'Last week, at his house, when you were all drinking after the meal, I had a little look round.'

'Snooping, you mean.'

Tara looked down at the plastic table cloth, tracing the red and white checks with her finger. 'There's a room upstairs that obviously belongs to a little girl.'

Violet's arms were folded now, a frown registering on her brow, her silence making Tara unsure whether or not to continue. 'Erm . . . well, I also found a photo hidden away of a woman and her daughter.' Violet still didn't speak. 'And . . . and . . .' Tara floundered. 'In the lounge, there used to be a big picture over the fireplace, but he's taken it down and I think . . .'

'*The Haywain*,' Violet said.

'What?'

'*The Haywain*. It's a painting by Constable. Larry's sent it away to be re-framed.'

'Oh, right . . . well . . . um . . . what about that room then?'

'It's Becky's.'

'Who the hell's . . .?'

'His niece. She comes to stay sometimes. He keeps a room for her. It's a big house, he's not got any kids of his own and he's close to his sister.'

Tara thought about the photo stuffed under the towels. 'His sister?'

Violet nodded. 'Do you have anything else to say?'

'I just don't want you to get hurt, Mum. I'm sorry.'

'Tara, you don't need to look for problems, OK?' She gestured around the spartan room. 'Don't you think we have enough to worry about? Do you think this is the kind of place I wanted to raise my daughter? This wasn't part of the grand plan. Living over a bloody hardware shop, without a proper job and with a lonely old man who thinks . . .'

Tara glared at her mother and nodded towards the door, where Alf stood listening.

'Who thinks what, Violet?'

'Oh, Alf, I didn't see you there.'

166

'Obviously.'

'I'm sorry, Alf. You know we love living here. I don't know what would've happened to us if you had not taken us in that night. Please don't think we're ungrateful.' She kissed him on his cheek. 'And we're both very fond of you.'

'Aye, and I'm fond of the pair of you an' all.'

Violet released her grip on his arm. 'Anyway, I need to crack on with this cake. What time's her ladyship coming?'

'Four.' Alf scuffed his foot on the lino. 'We need to have a bit of a spring clean in here too.'

'Leave it all to us, Alf. You just take a seat over there from which you can issue instructions. Tara, fetch the dustpan and brush.'

'Why me? I thought I was helping with the food.'

'Tara, don't argue, you can do both.'

A few hours later, the three of them stood back and admired all their hard work. The little square table creaked under the weight of the food. Tara had made fish paste and cucumber sandwiches, cutting off the crusts at Alf's insistence, but saving them for the birds as he was not fond of waste. There were several Tupperware bowls filled with crisps, Twiglets and cheesy balls, cocktail sausages on sticks and a jar of pickled onions. Violet's sponge had pride of place in the middle on one of Ethel's cake stands, a thick dusting of icing sugar disguising the fact she had left it in the oven a little too long. The tinned peaches had been decanted into a crystal fruit bowl and the evaporated milk poured into a matching jug.

'You've done me proud, girls,' said Alf. 'I've never seen me kitchen looking this clean.' He glanced down at the lino. 'I'd forgotten what colour that was.' He rubbed his hands together. 'Now, how about a small sherry whilst we wait for our Judith?'

'Not for me, thanks, Alf,' said Tara. 'If it's owt like that Cinzano, I think I'd be sick.'

'Right you are. Violet?'

'Go on then. Just a small one for me, Alf.'

By the time five o'clock came, Violet had had one too many sherries and coupled with the fact she had nothing in her stomach was beginning to feel rather light-headed. 'Is she always this late, Alf?'

'Um, well she's very busy. You know what politics is like, things can 'appen when you least expect them.'

'Can I have a butty, Mum? I'm starving.'

'Tara, what've I told you? People in Africa are starving, you're just feeling a bit peckish. Alf, can Tara have a sandwich?'

He looked at the clock. 'Give it another half hour can you, lass?'

'But . . .'

Violet glared at her. 'Alf said wait.'

At six o'clock Violet's stomach was rumbling so loudly, Alf was on the verge of calling a plumber.

She patted her stomach. 'Goodness me, I'm sorry about that.'

'You need to eat, Mum,' Tara urged. 'We all do.'

'Alf?' asked Violet. 'What do you think? Shall we start without her? It is getting rather late.'

Alf peeled back the net curtain. 'Aye, perhaps we better had.' His breath had fogged up the window and he wiped the glass with his sleeve before continuing to gaze down the street. 'She'll be here. She's a good lass really, just so driven. Her career is very important but she won't let her old dad down.'

Violet handed round the plates and Tara loaded hers up, wolfing down sausages as she did so.

'Hmm . . . that's better,' she mumbled.

'Tara, please don't talk with your mouth full.' Violet stared at the empty plate on Alf's lap. 'You not eating, Alf?'

'Oh, I will soon enough. I've just got butterflies in me tummy, I'm that excited to see our Judith.'

Out in the hall, the telephone rang and Alf began to rise from his chair. 'That'll be her.'

Violet pressed him back down. 'Leave it to me, Alf. I'll go and find out what time she expects to arrive.'

She closed the kitchen door behind her before lifting the receiver. 'Hello.'

'Oh! Who is this?' The question came out on a huge yawn. 'Oo, excuse me.'

'It's Violet, who's speaking, please?'

169

'Can I speak to Alf Bickerstaffe?'

Alf *Bickerstaffe*. How many Alfs did she think lived here? 'Is that Judith?'

'Yes, is he there?'

'You're over two hours late,' Violet hissed. 'Where've you been?'

'I'm sorry, who *are* you?'

'I'm the mug who's been working her fingers to the bone preparing for your state visit. Now what time will you be here?'

In the long silence that followed, Violet could hear the sound of glass clinking and a voice saying, 'Where shall I put these empties, Jude?'

'Erm . . . I'm not coming, something's come up, something important.'

'Something more important than seeing your own father?'

Judith's voice adopted a hard edge. 'Look, you . . . you . . . whoever you are, I don't have to answer to you. I'm not coming, alright? Tell him I'll be in touch.' She slammed the phone down, leaving Violet protesting to the dial tone.

She returned to the kitchen, clasping her hands together to stop them shaking with rage. She looked at Tara and shook her head. Alf was staring out of the window again, his back to them. 'She's not coming, is she?'

'She said she's really sorry but she's been called into work on some kind of erm . . . political . . . emergency.

Obviously, she couldn't say what it was about because it's all top secret. She thought she would be able to get away but now it looks as though she might have to work through the night.'

'Work through the night? Well, it must be something big then. Poor Judith, she works too hard.'

Hmm . . . parties too hard more like. 'She was so looking forward to seeing you and is really disappointed. She told that Mrs Thatcher that she really had to travel to Manchester to see her dear old father but she wasn't to be swayed apparently. I mean, you can believe it, can't you? From what I've seen on the telly, that Mrs T is not to be argued with.'

'So, she's not coming at all then?' Alf's plaintive expression made it difficult for Violet to speak. She swallowed down the mixture of anger and sadness. 'No, she's not, Alf. I'm so sorry.' She took hold of his hand. 'How about I cut you a nice big slice of my cake, eh?'

'Aye, go on then. No sense in it going to waste, is there?'

Violet picked up the knife and plunged it into the cake, causing a puff of icing sugar to rise into the air.

'Perhaps I'd better ring her,' said Alf. 'Check she's alright. I don't want her to think I'm not worried about her.'

Violet handed him his plate of cake. 'No, Alf, you can't ring her. She was ringing from the office. She's in a top-secret meeting, been squirrelled away all day, she has,

171

and it was only on a visit to the loo that she managed to sneak out and make the telephone call.'

Alf smiled. 'Ah, that's our Judith all over. So considerate. I hope she hasn't been worrying about me all day.'

Violet stared at him, biting her lip. 'I'm sure she hasn't, Alf.' She turned to Tara, who was on to her third piece of cake. She spoke through clenched teeth. 'She's a bloody selfish cow, that's what she is.'

'It's your birthday in a couple of weeks, isn't it?' Tom stood clutching the stack of firelighters Alf had asked him to put in the back on account of folks not wanting to start fires now that the weather had really warmed up.

Tara looked up from the till. 'Yes, it is. Fifteen, eh? God, I feel old.'

Alf gave a snort from the corner of the shop. 'Wait until you get to my age, then you can complain about gettin' old.'

'You're off on your hols shortly after, aren't you?' asked Tom.

She nodded. 'Mmm . . . and I'll have to take an extra week off school.'

'Lucky you. Listen, I was wondering if you fancied doing something for your birthday? Nothin' flash, I'm not made of money.' He nodded towards Alf. 'Not on what he pays me.'

Before Tara had a chance to answer, the shop bell rang and Violet breezed in, her hands full of shopping bags,

Larry trailing after her. 'Wait until you see this lot, Tara. Larry's been treating me to a few bits for our holiday.' She dumped the bags on the counter and began to pull out bikinis, sarongs, a big floppy hat and an enormous pair of sunglasses.' She kissed Larry on the cheek. 'Thanks again, darling, you're too kind.'

He took hold of her chin and pressed his lips to hers. 'Worth every penny, Princess. You're going to look ravishing. I'll be the envy of every bloke on the French Riviera with you on my arm.'

Violet could not keep the excited squeal out of her voice.

'Did you hear that, Tara? We're going to St Tropez.' She delved into a bag and brought out a pair of tight denim shorts. 'We didn't forget you, love. Larry chose them.'

'Gee, thanks, Larry.' Tara held the shorts at arm's length. The Sindy doll she'd had as a kid would have struggled to get into them. 'But you really shouldn't have.'

Larry dismissed her comment with a wave of his hand. 'It's nothing.' He patted Violet's bottom. 'Now come on, let's get you upstairs and you can model this lot for me.'

Tara glanced at Tom as she stuck her finger in her mouth and heaved. 'Pass the bucket,' she whispered.

Larry and Violet were lying together on top of the bed, their legs entwined, as Tara entered the room. They didn't even make any attempt to pull apart. 'Don't mind me,' Tara said, shrugging off the tabard she wore for the shop.

Violet had taken to bringing Larry back to Alf's of late. Mercifully, he couldn't stay the night, not with there only being the one bed, but Violet was keen to let Larry see the cramped conditions in which they were forced to live. She was convinced it was only a matter of time before he invited them both to live with him in his mansion. Tara was none too keen though. She couldn't stand the thought of having to watch them pawing each other on a daily basis, plus it would mean catching two buses to school instead of one.

'I'm going to make a start on the tea, Mum. Larry, are you staying?' she asked, wondering how on earth she was going to divide a pork chop into two.

'Oh, no, nothing for me and Violet, we're going out for a meal.'

'Again?'

Violet scrambled off the bed. 'Come with us, Tara. That's alright, isn't it, Larry?'

He nodded. 'Fine by me, love.'

'Nah, you're alright. I promised Alf I'd do those pork chops for him. I don't want to let him down.'

'You're a good kid, our Tara, but it's Saturday night. Would you really rather spend it with an old man in this . . .' she gestured round the room, 'this . . .'

'I'm going to the pictures with Tom later,' interrupted Tara. 'So you can swan off guilt-free.'

'Don't be like that, Tara. We'd have loved you to come with us. We're going to try out that new Indian.'

174

'Well have a great time then. Erm . . . excuse me.' She rushed down the stairs. Tom was just turning out the lights and preparing to lock the front door. 'Tom, don't go.'

He turned around, his hand on his chest. 'Tara, you frightened the life out of me. What do you mean, don't go?'

'Mum and Larry are going out. I wondered if you'd like to stay and have her pork chop. It seems daft you going all the way home only to come back later for the pictures.'

'Hmm . . . I suppose it does. We always have a chippy tea on a Saturday so I'll have to ring me mam and let her know. Do you think Alf'll let me use the phone?'

'If you put your tuppence in the pot he won't mind. Go on.'

She was quite proud of her effort, even though any idiot could grill chops and boil up some potatoes and peas.

Alf scraped round his plate, licked his knife and declared it the best meal he'd ever eaten. 'You'll make someone a good wife one day, Tara lass.'

Her face instantly colouring, she changed the subject. 'Alf, you know on Wednesday?'

'Wednesday? What about it?'

'Would you come into town with me and help me choose Mum's birthday present. I want to get her something special. I'll be back from school about four so we can go then.'

'Wednesday's half-day closing, lass.'

'Oh, yeah, course. Thursday then. I won't stay behind at school for badminton.'

'What about young Tom here? Can't he go with you?'

'I suppose he could but I really want you to come with me, Alf.' She patted Tom's arm. 'No offence.'

Alf pushed his chair back from the table, placed his hands on his knees and stood up as straight as his curved spine would allow. 'That's settled then, Thursday it is.' He shuffled over to the sink and squirted a blob of Sunlight into the bowl, the lemon fragrance instantly quashing the smell of cold boiled potatoes and congealed fat. 'I'll do t'pots,' he declared. 'You two go and put your feet up.'

Tom held onto Tara's hand for the short journey between the kitchen and the bedroom. 'Thanks for tea, it was lovely.'

'Well, it was hardly Cordon Bleu,' she replied, smoothing the crumpled eiderdown. 'Erm . . . there are no chairs, just . . . well . . . this.' She indicated the bed.

Tom hopped on, leaned back against the pillows and clamped his hands behind his head. 'I'm going to miss you, you know.'

Tara climbed on beside him, making sure she kept to her side and didn't venture into the no man's land between them. 'It's only for three weeks. I'll be back before you know it.'

Tom turned on his side, his hand propping up his head. 'Come here.'

'What?' Tara laughed. 'I am here.'

'Come closer,' he whispered.

She glanced towards the door.

'It's alright. Alf's not going to bother us. He's not that clueless. Come on.'

She shuffled a couple of inches to the left and lay as rigid as an ironing board, her arms by her sides, her eyes fixed on a damp patch on the ceiling. She felt the mattress bouncing as Tom edged closer to her and then his breath was on her cheek. 'That's better.'

She desperately wanted to turn to look at him but knew if she did their faces would only be inches apart. He was bound to move in for a kiss and she was sure she still had a bit of pork chop wedged between her front teeth.

'Tara?'

She ran her tongue round her mouth, searching out any debris from the evening meal. 'Yes.'

'What do you fancy seeing at the pictures?'

She exhaled a calming breath and tugged at her collar to let some air out. 'I don't mind . . . you choose.'

'We could just stay in and . . .'

Tara leaped off the bed as though she had been electrocuted. 'And what?'

'Calm down, Tara, why're you so jumpy?'

She glanced towards the door again. 'I'm not, it's just what if Mum comes back or Alf barges in wanting to know if we want a cuppa? It would be just like him.'

'We're not doing anything wrong, Tara.'

She sat down so hard on the edge of the bed that a spring in the mattress gave a loud cartoon-style *boing*. 'I really like you, Tom.'

'Good, because I really like you.'

'I don't want to rush things.'

He cast his eyes to the ceiling. 'Well, I'd never have guessed.'

She whacked him across the arm, not quite as playfully as she had intended. 'Let's just go to the pictures, shall we?'

'Deal, as long as we can sit on the back row.'

21

'What did you have in mind?' asked Alf.

Tara peered in the jeweller's window. 'Hmm . . . I'm not sure, but I'll know it when I see it.'

'How much have you got saved up, lass?'

'Oh, enough, I hope.' She linked her arm through Alf's. 'Come on, let's have a look inside.'

In spite of the brilliant sunshine outside, the interior of the shop was dark, the only light coming from the spotlights directed onto the glass display cases. A man in a pin-striped suit shuffled forward, his hands clasped in the prayer position. 'May I help you?'

'I'm looking for a present for me mum,' ventured Tara. 'Something special. It's for her thirtieth birthday.'

'Well we have quite a selection. Do you have a budget?'

Tara dug her hand into her back pocket and fished out ten dog-eared pound notes. The jeweller raised his eyebrows. 'Is that it?'

Tara nodded. 'It's all I can manage.'

'In that case I think you'd be better served by visiting the indoor market. I don't mean to be rude but . . .'

Alf stepped in, jabbing his finger at the jeweller. 'Get

yer key and go and open that cabinet over there.' He jerked his head towards the window. 'The one with all them silver necklaces and whatnot.'

The jeweller stared at them for a long moment, gave a half-bow and silently retreated to safety behind the counter. Wordlessly, he opened a drawer, took out a small brass key and opened the display case. He pulled out a navy-blue velvet cushion, the silver necklaces sparkling under the warm lights. 'This one?'

Alf nodded and placed his elbows on the counter. He took out his glasses and peered more closely at the jewellery, pointing to a silver heart-shaped locket. 'Can we have a look at that one?'

'Certainly, sir.' The jeweller carefully lifted the necklace and laid it across Alf's palm. 'It's a beautiful piece, if I may say so. High-grade silver, 1960s, if I'm not mistaken.'

'What, you mean it's not a new 'un?' asked Alf.

'It's second-hand, yes, but as you can see it's in immaculate condition, no scratches and the inside is pristine too.' He dug his nails into the edge of the locket and prised it open. 'See.'

Alf turned to Tara. 'What do you think?'

She took the necklace from him and held it against her chest. 'It's gorgeous.' She fingered the stylised foliage design which had been engraved on the front. 'I could put a photo of me inside. That would be really special.'

Alf nodded. 'How much?'

'Thirty pounds.'

Tara placed the locket back on its velvet cushion. 'Sorry for wasting your time. Come on, Alf.' She turned to leave.

'Wait,' Alf said, turning to the jeweller. 'We'll give you twenty-five.'

'Alf, come on, I've only got ten.'

He ignored her, took out his worn leather pouch and retrieved a roll of notes. 'Twenty-five,' he tried again. 'What do you say?'

Tara edged forward. 'Alf, what're you doing?'

'Leave this to me, Tara.'

The jeweller drummed his fingers on the glass case, then searched his drawer for a pad and pencil. He lifted the pencil and dabbed the nib onto his tongue, before scribbling some figures down. He frowned then gave a dramatic sigh. 'Twenty-eight, but I'll engrave a message on the back for free.'

Alf extended his hand. 'Done.'

'Alf, I can't afford that much.'

'Just give me the ten, Tara. I'll make up the rest.'

'But it'll take me months to pay you back.'

'Tara, you pay me back every single day. You and yer mum have brightened up my life no end. Just hearing the two of you laughing together, or Violet singing in the bath, it's a treat, I can tell you. The acoustics in that bathroom, well, it's like she's singing at the Free Trade Hall.' He patted his stomach. 'And look at this. I've put on at least a stone since I've been eatin' proper like. It's no fun cooking for one.'

The jeweller cleared his throat. 'Erm, if I may interrupt for a minute.' He thrust the note pad across the counter. 'If you could just write down the message you'd like engraving on the back.'

'Go on then, Tara,' urged Alf. 'Before he changes his mind.'

22

The morning light sneaked through the gap in the curtains, casting a dagger of sunshine across the carpet. The open window allowed the blackbird's song to intrude on his thoughts. Larry hated the dawn chorus, but she liked to sleep with the window open and he would do anything for her. He clamped the pillow over his head but the birds seemed to compete with each other and the resulting crescendo had him leaping out of bed to close the window on the irritating avian choir.

She stirred under the covers as he crept back into bed beside her. She had her back to him but he curled his body round hers, moved her hair to one side and kissed the top of her shoulder. 'Morning, beautiful.'

She reached behind and tugged at his hair. 'Mmm . . . what time is it?' Her voice was thick with sleep, giving it an even more seductive edge.

He ignored the question and instead traced his finger down her spine.

She wriggled under his touch and turned to face him. 'Oh, Larry.'

He eased her onto her back and climbed on top, her

183

body pinned helplessly beneath his as he kissed her neck. 'Larry, we need to talk.'

'No, we don't, Carol. Please not now.'

She gripped his shoulders and spoke more firmly. 'Larry, stop it.'

He propped himself up on his hands and gazed down at her flushed face. 'I knew you'd come back, Carol. I always knew it.'

'Larry,' she whispered. 'Last night was a mistake. I should never have come round.'

He flopped back down to his side of the bed, the satin sheets twisted around his legs. 'But you did, Carol, you did come round and more to the point you're still here.' He reached for her hand. 'And what we had, it's all still there, isn't it? Nothing's changed. You may wear my brother's ring but it's me you love.' He squeezed her fingers. 'That's right, isn't it, Carol? It's me you love, not Martin.'

She sat up, swung her legs out of bed and placed her head in her hands. Larry crouched beside her hunched form. 'Carol?'

Yesterday's mascara framed her eyes. 'It shouldn't have happened, Larry. I was upset. Martin said some terrible things but he does that when he's been drinking. And I'm not completely blameless myself. I know which buttons to press to get him riled.'

He glanced at the empty champagne bottles on the bedside cabinet, the two crystal glasses, one still adorned with Carol's red lipstick. 'But I thought . . .'

'I'm sorry, Larry.' She reached for the sheet and wrapped it round her naked body. 'What time's your ferry?'

'What? This evening, but I'm not going now, not after this.'

'This . . . this isn't anything, Larry. We're over. I've moved on and so have you.'

'Violet? She's nothing compared to you. You're the one I love, always will.'

She leaned back on the pillow, reaching for her cigarettes. She spoke to him through the haze of smoke. 'Tell me about her.'

'What for?'

'I want to know . . . really.'

He took a long drag of her cigarette. 'What do you want to know?'

'Is she beautiful?'

He passed the cigarette back and forced himself to think about Violet. Her hair a mass of dark bouncy waves, her skin as smooth as an eggshell, her waist the diameter of a Barbie doll's. Her infectious laugh never far from the surface. 'Yes, she is.'

Carol blew out a puff of smoke, tapping some ash into an empty champagne glass. 'Does she make you happy?'

'Not as happy as you make me,' he said, sliding his hand under the sheets.

He knew Violet deserved better. He'd made her all

kinds of promises he couldn't possibly keep, but how was he to know she would fall for him? He'd used her as a distraction, a mechanism for getting over Carol which had almost worked. Except Carol was now lying naked in his bed.

23

'Right, have we got everything?' Violet scanned her list and began to rattle off the essentials in rapid succession. 'Passports, money, toothbrush, sunglasses, sun cream.' She picked up the Ambre Solaire and unscrewed the cap, thrusting the bottle under Tara's nose. 'Ooh, smell that, our Tara. It's like sunshine in a bottle, that is. I can't wait until I'm pegged out on me towel, skin all glistening with oil, turning a lovely golden brown.'

'Mmm . . . like a sausage on a barbecue, you mean.'

Violet regarded her daughter's wan face. 'It wouldn't do you any harm to get some colour into them cheeks either.'

'Will it be really hot, do you think?'

Violet stuffed another bikini into her case. 'Yes, of course it'll be hot. Like it was here a couple of years ago, hotter probably, but at least we'll have the sea to go in. We won't need to rely on a paddling pool in the back garden.'

'Do you think Alf'll be alright on his own?'

Violet stopped folding a t-shirt and let it drop to the bed. 'I'm sure he'll be fine, love. It's only three weeks and he was OK before we came along.'

'But what about when we get back? Do you think Larry will finally ask us to move in with him?'

Violet absently rubbed at the third finger of her left hand. The excitement caught in her throat and her reply came out as a girlish squeal. 'I really think he will, Tara. Won't that be fantastic though? You'll have your own bedroom, perhaps even your own little lounge if we can persuade Larry to shift his pool table. Oh, don't look so glum, Tara. You'll be able to get a record player, have your mates round and Tom of course. It'll be fun, the three of us living together. We'll be a family.'

'But I'm not sure he likes me, Mum. There's something weird about him.'

'Stop it, Tara,' Violet snapped, picking up the t-shirt and making a haphazard attempt to fold it. 'I'm not listening to this nonsense again. Larry adores you. He wouldn't be taking you on holiday with us if he didn't.'

A hesitant tap at the door made them both turn around.

'Come in,' said Violet.

Tom stuck his head round the door. 'Need any help with your cases?'

'Ooh, you're a good lad, Tom.' Violet closed the lid on her bulging suitcase and sat down on top of it. 'Tara, do the catches up, will you?'

They waited out on the street, the early morning sunshine not quite strong enough to have any impact on the temperature.

188

Alf clutched his arms across his chest. 'Brrr . . . it's a bit nippy for May, in't it?'

'You go in, Alf,' said Violet. 'No need for you to wait out here catching your death.'

'Erm, I'm good for a few years yet, Violet Dobbs, thank you very much. And anyway, I want to wave you off.'

Tom took hold of Tara's hand and pulled her to one side. 'I'll miss you.'

She managed a smile. 'Good, you better had.'

He placed his finger under her chin and tilted her face towards his. 'Bye, Tara.' He landed a soft kiss on her lips, lingering there for so long she was sure Violet and Alf would have felt compelled to avert their eyes in embarrassment.

'Bye, Tom.' She hugged him hard, burying her nose in his freshly laundered t-shirt, absorbing every detail of him and committing them to memory, terrified she would forget him.

Violet bounced on the balls of her feet like an impatient toddler. 'Where is he?' she asked for the umpteenth time. 'He should be here by now. It's not as if there's much traffic at this time on a Saturday morning.'

'You've plenty of time, lass,' said Alf. 'Your ferry's not 'til eight o'clock tonight.'

Violet stared down the empty street. 'I hope he's not had an accident.' Her voice rose in panic at the sudden realisation that this was exactly what must have happened. 'He's half an hour late, Alf, he must be dead.'

'Bloody hell, Violet! There are numerous other explanations. Don't assume the worst.'

She faced Alf, arms akimbo, challenging him. 'Like what?'

He shrugged. 'I dunno, do I? Flat tyre, overslept, couldn't find his passport, forgot to cancel the milk and that's just off the top of me head.' He tutted and turned to Tara. 'Have you 'eard this?'

'Alf's right, Mum, calm down. He'll be here.'

At the sound of a distant hum of an engine, Violet told them all to shut up, even though nobody was actually talking. 'Do you hear that?' Her fingers covered her mouth as she waited for the car to come into sight. 'It's him,' she squealed, picking up her case. 'Tara, get your stuff, he's here.'

Larry brought the car to a smooth halt and flicked on his hazard warning lights, as was accepted practice if you parked on double yellow lines, although some traffic wardens didn't agree. He stepped out of the car and clapped his hands. 'Who's ready for a holiday?'

Violet's feet felt welded to the pavement, like she was wearing concrete boots. She dropped her case, the impact causing it to spring open and spill her clothes onto the street. 'What . . . what's this?'

Larry frowned. 'What are you talking about, Violet?'

'The car, Larry. Why've you come in this one?'

'Err . . . because it's a soft-top, Violet, and we're going to the continent, you know, where it's hot.'

190

She walked over and hissed in his ear. 'It's only got two seats, Larry.'

He laughed. 'Well how many do we need?'

She jerked her thumb at Tara. 'Three, obviously.'

He opened his mouth to speak but his brain was clearly having difficulty catching up. 'Oh . . . did you . . . did you think Tara was coming with us?'

The fact he seemed to find this amusing did little to quell Violet's simmering fury. She clutched his bicep, resisting the urge to dig her nails in, and steered him round to the other side of the car. 'You said she could come with us.'

'When? I've never said she could come with us. Why would I want . . .' He stopped. 'Why would your daughter want to come away with her mum and her boyfriend?'

Violet rubbed her forehead and tried to recall the conversations they'd had about the holiday. They'd talked about it freely in front of Tara but there had never been an explicit discussion which involved taking her with them. Violet had made a huge assumption. She sneaked a look at Tara, who was hanging onto Tom's arm but staring down at the pavement. 'I can't go away for three weeks and leave her behind, Larry. It's not fair, she deserves a holiday too.'

'Well, I suppose I could go and get the Rover.' His words were hollow, no conviction.

Tara stepped forward. 'It's alright, Larry. I was never that keen on spending three weeks with you anyway.'

'Tara! Don't be so rude. Larry's just said he'll go and fetch the other car, now apologise at once.'

'Honestly, Tara,' Larry relented. 'It's a genuine mistake. I feel awful about it.'

Alf stepped in. 'Come on, Tara, he's said he's sorry.'

Tara looked at Tom who nodded his agreement.

'Please come, Tara,' implored Violet. She bent down and scooped her clothes back into the case. 'I'm not going without you so you'll spoil it for all of us if you don't say you'll come.'

Tom nudged her arm. 'Go on, Tara.'

She let out an irritated sigh, dropping her shoulders in defeat. 'Oh, alright then.'

'Hurray, that's wonderful. Isn't that wonderful, Larry?' Violet stared at him for confirmation.

'Y . . . yes, it certainly is.'

Everybody but Tara was fooled by Larry's response. Her mum stood on tiptoe and kissed him on the cheek, Tom clapped him on the back and even Alf shook his hand. They were all so busy fawning all over him that they hadn't seen him bite down on his bottom lip and roll his eyes skywards. She was not welcome on this trip and in spite of what he said, his body language spoke only of disappointment. Tara picked up her case and turned towards the shop. 'No need to go and get your other car, Larry. I've changed my mind.'

Violet threw her arms in the air. 'Oh, for God's sake,

Tara. Are you doing this just for attention? Stop being such a spoiled brat.'

Larry seized his chance. 'Well, if she doesn't want to come . . .'

'Shut up, Larry. I'll handle this.'

Tara was already heading back to the shop, her case weighing heavily in her hands. She pushed open the door and hefted the case onto the counter. Violet rushed in behind her and started to speak but Tara silenced her with a raised palm. 'Don't say anything else, Mum. I've made up my mind.' She opened her case, ferreted under a pile of underwear and brought out a small gift-wrapped box, the red bow on top now flattened. 'I want you to go on holiday with Larry and I want you to have a great time.' She passed the box to Violet. 'Don't open it until your birthday.'

Violet took the box and gingerly fingered the bow, trying to tease it back to life. 'It won't be the same without you, Tara.'

'No, it'll be better,' Tara smiled. 'You don't need me around, playing gooseberry. I'll be fine here with Tom and Alf.' She stepped into Violet's arms and gave her one long last hug. 'I love you, Mum. Now go. Go and have the time of your life and don't forget to send me a postcard.'

Violet pressed her lips to Tara's forehead, then clasped her face between her hands. 'I'll miss you, Baby Girl.'

Later, as she lay on top of the bed, her arms and legs spread out wide, taking advantage of the space, Tara knew she had made the right decision. Something did not feel quite right and no matter how much she tried to isolate it, she could not grasp what it was.

24

The temperature hadn't climbed high enough to merit driving with the top down, but Larry needed to feel the wind in his face, the sound filling his ears, blocking out everything else. He snapped a glance at Violet beside him, her hair flying in all directions as she peeled off the strands which had stuck to her lipstick. They'd driven in silence for the past two hours. Competing with the wind made conversation difficult but that suited Larry. It gave him plenty of time to think.

Violet squeezed his forearm. 'Can we stop at the next services, Larry?'

He nodded, manoeuvring the car from the fast lane in preparation for the exit. He laughed to himself. Moving from the fast lane to the slow one was exactly how his life was panning out. He flicked on the indicator and pulled onto the slip road. 'Five minutes, OK?'

'Aren't you coming?'

'I'll just stretch my legs here.'

He watched as she hurried into the building, her short skirt revealing the imprint of the leather car seat on the back of her legs. He rested his head on the steering wheel,

his furred-up tongue a physical reminder of all the champagne he had drunk the night before. He closed his eyes
and allowed himself to think about Carol. She'd left him
in no doubt that she wouldn't be returning. His future
lay with Violet, she'd said. But Carol was wrong. Once
Violet realised the extent of his duplicity, there would be
no future for them beyond the next three weeks.

Violet rubbed her hands together in an effort to dry them.
No paper towels, no toilet paper, a floor which was so
sticky she'd had to walk on tiptoe, it was no wonder Larry
had preferred to wait in the car. She spotted a payphone
on the wall near the exit and hesitated, wondering whether
to call Tara. She could see Larry through the glass doors,
leaning against the car, kicking at a stone. The episode
with Tara had meant he'd been quiet the whole journey.
It had given her time to think, though, to see things from
his point of view. Why would he want her teenage daughter
tagging along? She stopped then as the realisation hit her,
the force so sudden she might as well have walked straight
into the glass door. He was going to propose. God, it was
so obvious she couldn't think why she'd been blind to it
for so long. She'd almost ruined everything. *Violet Valentine.*
She liked the sound of that. There was a fancy word for
it . . . alliteration or something. She walked towards him,
smiling, holding out her hands.

He lifted his head. 'What are you looking so pleased
about?'

196

'I love you, Larry.'

'Oh, well . . . that's nice.'

'Nice? It's customary to say it back, you know. You're such a tease, Larry.'

He was trying to throw her off, she knew that now, but she'd go along with it. It would all be worth it when he placed that ring on her finger. And she knew just when he was going to do it. On her birthday.

'I feel really bad for saying this but I'm glad you didn't go, Tara. I'm sorry, I know that makes me a selfish sod but . . .'

Tara finished counting out the pound notes for the float. 'I'll let you into a little secret, Tom. So am I.' She glanced towards the back of the shop where Alf was busy pricing up a new delivery of paint stripper. 'I wasn't happy leaving him to be honest. Oh, I know he was alright before we came along and all that but he's used to having us around now and that Judith is as much use as an ashtray on a motorbike.' She closed the drawer on the till a little more savagely than she'd intended. 'And imagine having to spend three weeks with them two pawing each other.' She shuddered. 'No, I'm best off here with you and Alf.'

Tom took a step closer and whispered in her ear. 'Fancy coming into town tonight?' He ferreted in his back pocket and fished out a packet of ten Consulate.

'Fags? Oh, I don't know, Tom. Mum would go mad.'

'Your mum's not here, Tara. Come on, they're menthol, five each. We can chain smoke them in Spud-U-Like.' She imagined Violet and Larry winging their way to Dover, music blasting out of the radio, Violet's hair whipping round her face, Larry laughing and resting his hand on her knee. They probably hadn't given her a second thought since they sped away this morning.

'Go on then, Tom. Honestly, you're such a bad influence.'

A low gurgling sound from the back of the shop stopped them both. 'Alf?' Tara sprang forward, knocking over the paintbrush display as she raced to his side. 'What's up, Alf?' He began to cough, his eyes watering as he thumped his chest. 'Bloody hell, I feel as though I'm going to bring a lung up.'

She guided him to the stool behind the counter. 'Sit here, Alf. Tom, fetch a glass of water.' She massaged Alf's shoulders until the coughing subsided. Tom handed him the water and he took a grateful gulp. 'Aye, that's better. I think I must've swallowed a fly or summat.' His chest heaved with the exertion, his eyes still watering.

Tara glanced over Alf's head at Tom. *I'll stay in with him tonight*, she mouthed. Tom went to protest but she silenced him with a look, no words necessary.

Violet had never travelled on a ferry before, or any kind of boat for that matter, so how was she to know that she'd be as sick as a dog? Larry had been sympathetic at first, but half an hour into the crossing, he'd grown tired of holding back her hair as she vomited over the handrail. 'Violet, love, you've nothing left, come inside and sit in the warm.'

Her shaky legs would not co-operate. 'You go, Larry. I'll just stay here. How much further to go?'

He looked at his watch. 'Another hour, just under maybe.'

'Oh God, no.' She turned away and retched again, her stomach muscles aching. She felt Larry rubbing her back, small circular motions which served no purpose other than to irritate her further. 'Larry, will you just go back inside and leave me alone.' She couldn't imagine a more unedifying sight.

To his credit, he did hesitate for a second or two. 'Well, if you're sure. They're serving a nice scampi in the basket in the restaurant and I am a little peckish.'

Scampi! The juices began to flood her mouth again. Was he doing this on purpose? She wafted him away, gripped the handrail and fixed her gaze on the black horizon.

It felt like a miracle. Within thirty seconds of driving off that blessed ferry, all her biliousness had evaporated. Her stomach was hollow and her mouth felt like the bottom of a budgie's cage but here she was in France. Abroad, for the first time in her life. It was dark as they left Calais and driving on the wrong side of the road unnerved her.

She looked at Larry for reassurance, his forehead registering a slight frown as he navigated the unfamiliar roads. She leaned across to kiss him but he visibly recoiled and nodded towards the glove box. 'Your breath stinks. There're some extra strong mints in there.'

'What's the matter, Larry? You seem annoyed with me for some reason. I can't help it if I was seasick. I've never been on a boat before. Unless you count those pedal boats in the shape of swans down the local park.'

He didn't speak but kept his eyes focused on the road ahead, the clenching of his jaw further confirmation that he was in a foul mood. She lolled sideways and rested her head on his shoulder. She felt him stiffen and tighten his grip on the steering wheel. 'Please relax a bit, Larry, we're on holiday now. Don't spoil it.'

She would later spend more time than was good for her reflecting on what happened next. Larry seemed to snap and brushed her arm out of the way more savagely than he had surely intended. His hand hit her in the face, the sharp diamond of his signet ring catching her on the lip. The shock rendered her speechless and she didn't cry out, but merely turned and stared out of the passenger window, the metal tang of blood mixing with her bitter tears.

25

It wasn't exactly how she'd planned to spend the school holidays. She should have been pegged out on the beaches of St Tropez or Cannes or whatever other pretentious place Larry had lined up for them. And yet she was happy here, minding the shop for Alf while he was tucked up in bed. Turned out he hadn't swallowed a fly as he'd self-diagnosed but had developed some sort of chest infection. The doctor had been and prescribed some antibiotics which still sat on his nightstand, untouched.

'I'm not going to bother with all those fancy medicines. Never did owt for my Ethel.' He brandished the pot of mustard powder at Tara. 'Here, this is what we need. One part dry mustard, three parts flour, mixed with a little water.'

Tara took the little yellow box. 'Plain or self-raising?'

'Yer what?'

'The flour? Plain or self-raising?'

'It doesn't matter, Tara. I'm not asking you to bake a cake.'

Tara mixed up the mustard poultice in the kitchen, the smell making her eyes water. Alf was a stubborn so-and-so. It was a good job Violet was away because she'd have force-fed him his pills, with as much finesse as a plumber unblocking a drain. 'Here we are, Alf. Open up your pyjama top.'

She sat down on the bed and waited for Alf to undo his top, fighting the instinct to take over as she watched him fumble with the buttons. She managed not to gasp as he revealed his chest. The skin was so pale it had a silvery hue to it and his ribs were clearly visible. So much for all the weight he was supposed to have gained. Tara took the spatula and spread the mixture over his chest, smoothing it out with the precision of a master sculptor. Alf closed his eyes, a faint smile on his lips, his breathing becoming a little more rhythmic. 'I wish you'd take the tablets, Alf.'

He lifted a hand. 'Stop fussing, Tara. This is fine. I can feel it working already. These old-fashioned remedies are much better. I remember when I were a lad, we rubbed lard on my grandad's back.'

Tara wrinkled her nose. 'Lard?'

'Aye, he went downhill really fast after that.'

In spite of herself, Tara laughed. 'This isn't funny, Alf. Shall I ring your Judith?'

Alf's eyes flew open. 'What for?' He grabbed Tara's arm. 'You think I'm done for, don't you? What did the doctor say? Tell me, Tara.'

'The doctor said you should take your pills, Alf.'

'He didn't say anything about me popping my clogs then?'

The thought had never occurred to her. Alf was a tough old boot, he'd go on for ever. 'You're not going anywhere, Alf.'

'Actually, I need to point Percy at the porcelain, love.'

This was where she drew the line. She would cut his toe nails, clean his false teeth and spread obnoxious unguents onto his chest, but toilet stuff was not in her remit. She called downstairs. 'Tom, can you come up here for a minute?'

She passed Tom on the narrow staircase. 'Toilet, is it?' he asked, only the trace of a grimace on his face.

''Fraid so. I'll mind the shop.'

She stopped beside the telephone in the hall and picked up the receiver to check for a dial tone. It had been two weeks since Violet and Larry had left and in all that time Tara had not heard a thing from them, not even a lousy postcard. But today was Violet's birthday, she had promised to call and Tara knew Violet would not let her down.

France had been a revelation to Violet and nothing at all like she had gleaned from magazines, books and daft comedy programmes. She hadn't seen a single Frenchman wearing a striped t-shirt with a string of onions round his neck and a beret on his head. She could spot a native French woman from the other side of the street though. They were always immaculately dressed, usually in some sort of flowing white ensemble with large sunglasses and huge floppy hats protecting their delicate skin from the sun. They seemed to exist on tiny cups of strong black coffee, fizzy water and Gauloises. Violet pulled down the sun visor and peered in the mirror, hardly recognising the tanned face which stared back at her. Her eyes and teeth stood out against her darkened complexion. She smoothed out the skin on her neck and turned to Larry, raising her voice to compete with the rush of wind. 'You don't think the sun's aged me, do you, Larry?'

'No, I don't, Violet. You're even more beautiful than when we stepped off that ferry. Mind you,' he chuckled, 'that shade of green really didn't suit you!'

She'd been careful to apply the sun cream, avoided the midday sun and had religiously applied the After Sun. Larry's skin had taken on the hue of a freshly creosoted fence and his sandy hair now sported blonde highlights that any self-respecting woman would have paid a fortune for at the hairdresser's.

'How long until we're there?' asked Violet, not for the first time on this trip.

The day before, they had left France, crossed the Pyrenees and were now heading to a medieval village in central Spain which Larry had been told about by a toothless indigent farmer, who had sold them a jug of milk.

He glanced down at the map, the car drifting to the left.

Violet instinctively reached for the steering wheel 'Careful, Larry. Here.' She grabbed the map. 'Let me look. What's the name of the village again?'

'San Sedeza. Only another half hour, I reckon, but it'll be worth it from what that chap was saying.' He placed his hand on her bare thigh, moving it slowly upwards. 'I cannot think of a more special place to spend your thirtieth birthday.'

'Thank you, Larry,' she sighed. 'It's going to be perfect.' She fell silent and played with her necklace. 'It's a pity we couldn't find a working phone box though. I promised Tara I would ring today.' She unclipped the chain and held the locket in her hands. 'It's beautiful, isn't it, Larry? She must've saved up for months to be able to afford this. And to have it engraved too. It's so special.' She dug her nails into the side and prised open the locket. Tara's face beamed back at her and Violet had to swallow hard to quell the unexpected tears.

The old farmer had certainly not exaggerated the medieval splendour of the hill top village. Surrounded by a wall, it was replete with cobblestoned streets and crumbling biscuit-coloured cottages, their window boxes festooned with vivid red geraniums. A tired-looking donkey pulling a ridiculously overloaded cart ambled past, flicking away the flies with his furry ears.

In the distance, forested hills stood out against the unblemished sky.

'My God, Larry. It's stunning,' Violet said, fanning herself with the road map. 'That was quite a climb but worth it.'

Larry took hold of her hand. 'Shush, listen.'

There was no road noise, no sound of conversation, no music blaring, only the scratching of cicadas in the trees above. Larry had parked the car under the shade of a pine on a piece of scrub land at the bottom of the hill. They'd soon learned that the sun was capable of heating the red leather seats to the point where third-degree burns were a serious possibility. Cars were prohibited from entering the village itself, a law that was enforced by the narrow archway in the wall which only a donkey cart was capable of squeezing through. Violet was still struggling for breath after the steep climb. 'Can we just sit for a minute, Larry? Here on this wall.'

Larry pointed at the sky. 'Look at that.'

Forming a protective peak with her hand, she followed his finger. 'Wow, what are they?' A large bird with a fluffy white head and an incredibly wide wingspan soared on the thermal currents.

'Griffon vultures,' Larry confirmed. 'I read about them in the guide book. Carnivorous, they are. They feed on the carcasses of dead animals. Bloody good eyesight too. From the air they can spot a carcass from four miles away.'

Violet nudged him. 'I didn't know you were into birds, Larry.'

He stared at her for a second. 'There's a lot you don't know about me, Violet.'

He unfolded a piece of paper and read the name of

the hostelry which the old farmer had recommended. 'He's probably on some sort of back-hander,' he muttered. 'Goes on all over the world.'

'This whole village is asleep,' whispered Violet as they walked into the square. She pointed to the green shutters on the windows. 'Look, the houses have their eyes closed.'

'Bloody hell,' Larry cursed, looking at his watch. 'They must all be having a siesta.'

'It feels a little creepy.'

A black dog lay on the cobbles underneath a veranda, his belly heaving up and down, his tongue lolling out of the side of his mouth. He lifted his head as he heard them approach. 'Don't touch him,' warned Violet. 'He's probably got rabies.'

'He hasn't got rabies, Violet. You pay too much attention to the scaremongering tactics of the *Daily Mail*.' Larry clicked his fingers at the dog who hauled himself to his feet and waddled over, his tail wagging languidly. 'Hello, fella. Where is everybody then?'

'Larry, he's a Spanish dog, he won't understand English.'

'Oh, right, because if I'd spoken to him in Spanish he would have given me a coherent answer, I suppose.'

A young girl appeared from the back of the *panadería*. Her sunken eyes were rimmed with fatigue, her sallow skin looking as though she never saw the light of day. She wore a thin cotton dress which may have fitted her once, but now hung shapelessly from her slender frame. 'Can I help you?' she offered.

Larry showed her the piece of paper and the young girl looked down at the scrawl. 'Over there.' She pointed across the main plaza. 'It's . . .' She stopped at the sound of a voice calling from inside the *panadería*. 'Gabriela, who are you talking to?'

She passed the note back to Larry. 'Sorry, I've got to go.' She disappeared into the shop, her shoulders hunched, her lank hair falling round her face.

'Strange girl,' said Violet.

'Mmm . . .' agreed Larry. 'I've seen more vibrant-looking corpses.'

26

It was gone five by the time they were able to secure the room at the inn and they were both ready for a little siesta themselves. Larry threw himself down on the bed. 'It's hard work doing nothing all day.'

Violet crawled on beside him. 'You're not doing nothing though, Larry. You're driving for miles on end, on the wrong side of the road, squinting into the bright sun. It's a wonder you're fit for anything come the afternoon.'

He rolled onto his side and stroked a finger along her collarbone. 'How about a little nap then?' He peeled the straps from her sun dress.

'Oh no, Larry, I'm all hot and bothered. Let me take a quick shower.'

She went to move off the bed but he grabbed her wrist and hauled her back. 'It's fine, Violet.' In one swift move he manoeuvred her onto her back and straddled her, pinning her arms above her head as he leaned down and kissed her neck. She lay captive beneath him, his weight almost too much to bear, his unshaven skin chafing against hers. She instinctively crossed her legs but he prised them apart again and wedged his knee in between. 'No,' she screamed. 'Stop.'

'What's the matter? You've never objected before.'

She closed her eyes. 'I'm sorry, Larry. I know it wasn't your intention to be . . . forceful but it's just when you held my arms like that . . . it reminded me . . .'

'Forceful? Jesus Christ, Violet. What do you take me for? I was only being playful.'

She imagined another face hovering above her, one pitted with old acne scars, a bulbous red nose testament to his drinking habits. She could almost taste his sour breath. She opened her eyes again and looked at Larry. 'I'm sorry,' she whispered as a hot tear slid backwards and soaked into the pillow.

Larry climbed off her and flopped onto his back. 'What's going on, Violet?'

'Nothing: it's not you, honestly.' She propped herself up and looked him in the eye. 'You haven't done anything wrong, Larry.' She laid her head on his chest, his breathing slowly returning to normal. 'I promise you, Larry. It's not you.'

For a long time they lay in silence watching the lazy fan above them, each hypnotic revolution making their eyelids grow heavier. Violet succumbed and closed her eyes. She felt Larry nudging her. 'Oi, sleepy head, look lively. I've arranged a special treat if you feel up to it.'

Violet yawned and stretched her arms, injecting as much enthusiasm as she could muster into her reply.

'Ooh, sounds mysterious, Larry. Where're we going?'

'I'm not telling you. Just be ready in half an hour with your glad rags on.'

Tara thumbed through Alf's battered address book, searching for Judith's telephone number. In spite of what Alf said, Tara thought his daughter deserved to know that her father was poorly. She wouldn't need to put herself out to the extent of making a two-hundred-mile journey north, but she could at least send a card. There was nothing listed under Bickerstaffe though, nor indeed Judith. Perhaps she used a different surname now, one that was more suited to the high echelons of power within the corridors of Westminster. It only took a few more minutes to find her number under 'O' and Tara smiled to herself at Alf's simple categorisation of his daughter – Our Judith. She dialled the number, hoping that Judith wasn't working late, but thankfully she picked up on the third ring.

'Judith Bickerstaffe.'

'Oh . . . er . . . hello, Judith. It's Tara here. Tara Dobbs.'

'Tara Dobbs from?'

'Erm . . . from Manchester. Me and my mum lodge with your dad.'

There was a brief pause and Tara realised Judith must be expecting the worst news. 'Don't worry, your dad's not dead,' she blurted out. 'He's . . . just . . . erm . . . poorly, a chest infection. The doctor's been and told him to take some pills, which he won't, but he needs plenty of rest and me and Tom are looking after him so you don't need to worry but I just thought . . .'

'Slow down, will you,' interrupted Judith. 'Do I need to come up?'

'No, you don't *need* to make the pilgrimage north, but he'd love to see you, I'm sure.'

Judith let out an irritated sigh. 'I've got a lot on here. Just put him on, will you?'

'Oh, sorry, no, he can't come to the phone. He can't manage the stairs, see.'

There was a brief silence, filled by Judith tapping her fingernails on something. 'Well, thanks for letting me know then. Leave it with me, erm . . . what did you say your name was?'

She was about to furnish Judith with the answer when she felt the vibrating of the floorboards, accompanied by Tom's thunderous footsteps as he vaulted down the stairs. 'Tara, quick. It's Alf.'

'I've got to go.' Without affording Judith the courtesy of a goodbye, she slammed down the receiver and followed Tom up the stairs.

Tom pointed to the bed. 'I found him like this. I'd only gone into the kitchen to fetch a glass of water.'

Tara knelt by the side of the bed and took hold of his hand. 'Alf, can you hear me?'

She placed her ear on his chest, relieved to hear the faint thrum of a heartbeat. 'Alf,' she tried again, gently shaking his shoulders. She turned to Tom. 'Call an ambulance.'

With the lengthening of the shadows, the relentless heat of the sun had abated. They had been driving for almost an hour, climbing in altitude until Violet's ears popped and her stomach groaned in protest at the lack of food. She could feel a trickle of sweat running down her spine and fretted that when she eventually climbed out of the car the fabric would be stained a darker shade of red. She knew that this evening would be forever ingrained on her memory, one she would be able to tell her grandchildren about. They would listen wide-eyed as she retold the tale about how their grandfather had proposed in a mountain-top restaurant, surrounded by bougainvillea-covered terraces, the scent of pine trees, rosemary and lavender hovering in the air.

They were escorted to a table in the corner, only a dry-stone wall separating them from the river at the bottom of the gorge far below. Violet peered over the wall, a sickly feeling in the pit of her stomach, but whether it was excitement or vertigo, she could not tell. 'Where did you find this place, Larry? It's in the middle of nowhere.'

He tapped the side of his nose. 'I have my sources.' He clicked his fingers at the waiter. 'A bottle of your finest vintage cava, please.'

Violet shuffled in her seat. This was it, there was bound

to be an engagement ring in the bottom of her glass. She picked up the menu but out here in the sticks it was all in Spanish. It'd been bad enough grappling with the menus in France but at least she had retained some words from her school days.

Larry reached over and plucked the menu from her hands. 'No need to look at that. We're having the house speciality.'

'Oh, and what's that?'

'Suckling pig.'

'Suckling pig?'

'That's right. *Cochinillo*, they call it.' Larry cleared some space on the table as the waiter arrived with the cava and opened it with a flourish. He raised his glass to hers. 'Happy Birthday, Violet.'

She clinked her glass against his. 'Happy Birthday to me.' She peered into her glass before taking a careful sip.

'Anyway,' she continued. 'This suckling pig.'

'What about it?' he asked, refilling his glass.

'It sounds like a baby pig, you know, a piglet.'

'It is, Violet. Slaughtered between two and six weeks usually. Only ever been fed on its mother's milk. After six hours on the spit it just falls off the bone. Delicious.' He smacked his lips and laughed.

She took a swig of her cava, squinting at Larry through her glass. Not for the first time an unwelcome nugget of doubt crept in, almost unobserved but nevertheless hovering in the shadows. It was difficult to identify with any certainty but Larry was different somehow. It had all started on the morning he collected her for their holiday. Turning up late and in the wrong car, meaning Tara had been left behind. Violet had been so excited about the holiday that she'd overlooked the way he had behaved but something had not been quite right then. He was cold, distracted and picky, as though she got on his nerves. Even on the ferry when she'd been sick, his patience had run out and she'd felt like a nuisance. And then of course there was the split lip. He had been full of remorse and she'd believed him when he said it was an accident. But was it? She began to feel light-headed and it had nothing to do with quaffing cava on an empty stomach. She stood up. 'Larry, I just need to go to the bathroom.'

She leaned over the sink and stared into the mirror. How much did she really know about Larry? Had the fact he was wealthy turned her head? God, she hoped she wasn't that shallow. She twisted the cold tap and held her wrists under the flow. Perhaps she was so desperate to forge a secure future for herself and Tara she had grabbed onto Larry the way a drowning man grabs onto a life belt. She sat down on the edge of the toilet and pinched the bridge of her nose. Did she really love Larry or did she love the idea of being a suburban housewife whose only worry was where the next invitation to cocktails was coming from? Larry already had a gardener and a domestic help who did all his ironing so there would be nothing for her to do but . . . but what? Larry would be out at work all day and she hadn't even got to the bottom of what it was he actually did. Whenever she'd enquired he'd simply patted the back of her hand and muttered something about brokering stocks and shares, whatever the hell they were. Her life would be an endless round of coffee mornings and Tupperware parties. She peered round the door and stared at him. He was handsome, no doubt about that. He was generous too but there was something that didn't quite fit. He could be moody and had scant regard for her feelings sometimes. 'Oh, Violet Dobbs, you silly cow. Why didn't you ask yourself all these questions before?' She should've listened to Tara. She stared at her reflection, the rush of heat to her cheeks visible through her tan. She tilted her head and stared at the ceiling, her voice a cautious whisper. 'I'm so sorry, Tara. I should have listened to you. Larry's not right for me . . . for us. I don't know why I couldn't see that.' She inhaled a purposeful breath. Saying the words out loud made her more determined. 'I promise you, Tara, I'll never, ever put a man before you again. It'll just be the two of us from now on, Baby Girl.'

Picking up the threadbare towel, she blotted her face and returned to the table.

Larry took hold of her hand. 'You look a little flushed, Violet.'

'Do I? Well it's flippin' hot, isn't it?'

'I've ordered the pig.'

'Oh, um . . . great.'

He let go of her hand and reached into his jacket pocket, pulling out a small black box. He passed it over the flickering candle. 'For you.'

Violet had waited for this moment most of her adult life. She should be feeling euphoric but instead her mouth was so dry she almost choked. 'What . . . what's this?' she managed, taking the box.

'Open it.'

Steeling herself, she lifted the lid. Her gasp of relief must have been audible to the diners at the adjacent table. 'Oh, Larry! It's . . . lovely.'

He grabbed hold of the box and took out the thin silver chain, a single oval-cut diamond hanging from it. 'Two carats,' he confirmed. He pointed to Violet's throat. 'Now get that thing off and I'll put it on.'

Violet clasped the locket. 'Well, I'll put yours on another time. I'd rather wear this one for now.'

Larry clenched his jaw then drew in a deep breath through his nostrils. When he finally spoke, his voice was measured, bordering on menacing. 'You'd rather wear that cheap tat than a diamond necklace? Have you any idea what that cost?'

'Well, it's just that Tara's not here, I've not been able to speak to her and it makes me feel close to her.'

Larry shook his head. 'Women! I'll never understand them.' He shouted over to the waiter, not even affording him a polite click of his fingers. 'Oi, Manuel, fetch us a bottle of the Rioja, will you?'

217

The waiter frowned but he had obviously picked up on the word Rioja because moments later he appeared with the bottle and placed it in the middle of the table. Without a word, he uncorked it then tipped a small amount into each of their glasses. Larry stared pointedly after him before picking up the bottle and filling his glass to the top.

'Careful, Larry, you're driving, remember.'

He slammed down his glass. 'Give it a rest, Violet. It's like coming away with the Gestapo.'

'The roads are awfully winding, and there's a bloody steep drop into the gorge.'

'Feel free to drive if you're worried.' He took a gulp of the wine.

'I can't drive, Larry, as full well you know.'

'Don't lecture me then.'

Her vision was blurred, the tears standing in her eyes ready to spill out with just one blink. She stared at Larry until she could stand the stinging no more. She closed her eyes and two fat teardrops rolled down each cheek.

'Oh, Christ Almighty, here come the waterworks.' Larry passed her a napkin. 'Here, you're making a show of us.'

Violet dabbed her cheeks. 'I'm sorry, Larry,' she sniffed. 'I'm just a bit emotional because I miss Tara. We've never been apart for so long and I'm worried about her.'

'That kid can look after herself, from what I've seen.'

'She's only fifteen. We shouldn't have left her.'

Larry relented with a sympathetic smile. 'Look, we'll ring her tomorrow if you like, I promise. We'll drive around until we find a phone box and to hell with the expense.'

Violet blew her nose as delicately as she could. 'Thank you, Larry.'

'Good, now can we just enjoy our evening?' He craned his neck in search of the waiter. 'Where's Manuel with that bloody pig?'

Tom and Tara sat in the visitors' waiting room. The bright orange plastic chairs had not been designed for comfort, or ease of cleaning, given the layers of grime that were embedded in their pores. The smell of stale body odour mingled with the antiseptic spray the nurse had just dispensed with a look of distaste.

Having been unable to absorb a single word, Tara flung the magazine back onto the coffee table. 'What's taking them so long?'

'They're busy, Tara,' said Tom. 'Don't worry, Alf's in the best place now. They'll make sure he gets the medication he needs.'

She glared at Tom. 'Are you saying this is all my fault? Because I didn't insist he took the tablets?'

'I'm not saying that at all, Tara. Alf's a grown man capable of making his own decisions.' He squeezed her hand, injecting a forceful note into his voice. 'None of this is your fault.'

She laid her head on his shoulder. 'If anything happens to him . . .'

He cut her off. 'It won't.'

Violet clung onto Larry's arm as they left the restaurant, a combination of Rioja, high heels and a patch of rubble masquerading as a car park making her unsteady on her feet. Although it had got off to a rocky start, the evening had not been a total disaster after all. She had had to steel herself when the waiter delivered the suckling pig on a silver platter. He had lifted the dome with all the drama of a magician pulling a rabbit out of a hat and there, curled into the foetal position, his once-pink skin darkened by the flames to a sizzling bronze colour, lay the piglet in all his porcine glory – head, trotters, curly little tail, the lot. He looked as though he was asleep in his cosy nest of lettuce.

Larry opened the car door for Violet and she slid into the passenger seat. He leaned in and kissed her full on the mouth, his lips still coated with piglet juice, his breath reeking of red wine. She wafted him away. 'Are you sure you're OK to drive?'

'God, not this again, Violet.' He gestured with his hand across the valley. 'There're no coppers round here. And even if I do get pulled over,' he patted his breast pocket, 'I've got wads of cash in here.'

The sun had dropped behind the hills hours ago and yet it still wasn't quite dark. The sky looked as though it had leaped off an artist's easel with its hues of violet and navy. Deep down in the gorge below, the emerald river snaked its way along the valley floor, carving out the canyon just as it had done for millions of years.

Violet leaned against the head rest while Larry fumbled with the key, blindly trying to find the ignition and cursing under his breath. The car finally coughed into life and he ground the gears into reverse. 'Right, let's go for a spin, shall we?' He produced a bottle of Calvados from between the seats. 'How do you fancy an al fresco nightcap?'

'It's a long journey, Larry. Can we just get back to the village first?'

'God, Violet, when did you become so boring?' He wedged the bottle between his legs, revved the engine and then sped off with such gusto a shower of gravel flew up from beneath the tyres. Violet gripped the sides of her seat as the throaty engine roared in protest, crying out for Larry to change up a gear.

She stared at the white needle on the speedometer, slowly advancing towards sixty. She shouted above the noise of the engine. 'Larry, are you insane? Slow down, will you?'

He turned to face her, laughing. 'Whoa! It's exhilarating, Violet.' The needle quivered its way towards seventy and Violet covered her face with her hands. She felt Larry grappling with her, trying to prise her fingers away from her face. 'Come on, Violet, relax, you're in safe hands.'

'Keep your bloody safe hands on the wheel, Larry,' she

snapped, but the rush of wind carried her voice away. 'This isn't the way back either. Why are you climbing further up the mountain? Larry, listen to me.'

He took the first bend far too fast, the car seemingly tipping onto two wheels as she was flung into Larry. She screamed, instinctively grabbing for the steering wheel.

'What're you doing, you daft cow?' He pushed her back into her own seat. 'Are you trying to get us killed?'

She was crying now and this time she didn't care if he noticed. 'Larry, please. I want to go home. I want to get back to Tara.'

But he merely grinned and pressed his foot to the accelerator.

27

2018

I'd chosen a table that was partially screened by pot plants but still afforded me a view of the front door, thus ensuring that I would see him before he saw me. I'd arrived deliberately early because the last thing I wanted was a hurried entrance, me huffing and puffing, face like a beacon and tripping over my words. I picked up the menu and studied the drinks list. When did ordering a coffee become so complicated? Just when you think you've got to grips with the difference between a cappuccino and a latte, along comes a flat white or a cortado and something termed a chai latte which turns out not to be coffee at all but a syrupy mix of frothy milk and spices.

'Are you ready to order?' The waitress was at my side, pad and pen poised.

'Not quite. I'm waiting for a friend.' I swirled my finger above the table where the remains of the previous occupant's beverage was still in evidence, along with the crumbs from his flaky pastry. 'Would you mind clearing all this away?'

She looked at me as though I'd asked her to take in a family of refugees, then called to a colleague who I gathered must be beneath her in the hierarchy of the village tea rooms. 'Toyah, fetch a cloth and come and clear this lot up.' She gave me a sweet smile and assured me she would return when she saw I had company.

Outside, a gale gathered momentum and every time the door opened, a gust sent the wind chimes into over-drive. The metallic jangling was starting to get on my nerves.

I sat fidgeting for another ten minutes until finally, along with a mini tornado of leaves, he came through the door and stamped his feet on the mat. I half-stood and called out his name. 'Tom, over here.'

He looked my way and for a split second I could tell he didn't recognise me. Sure, he knew it must be me because we'd arranged to meet here, but forty years is a long time in anybody's book and I knew I looked nothing like the fifteen-year-old I was the last time we'd seen each other.

'Tara,' he cried, slotting his umbrella into the stand. He came over, his arms outstretched, and gave me a kiss on both cheeks. 'You haven't changed a bit.'

I was about to suggest he needed a pair of glasses when the waitress appeared again. 'What can I get you?'

Tom smoothed out his wind-ruffled hair. 'Oh . . . erm
. . . just a pot of tea, please. Tara?'

'Oh, go on then, pot of tea for two,' I confirmed.

'So,' he began. 'This is nice.' He splayed his hands on
the table. 'Forty years, eh?'

I was surprised by how good it felt to see him again.
He still had all his hair and his own teeth from what I
could make out. He was a little grey round the edges, but
the years had been kind to him. He didn't really look like
David Essex now but I suppose David Essex doesn't
look like David Essex any more either.

'Yes, a lifetime,' I replied.

'I couldn't believe it when Mum said you'd been in
touch.'

'I couldn't believe she still lives in the same house.'

Tom shook his head. 'She's immovable. Ever since Dad
died she's become even more determined to stay in that
house. All the memories are there, she said. I pointed out
that she'll still have her memories wherever she lives, but
she's a stubborn so-and-so. The only way she's leaving is
feet first.'

I glanced at his left hand. 'You're married, I see.'

He only hesitated for a second. 'Widower, actually. Been
two years now.'

'Oh, Tom, I'm so sorry.'

'Cancer,' he confirmed. 'It was a blessed relief in the
end, to be honest.'

I'm no good in situations like this but Tom saved me

by enquiring about my own marital status. I twisted my wedding ring. 'Divorced . . . well, technically separated. Also two years.'

He nodded sagely but I couldn't tell what he was thinking. The waitress returned and filled the table with an inordinate amount of crockery for just two cups of tea.

Tom lifted the lid on the tea pot and stirred the contents. 'I'll let it brew for a bit.'

As the years fell away I suddenly felt like crying, although that wouldn't have been enough. I actually felt like sobbing until there were no tears left and I was reduced to a quivering hollow shell. Obviously, that was a non-starter so I had to pull myself together. I'm used to it.

'Just like old times,' I said. 'Do you remember the café we used to go to? The one in the bus depot?'

'Aye, with the sticky floor and the dodgy paraffin heater.' He nodded towards the waitress who was balancing a tray of lattes. 'When you could just go up to the counter and order a mug of coffee without having to answer a million questions about it.'

I found myself smiling and my spirits lifted a little. There I was, sitting across the table from my first love. Circumstances beyond our control had separated us and I wondered, not for the first time, whether we would still be together had things been different.

'OK,' said Tom, putting his cup down and folding his

arms on the table. He leaned in slightly. 'What can I do for you?'

I was flustered then. I'd thought the inane chit-chat would continue for a bit longer before I had to get serious. Still, maybe he was in a rush, perhaps he'd got work or something. I realised that I knew nothing about his life now. I reached down and pulled the little box out of my bag. I noticed his eyebrows rise but he said nothing.

I hardly knew where to begin so I took the lid off the box and gingerly lifted out the silver locket, letting it rest in my palm. Tom took hold of my fingers and drew my hand closer. 'What's that?'

I turned the locket over so he could see the inscription. He whipped a pair of reading glasses out of his top pocket and read aloud. 'Happy 30th Birthday, Love Tara. 4.6.78.'

He stayed silent for so long that I was forced to speak. 'It's the locket I bought for Mum for her birthday. Do you remember?'

He reached for the locket and let the chain trail through his fingers. 'I did still think about you, you know. After we lost touch, even many years after, I often wondered how it all turned out.'

'It didn't turn out well, Tom.'

He closed his eyes briefly and took a deep breath. 'Go on.'

I summed up the past forty years as best I could, ending

with the story of the solicitors and Loxton's safe deposit company.

Tom rubbed his face. 'I'm so sorry, Tara. I had no idea.'

I brushed aside his apology. 'It's fine, Tom. It wasn't your problem. We were over, remember?'

'Still, that must've been tough to deal with on your own.'

'I had Nan, we supported each other.'

He offered a brief smile at the mention of Nan. 'How is she? Is she still . . .'

'Alive? Yes, she is . . . just about. She's got lung cancer.'

'Oh, I'm sorry . . .'

I held my hand up. 'Tom, please. I don't want to cry. That's not why I'm here.'

'Have you any idea what happened to Violet?'

'None whatsoever, Tom. She just disappeared. Neither her or that Larry have been seen or heard of since. The last time I saw her was that Saturday morning when you and I waved her off.'

'And you've heard absolutely nothing? Have you tried to find her?'

I thought I detected a slightly accusatory tone in his voice but it was probably me being paranoid. 'It's a bit difficult when you have no idea where to start looking. Nan and I went to Dover, if you remember, we put posters up and asked around, caught the ferry to Calais and did the same there, but we had no idea where she went after that.'

'So how did the locket end up in a safe deposit box?'

'I have absolutely no idea, Tom.' I opened the locket and stared at my fifteen-year-old self. 'But I intend to find out.'

28

1978

Although she didn't know it then, the scent of a hardware store would always transport Tara back to this night. Fertiliser, mothballs and freshly milled sawdust would forever remind her of the home they'd shared with Alf. When they arrived back from the hospital, Tom unlocked the front door and swept aside the multi-coloured plastic strips hanging from the frame. The taxi waited at the kerbside, engine running and its meter still ticking. Tara sat on the stool behind the counter and waited for Tom to raid the jar on Alf's mantelpiece to pay the fare. Alf wouldn't mind.

'Right,' said Tom, after he'd paid the driver. 'I'm staying here tonight.'

Tara squinted at the clock. 'It's gone two, Tom, half the night's already over.'

'I phoned Mum from the hospital and told her I'm staying here so it's all settled. Come on.' He helped her off the stool and guided her through to the back. She stopped at the door to the hallway where Alf's shapeless brown overcoat that he wore in the shop hung on a rusty nail. She lifted it off and brought it up to her nose. His distinctive smell still lingered on the collar; a mix of pipe tobacco and medicated shampoo. She tucked it under her arm and climbed the stairs.

She sat down on the edge of the bed, her stomach hollow but the thought of food enough to knock her sick. 'Can you open a window, please, Tom?'

He lifted the sash, allowing a warm breeze to ruffle the curtains. 'Erm . . . where do you want me to sleep?'

'Oh, I don't think either of us will be getting much sleep, Tom.' She lay down on top of the eiderdown and patted the space where her mother normally slept. 'Lie here, next to me, will you?'

Tom sidled onto the bed and opened his arms. 'Come here.' She slid across and nestled her head against his chest. 'Why did he have to die, Tom?'

He cradled her head, repeatedly kissing her hair. 'I don't know, Tara, but at least we were with him. He didn't die alone and he knew he was loved.'

She rubbed away her eyes, trying to erase the grittiness. 'I wish Mum was here.'

She slipped off the bed and padded out onto the landing towards the kitchen.

'Where are you going, Tara?'

Tara ignored him and opened the cupboard in the

corner. She took out the fur coat and rubbed the collar against her cheek, Alf's final words echoing in her ear. *Make sure Violet gets the mink.*

She couldn't imagine that anything was hotter than this, not even hell itself. Blind as she was, she found it impossible to locate the heat source but that didn't stop it searing her skin and boring through her eyelids. She was lying on her back, a position she'd always found unnatural, even in the comfort of her own bed. She dug her fingers into the ground, wincing as the sharp stubble pierced under her fingernails. Pain, that was good, surely? It meant she wasn't dead. Hours passed, or maybe it was only minutes, she had no way of knowing. She didn't know anything anymore. Her lack of sight had heightened her other senses and she could hear birds overhead, a wooden-sounding chattering. Wait a minute. She knew something about those birds. She willed the information to reveal itself, straining every sinew because she knew it was important. When it came to her, she wished she hadn't bothered. The griffon vultures were circling and that could only mean one thing. She was dead after all.

She turned her head towards another sound, a scrabbling of feet and a whoosh of fabric. She forced her eyes open, recoiling from the dazzling sunshine. An angel knelt down and touched her forehead. The rush of relief overwhelmed her. At least she'd made it to Heaven.

'Can you hear me?'

She'd expected a light, harmonious voice but this was deep, heavily accented and not at all angelic. She tried to speak but the words wouldn't come. She closed her eyes again and succumbed to the enveloping exhaustion.

29

Tara stood with head bowed, one hand in Tom's, a clump of soil in the other. She didn't want to let go of his hand but was conscious that her nose was running and no amount of sniffing was adequate to stem the flow. She turned and wiped it on her shoulder, leaving a faint trace of slime on the black shirt. She concentrated on the vicar's words. *Earth to earth, ashes to ashes* and all that malarkey. She stared across the grave at Judith, who held a gloved forefinger under her nose, occasionally flicking away a tear. The coffin was lowered into the grave and the vicar gave the signal for the mourners to throw in their soil. Tara reacted immediately, her clump hitting the brass plaque bearing Alf's name. There was no way she was letting Judith go first.

The vicar closed his Bible and turned to Judith. 'Again, please accept my condolences. Take as much time as you need.' He gave a bow and backed away, leaving Judith rummaging in her handbag for a tissue.

'Shall we go?' Tom asked Tara, giving her a gentle tug.

'At least she turned up for his funeral,' replied Tara, staring at Judith. 'Look at her there with her crocodile tears. She's pathetic.'

Tara blew a final kiss at the coffin and turned away, leaning against Tom for support as they walked towards the gate.

'Wait.' They both hesitated at the sound of Judith's shrill command.

'What does she want? Ignore her, Tom, just keep moving.'

Judith caught up with them in spite of the fact her stiletto heels sank into the grass as she walked. 'Has your mother turned up?'

'Not yet.'

'Well, do you have any idea when she'll be back? I can't wait for ever, you know.'

'I've told you, she was due back four days ago, but she must've got held up. I've no way of contacting her but don't worry, she'll be back and you'll get your rent then.'

Judith gave a dismissive wave of her hand. 'This isn't about the rent. The shop and flat are going on the market as soon as probate comes through and even I have qualms about chucking a kid out onto the street.'

Tom placed a protective arm around Tara. 'You can't do that, Judith.'

'Believe me, erm . . . what did you say your name was?'

'Tom.'

'Believe me, Tom, it's the last thing I want to do but business is business. I have no need of Father's hardware emporium, surely you can understand that?'

'But I don't have anywhere to go until Mum gets back,'

Tara reasoned, her voice suddenly sounding small and pitiful against Judith's clipped, efficient tones.

'I'll tell you what I'll do. Even though your mother's arrangement with my father was casual, I'll let you stay there until she returns or until the business is sold, whichever comes first. I can't say fairer than that. Now, can you keep the shop going in the meantime?'

'You're unbelievable, you are,' said Tara. 'No, I can't keep the bloody shop going. I'm only fifteen. I'm still at school.'

Judith appeared momentarily flummoxed. 'Oh . . . of course, silly me. Right well, if you're not going to be working in the shop, there seems little point in you continuing to live above it.'

'Hang on,' Tom interjected. 'You just said she could stay there until it was sold.'

Judith narrowed her eyes, steering the conversation in another direction. 'Why do you think your mother hasn't returned?'

'I don't know,' said Tara. 'But she will come back. If something had happened to her then we would have heard about it. My mum is very, what's the word . . . spontaneous. They'll have gone off to see some castle or vineyard or something. She knows I'm alright here with Tom and . . . Alf . . .'

Judith seemed to relent. 'Would you like a lift back to the shop?'

Tom looked at Tara. 'Shall we? Saves getting the bus.'

Tara nodded. 'OK, ta.'

Somebody had left a small bouquet outside the shop door, a simple bunch of forget-me-nots bound at the stems with tin foil. Judith picked them up and read the card aloud.

Rest in Peace, Alf. You were a true gent. Maggie from the Post Office.

'How sweet,' she said, thrusting the flowers in Tara's direction. 'Now would you mind giving me a hand with clearing some stuff out? I've got a house clearance company coming tomorrow but I'd better check there's nothing of any value. Tom, if you're not doing anything, you can open the shop.'

'Don't you think it's a bit soon?' asked Tara.

'Soon? My father's dead, what's the point of hanging about? If he was here he'd say the same thing.'

How Tara wished Violet was here. She'd have no trouble putting Judith in her place.

Tom pulled a face behind Judith's back. 'I'll go and open up then.'

Tara's breakfast bowl was still on the table, the remains of her Weetabix welded to the surface. She'd left the bottle of milk out too. Judith picked it up and sniffed the contents. 'Urgh! Pour that away, will you? Don't you have a fridge?'

'Sorry, I was a bit distracted this morning, probably because I had a funeral to go to.'

'Yes, well, I'm going to need you to keep this place clean and tidy and the smell of rancid milk isn't conducive to a quick sale.' She looked around the kitchen, not bothering to hide her distaste. 'God knows how I'm going to sell this hovel.' She glanced at Tara. 'No offence, love, but I'm surprised it survived the slum clearances.'

'Me and my mum like it here. We were desperate when your dad took us in.'

'Hmm . . . you must've been.' Judith clapped her hands together. 'Right, have you got a bin bag?'

30

2018

Tom looked at the locket again, shaking his head. 'I don't know what to make of it, Tara, it's just so unbelievable.'

'You're not kidding. And I didn't know who else to call. I'm sorry.'

'Don't be sorry, I'm glad you did.' He tugged at his sleeve and sneaked a look at his wristwatch.

I signalled to the waitress by writing on my palm with an imaginary pencil. 'Four fifty, love,' she shouted. I stood to leave. 'I won't keep you any longer, Tom. I just . . . well, I just . . . oh, I don't know, I just wanted to tell someone who was there, that's all.'

He whipped out his wallet. 'I'll get this.'

'Oh no you won't,' I said, a little too forcefully. 'This is on me.' I thrust a fiver over the counter before he had a chance to argue further.

Out on the street, he turned his collar up against the battering wind. I could feel my hair lifting, no doubt standing comically on end. 'Well, goodbye then, Tom.'

He leaned in for an embrace and kissed me on the cheek. 'Bye, Tara. It was good to see you again.' He took hold of my hand. 'I'm really sorry this happened to you. You don't deserve it and I hope you find the answers you've been searching for.'

'Me too, Tom.'

I turned to leave but he followed me. 'Oh, are you going this way too?'

He pointed down the street. 'Yes, my car's parked at the end of this road.'

We walked on in excruciating silence for a few paces. I couldn't think of anything else to say so I hummed a little tune instead.

Tom stopped at the corner. 'Well, this is me.' And then he surprised me so much I was left gaping like a moronic idiot. 'Look, why don't we have dinner? It doesn't feel right leaving it like this.' He interpreted my silence to mean I wasn't all that keen. 'I'm sorry, no, you're right, just ignore . . .'

'I'd love to,' I almost shouted. 'When?'

'Oh, great . . . erm . . . tomorrow night? I'll pick you up at seven. Now I really must dash, text me your address.'

I watched as he jogged over the road. I felt as though I was on a film set, a cheesy rom-com. I imagined a camera zooming in on my grinning face. If it had been a film, I would've thrown my arms out wide and spun round the lamppost. But it wasn't and I'm not one for drawing attention to myself, so I merely bowed my head and made my way calmly along the pavement like the respectable middle-aged woman I am.

Moira's car was parked in the driveway when I got home. The sight of the battered little Renault made me smile and I quickened my pace. I knew when I opened the front door the smell of furniture polish would hit me along with the comforting drone of the vacuum cleaner. Dear Moira. I'd come to regard her as a surrogate mother, even though she's only ten years my senior. Even before I had my key in the door, I could hear the commotion going on inside. There was so much shouting and screaming it sounded as though the entire Jeremy Kyle audience was crammed into my kitchen. Moira was standing with her hands embedded in her hair, struggling to remain calm whilst trying to assert her authority over the two little girls who were squabbling over a packet of Percy Pigs.

I dropped my handbag onto the counter and raised my voice above the din. 'What the f . . .' I remembered the girls. 'What the heck is going on here?'

Moira spun round and almost dropped to her knees with relief. 'Tara, thank God.'

Ralph's girls stopped arguing for a second. 'Auntie Tara,' cried one. I didn't know which one because, let's face it, I hardly see them and frankly I don't need to know which one is which.

'Auntie flamin' Tara?' I repeated. 'Who said you could call me that?'

One of them stuffed a squashy pink pig into her mouth and shook her head. At two years old, I didn't even know if she'd understood the question. She pointed to her sister. 'Lily hit me.' She pouted and rubbed her head.

Moira stepped in. 'Their mother brought them round soon after you left. Said it was an emergency.'

'Hmm . . . broke a nail, did she?'

'I said she couldn't just dump them here when you weren't in but she said she'd cleared it with you already.'

'Did she now?'

This was all I needed. I wanted to be alone to just think, and I didn't have the time, the inclination or the energy to sort out Ralph's mess.

Moira wrung her hands. 'I'm sorry, love. I tried to call you but you didn't pick up.'

'My phone was on silent. I didn't want to be disturbed.' I gave Moira a reassuring pat on the arm. 'Leave this with me.' I called to the girls who were digging their sticky little mitts into my sheepskin rug. 'Right, Lily, Jasmine. Come on, you two, we're going for a little ride.'

I bundled them onto the back seat of my car and fastened their seat belts. I didn't have booster seats, so the belts rested against their necks. If I needed to brake hard, they'd be decapitated. 'Wait here,' I commanded, running back into the house. I returned with the seat cushions from the settee. It wasn't ideal, but there again, there was nothing ideal about the whole situation.

Ten minutes later I arrived at Ralph's office. There was

a new logo, RAA, embossed in gold script on the smoked glass door. First impressions would conclude Richard's Advertising Agency would deliver an effective campaign. I mean, Ralph's hardly Maurice Saatchi but he's good at his job. I grabbed hold of the girls' hands and marched into reception, their little legs struggling to keep up. The receptionist told me Ralph was in a meeting with a prospective new client. I couldn't believe my luck. I could hear her frantically calling after me as I strode along the corridor towards his office. One of the girls had begun to cry and the other one declared she'd done a poo. Perfect! It was almost enough to make me believe in a higher power. I looked up and mouthed a silent thank you, just in case. I had to go through Mrs Blue Rinse's office to get to Ralph but mercifully she had deserted her post and the way was clear.

I didn't bother to knock on Ralph's door and as it flew open I saw him look up from his desk, his mouth open, immobilised with shock. The client in the seat opposite spun round in her chair, only managing a bewildered frown at this gross interruption.

I pushed the girls into the room as gently as my temper would allow. After all, none of this was their fault. 'Can you please inform your girlfriend that my house is not a free-for-all crèche and she can't just dump the kids you spawned together and swan off to get her eyebrows knitted whenever she feels like it.'

The client seemed to find something amusing.

'Threaded,' she stated. 'You get your eyebrows threaded, not knitted.'

I looked at her perfectly arched eyebrows and bowed to her greater knowledge of micro-grooming techniques. 'Thank you for that. At least I've learned something today.'

Ralph pulled one of the twins onto his knee, wrinkling his nose at the stench now emanating from her nappy. I cast my mind back to when our Dylan was that age. I'm sure he was out of nappies. 'I'm sorry, I didn't know . . .' he said.

'I'm not interested, Ralph. They're all yours.'

I stomped towards the door, then stopped to give him my parting shot. 'Oh, and I am not their Auntie Tara.'

Moira was still beavering away when I returned. 'They're little monkeys, aren't they?' She rummaged in the pocket of her tabard and shoved a note towards me. 'Here. Fella called Jamie rang. Said he was from a solicitor's. Ernest something or other.'

'Irwin Fortis?'

'Aye, that's the one. Chap said there's been a cock-up.'

'Is that a new legal term then?'

'Well, I'm paraphrasing, but he wants you to call him urgently.' She folded her arms and nodded sagely. ''Ere, it'll be about that locket, I reckon.'

My heart beating hard in my chest, I reached for my phone and punched in the number.

31

The receptionist picked up on the third ring and sang her greeting to me. 'Irwin Fortis, how may I help you?' I cleared my throat and adopted a business-like tone. 'Can I speak with Jamie, please?'

'Jamie Mac or Jamie Ewing?'

'Erm, I'm not sure, he called me and didn't leave a surname. He's tall and he's quite young . . .'

'In that case, it's definitely Jamie MacKenzie you want. I'll put you through.'

As I waited for the inept Jamie to come on the line, I was forced to listen to a medley of Christmas carols, which caused me to glance at the calendar even though I knew full well it wasn't even the end of November. 'Jamie MacKenzie, how can I help you?'

'Jamie, it's Tara Richards here, returning your call.'

I could hear him tapping his pen. 'Tara Richards?'

'That's right.' The fact he seemed to have forgotten who I was didn't instil me with much confidence.

There came a shuffling of papers down the line. 'Aah, yes,' he said triumphantly. 'I'm glad you've called . . .'

'You asked me to,' I said incredulously.

He lowered his voice and I struggled to hear him. 'When you came in last week, when I gave you the key, you remember?'

I tried to remain calm. 'Yes, Jamie, of course I remember.'

He laughed nervously and reduced his voice to a mere whisper. 'Well, I forgot to give you something else . . . a . . . a letter.'

Lord have mercy! It's for people like him we have to have instructions on shampoo bottles.

'A letter?'

'Yes.'

'Who from?'

'I don't know, it's sealed. It's for your eyes only.' He managed another nervous laugh.

'Well, you'll have to stick it in the post, I'm afraid. I'm not coming all the way to London to collect a letter.'

He seemed unsure. 'You're not passing anytime soon then?'

Passing? Has he ever looked at a map? 'No, Jamie, I'm not passing. Please put it in the post and we'll say no more about it.'

He let out a sigh of relief. 'Thank you, Mrs Richards. I'll do it recorded delivery and once again, I'm really sorry.'

'Apology accepted, Jamie, but for your sake, career-wise, I hope you've got a Plan B.'

Moira was hovering by the mantelpiece as I ended the call. 'Everything OK?'

'That dozy intern should have given me a letter when he gave me that key. He's going to post it to me.'

Moira widened her eyes. 'Oh, well good, perhaps that'll explain everything.'

32

Forty years had gone by since I sat in front of a mirror contemplating a date with Tom, only this time I didn't have my mother to help me produce a miracle. No, this time I had to call in the professionals. The stylist stood behind me tapping her scissors on her palm. I tried to concentrate on what she was saying but my mind kept wandering to the letter. Who had written it and what did they want to tell me? And, most mystifyingly, why had it taken so long to reach me?

The hairdresser brought me back to the task in hand. 'Well, that's my suggestion but why don't you tell me what you want?'

'What? Oh, sorry, I was miles away.' I stared at her reflection in the mirror and flattened out my parting. 'This grey needs to go and the overall colour needs warming up. Then I want you to cut out all these split ends and give it some shape.'

She picked up a strand of my hair and squinted at it. The look on her face suggested it was a clump of hair she'd just pulled out of the plughole. 'How long is it since you've had it cut?'

I tried to think. I knew I'd had it cut for Moira's son's wedding but that was back in February. Had it really been nine months?

'Oh, not for a long time,' I admitted. The truth is, going to the hairdresser's is one of my least favourite things to do. Sitting in a chair, wilting under a black cloak with a pile of *Hello!* magazines to wade through is not my idea of fun.

'I'm going to have to cut a good three inches off,' she declared, as though this was some kind of punishment for letting myself go.

'Do what you have to.'

Even though we'd only known each other five minutes, she gave my shoulders an affectionate squeeze. 'You're going to look amazing after I've lopped this lot off. Long hair drags down your features. You've got great bone structure, you need to show it off.' Frowning, she peered at herself in the mirror. 'I wish I had your cheekbones.'

'Oh,' I replied, genuinely embarrassed. 'Thank you.' I've always been hopeless at accepting a compliment.

Three hours later I left the salon. That's another reason I hardly ever visit the place. I was pleased with the result though. My hair moved in bouncy auburn waves as I walked down the street and I couldn't help but admire my reflection in the shop windows as I breezed past.

I needed to be back home before one to sign for the letter Jamie had posted. There was just time to nip into Next and treat myself to a new top to go with my staple black trousers and heeled boots. I went for a daring fuchsia colour in satin which would look great teamed with my cream leather jacket.

As I turned into my road, I could see the postman with his bike propped up against my hedge. He was ferreting in his sack as I pulled onto my driveway. He looked up, waving the letter. 'Another recorded delivery,' he stated.

I climbed out of the car and grabbed the bags off the back seat. 'Yes, I'm expecting it.'

'I like your hair, suits you, makes you look younger.'

I took the letter and signed his little machine. 'Thank you.'

I dropped the bags in the hall and scurried through to the kitchen, tugging open the manila envelope as I went. Inside there was another envelope with an Irwin Fortis compliment slip attached to it.

Again, my sincere apologies for the oversight, Jamie.

I sat down at the breakfast bar and smoothed out the bulging envelope. The paper was crisp with age and smelled of old hymn books. My hands shook as I picked up the letter knife and eased it under the flap. There appeared to be several sheets of paper inside. The heat began to rise from my toes, flooding my body until my armpits prickled and I could feel the moisture on my top lip. Opening the back door, I leaned against the frame, wafting my blouse to let the cool air in. I stared at the letter, thick with promise. Part of me wanted to rip it open and greedily gobble up the contents. Another part of me, the more vulnerable side that I rarely showed to anybody, wanted to run and hide. It may appear that I have a tough exterior but that has been my way of coping ever since that life-changing day my mother drove off with Larry and never returned. I had no idea what answers lay in that envelope but I was sure of one thing. I couldn't do this on my own.

I lit a calming lavender-scented candle and sat down at my dressing table, staring at my reflection. My expertly coiffured hair was at odds with my pale make-up-free face. As I smoothed on my foundation I thought about the last time I'd seen Tom.

He'd come to visit me in Lytham and when it was time for him to leave, I went with him to the coach station. He'd accepted a place at Thames Polytechnic but we promised each other that it wouldn't be the end of our relationship. In spite of the distance between us, we knew we could make it work. We'd been through so much together and we weren't going to let a mere two hundred and fifty miles scupper what we had. Our love was real and tangible; but in spite of our promise I never set eyes on him again until yesterday. The phone started ringing downstairs in the hall but I chose to ignore it.

I was ready by ten to seven and even though I say it myself I didn't look half bad. The new top was flatteringly roomy and didn't cling to my doughy stomach. My bottom and hips have always been on the slim side and the gently tapering trousers grazed the top of my patent-leather ankle boots and made me look taller than I am. I'd managed to find an old pink lipstick which perfectly matched the colour of the new top and my trusty Swarovski earrings dazzled under the lights. I picked up the letter again, pressing it to my nose. Tom and I would read it together and at that moment I realised there was no one I would rather have by my side.

I froze as I heard the key in the front door. Bloody Ralph, who the hell did he think he was? I'd told him that key was for emergencies only, but we seemed to have different opinions on what constituted an emergency. I resolved to take it off him. I tottered towards the front door on my heels, ready to intercept him in the hallway, but as the door opened my fury dissolved in an instant. 'Dylan! What on earth are you doing home?'

He dumped his holdall on the floor. 'Surprise!' He gave me a big hug then stepped back and frowned. 'You're going out?'

'Well, yes, I was, but I won't go if you don't want me to. Come here.' I gave him another hug and my cheek rubbed against his bristles. I grabbed hold of his chin. 'What's all this? Don't they have razors up in Newcastle?'

A note of irritation crept into his voice. 'Nobody shaves any more, Mum.'

It was a ridiculous statement but I let it go. 'Why didn't you tell me you were coming? I could've picked you up from the station. No sense in wasting your money on a taxi.'

'I tried to call you on the home phone and on your mobile but got no answer. It was a spur of the moment thing. Dave's sister's having a twenty-first in town tonight and he asked me if I wanted to go. It'll be great to see the lads again.'

'Oh, so you haven't come to see me then?'

'I've come to see you as well, Mum.' He pushed past me and went into the kitchen. 'How's Nan?'

'Nan's doing OK, considering. She told me you'd rung her. Brightened her day, it did.'

He opened the fridge and stared into it. I saw the look of disappointment cross his face. 'Not got much in, have you?'

'There's an emergency lasagne in the freezer, you can have that.'

At the sound of the doorbell, I left him ferreting in the freezer and went to answer it.

'Hi, Tom,' I said. 'I'll just grab my handbag and I'll be right with you.'

I left him on the doorstep and dragged Dylan's holdall into the kitchen. 'Feels like you've brought a ton of bricks home.'

'Oh that,' he said casually. 'It's my dirty washing.'

'Aah, right, well the utility room is that small one off

the kitchen and the washing machine is the big white thing with the round glass door.' I swung my bag onto my shoulder. 'See you later, don't wait up.'

Tom gave a low whistle when he saw me again. 'Wow, you look . . . amazing. I like your hair, it suits you, makes you look younger.'

'You sound just like the postman.'

I smiled at his frowning face. 'Never mind.' I linked my arm through his. 'There's been a development.'

'Oh?'

I patted my handbag. 'It's all in here. I'll tell you about it at the restaurant. Believe me, Tom, it's not something I want to read all by myself.'

33

We followed the waitress to our table, Tom's palm gently touching the small of my back. He pulled a chair out for me and as I sat down the waitress flicked open the folded napkin and laid it across my lap. It was as though I was incapable of doing anything for myself.

'Can I get you some drinks?' the waitress asked

'Sure,' said Tom. 'Tara, what do you fancy?'

'I don't know. What will you have?'

'Well, I'm driving but I suppose one won't hurt.'

The waitress stifled an impatient sigh as she hovered with her iPad.

'G & T?' suggested Tom and I quickly agreed, if only to get rid of the waitress; but no, she wasn't finished just yet.

'Any preference? Bombay Sapphire, Gordon's, Hendrick's?'

'Gordon's is fine,' I said.

She tapped away on her iPad. 'Schweppes or Fever Tree?'

I shook my head. 'Either, you choose.'

'Ice and lemon?'

Whilst I had to admire her attention to detail, on what planet did someone drink a gin and tonic without ice and lemon?

'Yes, please.'

She stabbed at the iPad again and toddled off.

'When did everything get to be so complicated?' I said, picking up the menu and fanning myself. 'Is it hot in here or is it just me?'

Tom shrugged off his jacket. 'It is a bit warm.' He leaned so far across the table I was worried his tie was going to catch fire on the candle. 'So, you said there's been a development.'

'Yes.' I nodded. 'I should've been given a letter with the locket but the numpty down at Irwin Fortis forgot. I've got it now though.'

'Oh, and what does it say?'

I looked down at the table, my voice small and pathetic. 'I don't know. I haven't opened it yet.'

'Why not? You might finally have the answers you've been looking for.'

The dismay in his voice forced me to try and explain something I could hardly understand myself. I can see why he would think it natural for me to rip open the letter and perhaps finally find out the truth. But it wasn't as simple as that. As long as there was no proof otherwise, I could dream that against all the odds my mother was alive and well somewhere. Where there was ignorance, there was hope. I tried to articulate my reasoning but even to my ears it sounded hollow. 'I've waited forty years to find out what happened to my mother. Let's face it, Tom, it's hardly going to be good news. Either she's dead or she didn't come back because she didn't want to. And I'm not sure which is worse.'

The waitress returned with our drinks and plonked them on the table. 'Are you ready to order?'

We hadn't even glanced at the menus. 'No, not yet,' said Tom. 'Can you give us five minutes?'

'I understand what you're saying, Tara. It's been forty years; another couple of hours isn't going to make any difference. You need to steel yourself, and whatever the letter says, I'm here with you, OK? Just like I was back then when she didn't come home.' He reached over and squeezed my hand. 'We'll open it together.'

I managed a smile and wondered not for the first time why I ever let him go.

'We'd better have a look at the menu,' he said. 'I can recommend the fish pie.'

'Oh, you've been here before then?'

'Once or twice. Penny liked it.'

I shuffled in my seat. 'Was Penny your wife?'

'That's right, she was.'

I struggled to think of something to say. I could talk about my ex all day long because he was still a living, breathing person who barged into my life with annoying regularity. Talking about a late spouse, though, that was a whole different ball game. 'Erm, do you still miss her?' I cringed and took a slug of my gin. Why did I always say the wrong thing? Of course he must miss her.

'Yes, I always will. The girls help though.'

I wiped my lipstick off the glass with my thumb. 'Yes, I'm sure they do. How old are your daughters?'

'Meg's twenty-one and is on a gap year in Thailand and Hannah's eighteen. She's at uni studying the club scene and drinking culture of Liverpool.'

I frowned. 'Really? That's a course now, is it?'

He stared at me. 'No, it's not. It was a joke. She's doing geography.'

God, I'm so dense at times. 'She's the same age as our Dylan then. He's studying medicine at Newcastle.' I tried to keep the pride out of my voice and just managed to stop my chest from inflating.

Tom gave a quick whistle. 'Wow, he must be very bright.'

'Yeah, he takes after his dad.'

'Hey, don't do yourself down, Tara.' He picked up the menu again. 'Come on, how about we have this sharing platter thingy for starters and then the fish pie? Unless there's something else you'd prefer?'

I slammed my menu shut. 'It sounds perfect.'

There was more dabbing at the iPad as the waitress took our order and then she plonked down a basket of bread which we hadn't ordered and neither of us particularly wanted and yet I knew we'd have cleared the lot before our starter arrived. It's something to do with your hands and helps to fill the silences.

'Tom,' I began, as the gin loosened my tongue. 'I really did love you, you know.'

He put a slab of rock-hard butter on his bread and made a futile attempt to spread it. 'And I loved you too.' His words were coated with sadness and I swear his voice almost cracked.

An unexpected lump formed in my throat and it had nothing to do with the doughy bread. 'And you never forget your first love, do you?'

He rocked back in his chair and laughed, instantly lightening the mood. 'Do you remember the first time we . . . you know . . .' He lowered his voice 'Did it?'

I could feel myself blushing like the fifteen-year-old I was back then. 'How could I forget?'

It happened when he came to Lytham. Nan went off to bingo and we took advantage of the empty house. We lay on my single bed, the bright orange walls crowding in on us, Leo Sayer's 'When I Need You' on the turntable. For years after I couldn't listen to that song without crying. We were both nervous and whilst Tom was no choir boy, he did lack the experience to make me feel as though I was in capable hands.

'There was an awful lot of fumbling as I recall.'

Tom dabbed at his mouth with his napkin. 'Didn't last too long either, did it?'

I groaned inwardly. I hadn't had nearly enough alcohol to

259

make this conversation comfortable. 'Well, it was a long time ago. I expect we've both learned a few moves since then.'

The waitress saved me by bringing over the sharing platter on a huge breadboard. 'Any more drinks?'

'I could use another,' I said to Tom.

'Make it a large one,' he told the waitress. 'And I'll have a Diet Coke.'

'So,' he said when she'd gone. 'You're divorced.'

I wasn't quite sure how to answer. 'Not divorced, separated. We're not on bad terms though. We can just about manage to be in the same room.'

'Oh well, that's nice,' he declared. 'Best to be grown-up about these things, especially when kids are involved. Dads always seem to come off worse in a divorce or separation, don't they? You know, having to have visiting rights to see their own kids, it must be . . .'

I cut him off. 'Ralph left me for his pregnant secretary actually.' I had to nip this sympathy for Ralph thing in the bud. I gave a tight smile as Tom held his loaded fork midway between his plate and his mouth.

'Oh . . . how . . . well, I mean, that's . . .'

I dismissed his concern with a flick of my hand, warming to my theme. 'Been cheating on me for years, he had. Serial adulterer. I thought he'd calm down a bit in his old age, but no, he gets his dozy secretary pregnant and she spawns twins.'

Tom choked on his food and took a swig of Diet Coke. 'Twins?'

'Mmm . . . you couldn't make it up, could you?'

He shook his head. 'I'm sorry, Tara. You don't deserve that.'

'Oh,' I replied in mock surprise. 'Apparently, I do. Once I'd had Dylan I didn't pay Ralph enough attention. I put the needs of my baby before a thirty-seven-year-old man-child.' I realised I needed to stop. I felt my chest flushing and that's not a good look for anybody. I took a deep breath and pushed my fingers into my breastbone. The first burning sign of indigestion was on the horizon.

'But you're not divorced?'

Tom said this in a manner which led me to think he wasn't convinced that Ralph was the philandering, duplicitous two-timer I made him out to be.

I moved some food around my plate whilst I searched for a convincing answer I'm not even sure I'd believe myself. 'Divorcee,' I said eventually. 'It's such a . . . disappointing label. It just reeks of failure.' I felt the tears begin to prick. 'Anyway, that's enough about my troubles. Let's just enjoy our meal, shall we?'

The rest of the evening passed by in a rather pleasant mixture of reminiscing, talking about what we did now and our respective children. We hardly noticed the elephant in the room. Or rather the one in my handbag.

We were on our coffees before Tom brought it up again. 'Shall we have a look at that letter then?'

I glanced around the restaurant. It was still lively, the music was a little too intrusive and I could see a waiter coming around the corner with a birthday cake ablaze with candles. There was much whooping and clapping as the birthday boy spotted his cake before his friends broke into a chorus of 'Happy Birthday'. For some reason, we all joined in, even though most of us didn't know him from Adam. 'I'd prefer to wait until I get home,' I said.

'Oh,' said Tom, looking crestfallen. 'I thought you didn't want to open it alone.'

'I don't. I was hoping you'd come in with me.'

'Of course I will.' He brightened. 'Shall I ask for the bill then?'

34

I was annoyed but not surprised to find the kitchen a complete tip when we got back.

'Dylan's home,' I said to Tom by way of explanation. I didn't want him to think I was this slovenly. 'Honestly, all he had to do was heat up a ready-made lasagne and yet it looks as though he's prepared a feast for the court of Henry VIII.'

I began to clear away. I couldn't imagine why Dylan had had to use so many cooking implements and dishes, all of which had failed to make their way into the dishwasher.

'Surprise visit,' I continued as I chiselled away at a blob of lasagne. 'Some party in town or something.' I indicated the chairs by the wood burner. 'Have a seat, I'll be with you in a minute, I just need to . . .'

Tom draped his jacket over the chair and sat down. 'Tara, I can see what you're doing. Come on now, that's enough. Leave all that. It's time.'

He was right of course. The time for procrastination was over. I took the letter out of my bag and sat down in the chair opposite Tom. I passed it over to him. 'Will you read it for me?'

'Yes, if you're sure.' He positioned his glasses on his face, slid his finger under the flap and pulled out a wad of pages. He cleared his throat and looked at me. 'Ready?'

I was holding my breath and couldn't speak so I closed my eyes and nodded. I could hear the rustle of the paper as Tom unfolded it. He began to read, his voice steady and reassuring. I was so grateful he was there with me.

16th May, 1981

Dear Tara

My name is Br Isidore and if my instructions have
been followed, then you now have in your hands a
locket. One which you will recognise, even though it
may be many years since you last saw it.

It was 5th June 1978 when I found it. The day was
unforgivingly hot and under my hair shirt and heavy
white robes I was itching and sweating. I had been
walking for around three hours when I found I could
go no further and I was forced to sit down and rest.
I lay back on the rough stubble and closed my eyes.
At first I thought I was dreaming but then I felt it
again, a brush stroke as soft as gossamer (I think this
is the correct word) on my cheek. I sat up and there

265

it was about an arm's length away from me sitting on the petals of a yellow flower – a butterfly, a Mazarine blue. I rose to my feet and the butterfly flew on ahead then landed on a nearby bush and waited. I followed it along the dirt track almost in a trance as it fluttered from bush to bush, its bright blue wings guiding me. It was then I noticed it. It was the splash of red that caught my eye. The dress she was wearing had come up to her thigh and I tugged it down to save embarrassment. Her eyes, they were closed and her dark hair was thick with blood. I do not know how long she had been like this, lying out in the sun, but her lips were dry and cracked and her shoulders and chest were blistered. She had blood and rough skin on her knees, grazes, I think is the word. On her hands too. Like she had been going like a baby on her hands and knees. I put my arms under her shoulders and eased her head into my lap. 'Where am I?' she whispered. It was as though she had fallen from the sky and it was a miracle that I had found her. I looked around for the Mazarine blue. It had gone.

I gathered the girl in my arms. Before setting out from the *monasterio*, as well as wearing my hair shirt, I'd chosen to walk without sandals for I knew each painful step would atone for my sins and bring me closer to God. On and on I walked, ignoring the agony of my lacerated soles and the sweat running into my eyes. I began to recite the Lord's prayer and the girl's eyes fluttered open at the sound of my voice. Every excruciating step was a reminder of what I had done, a reminder of the events that had brought me to this place and why I had to atone. I held the girl in my arms, like a mother would hold her baby. She was of slender build but even her meagre weight was beginning to make me tired. My back ached and my hair shirt beneath my robe scratched at my skin, rubbing away the layers and leaving a raw mass which I knew would make sleep impossible later.

By the time I arrived back at the *monasterio* I was on the point of exhaustion, severely dehydrated and almost delirious with pain. I hurried to my cell and laid the girl down on my bunk.

I dabbed at the mixture of blood and hair with a wet cloth, making her wince. I asked if she could tell me her name but she shook her head, then closed her eyes. Several minutes passed before she opened them again. 'Violet,' she said. 'My name is Violet Skye.'

My dear Tara, thank you for bearing with me. My English is not bad, I think. It has certainly improved over the last three years. Communicating with Violet has helped with that. When I first found her, I had no clue as to her identity. She wouldn't talk much and seemed distant and afraid. It was about a week later when I returned to the place I had discovered her. I thought perhaps she may have been carrying a handbag or something. Scratching around in the sandy soil I saw something glinting in the sunlight. It was a silver locket bearing the inscription: Happy 30th Birthday, Love Tara. 4.6.78. There was a photo of a young girl inside. Is that you, I wonder? Are you Violet's sister, daughter, niece, friend? When I showed it to Violet she frowned and pushed it away, saying it wasn't hers and she had never seen it before. I think she's wrong. We are so isolated up here that the chances of someone else losing a necklace in the exact same spot that I found Violet are just too remote to envisage. To this day, some three years later, all I know is her date of birth and her name. It's important for you to know that Violet does have some memories but they are not happy ones. It's clear that she has suffered some sort of traumatic brain injury, evidenced by the wound on her head. This has resulted in a degree of amnesia but she is able to recall somewhat disturbing events from childhood.

Now the time has come for me to take my solemn vows. I am permitted one last visit home to say goodbye to my family but I did not make that final visit. Instead I went to England. There was nothing I could say to convince Violet to go with me so I went alone, without telling her. It was the only way I could think of to help her. The locket has been placed in a safe deposit box and the key to that box and this letter have been given to the oldest firm of solicitors in London that I could find. I have engaged the services of a private investigator to trace your whereabouts, recompensing him with everything I have. I have no further need for it. If he is successful, then he will inform Irwin Fortis and they will contact you.

Tara, I have no way of knowing whether his search will be long, short or even fruitful, but I hope that now you are reading this letter, you will at least have some answers. We will take care of Violet here for as long as she wants us to. She has no happy memories of her past life, but I can assure you she is safe here with us. And she is happy now.

With my sincerest best wishes,

Brother Isidore

Tom finished reading and exhaled a shuddering breath. 'Well, well, well.'

I can't imagine how I must have looked. My face was wet with tears and my eyes stung behind my contact lenses. 'She . . . she didn't leave me, Tom.'

He shuffled off his chair and sat down on the floor at my knee. He passed me his handkerchief.

'What the hell happened to her, Tom? How did she end up like that?'

Tom peered at the letter again. 'This letter certainly presents more questions than it answers.'

'Give me that, will you?' Tom handed me the letter. '16th May 1981. That's thirty-seven years ago. How did it take so long to find me?'

Tom thought for a second. 'Well, for a start they didn't have the right name and thirty-seven years ago we didn't have records as readily available as they are today. There was no internet with websites dedicated to finding our ancestors.'

I flipped to the last page of the letter. 'And what does he mean by "disturbing" events from her childhood?

This is just too much to take in.' Another thought occurred to me. 'Do you think there's a chance she's still alive? She'd only be . . . what . . . seventy?'

Tom smiled, his knees cracking as he struggled to his feet. 'There's only one way to find out.'

Offering his hand, he pulled me out of the chair. We stared at each other for a second. His hand was warm in mine and I could smell the Imperial Leather on his skin. 'Go to Spain, you mean?'

'You've nothing to lose, have you?'

He was right, I hadn't. I'd been forced to grow up without the one person who loved me above all else, without my guiding light, my beautiful, funny, talented mother. I didn't just want to find her, I needed to. And time was not on my side.

35

1978

Violet stared out of the window, absently caressing the stubble just over her right ear. She couldn't remember them shaving her head and yet the proof was right there under her fingertips. The graze had healed over but the bone underneath was still tender and the bruise still visible, although it had gone from dark purple to a greeny-yellow. Nine days had crawled by since Br Isidore had found her and not one of those days had passed without her wishing she'd died. The brothers were kind enough but most of them didn't speak any English and kept their distance.

There was a hesitant tap at the door. 'Come in.'

Br Isidore stuck his head round. 'You awake?' His dark eyes were half-closed and his whole body seemed to sag under the weight of his robes. Although it was still early for Violet, Br Isidore's day had begun before sunrise with Vigils, an hour-long scripture followed by the reciting of twelve psalms he'd had to learn by heart. Straight after that, the brothers attended Lauds, another hour-long service in which Br Isidore confessed he had to chew on peppercorns to stop himself nodding off.

'How are you feeling today?' he asked. Violet could listen to his melodic accent all day.

'No pain, just . . . numb.'

He scratched away at his chest beneath his robe, his face twisted with obvious discomfort. 'Well that is something.'

'What's the matter, Br Isidore? You look as though you're the one in pain.'

'No pain, Violet, more like . . . oh what is the word now . . . *irritante*. It's the hair shirt. I'm wearing it to remind me of my sins.'

She smiled. 'You? A sinner? I've never met a more caring, compassionate man in all my life.' She stopped and frowned. 'At least I don't think I have. I can't remember.'

'There's something I need to talk to you about.'

'I know. I heard you and Br Florian talking. I obviously couldn't understand what you were saying but I heard my name and his body language spoke volumes.'

'No,' he said, emphatically. 'You have this wrong. Br Florian is as worried about you as I am. You have a life, Violet. Somebody, somewhere, they miss you, no?'

She shook her head. 'There's nobody missing me, Br Isidore. I might as well have died out there on that mountain. In fact, I wish I had.'

'No, no, no . . . you mustn't say that.' He lifted his leg and kicked the door shut. 'I have found something that I think is yours. *Ayer* . . . I mean, er . . . yesterday, I go

273

back to the place where I find you. I think maybe you have a *bolso* with you or something that I missed before.'

'A *bolso*? I'm sorry, Br Isidore, I don't know what you mean.'

'You put your things in. Like your money and your *pasaporte*.'

'You mean a handbag?'

'Ah, *si, si*, a handbag. There was no handbag but I did find this.' He reached into his pocket and brought out a silver chain, a heart-shaped locket on the end. He dropped it into her palm.

She gave it a cursory look before handing it straight back. 'It's not mine.'

'Look again, Violet. It has an *inscription*.'

She moved away and resumed her position at the window. Br Florian was scattering corn for the chickens, his white robe blowing in the gentle breeze. 'I've told you, it's not mine.'

He ignored her protests. 'It says "Happy 30th Birthday, Love Tara. 4.6.78."'

The chickens were clustered round Br Florian's feet, their heads bobbing up and down as they scratched around in the dust for the corn. He picked up a basket and lifted the lid on the hatch box, taking out several brown eggs.

'Violet?'

'Br Florian is collecting the eggs. It'll soon be time for breakfast.'

'Forget the breakfast, Violet. This is *importante*. It is perhaps . . . I'm sorry, I don't know the English word . . . but it is a *pista*. It might lead us to find out where it is you come from.'

She closed her eyes. She didn't know who she was exactly or where precisely she had come from. She knew one thing for sure though. She had no desire to return.

'If this is your necklace, Violet, then this Tara, maybe she be worried out of her mind.'

'Br Isidore,' she said firmly. 'If that necklace did belong to me, then that would make me thirty years old. That's just not possible, Br Isidore, and I'll tell you why, shall I?'

He sounded as though his patience was about to desert him. '*Sì,* please do.'

She placed her hands on her hips, squaring up to him. 'Because I'm only fourteen, that's why.'

He responded with a laugh, although it wasn't an unkind laugh, more of a disbelieving one. 'You are not fourteen years old, Violet Skye.'

She folded her arms, her stance even more defiant. 'You don't know me, Br Isidore. How dare you say that?' She raised her fists and pounded them into his chest.

He took a step backwards, gently taking hold of her wrists. 'Violet, please. In this moment you act like a fourteen-year-old but this is not helping.'

She stared into his face, his eyes full of concern, but it could just as easily have been pity. She let her arms

275

hang limply by her sides. 'I'm sorry.' She rubbed at her temples. 'I'm just so confused.'

'When is your birthday?'

She sighed and positioned herself at the window again, staring into the distance at the dappled sky, the sun casting a watery glow over the mountains beyond. She couldn't turn round to face him, couldn't bear to see the despair in his eyes. She leaned her head against the cool glass. 'I can't remember.'

She felt his hands on her shoulders. 'Come, sit down.' She allowed herself to be guided to the small wooden table in her cell. Even though the monks insisted they were not prisoners she found it ironic that their rooms were referred to as cells. They were certainly spartan; just a bed and a desk at which to work and study and take meals alone if they so desired.

Br Isidore pushed her gently into the chair. He prised the locket open with his thumbs and laid it on the desk. 'Do you know her?'

Violet bowed her head and squinted at the photograph of a young fresh-faced girl, her head tilted as she smiled for the camera. 'She's very pretty.'

Br Isidore lowered his head and peered more closely. '*Si*, she certainly is, but do you know her?'

She could hear the hope in his voice, almost pleading with her to remember something. After all he had done for her, she hated to disappoint him. She snapped the locket shut. 'I'm sorry, Br Isidore, but no, I don't.'

36

They stood at the end of the tree-lined avenue, hesitant, bewildered and with no idea what it would achieve, but they'd both agreed it was better than doing nothing.

'Are you sure you're ready for this?' Tom asked.

'The only thing I'm sure about is Mum was due back eight days ago and I just know something is very wrong.'

'But she's hardly likely to be holed up at Larry's house.'

'I don't have anywhere else to look, Tom. Do you have any better ideas?'

He sucked in his breath. 'Come on then.'

Tara nodded and moved forward, each step taking her nearer to finding out what had become of her mother. Perhaps she and Larry had fallen out and he had returned on his own, abandoning Violet in a foreign country, forcing her to make her own way home. She could imagine Larry doing that. She had never liked him.

The wrought iron gates were open and Tara quickened her pace as she stomped across the gravel, the urge to find answers suddenly overwhelming. She pressed so hard on the doorbell that it became stuck and continued to emit its piercing sound even after the door had been opened. 'What on earth . . .?' Tara stared at the woman as she fiddled with the doorbell, loosening the button until a blessed silence descended.

'Can I help you?'

It was difficult for Tara to get her words out, not because she couldn't think of anything to say but quite the opposite. She lurched towards the woman, her pointed finger almost connecting with her chest. 'I bloody knew it.' She turned to Tom. 'I told you he was married, didn't I? She's the one from the photograph. Where is he and what's he done with my mother?'

It was to her credit that even in the face of this door-step ambush, the woman retained her composure. 'If you could just stop shouting for a minute, I might be able to help you.'

Her quiet tone and calm demeanour enraged Tara even more. 'Your husband has been having an affair with my mother.'

'Tara,' said Tom. 'Calm down, this isn't her fault. She's been wronged too.'

The woman took a sharp intake of breath, the first flash of doubt registering in her narrowed eyes. 'My husband is here with me and I can assure . . .'

Tara was panting so hard she was on the verge of hyper-ventilating. She reached out to Tom for support. 'Well go and fetch him, then; let's see what he's got to say for himself.'

A deep voice came from somewhere within the house. 'Who is it, darling?'

He appeared at his wife's side a second later. His jet-black hair was slicked back as though he had just climbed out of the shower and a soapy smell clung to his dark skin. He wore the whitest, crispest shirt Tara had ever seen, the top few buttons undone to allow her a good view of the gold chain round his neck.

The woman introduced him. 'This is my husband.' She pointed at Tara. 'This one here says you're having an affair with her mother.'

'No, not him,' dismissed Tara. 'He's not the one. It's Larry who's having an affair with my mother. I don't understand; where's Larry? You're his wife, aren't you? I've seen your picture.' She barged her way past them both and stood in the hall. 'Larry, Larry,' she shouted. 'Get down here now and tell me where my mum is.'

'I'm really sorry about this,' said Tom. 'There's obviously been a misunderstanding. We're looking for Larry Valentine. Do you know where he is?'

A look passed between them before the man opened the door a little wider for Tom. 'I think you'd better come in.'

Nothing made sense anymore and, verging on hysteria, Tara bolted up the stairs, two at a time.

'She's just upset,' Tom said. 'Her mum's missing and . . .'

The man offered his hand. 'Look, I'm Christopher Carter and this is my wife, Nancy. And you're right, Larry Valentine does live here.'

They could hear Tara upstairs, crashing around, slamming doors, all the while calling out for Larry.

Nancy looked at her husband. 'I'll go.'

They were seated in the conservatory, Christopher Carter in the big peacock chair, everybody staring at him expectantly. It was like a horrific episode of *Jackanory*. Christopher touched his fingertips together, drew a deep breath and closed his eyes. Tara glanced at Nancy, who fiddled with the necklace round her throat.

'OK,' began Christopher, so loudly that Tara jumped. He slapped his thighs, stood up and began to pace the floor like a police officer who was just about to crack a major case. 'My wife, myself and my daughter left for South Africa in January. I had some business to attend to.' He absently rubbed at the diamond signet ring on his little finger. 'I'm a jeweller,' he explained, even though nobody had asked. 'Anyway, we extended the trip to take in the Garden Route, a safari lodge, the wine lands and what have you, before flying on to Australia, where we expected to remain until the end of June.' He nodded towards Nancy. 'My wife has family there.'

'But it's not the end of June yet,' Tara interrupted.

'Well, that's families for you,' said Nancy, with a small laugh. 'Let's just say we had perhaps outstayed our welcome.'

Tara shuffled to the edge of her seat and leaned forward. 'You said Larry Valentine lives here. Where . . .?'

Christopher held up his palm to silence her. 'I'm getting to it.'

Nancy's patience seemed to run out. 'For God's sake, Christopher, put the poor girl out of her misery.' She turned to Tara. 'Larry does live here, but not in the house. He lives in a converted garage in the garden. He's our gardener-cum-chauffeur-cum . . . oh, I don't know, handyman, I suppose.'

Tara opened her mouth to speak, but no words came. Her brain could not come up with a coherent question and her instinct was to laugh. It was all too much to take in.

'So,' interjected Tom. 'Larry's not wealthy then? This house doesn't belong to him . . . the cars . . . everything?'

'All mine,' said Christopher. 'Larry was supposed to be house-sitting for us whilst we were away.' He turned to his wife. 'I said it was a bad idea, but . . .'

She skewered him with just a look. 'Not now, Christopher.'

'We came back a little earlier than expected and Larry was nowhere to be found. He obviously left in a hurry because the bed . . . *our* bed . . . was unmade and there were two glasses of champagne, one stained with lipstick, on the bedside table. The ashtray was full of cigarette ends too and some of them had lipstick on.'

Tara frowned. 'But my mum didn't stay here the night before they went away. He picked her up at Alf's, he was late and . . . in any case, she doesn't smoke.'

Nancy raised her eyebrows. 'Mr Valentine certainly has a lot of explaining to do, it would seem.'

'Obviously the police are involved,' said Christopher. 'I've reported the Jag as stolen, plus there's some money missing from the safe and a diamond necklace belonging to my wife has also been taken, as well as other bits and bobs of jewellery.'

Tom looked at Tara. 'It seems like we've all been taken for a ride.'

Tara clenched her jaw, her eyes misting over. 'If he's hurt my mum, I mean it, Tom, I'm going to kill him. If it takes the rest of my life, I'm going to track him down and I swear to you, I *am* going to kill him.'

37

Tara laid the red sequinned dress on the bed and placed the tissue paper on top before carefully folding the dress into a neat square. The long fishtail dress was a little more awkward to pack and she decided to roll it up instead to minimise the creases. She glanced around the spartan bedroom, now stripped of its adornments. The cracked washstand had gone to the tip, the flea-bitten curtains had been torn down and stuffed into the rubbish bin. The only item of furniture remaining was the cast-iron bed she had shared with her mother but that too was on its way, sold to a young couple who had recently married. They had declined to take the mattress though and Tara could hardly blame them. It dipped so much in the centre that she and Violet had often found themselves huddled together in the middle of the night, pinned down by the sheer weight of the bed clothes, rogue springs digging into their hips.

Tom stood in the doorway. 'You ready?'

She shook her head. 'I'll never be ready.' She pointed to the two suitcases by the door. 'Not much to show for fifteen years, is it?'

Tom picked up the cases. 'Dad's downstairs. Come on.'

'You go ahead. I'll just be a minute.'

She closed the door behind him and took the mink coat off the hook. It'd been stuffed inside a pillowcase since Alf died, hidden away from Judith's grubby little paws. Alf's dying wish was for Violet to get that mink and Tara was determined that Judith wouldn't snaffle it. She gripped the iron bedstead and inhaled the familiar biscuity scent of the room. She would never forget this place and the refuge it had provided her and Violet when they had been so desperate. She would always remember Alf's kindness, his companionship and his funny little ways, which had endeared him to them both. She ran her hands over the tally marks she had drawn on the wallpaper behind the bed. Like a hostage counting off the days he had been held, she too felt like a prisoner, a prisoner of circumstances which were out of her control. She counted them again, even though she knew how long it had been since Violet had failed to return. Thirty-eight days, almost six weeks. Tara had never felt more helpless. The police were only vaguely interested in finding Larry Valentine because he had stolen the car and jewellery, and seemed reluctant to entertain the notion that he had kidnapped Violet. Tara didn't know where to ask them to look, couldn't even narrow it down to a country. As far as the police were concerned, Violet had gone off with Larry willingly and was probably in on the whole duplicitous episode. Now, the shop and flat had been sold and not for the first time in her life, Tara was being moved on against her will.

The journey west had taken a little over an hour and for that entire time, neither of them had said a word, each lost in their own thoughts. As the sea came into view and they joined the coast road, Tom nodded out of the window. 'Be nice living by the sea, Tara.'

She pulled a face. 'It's Lytham, not the Bahamas, Tom.'

'Still, beats the wet streets of Manchester though.'

'It looks boring, there'll be nothing to do. I bet it's full of old people. People like my nan.'

Tom's father had also been quiet, preferring instead to listen to his fancy 8-track with the volume turned up unnecessarily high in Tara's opinion. He pulled up outside a newsagent's and turned off the engine. Tara felt as though she'd gone deaf.

'Thank Christ for that,' she muttered.

'I'm just popping in here for the Pink,' declared Mr Marshall.

'The pink what?' Tara asked Tom when he'd got out and slammed the door.

'The newspaper. He wants the football results to check his coupon. He's been doing the pools for years and every week he's convinced he'll win the jackpot.'

'Hmm . . . it'll take more than a pools win to solve my problems.'

Tom leaned across and kissed her on the mouth. 'Gives us a few more minutes together.'

'Do you think we'll ever see each other again, Tom?'

'Yes,' he said emphatically. 'Yes, we will, I promise. I could get the coach or the train and when I get a job I'm going to start saving up for driving lessons.'

'I wish I'd left school already. It's going to be awful not seeing you.'

'I know, but I've got to knuckle down and find a job. Keep me mum and dad off me back.'

'Eh up, your dad's here.' She shuffled over to her side of the seat.

Mr Marshall threw his pink newspaper onto the passenger seat and rifled through the glove box. He took out the *A–Z* and flicked to the index of street names. 'Righteo then, let's have a look here, shall we?'

Tom leaned in between the front seats and handed a piece of paper to his father. 'It won't be in there, Dad. Here, I've written the directions down on this.'

Ten minutes later they pulled into Elm Close, a tiny cul-de-sac surrounded by eight nearly identical semis, the colour of the front doors being the only discernible difference between them. A couple of kids were playing hopscotch in the middle of the circle and did not look best pleased when Mr Marshall honked his horn and sent them scurrying to the pavement.

A chap who was crouched down messing about with the exhaust on his motorbike wiped his brow and looked across at them. He narrowed his eyes and blatantly peered into the car. In another house, the curtains at an upstairs window twitched, the occupant within no doubt having a good gawp.

'Well, here we are then,' announced Mr Marshall, for want of anything more useful to say. 'I'll get your cases out.'

'This is it then, Tom.' Tara had promised herself she would not cry. She pressed her closed fist into her lips.

Tom nodded towards number eight. 'Doesn't look too bad.'

'Compared to some of the places I've lived, it's a palace.' She turned back to him. 'I'll never forget you, Tom. I couldn't have got through the last few weeks without you by my side.'

He stroked her cheek. 'Don't make everything sound so final. This isn't goodbye.'

'It is, Tom. We need to be realistic.' She gazed around the cul-de-sac, her eyes settling on number eight. The windows were shrouded in net curtains which were possibly once white but now had a greyish hue. The garden gate hung on determinedly by one hinge and a solitary garden gnome with only one arm sat by a dried-up pond. 'This is my home now, Tom. Until Mum gets back anyway.'

'Hopefully that won't be too long then. I'll pop into Alf's from time to time,' said Tom. 'Check the new owners haven't heard anything from Violet.'

'Thanks. They've got this address so my mum will know where to find me . . . . if she wants to.'

Mr Marshall opened the back door. 'Are you two coming or not?'

'I'll write,' said Tom. 'And I'll phone too, on Sundays when it's cheaper.'

Tara climbed out and stood on the pavement. In spite of the warm evening, she draped the mink coat over her shoulders, leaving her hands free to carry the cases. The door to number eight opened.

'Coo-ee, there you are. Don't stand on ceremony, come inside. Let me get you a cuppa, all of you, you've had a long journey. I've just made a fresh batch of rock buns too.'

Tony Marshall held up his hands. 'We'll be on our way thanks all the same, Mrs Dobbs.'

'Don't let the name put you off. They're not like rocks at all, in fact they're very light. And call me Beryl.'

Tara stared at her grandmother. She'd only ever seen a photograph of her, a black and white one at that. She wore a flowered housecoat and had a pair of furry slippers on her feet. A headscarf covered her roller-clad hair and a cigarette clung to her bottom lip. 'Tara, is that you? Why, you look like a little Yeti shrouded in that thing. Come here, love. Let's get you inside.'

Tom bent his head and whispered in Tara's ear. 'She seems nice.'

Beryl hurried down the path and opened the front gate.

'You've made good time then. Caught me on the hop, you 'ave.' She patted her head. 'Still got me curlers in.' She opened her arms. 'Got a hug for your nan then, Tara?'

Tara hesitated but after a nudge in the back from Tom took a step forward into her grandmother's eager embrace. She smelt of liver and onions. Admittedly, her knowledge of grandmas was virtually non-existent, but she'd imagined a more floral scent, lavender or lily of the valley perhaps.

Mr Marshall cleared his throat. 'Erm, we'd better get going, Mrs Dobbs.'

'I've just told you, it's Beryl. Can I at least pack you a couple of buns for your journey?'

'No need. Come on, Tom, say your goodbyes.'

Tom placed his hands on Tara's shoulders, not seeming to care that he had garnered a small audience. His father, Beryl and the two little girls who had been playing hopscotch all stood and listened intently to what he had to say. 'She'll be back, Tara. Your mum loves you more than anything else.' He tilted her chin, forcing her to look at him. 'And I love you too, Tara.'

She swallowed down a small laugh, her heart thumping and fluttering like a budgie trying to escape the confines of its cage. If she never heard those words again for as long as she lived, this moment would always be enough.

'I love you too, Tom.'

Beryl clapped her hands. 'Right you are. Come and visit whenever you like. Don't be a stranger.'

Tom and his father climbed back into the car, Tom in the front seat this time. As they pulled away, he leaned out of the window, waving furiously. Tara returned the gesture and watched until they were almost out of sight. Her grandmother turned her round abruptly. 'Don't watch anymore.'

'Why not?'

Beryl cast her eyes skywards. 'Has your mother not taught you anything? If you wave to someone until they're out of sight, it means you will never see them again.' She folded her arms and nodded as though she had just delivered a piece of irrefutable evidence in a courtroom rather than an old wives' tale.

Tara followed her grandmother through to the front room which was crammed with furniture, patterns everywhere. Floral curtains, paisley carpet and a tartan three-piece suite. The expression *less is more* had evidently passed her by. The mantelpiece was adorned with a row of Whimsies. At either end stood matching china poodles, as though they were the guardians of the cheap pottery forest animals. Above the fireplace, on the chimney breast, was a framed portrait of the Queen in all her coronation regalia.

Beryl straightened one of the Whimsies, a hedgehog if Tara was not mistaken.

'Do you collect them?' asked Beryl.

'Erm, no.'

'Aye well, 'appen you're right. Take some dusting they do.' She gestured towards a mahogany display case on the wall. 'See all them thimbles in there? Every Saturday morning, I take them down and give 'em a good once over with a damp cloth. I'm house proud, you see?' She said this as though it was an affliction she had no control over, some kind of incurable disease she just had to live with.

Tara glanced at the net curtains but said nothing.

'Come on then, give us your cases and let's get you settled in.'

Tara had been allocated the box room and even though the orange-painted woodchip was enough to induce a migraine, for the first time she could remember she had a bedroom all to herself. Beryl, or Nan as she was insisting on being called, had done a thorough job with the Pledge and a duster. Even the net curtains didn't seem quite as grubby as their counterparts downstairs.

Tara had picked her way through tea: salty bacon ribs which had been on the boil since yesterday and thick slices of white bread and butter. Now she sat by the window and pulled the net curtain to one side. The sound of the ice cream van and its tuneless rendition of 'Greensleeves' had brought out a cluster of excited children, their fists clenched around the contents of their piggy banks.

Beryl looked up from her Mills & Boon. 'Want one?'

'Oh, no, it's OK, thanks.'

Beryl uncurled her legs from underneath her and disappeared into the kitchen. She returned a few seconds later with a bowl and brandished it at Tara. 'Ask him to fill this with raspberry ripple, will you? And extra sauce on top too.'

'Me?'

'Yes, you. It'll be a chance to say hello to the other kids. Sandra's out there. You two'll be in the same class come September. She'll be able to tell you all about your new school.'

'September! We don't even know if I'll still be here in September. Surely Mum'll be back by then.'

Beryl sighed and put the bowl down on the coffee table. 'We don't know that, luvvie. Maybe she will, maybe she won't. And if she is back, then you can still live here, the three of us. I mean, it's not as if you have anywhere else to go, is it?'

Tara looked out of the window again. It was easy to spot Sandra in the queue, the only girl anywhere near Tara's age. Her hair had been cut short, dyed a shocking pink then teased into spikes. She wore a short tartan skirt and what appeared to be a studded dog collar around her neck. She had piercings in her eyebrows, nose and ears. She pulled a long piece of bubble gum out of her mouth and wound it round her finger. A little boy in National Health specs tried to push his way in front of her but

Sandra twisted his ear so hard, he burst into tears and ran home.

Tara let go of the curtain and turned away. 'Erm . . . Nan.'

'What is it, love?'

'I need you to help me find my father.'

For a split second, Beryl couldn't even find her voice. 'Your . . . father?'

'Yes, you must know something about him. Mum said he was her boyfriend when she was my age. Surely you remember him?'

'She told you that, did she?' She reached for her cigarettes. Tara looked up at the ceiling; the patch over her Nan's chair was stained yellow with nicotine. 'I don't remember him, love.' Her voice sounded as though she'd swallowed a shovel full of gravel.

'Please, Nan, think. You must remember him. Mum said she loved him very much. She never told him about me because he moved to Mongolia with his parents. I've had a look at Mr Long's atlas – he's my geography teacher – and it's miles away.'

Beryl choked on the cigarette. She thumped her chest, her eyes watering. 'Mongolia! As in Outer Mongolia? What on earth has that got to do with the price of fish? I thought that was a made-up place like that whatsit . . .' She twirled her finger in the air, searching for the answer. 'Ooh, what's it called now . . . Timbuktu, that's it.'

'Timbuktu *is* a real place, Nan. It's in Mali, in Africa.'

Beryl frowned. 'Are you sure? Well, I'll go to the foot of our stairs. I never knew that.' She narrowed her eyes and tilted her head. Tara could almost hear the cogs whirring.

'What about Back-of-Beyond then?' she asked.

'What about it?'

'Well is that a real place too?'

'No,' replied Tara, trying to keep the exasperation out of her voice. 'Of course it isn't. Nan, we're wandering so far off the subject, we'll need a road map to find our way back.'

She sat on the faux-leather pouffe next to her nan's slippered feet and repeated her earlier question. 'Nan, do you remember my father or not?'

Beryl took another long drag, the end of the cigarette glowing brightly. She stubbed it out in the ashtray and reached for another. 'Our Violet was popular with the lads,' she said eventually. She clicked her lighter several times until the elusive flame appeared. 'I'm sorry, love. I don't remember her being fond of anyone in particular, but in any case, if he moved to that Mongolia whatsit, then that's that. You can't pack up your stuff and go looking for him out there, can you?'

'Suppose not.'

'Look, you've lasted this long without him and now you've got me to look after you. Do you think you can forget about him now, eh?'

'Are you sure there's nothing about him you can remember?'

Beryl stared at the ceiling. She took a deep breath in through her nose. Several minutes passed before she spoke again. 'OK, then, I'll tell you what I know.'

38

'I blame myself, I do,' said Beryl.

It certainly wasn't the opening gambit Tara was expecting. 'You blame yourself for Violet getting pregnant?'

The cigarette Beryl had been holding now had a long piece of ash clinging on precariously. 'Well, I blame myself and I blame Hitler.' The ash fell off and landed in her lap. She didn't seem to notice.

'What has Hitler got to do with Mum getting pregnant?'

Beryl frowned as though the answer was obvious. 'If he'd not invaded Poland then we wouldn't have gone to war and then the Americans wouldn't have had to send over all them rakish GIs. It was no wonder we fell for them. They seemed so exotic, chewed gum and that. And they ate pizzas. How were we supposed to resist all that, eh? By the summer of 1942 there were thousands of them. Lost my virginity at fifteen, I did.' Beryl shrugged. 'You see? It was all Hitler's fault.'

Tara nodded. It was certainly a slant on history not covered by her school syllabus and she was struggling to see what this had to do with Violet.

'Anyhow, I got caught with your mum in September 1947. The father wasn't a GI sadly, they'd all gone home by then. No, it was the lad who delivered our coal. Strong arms he had, all that heaving sacks about had given him some hard muscles alright. Good-looking too even though his face was always covered in coal dust. It gave him an irresistible swarthy look. He took quite a shine to me too.' She glanced at Tara. 'Oh, I know you wouldn't think it now, but I was quite a looker in them days.'

Tara could well believe it. Beryl wasn't like other nans. She was tall and straight, a peroxide-enhanced halo of golden curls framing a largely unlined face. And she wore huge dangly earrings. And nail varnish. She wasn't that old either, fifty-one if Tara's maths was correct.

'Anyway,' Beryl continued, 'it wasn't to be. Didn't want owt to do with me once he found out I was in the family way.' She narrowed her eyes and wagged her finger at Tara. 'They're all the same, love. Quite happy to have their way with you but once they've knocked you up you don't see them for dust. Coal dust in my case.' She gave a little chuckle. 'It were a terrible shame in them days too. I was only twenty by this time and my mum and dad were none too pleased either. To their credit though, they didn't chuck me out.'

'He came back though, did he? The coal boy.'

Beryl produced a tar-laden laugh. 'No, love, he didn't.'

'Oh, dear, I'm . . . erm . . . sorry.' Tara shifted her position on the pouffe and waited for the next instalment.

'New Year's Eve 1947 it was when I met George in a pub back home in Manchester.'

Tara recognised the name. 'My grandfather?'

'That's right. I told him from the off that I was three months gone but he wasn't bothered. He was so smitten I could have told him I was expecting triplets and he wouldn't have run for the hills. We moved over here for the sea air and all that and George found a job in a sweet factory. We were married before our Violet was born and I put his name on her birth certificate. She was conceived on the wrong side of the blanket, see, and I didn't want her to live with the label of being illiterate.'

'Illegitimate, Nan.'

'Oh, aye, I always get them words muddled up. Prostrate and prostate's another two. I mean who makes these words up? If it were up to me then . . .'

'Nan,' interrupted Tara, trying to keep Beryl on track. 'So George wasn't Violet's real dad then? Did she know?'

Beryl nodded. 'Yes, she did, but not at first. It all came out in the school playground. You know how cruel kids can be. Taunting her they were. It was that boss-eyed kid from number three mainly.' She pursed her lips. 'I'll never forgive the interfering little tw . . . twit.'

'Where's George now then?' asked Tara. 'I thought he would've been home by now.'

Beryl lowered her eyes and fiddled with a loose button on her cardigan. 'I'll have to get my needle and thread out before this comes off altogether.'

'Nan?'

Beryl looked up, her face blank. 'George is dead, love.'

'What?' She wasn't sure what she was supposed to do. Show some emotion, give her nan a hug and offer her condolences? She leaned forward and patted Beryl's knee. 'I'm sorry, Nan.'

Beryl reached for her cigarettes again and held one between her fingers without bothering to light it. 'When our Violet got pregnant, George threw her out. I wanted her to stay. We had a huge barney about it. I would've supported her just like my mum and dad did me but she was keen to go too. She wouldn't tell me anything about the father so that was it, she upped and left.'

'Didn't you go after her?'

'I tried but George stopped me.'

'But she was only fourteen.'

'Aye, fourteen going on twenty-four. She knew her own mind did that one.' Beryl nodded towards the window as she finally lit the cigarette. 'Close the curtains, love.'

'Why? It's not dark yet.'

'Just do it.'

Tara did as she was told and sat back down, the room now dim and gloomy.

'Thank you, love. Now, where was I? Oh yes, well, I went to the police, didn't I? I didn't tell George naturally, I knew he wouldn't like it. But I couldn't just leave it, I had to do something. I knew she wasn't in any danger, it wasn't like she'd been abducted or owt. Police would've taken more notice if she had been, I expect. But no, she was just another teenage runaway to them.'

'The police are not all that interested this time either,' said Tara.

'Well, she's a grown woman now, isn't she? They've got enough on their plates with that Ripper fella on the loose. What a maniac he is.'

Tara shuddered. 'Mmm . . . maybe you're right.'

'She rang from time to time, from a phone box, like, but she would never tell me where she was. Just that she was OK and I wasn't to try and find her. She rang when you were born and I begged her to come home but she wouldn't.'

'Was she with my father, do you think? Like I said, she always told me that they were very much in love but he didn't know anything about me and had gone off to Mongolia with his parents to trap fur. Maybe that wasn't true. Perhaps they were together.'

Beryl shrugged. ''Appen they were. All I know is Hitler's antics turned me into a promiscuous young girl and Violet obviously took after me.'

Later, as Tara lay under the covers struggling to sleep, she thought about Violet and how she must have struggled on her own with a baby to look after. In all her life, Tara had never felt anything other than loved and cared for. She climbed out of bed and crept across the landing to her nan's room. The door was ajar, the dim light within

300

pointing to the fact Beryl was still awake. She tapped on the door. 'Nan?'

'Come in, Tara love. What is it?'

'I can't sleep.'

Beryl was sitting up in bed reading, her face smothered in cold cream. 'Well that makes two of us then.' She laid down her book and patted the space next to her. 'Climb aboard.'

Tara nestled under the covers and snuggled up to her nan. She felt her kiss the top of her head. 'It's only been six weeks, love. Don't give up on her yet. She'll be back, I can feel it in me water.'

'I just want her home, Nan. I don't know how some-body can just disappear. Something terrible must have happened to her. She wouldn't just leave me, I know she wouldn't.' Tara closed her eyes, the comforting weight of her nan's arm around her shoulders.

'There, there,' soothed Beryl. 'I'm 'ere for you now. I may have let our Violet down but there's no way I'll let anything happen to you. You're safe 'ere with me and we'll look after each other until your mum gets back. What do you say?'

Tara managed a smile. This husky-voiced, chain-smoking grandmother of hers might not be Violet. But she was the next best thing.

39

The phone was ringing in the kitchen, the sound reverberating off the white tiled walls. Beryl's voice came from somewhere upstairs. 'Who on earth is that at this time, Tara?'

Tara smiled to herself. Every time the phone rang or the front door bell went, Beryl would ask the same question, as if Tara had some kind of psychic power or X-ray vision.

'I'll get it, Nan.'

She snatched up the phone. 'Lytham 3452.'

'Tara?'

She almost dropped the receiver. 'Tom, it's you, hi.'

'Thought I'd wish you luck on your first day at your new school.'

'You only spoke to me on Sunday.' She twirled the coiled flex of the telephone between her fingers, her wide smile making her cheeks ache.

'So, who's counting? I miss you, Tara.'

She'd been in Lytham for a little over six weeks and just as Nan had predicted, she'd had no choice but to start a new school. 'I miss you too, Tom. When are you coming to see me again?'

He'd managed only one visit in all that time, a trip by coach in which he'd been the only passenger without a flat cap or a blue rinse.

He sounded hesitant, nervous even. 'It's going to be difficult. I . . . erm . . . look, I wasn't just ringing to wish you luck. I have some news. It came in the post yesterday.'

'You're worrying me, Tom.'

At the sound of Nan coming down the stairs, she lifted the phone and, as far as the flex would allow, crept into the larder and closed the door. 'Tell me.'

'I'm not going to find a job, Tara. I've got a place on a course.'

She laughed with relief. 'That's fantastic news, Tom. Mechanical engineering, like you wanted?'

'Yes. It's at Thames Polytechnic.'

She came out of the larder as she heard her nan filling the kettle. 'Tom's going to university, well . . . a polytechnic.'

'Is he? Ooh, the clever lad.' She set the kettle on the stove and lit the gas. 'Brew, love?'

'That'll be lovely.'

'It won't be lovely, Tara. Have you any idea where Thames Polytechnic is?'

'Sorry, I was talking to Nan. No, I don't. Where is it?'

'London, two hundred and fifty-odd miles away.'

They both fell silent, the implications unspoken but looming large. Tara was the first to speak. 'That's a long way, Tom, but we'll make it work. When do you start?'

'Next week. I'm going to stay with my aunt to start with. She's got a spare box room.'

As the doorbell rang, Nan glanced at the kitchen clock. 'Who on earth is that at this time?'

'Honestly, Nan, I don't know. Go and answer it.'

'As I was saying, it's a long way and I don't know how often we'll get to see each other so if you want to see other boys then . . .'

She slid back into the privacy of the larder. 'Are you chucking me?' she hissed.

He was silent for a moment. 'I don't know what to do, Tara.'

'Tara, where've you gone, love?' Nan was back. 'It's Sandra come to call for you. Says you can walk to school together. Tara?'

'I've got to go, Tom.' She cupped her hand round the receiver and whispered, 'Everything'll be alright. I love you.'

'There you are, Tara. Look, Sandra's here.' Beryl pointed unnecessarily to the spiky-haired girl who was now standing in the kitchen. She had certainly adapted the school uniform to suit her own particular brand of fashion. Fishnet tights and bovver boots were not a look everybody could carry off. Tara looked down at her own grey socks and sensible black shoes. She thought she'd been daring in going for a heel above the regulation two inches.

'Y'alright?' asked Sandra, chewing gum both visibly and audibly.

'Her boyfriend's just got a place at pyrotechnic college.' Beryl beamed.

Sandra seemed uninterested. 'Great.' She lifted the lid on the teapot. 'Any tea in there for me? I've not had me breakfast.'

'Sit yerself down, Sandra. I'll do you a bowl of corn-flakes.'

Since moving to Lytham, Tara had barely spoken to Sandra, so she was more than a little surprised that she'd come to call for her.

They waited at a pelican crossing for the lights to change. 'Thanks for walking with me, Sandra. I'm really chuffed.'

Sandra shrugged. 'I didn't want to but your nan gave me two quid to do it and told me not to say anything.'

Tara bit back her annoyance. 'Then why did you?'

'Two quid's two quid, innit?'

'I meant why did you tell me?'

'Dunno. Didn't want you thinking I'd gone all soft, I suppose.'

As the lights changed, they crossed the road, Tara acknowledging the cars with a polite wave. 'We could be friends, you know.'

Sandra scoffed and looked Tara up and down. 'No offence but you're a bit . . . straight. I mean you've even got your top button done up.'

Tara unfastened the button and pulled at her tie, loosening the knot so that it lay skew-whiff across her shirt. 'Better?'

Sandra nodded and gave a half-smile. Her lips were edged with black liner and she wore a ring through her nose, like a bull. 'So, that boyfriend of yours is off to London then?'

'Yes,' Tara sighed. 'It'll be difficult but we'll manage.'

'You two slept together yet?'

Tara blushed. 'Well, that's none of your business.'

Sandra laughed. 'Thought not.'

Tara seized the chance to get one over on Sandra. 'Actually, that's where you're wrong. For your information, we have done it, so there.'

Sandra seemed impressed. 'Well, bugger me. Who'd have thought?' She picked away at her black nail varnish. 'Love him, do you?'

'Yes, I do. I don't make a habit of going around sleeping with people.'

Sandra pulled a packet of cigarettes from her school bag. 'Want one?'

'No thanks, I don't smoke.'

'Course you don't.'

'What's that supposed to mean?'

'Nowt, don't be so touchy.' She lit the cigarette and exhaled a cloud of blue smoke. 'It won't last, you know.'

Tara kicked at a rusty Coke can in the gutter, sending

it clattering along the street. 'Shut up, you don't know anything about us.'

'Trust me.' Sandra took another long drag, narrowing her eyes as she looked at Tara. She waved the cigarette in the air. 'And I'll tell you summat else for free.'

'If you must.'

'Your mum ain't coming back either.'

Tara stopped and pulled on Sandra's sleeve. 'Take that back.'

'Gonna make me?'

She dropped her school bag to the ground and rolled up her sleeves. 'If I have to.'

'Ooh-er,' mocked Sandra. 'I'm really scared.'

Tara hadn't planned to spend her first morning at a new school in the headmistress's office, but punching another pupil in the face generally made plans go awry.

Mrs Grimshaw sat across the desk, her fingers steepled and her glasses perched on the end of her nose. 'I'm really disappointed in you, Tara.' She glanced at the file on her desk. 'I'm looking at the report from your previous school and it appears it's not the first time you've attacked another pupil.'

Tara frowned. 'I've never attacked anybody, Mrs Grimshaw.'

The headmistress ran her finger along the report. 'Lisa Cooper?'

'Oh, that was different. She said some awful things about my mother.'

'Really, and what did Sandra Hobson do to deserve your wrath?'

Tara looked at the floor, her voice quiet. 'She said my mother . . .'

'Speak up, girl, I can hardly hear you.'

Tara raised her voice, almost shouting. 'She said my mother was never coming back.'

There was a knock at the door and the secretary bobbed her head in. 'Mrs Dobbs is here now.'

'You called my nan?'

'This is a very serious matter, Tara Dobbs. We may have to get the police involved.'

Tara slouched in her chair and folded her arms. 'It's got fuck all to do with you. It didn't even happen on school premises.'

Mrs Grimshaw ignored the remark, turning to the secretary instead. 'Send Mrs Dobbs in, will you?'

Tara sat up a little straighter as her nan walked in. She could hardly bear to witness the disappointment written across her face. 'Sorry, Nan.'

'Could I just have a minute with my granddaughter, please, Mrs Grimshaw?'

The headmistress stood. 'I'll just be on the other side of that door.'

Nan sat down next to Tara. She opened up her handbag and pulled out a bag of Murray Mints. 'Want one?'

In spite of herself, Tara smiled. Nan always tried to make everything better with sweets. 'No, ta.'

Nan shook her head, the plastic spotted rain hood rustling. She took it off and shook the droplets of rain onto the carpet. 'What am I going to do with you, eh?'

Tara stared out of the window. There really was no answer to that.

'You can't go around thumping people, our Tara. Violence is not the answer, it never is.'

'Hmph . . . wonder why we've had two World Wars then.'

'Less of the cheek, young lady, it doesn't suit you.'

'She had it coming.'

'Sandra? What did she say?'

'That me and Tom wouldn't last and that me mum was never coming back.' A tear slid down her cheek and she took a savage swipe at it.

'You can't let things get to you, love. Sandra doesn't know her arse from her elbow.'

'What if she's right though? What if Mum never comes back? I couldn't bear it, Nan. I love living here with you but you're not me mum and I want her back.' She stood up having difficulty breathing. 'What has happened to her, Nan? Everything's just so . . . so fucked up . . .'

'Language, Tara.'

She stared at Nan, lowering her voice to a whisper. 'Gosh, you sounded just like her then. She was always telling me to mind my language.'

She was standing by Mrs Grimshaw's desk, the files ordered into neat piles, the pencils freshly sharpened.

'Aargh!' she suddenly screamed, her voice cracking. 'I want my mum back, I need my mum. Nan, you've got to help me, I can't . . .' She tried to inhale but couldn't find any breath. Without words to convey her rage, she swept her arm across the desk, sending the files, pens and an industrial-sized stapler crashing to the ground.

Nan was on her feet. 'Tara, calm down. You . . .'

Tara wasn't finished. She picked up the headmistress's mug of coffee and hurled it at the wall, where it smashed into Mrs Grimshaw's fancy diploma or whatever the hell it was. The glass shattered as Mrs Grimshaw reappeared, her over-plucked eyebrows half-way to her hairline, her shocked secretary bringing up the rear.

Tara slid down the wall and hugged her knees, rocking back and forth, the sobs coming freely. 'I just . . . I just miss my mum.'

'Tara Dobbs,' shouted Mrs Grimshaw. 'You leave me no choice but to . . .'

Nan threw her a venomous look. 'Shut up you. I'll handle this.'

She sat down on the floor next to Tara. 'We'll find her, Tara, we will. As long as I have breath in my body, I'll never stop looking.' She took hold of Tara's chin. 'Look at me. I promise you, we will find her.'

She unzipped the secret pocket inside her handbag and pulled out her building society passbook, running her finger down the final column. 'Mmm . . . I think I can manage it. Had a small bingo win a month or two back. I've been saving for a twin-tub but this is more important.'

'What is?' Tara sniffed.

'You and me are going on a little trip, Tara. We'll find our Violet and bring her back here where she belongs.'

'I don't even know where she went, Nan, other than she caught the car ferry from Dover.'

Nan snapped her bag shut. 'Well, that's where we'll start then. We'll put some posters up around the port.'

'It'll be impossible.' She linked her arm through Nan's. 'But thank you anyway.'

'Tara, just because something seems impossible doesn't mean you shouldn't try. If everybody thought like that we wouldn't have put a man on the moon, nobody would have climbed Everest. I never believed I would ever meet my granddaughter and yet here you are sitting right beside me.'

Tara smiled. 'Being a right pain in the arse.'

Nan turned to the headmistress. 'Tara will be absent from school for the next couple of weeks.'

The headmistress began to speak but Nan held up her hand. 'I don't expect any arguments. I made a promise to this young girl here and I intend to fulfil it.' She swept her arm around the office. 'Tara, help get this lot cleared up and then we'll make the arrangements. We'll have your mum home before you know it.'

40

2018

I had the worst night's sleep in a long time. Every time I closed my eyes I was plagued with visions of my poor mother's broken body and, for some reason, that monk's bloody feet. Over the years I had driven myself almost insane imagining what had happened to my mother but in not one of those scenarios had she been alive and well because if she was, she would have found her way back to me. Long ago, I buried the pain of losing her. I had to or else I would've gone under. And now I had been offered a crumb of hope.

I pulled on my dressing gown and headed out onto the landing just as Dylan's bedroom door opened. Out came a young girl with jet-black hair, her face pure white except for the dark rings of mascara framing her eyes. She looked like Morticia, if Morticia had spent the night sleeping under a hedge and had then been dragged through it backwards. 'Morning,' she said through a yawn, then padded off to the bathroom, her t-shirt barely covering her buttocks.

I went into Dylan's room. He was sound asleep, one leg hanging out of the bed. I resisted the urge to grab it. 'Morning, Dylan.'

He opened his eyes, his furred-up mouth trying in vain to form some words. He frowned, feeling around in the empty space next to him. He lifted up the duvet and peered under it.

'She's in the bathroom,' I offered, helpfully.

'Oh, shit. Sorry, Mum.'

'You're not at uni now, Dylan. It's not acceptable to bring random strangers home for me to bump into on my own landing.' I sat down on the bed. 'I hope you're being careful because . . .'

'Christ, Mum, not now.' He pressed the heel of his hand into his forehead.

'When then? Because it'll be too late once you've got some girl up the duff.'

He shuddered. 'No one says *up the duff* anymore, Mum. Don't worry, everything's under control.'

I heard the toilet flush. 'Ssh, she's coming back. Look, I need to talk to you about something else. When's she going?'

'I don't know, Mum. I can't just turf her out after we've just . . .'

Mercifully, he left the sentence hanging. 'What a gentleman you are.' I stood up. 'What's her name, by the way?'

He slumped back onto his pillow and laid his arm across his eyes. 'Erm . . . I wanna say . . . Sadie?'

The door opened and in she walked, toothpaste all round her mouth. 'That's better.' She held out her hand to me. 'Hi again. I'm Abigail.'

I turned to Dylan. 'Not even close.'

We were sitting at the breakfast table, a huge antique pine thing that still bore the scars of our family life. I traced my finger over a patch of navy-blue ink which had seeped indelibly into the cracks in the wood. Dylan would sit at that table doing his homework, whilst I concentrated on preparing the tea. He was fourteen when his fountain pen sprung a leak and no amount of bleach or elbow grease had been able to shift the stain. There was also a circular scorch mark from a saucepan. Ralph, not known for his culinary expertise, decided to have a go at making treacle toffee one Bonfire Night. He wandered over to the table with a pan of the bubbling, molten toffee and, deciding it looked good enough to eat, stuck his finger in to taste it. Five-year-old Dylan's eyes were like a startled fawn's as a torrent of words he'd never heard before spewed from his father's mouth. Ralph had a blister the size of a whoopee cushion for days.

Dylan noticed my scrutiny. ''Bout time you got a new table, Mum.'

I was shaken out of my reverie. 'Never. Now then.' I clasped my hands together on the table and adopted a headmistress-like tone. 'There's something we need to discuss.'

He folded his arms and rolled his eyes but said nothing. I filled him in on the letter from Br Isidore. He listened intently, his shoulders dropping slightly as he realised this wasn't about him and his latest misdemeanour I might or might not know about.

'Wow,' he said when I'd finished. 'That's amazing. Are you going to tell Nan?'

I knew what I was going to do but I wanted to hear his opinion first. 'What do you think?'

'Tell her,' he said emphatically. 'You have to tell her, Mum.'

I gave an audible sigh of relief. 'Good, because that's exactly what I'm going to do.' I paused for a second. 'Fancy coming with me?'

He leaned back in his chair and placed his hands behind his head. 'Ooh, I dunno, Mum. I'm not great with things like this. I would rather remember her how she was. It really upsets me to see her so poorly. I hate it.'

'I see.' I looked down at the table, avoiding eye contact, because I knew exactly how he felt, but this wasn't about us. 'So, you'd rather do what's best for you then?'

He didn't reply but turned instead to look out of the window.

'She's your great-grandmother, Dylan. She adores you and I know it's hard but you have to think about what she would want. I'm telling you, if you walked into her room today, any awkwardness or sadness you might feel would be completely evaporated by the utter joy it would bring her.'

He thought about this for a moment and then nodded. 'You're right, Mum. Give me ten minutes and I'll be raring to go.'

It was about twenty minutes before he came back down but I didn't mind because I was witnessing a miracle. He'd had a shave. Without saying anything, I ran my fingers across his smooth cheek and smiled.

Nan sat in the chair, her puzzle book open across her knee, her pen stuck into her mouth as she ruminated over a clue. She looked up when she heard the door open.

'Tara, love. Ooh, you've had your hair cut. Makes you look even more lovely.'

Nothing got past my nan. It was good to see her out of bed for once and had she not been dressed in her nightie and slippers, with a drip attached to her arm, it would have been hard to tell she was even ill. Her face had been powdered and her hair rolled into a neat bun. I was so thankful that Dylan would not be seeing her at her worst.

I cocked my head towards the door. 'Look who I've brought.'

She turned to look. 'Dylan! Oh, Dylan lad. What are you doing over there? Come here so I can get a proper look at you.'

He walked up to the chair, leaned over and gave her a hug. 'Hi, Nan. You're looking well.'

Her eyes had filled with tears but I knew they were

tears of joy. I winked at Dylan and mouthed a 'thank you'.

She shuffled into a more comfortable position, wincing as a bolt of pain shot through her ravaged body.

'Shall I call someone?' I asked.

She wafted her hand. 'No point, love. I'm maxed up on the morphine as it is.'

I smiled at her youthful vernacular. She may have been diminished physically but her mind was as sharp as it ever was.

The door opened and a nurse stuck her head round. 'Oh, sorry, Beryl. I didn't know you had company. I've just clocked off but I wondered if you wanted me to do your nails?'

Angels, the lot of them. That nurse had just done a twelve-hour shift but before she went home she'd got time for one more act of kindness. My nan was terminally ill; did it really matter if her nails were done or not? At St Jude's it did. Everyone was treated as a human being first and a patient second.

'Come in, Charlotte love,' said Nan. 'You know our Tara.'

'Hi, Charlotte,' I said. 'How are you?' She gave me a little wave. Her hands had the red-raw look of someone who worked hard for a living.

'Charlotte,' said Nan, beaming with pride, 'say hello to our Dylan. He's a doctor.'

Dylan shook his head. 'A slight exaggeration. I'm a

first-year medical student, started two months ago. I haven't been allowed anywhere near a patient yet.'

I swallowed down the huge knot of regret that Nan would not live to see him graduate.

Charlotte laughed. 'Well, it's good to meet you anyway.' She turned to Nan. 'I'll leave you to it, Beryl. See you tomorrow and I'll do your nails then. I've got a lovely new colour, Elephant's Tusk. Don't worry, it's nicer than it sounds.'

She breezed out leaving a waft of hand sanitiser in the air. I made my excuses and hurried after her. 'Charlotte, wait.'

'What's the matter, Tara?'

'Nan seems so much brighter today. Perhaps I could take her home. Just for a bit. Give her a change of scenery.'

Charlotte placed her hand lightly on my forearm. 'I know it's difficult, Tara, but your nan really is in the best place. She makes a super-human effort when she knows you're coming in but . . .' She stopped and looked down at the floor.

'What is it, Charlotte?'

'We can manage her pain better here. There's someone to help twenty-four hours a day. And if she needs you, I will call you, whatever time, day or night.'

'What have you both been up to then?' asked Nan as I returned to her room. 'Tell me all about life on the outside.'

'You make it sound as though you're a prisoner here.' Which she was of course but Nan didn't do self-pity.

'Have you got a girlfriend yet, Dylan?'

He threw me a brief look. 'Erm . . . I'm keeping my options open, Nan.'

She leaned over and ran her finger down his cheek. 'Eee, by 'eck, our Dylan. You're going to break a few hearts, you are. What on earth happened to that cheeky little lad I used to babysit, eh? The one who couldn't stand girls. What was it you called them?'

Dylan smiled. 'Gross.'

'That's it, gross. You were funny, Dylan.' She pointed to the locker next to her bed. 'Fetch me my bag, will you?'

Dylan and I exchanged a knowing look. Whenever Nan asked Dylan to fetch her handbag, he knew he was in for a treat. Growing up, it had usually been a bar of chocolate, or a Matchbox car or some football cards. She opened the clasp on her bag and took out her purse. She brandished two twenties at Dylan. 'Treat yourself to something nice, Dylan.'

He shook his head. 'No, Nan, honestly, I can't take that.'

She gave a husky laugh. 'Well, I can't take it where I'm going, lad.'

I closed my eyes around a memory. I was just the same with Alf. He was always trying to give me money and I always refused, only finally accepting once I understood that it was he who gained the greater pleasure from the act. 'Take it, Dylan.'

'Thanks, Nan,' he said, stuffing the notes into his back pocket.

'I had dinner with Tom the other night,' I said, changing the subject. It seemed as good a place as any to start.

Nan didn't even frown or hesitate. 'Tom Marshall?' Sharp as a tack. It had been over forty years since she'd heard that name but her powers of recall were greater than mine.

'Yes, that's right. He said to pass on his regards to you.'

She fiddled with the satin ribbon on her bed jacket. She'd had it for years. I remembered when she knitted it. I'd sat at her feet with my arms out, the hank of pale pink wool strung across them whilst she wound it into a ball.

She patted her chest. 'I'm dying for a fag.'

I stared at her, my lips pursed, waiting for the irony of her words to sink in. When she caught up, she guffawed, setting in motion a gut-wrenching cough which I'm sure would've finished most people off. I couldn't help but laugh at Dylan's stricken expression. He certainly had a lot to learn.

'Here,' I said, reaching for the glass of water on her bedside cabinet. 'Have a slurp of this.' Her hands were shaking but she managed a few sips without any major spillages.

I took hold of one of her hands and rubbed the back of it. As soon as I'd read the letter from Br Isidore I knew I had to try and find my mother, not just for me, but for Nan. Especially for Nan. I knew her dying wish was to see Violet one last time and she'd never given up hope of finding her.

'Listen, Nan,' I ventured. 'Don't get your hopes up too much but I've received a letter from a firm of solicitors in London. It's a bit of a long story but it's about Violet.'

Her interest was immediately piqued, and she leaned forward. 'Go on.'

I filled her in on what I knew and showed her Br Isidore's letter and the locket. She let the chain slide through her fingers, her mouth open in wonderment. 'My Violet's still alive?'

'Well, I can't say for sure, but she was alive in 1981, Nan.'

'How many years ago is that?'

This had nothing to do with her ageing brain. She'd always been hopeless at maths.

'Thirty-seven.'

She wiped her eyes with her woolly sleeve. 'Well I never.' She squinted at the letter and then passed it back to me. 'Read it for me would you, love? Every word of it. Don't leave anything out.'

I took a sip of her water then began to read. I almost knew it off by heart I'd read it so many times. When I finished, Nan's eyes were closed and I feared she'd fallen asleep. I touched her arm 'Nan?'

She looked at me and smiled. 'She's still alive, Tara. Trust me.'

'Yes, I suppose it's possible.'

She reached out and grabbed my forearm, the strength

of her grip startling me. 'She's out there somewhere, Tara. Find her.'

As though the sudden exertion had exhausted her, she flopped back on the pillow, her words coming out on a wheezy breath. 'And don't take too long about it.'

We were both quiet in the car on the way home. A visit to the hospice certainly made you think about how lucky you were. There were two undertakers' cars in the car park as we left.

Dylan was the first to speak. 'I've asked Dad to come over for tea tonight.'

I braked so sharply that Dylan reached out for the dashboard.

'Oh, for God's sake, Dylan. What on earth did you do that for?'

'I've not seen him since September and I'm going back to Newcastle first thing tomorrow.'

I was flustered and turned on the wiper blades instead of the indicators. 'Well, can't you go there?'

He groaned. 'Oh, God, no. Not with them two little . . .' He searched for a word and settled on 'devils'.

'Last time I went there, Dad was late home and Susie had me reading them bedtime stories whilst she danced about in front of an exercise DVD. I'm not falling for that again. She says it's my duty to bond with them as I'm their . . .' he framed the next two words with air quotes, 'big brother.'

'Cheeky cow.' My son and I have always been able to strengthen our bond with our mutual loathing of Susie.

'Yes, so Dad's coming to ours if that's OK.'

'As long as he's coming alone,' I relented.

'Yes, he is, and I'll cook.'

My eyebrows shot up a bit but I managed not to scoff and I was proud of the enthusiasm I injected into my reply. 'Great, we'll swing by Waitrose on the way home.'

Dylan cooked the student staple that is pasta and chicken but to be fair to him, he'd actually peeled and chopped a garlic clove and made a nice sauce with some crème fraiche and parmesan. He'd even sprinkled over some fresh coriander.

'Mmm . . . this is actually alright, Dylan,' said Ralph, with his mouth full. He took a swig of his red wine. 'Better than anything Susie could rustle up. I'd say you've made quite a good fist of it.'

I stared at Ralph over the table. He'd taken up the place he'd sat at for over twenty years. We all had and it felt completely natural. Why did you have to ruin everything, Ralph? I didn't say that out loud of course. There was no need. He'd heard that question a million times and had never supplied a satisfactory answer.

'I'll come with you if you like,' Ralph said.

I blotted my mouth with my serviette. 'I'm not with you, Ralph. Come with me where?'

'To Spain obviously. I'll come with you to Spain, help you look for Violet.'

I flashed Dylan a look. A look which hopefully said something along the lines of 'now see what you've done'.

I hadn't intended to tell Ralph about the letter and the locket but it was obvious that Dylan had kindly filled him in.

'I don't think that's a very good idea, Ralph.'

'Why not? I could drive you. You know what you're like on those foreign roads.'

He sneaked a glance at Dylan and they shared a laugh, no doubt remembering how I once drove into a ditch in France to avoid a car which I thought was on the wrong side of the road.

'I'm not sure Susie would go for it, Ralph.' Everything starts or ends with Susie one way or another.

'You leave her to me, Tara. This is a family emergency.' He grabbed my hand and then Dylan's so we all joined up in an almost-complete circle. 'And we are family.'

I snatched my hand away. 'We were a family once, Ralph, and sitting round the table holding hands like the Waltons does not mean we still are.'

'Bit harsh, Mum,' said Dylan. 'Dad's only trying to help.'

I blew out my cheeks. 'Well, I'm sorry, Ralph, but you can't possibly think it's a good idea.'

'As a matter of fact, I do. I wouldn't have offered otherwise. You can't go on your own. You don't know what you're going to find.'

'Dad's right, Mum. I can't go with you so what choice do you have?'

'Erm, I do have other friends, thank you.'

Dylan widened his eyes. 'Like who?'

'Well, let me see, there's Sharon from work, although there's no chance we'd be able to take time off together, and then there's Sandra but she now runs a B & B on the Isle of Bute. And of course, there's Moira.'

'Moira?' Ralph interrupted. 'Moira's your cleaner, not your friend.'

'For your information, she's both. She was a massive support to me when you . . . you know . . .' I faltered. I just couldn't be bothered going into all that, especially with Dylan sitting here.

I poured myself some more wine. 'I've loads of friends I could ask but I wouldn't want to put them out.'

Ralph made a valid point though. I did not relish the thought of travelling to Spain alone but I wasn't sure taking Ralph would be the better option. I tried to put him off. 'I'll be going as soon as possible. Maybe as early as next week.'

'Suits me,' said Ralph, flatly.

That's the beauty of owning your own business. It's much easier to swan off at a moment's notice. 'Mmm . . .' I mumbled. 'I'll think about it.'

41

Naturally, I relented. I booked two seats on a flight to Madrid for the next week and Ralph insisted on paying. The other upside was that Susie did not take this news at all well. I picked up my phone and dialled another number. The singing receptionist answered on the third ring. 'Irwin Fortis, how may I help you?' She was exceptionally chipper for a Monday morning.

'Oh, hello. My name's Tara Richards. May I speak to Jamie MacKenzie, please.'

There was only a brief pause. 'Erm, Jamie doesn't work here anymore.'

Well, there's a surprise. 'In that case can I speak to the person who has taken over his . . . erm,' I searched for the correct word, '. . . caseload?'

'One moment, please. I'll put you through to Peter Fortis.'

'Thank you.' Blimey, I was getting the top man.

A few seconds passed. 'Peter Fortis speaking.'

I introduced myself and explained briefly my dealings with Jamie, leaving out the degree of his ineptitude. I didn't want to scupper whatever chance he might have had of getting a good reference. He had enough going against him as it was. 'So, I was wondering if you could let me have the name of the private investigator who tracked me down.'

I could hear him shuffling papers. 'I'll have to get back to you, I'm afraid. We're still going through Jamie's cases but it's like trying to nail jelly to the ceiling, to be honest.'

I felt a momentary pang of sympathy for poor Jamie. 'Thank you, I'd appreciate that.'

In the event it hadn't taken Peter Fortis long to find out the name I needed and he'd phoned me back within the hour. Perhaps there was hope for Jamie after all. The next day I found myself heading to London again. It's a good job my bosses at the medical centre are so understanding. Sharon and I job share our duties so as long as someone is manning reception then we can be quite flexible. I'd booked a seat in the quiet carriage, as I'm unable to tolerate other people jabbering away on their phones, especially as you can only hear one side of the conversation. It was therefore a little embarrassing when my usually dormant phone started to ring. I ferreted around in my bag and glanced at the ID. It was Tom. I bent my head and cupped my hand around my mouth. 'Tom, I can't talk right now, I'll have to call you back.' I ended the call with an apologetic smile at the frowning woman opposite. I was eager to know what he wanted, though, and briefly considered going to the loo and ringing him from there but it didn't seem appropriate. I decided on a text instead.

Sorry about that. I'm on my way to London. In quiet carriage with woman opposite giving me daggers. Call you when I get there.

I deliberated for much longer than the situation warranted about ending it with an X or not. I decided against it.

The office was at the end of a long corridor of identical offices. The top half of the door was plain frosted glass with the words 'Scotty Hamilton, Private Investigator' embossed in black-edged gold lettering. I knocked on the glass and when no reply was forthcoming I entered. The inside of the office was gloriously chaotic. Packing boxes and lever arch files covered the floor, the calendar on the wall was still showing August, even though it was 27 November, and the desk was totally obscured by used coffee mugs and towers of buff folders. Mr Hamilton wandered through from another room at the back, looking down at a file in his hands as he walked. He hadn't seen me and I suddenly felt like an intruder. I didn't wish to startle him so I scuffed my feet and quietly cleared my throat.

He looked up. 'Aah, Mrs Richards, I presume?'

A good start for anyone, especially a private investigator. He was younger than I'd imagined, younger than his shirt anyway, which was probably once white but appeared to have become acquainted with a rogue red sock during a boil wash. The buttons clung on determinedly against his pot belly.

'Yes, I apologise for my tardiness, signal failure some-where south of Milton Keynes. I hope you don't mind me barging in, Mr Hamilton. There was no answer when I knocked.'

He stuck out his hand. 'Not at all. Please, call me Scotty.' He indicated the chair opposite his cluttered desk. 'Have a seat. Just turf Mr Muggles out of the way.'

I hadn't noticed a ginger tom curled up on the chair. Great, I'm allergic to cats and now my black trousers would no doubt be covered in a layer of orange fluff.

'Thanks for coming,' Scotty said, even though it was my idea.

He picked up a buff folder from the top of the pile. 'Right, let's have a look.' 'Violet Skye' was written on the front and I held my breath as he flicked through some notes.

'As I told you on the phone, this case was first given to my father, Scott Hamilton, Snr, thirty-seven years ago, in 1981.' He produced a little chuckle. 'Obviously, before my time. I only picked up the case when I was having a clear-out.' He laughed again and swept his arm around the room. 'You should have seen it before.'

I laughed politely, willing him to get on with it.

'The problem my father had, apart from the fact that the internet had yet to be invented, was that he was working with the wrong name. It seems he tried various avenues but was always met with a brick wall. The case was put onto the back burner in 1984 and then, when no further progress was made, it was archived in 1987.

'Oh, I see, that's unfortunate,' I said, thinking of all those wasted years.

Scotty held up a finger. 'But, we never give up. When things are a bit slack, I review cold cases and I have to say that your mother's case wasn't just cold, it was frozen solid.'

'Yes, quite. You mentioned a breakthrough on the phone.'

He sat back in his chair and opened his palms. 'It was all relatively easy in the end. I searched Google for Violet Skye and eventually it led me to this.'

He pushed a photocopy across the table. It was an article from the *Manchester Evening News*, dated Tuesday 7 March, 1978.

The Skye's The Limit

The audience at The Amethyst Lounge was treated to a sensational performance last week, by newcomer Miss Violet Skye, 29. The regular Friday night crowd were unanimous in their appreciation of the quite astounding voice of this bright young star. I caught up with Violet, whose real name is Violet Dobbs, before she went on stage. 'It's a dream come true for me,' she said. 'To tread the same boards as Brucie, Lulu and Dusty is a huge honour. I keep having to pinch myself. I just hope I can repay the manager's faith in me.'

I can report that Violet had no need to worry on that score. Her performance was simply breathtaking and I predict that Miss Skye will be gracing the stage at The Amethyst Lounge for a long time to come.

Ian Cherry, Man About Town

There was a photo of my mother sitting in her dressing room, toasting the camera with a glass raised above her head. She looked so radiant and so full of life that I didn't trust myself to speak. My throat ached with unshed tears. Mr Muggles jumped onto my lap and I absently stroked his head.

'Are you alright, Mrs Richards?'

I nodded, gently placing the furry ginger one on the floor. I could let the tears fall now. I had a good excuse. 'I do apologise,' I sniffed. 'I'm allergic to cats.'

'Oh, sorry. You should've said.' He shooed Mr Muggles into the back room and closed the door but it wasn't enough to silence the cat's plaintive meows.

'We leave virtual footprints wherever we go,' Scotty continued. 'There's no hiding place, which is great if you want to be found, not so good if you don't. Anyway, once I had Violet's correct surname it wasn't too difficult and – *voilà!* – here you are.'

I continued to stare at the newspaper cutting. 'She was so beautiful.'

'She was and I can see the family resemblance if I may say so.'

331

I could feel myself blushing. 'Mmm . . . I wish.'

'There's a website dedicated to the old Amethyst Lounge. That's where I found this article. There's a section on there for people to share their memories. Your mother is remembered very fondly, you should take a look.'

I thought back to those days. She was only there for a couple of months before she went off on holiday. 'Thanks, perhaps I will.' I went to slip the cutting into my bag. 'Can I keep this?'

'Sure.' He reached for a rubber stamp and slammed it down on the front of the file. 'CASE CLOSED'.

He smiled at me and held up the stamp. 'It belonged to my late father. I know it's not exactly hi-tech, but I think he'd like the fact I still use it.'

'I wouldn't say the case is closed exactly. My mother's still missing.'

Scotty rubbed his chin. 'Our remit was only to find you, which we've done.'

I could feel my nose fizzing again. I needed to get out of that stuffy moggie-infused office. I thanked Scotty and bade him farewell. I turned to leave but then hovered in the doorway. 'Scotty, would you be interested in taking on a new case?'

'Certainly. I never turn work away.'

'I need you to help me find someone else.'

He picked up his pad and pen. 'Absolutely, fire away. Do you have a name?'

There was a sudden influx of bile in my throat and my teeth were clenched together so hard it was difficult to get the words out. 'The name's Valentine. Larry Valentine.'

42

It was only when I was out on the street again that I remembered I was supposed to call Tom.

'I thought you'd forgotten,' he laughed, when he answered.

'Sorry, I was late for my appointment, bloody signal failure or something. Anyway what did you want?'

'Charming.'

I ran my fingers through my hair. I hadn't intended to be so brusque. 'Sorry, I didn't mean it to come out like that. I've just met with the private investigator who tracked me down and I'm feeling a bit, I don't know . . . discombobulated, I suppose.' I remembered my mother's attempts to get me to pronounce that word. I was sure she had made it up. She held my hand up counting off the syllables. Dis—com—bob—u—lay—ted. The final syllable she tapped out on my nose. I could feel my chin wobbling and I was grateful he couldn't see me. I told him all about my meeting and the article from the *Evening News*.

'Wow, that's amazing. Fancy that. What are you going to do now?'

I took a deep breath. 'I'm going to Spain.'

'On your own? When?'

I ignored his first question and jumped straight to the second one. 'Next week.'

'You don't hang about, do you?'

I pictured Nan in her room, cocooned from an outside world she would never see again. 'I don't know how long Nan's got.'

There was a pause, which stretched into an uncomfortable silence, and I couldn't think of anything to say to fill it.

'Would you like me to go with you?' Tom asked.

'You?'

'Don't sound so surprised, Tara. I know how much your mother meant to you and I was rather fond of her myself.'

My heart hadn't galloped so fast since the mums' hundred-yard dash at Dylan's sports day. I caught a glimpse of myself in a shop window. I'd forgotten to close my mouth. Someone barged into me and I found myself apologising to them.

'Oh Tom, that would've been . . . well, I just can't believe that you'd . . . Oh God.'

'What's the matter?'

'Ralph's coming with me,' I blurted out. I closed my eyes and balled my hand into a fist. Damn, damn, damn.

'Your ex?' Tom didn't bother to hide his surprise.

'It was his idea and I never imagined for one minute

that you'd want to come, even though it would make a lot more sense, considering Ralph didn't even know my mother.'

'Never mind,' he sighed. 'But if there's anything else I can do just let me know.'

'There is,' I almost shouted before he had a chance to hang up. 'What are you doing tomorrow night?'

Charlotte was sitting by Nan's bed as I entered the room. 'How is she?'

The usually upbeat nurse sounded a little subdued. 'She's not been great today. I didn't ring you because I knew you were coming tonight.'

'Charlotte,' came Nan's raspy voice. 'I'm alright, stop worrying our Tara.' I could see Nan's hand fumbling for the control. Charlotte took over and Nan rose up like the proverbial phoenix from the ashes. 'Hello, love. Have you found my Violet yet?'

I sat on the edge of the bed. 'Give me a chance, Nan. I have booked the flights for next week though. Ralph's coming with me.'

'Who's Ralph?'

At first I thought she was joking. She was fond of saying 'He's dead to me, that man.' There was something different though. She was actually waiting for my answer. I beckoned Tom from where he was hovering by the door. 'Nan, you remember Tom?' And just like that, she was back in the room.

'Tom Marshall, as I live and breathe. Which I'm just about managing to do.'

He stepped forward. 'It's nice to see you again, Mrs Dobbs. It's been a long time.'

'Hey, less of the Mrs Dobbs. It makes me sound so old and I'm only ninety-one, you know. Call me Beryl.'

Charlotte made her excuses. 'I'll leave you to it. I'll be back to give you your meds later, Beryl.'

'Come closer, young Tom,' Nan said. 'Let me get a proper look at you.'

He leaned in and she took hold of his chin, squinting as she turned his face to the left then to the right, like a farmer inspecting his prize heifer. 'You've worn well, I'll say that for you.'

'Thanks,' he said. 'I'm not complaining.'

'Eee, I could set my watch by you back in the day. Every evening, one minute past six, the phone would go and I'd hear our Tara thundering down the stairs to answer it.'

Tom laughed at the memory. 'Kids today don't know they're born, do they? They're never off their phones. My Hannah can't go more than two minutes without some form of contact with her boyfriend. She has a complete meltdown if she can see he's online but has ignored one of her texts.'

Nan frowned. All this technology was beyond her. 'How are the twins, Ralph?'

Despite the warm room, I shivered. This was not like Nan at all. 'Nan, this is Tom, not Ralph.'

'Tom?'

I tried to remain patient and mouthed a silent apology to Tom. 'This is Tom from Manchester. My first boyfriend, remember?' Too late, I realised I'd adopted a completely different voice, as though I was talking to an imbecile.

Nan looked at me as though I was the idiot. 'Why are you talking like that, our Tara? I know who Tom is.'

'But you just said . . .'

Tom touched me on the arm and shook his head.

I understood and changed the subject. 'Anyway, I've booked to go to Spain next week, so hopefully I'll have some news when I get back. I'll only be away a few days.'

'I do hope you find her, love. I've not had a bad life but if I could have one wish before I shuffle off, it would be to see our Violet one last time. I need to explain everything. I could die happy then.'

Outside in the car park, I apologised again to Tom. 'She's not usually like that; honestly, she's so sharp.' I chewed at my thumb nail. 'It's worrying. And God only knows what she meant by needing to explain everything.'

'No need to apologise, Tara. I'm really glad I came.'

I gazed at his smiling face and saw nothing but kindness. 'So am I.'

43

I'd checked more than a dozen times but I couldn't resist the urge for one more look. I knew with absolute certainty that my passport and boarding card were in my bag but it's a compulsion. I heard Ralph's car pull into the driveway and I lifted the mink coat off the banister. It was perishing outside and the lawn sparkled with frost. I shrugged on the coat and was immediately transported back forty years. It still smelled of mothballs and paraffin. I stroked the fur and thought of Alf. The doorbell startled me and I hoisted my handbag over my shoulder and pulled out the handle on my case. 'Alright, Ralph, I'm coming,' I muttered.

He had a worried look on his face when I opened the door. 'What's up?'

'Erm, Susie's taking us to the airport. She insisted.'

'For God's sake, Ralph, I thought we agreed you'd drive then leave the car at the airport. It's only for a few days.'

'It's fine; it's better this way.'

'For who?' I mumbled, as I followed him down the path.

Ralph loaded my case into the boot and I opened the

rear door. There was no way I was sitting in the front next to her.

'You'll have to squeeze in between the twins,' Susie said, without looking at me.

Sure enough, both girls were strapped into their car seats, each sucking greedily on a bottle of milk. It was an awkward manoeuvre, but I managed to clamber over and wedge myself in the middle of the back seat. Thank God it was only a twenty-minute journey to the airport.

Instead of merely dropping us off, Susie insisted on parking up and accompanying us to departures. Somewhat mystifyingly, Ralph went along with this, even though it involved getting out the double buggy, which it took the pair of them a good five minutes to assemble.

Ralph's patience was stretched as thin as the skin on Susie's forehead. 'For God's sake, Susie. Surely you know how to put this thing up properly by now.'

She pouted her glossy bottom lip. 'Don't start, Ralphie. Not when you're going away.'

I bristled at the mention of this derivative of his name. I'm the only one who ever called him Ralphie.

He plucked one of the girls – Lily? Jasmine? – from the back of the car and settled her into the buggy. The other one, though, was having none of it. She arched her back as Ralph tried to press her into the buggy. I could tell he was becoming more and more flustered as the little girl began to wail, the acoustics in the multi-storey doing a sterling job of amplifying her histrionics. Finally, with the girls strapped, in we located the lift and traipsed in silence to departures.

'OK, girls,' said Ralph. 'See you in a few days.'

He crouched into the buggy and gave each of his daughters a kiss on the forehead. He then grasped hold of Susie by her shoulders and kissed her on the lips. She clamped her hand onto the back of his head and held him captive for longer than was acceptable, even for an airport departure terminal.

'I'll miss you,' he said, when he was finally freed.

His lips were stained the same colour as Susie's, leaving me in no doubt that she had marked her territory.

'Call me when you land,' she breathed, stroking his cheek.

He winked at her, reached out for her hand and pressed his lips into her palm. 'You can count on it.'

She flicked a tear from the corner of her eye. You'd have thought he was going off on a tour of Afghanistan.

I clutched the handle of my case. 'Bye then, Susie. Thanks for the lift and don't worry, I'll take good care of him.'

She didn't even bother to hide her scowl or her note of sarcasm. 'Thanks,' she said through a tight smile. Then her face relaxed and she dropped the brittle tone. 'And good luck with your search. I hope you find her.'

Even though it was the beginning of December, according to the digital thermometer out on the street it was fifteen degrees Celsius, or nearly sixty degrees in old money. I wasn't dressed for those temperatures and it came as a blessed relief to step inside the air-conditioned lobby of the hotel, with its shiny black tiled floors and trickling water feature. I felt a tiny bit ridiculous with a mink coat slung over my arm. Ralph slid our passports over the desk.

'Welcome to Madrid, Mr and Mrs Richards,' beamed the receptionist. 'We have a double room reserved for one night.'

I jumped in, rather dramatically it has to be said. 'Oh God, no, that's not right. Two single rooms, please.'

She frowned and tapped away on the keyboard, whilst I glared at Ralph. 'I'm so sorry, we only have a twin room available as an alternative to a double.'

I blew out my cheeks and fanned myself with my passport. 'That'll have to do then.'

She handed over two key cards. 'Second floor, room 212.'

Our meagre luggage had been confiscated by a liveried bell-hop who promised to bring it up to our room even though we were more than capable of carrying one small bag each. Once we were inside the lift I hissed at Ralph. 'A double room, really?'

He shrugged and wrinkled his nose. 'Sorry, force of habit.'

'Well, I wouldn't want to be in your shoes if Susie finds out we shared a room.'

'How will she?' He smiled at me. He knows me so well. I may be bitter but I'm not that spiteful.

I locked the door whilst I took a shower. Ralph might still be my husband but he hadn't seen me naked for over two years and I didn't relish the thought of him comparing my body to Susie's. When I emerged from the bathroom swathed in the hotel's stiff towelling robe, I found Ralph sitting on his bed, a bottle of champagne between his knees.

'What's this?' I plonked myself down next to him.

'I don't get out much these days, Tara.' He filled a flute and handed it to me. 'Cheers. And here's to a fruitful trip. I know how much this means to you.'

He looked more relaxed than I'd seen him in a long time and I wasn't even mad when it dawned on me that he'd made this trip for his own sake as much as mine.

I removed the towel turban and shook my hair free. 'Are you happy, Ralph?'

He adjusted his position slightly so that we were facing each other, only the champagne bottle between us.

'Mostly. Are you?' He reached out and scooped a wet tendril of hair out of my eyes.

'I suppose so.' I took another sip of my drink. 'We weren't really working, were we?'

'None of it was your fault, Tara.'

I leaned back in shock. This was a turn-up for the books. 'I thought I wasn't enough for you.'

'You were more than enough, Tara. I see that now.'

I supressed the urge to give a victorious punch of the air. 'Well, it's too late now, Ralph. You have another family.'

He lowered his gaze and fiddled with the foil on the champagne bottle. I moved my glass towards him. 'Any chance of a refill?'

He looked up, then almost in slow motion he leaned in to me until his face was only an inch away. My heart skipped like a teenager having her first snog behind the bike shed but I didn't recoil. I closed my eyes and waited for his lips to meet mine. The champagne had clouded my judgement and all the rules had flown out of the window. He didn't kiss me, his lips merely brushed mine as he lifted a hand to my neck, then let it trail down my front as he gently teased open the dressing gown. His hand was freezing cold as he slipped it inside and I gasped in shock more than desire. He placed the bottle on the floor, shifted his weight then pressed me down onto the bed. I knew it was imperative that I pushed him off; this could not go any further for so many reasons. He buried his face in my neck. 'You smell divine. What is it?'

'It's . . . it's nothing, just some hotel shower gel. Ralph?'
'Mmm.'

'Ralph,' I said a little more urgently. 'We can't.' I couldn't believe I actually felt sorry for Susie. The phone on my bedside table started to vibrate. 'Ignore it,' said Ralph.

'It might be important,' I said, pushing my palm into his chest. He lifted himself up and leaned across to squint at the caller ID, just as the phone stopped vibrating. 'Someone called Charlotte,' he said.

'No,' I shouted. 'Give me that phone.'

'Who's Charlotte?'

'A nurse from St Jude's. She knows I'm away so it must be important.' I thumped Ralph on the arm. 'I told you I needed to answer it. Now look what you've done.'

I drummed my fingers on the table as I returned the call and waited for Charlotte to answer. When she did, she got straight to the point. With my eyes closed, I listened intently. There was no need for me to say anything. After I hung up, I turned to Ralph. 'I need to go home.'

He held up his smartphone, already one step ahead of me. 'There's a flight at nine-thirty this evening. Two hours forty, so with the time difference it'll get you back to Manchester at ten past eleven, but there's only one seat left. There's nothing before that.'

I pulled the dressing gown across my chest and headed for the bathroom. 'Book me that seat, please, Ralph.'

44

It was just gone midnight by the time I arrived at St Jude's. Charlotte was waiting for me in reception, a limp smile on her lips. She took both of my hands in hers. 'I'm so sorry, Tara.'

'I'm not too late, am I?'

She shook her head. 'No, Beryl's comfortable and not in any pain but her breathing is laboured, very shallow.'

'You did the right thing in calling me. Can I see her now?'

'Yes.' She hesitated. 'But before you go in you should know that . . . um . . . Beryl's . . . confused. It often happens right at the very end, so don't take it personally if she doesn't recognise you.'

'Don't be daft, Charlotte. Of course, she'll recognise me.'

Nan's room was warm and dark, the only light coming from a lamp in the corner. I crept up to the bed and took hold of her hand. It felt ice-cold and for one dreadful second I thought she'd already left me but then I saw her chest rise ever so slightly.

'I'll bring in a pillow for you, Tara,' said Charlotte. 'And a nice cup of hot chocolate.'

I nodded my thanks then lowered my face to the bed, resting my forehead on Nan's hand. I couldn't bear to think of my life without her in it. Everything that I am today is because of her. I could not have asked for a better substitute for a mother. I think she felt she failed with Violet so seized on the chance to get it right the second time with me. Devastated as I was at the thought of losing her, I was also crushed that I hadn't been able to find Violet in time.

Charlotte came back in with the hot chocolate and a pillow. 'How is she?'

'Still with us.'

Charlotte picked up Nan's wrist and checked her pulse. 'It's very weak.'

Nan stirred then and moved onto her back. She opened her eyes and tried to focus. 'Where's George?'

My scalp prickled. 'George isn't here, Nan. He's gone, remember?'

Nan swivelled her head towards me. 'Violet, is that you? Oh, love . . . you came back.' All of a sudden she sounded younger and more animated than I'd heard her in a while.

'No . . .' I began, but Charlotte touched my arm and shook her head.

I understood what she meant, and my vision was instantly blurred by tears. I couldn't speak and my throat closed. Charlotte backed out of the room. 'Call me if you need anything.'

'Oh, Violet,' Nan continued. 'I've waited a long time for this day. I'm so sorry I let you down but believe me when I say I had no idea what George had done to you.' She stopped and took a few laboured gasps. 'For years, I never knew. Never suspected a thing. I just thought you were a stubborn lass who wanted to make it on her own. George told me the truth on his deathbed. Said he needed to get something off his chest so he could apologise and ensure his safe passage to heaven where God would forgive him.' She clutched at the bedsheet. 'And it's a bloody good job the coward did die, because I would've clamped a pillow over his miserable lying face and finished the job off myself.'

I covered my mouth with my hand. I could already feel the bile stinging as the awful truth began to develop like a photograph under water.

Nan fell silent for so long that I thought she'd drifted off to sleep, or worse. Then she started again, her voice quiet, almost a whisper. 'I don't blame you, Violet, but you should have told me George was the father of your baby. I would've believed you, you know. I would've kicked that bastard out and me and you could've brought up the baby together. You know I would've supported you, don't you?' She lifted her eyes and looked at me. I was incapable of speaking, so I nodded and gripped her hand tighter in reply. 'I've missed you so much, Violet,'

348

she continued. 'Not a day has gone by when I haven't looked out of the window, hoping to see you coming down the street, coming home where you belong.' She managed a little laugh. 'But you did come back. I knew in my heart you would. Now I've made my peace with you, I can slip away. Thank you for giving me the chance to apologise. You've no idea what . . .' Nan stopped and winced in pain and I stroked the back of her hand with my thumb. 'You've no idea what this means to me. I love you, Violet. I want you to know that. I never stopped loving you.'

She closed her eyes and felt silent. There was no point in me saying anything then. It had all been said.

It was about another hour before Nan breathed her last. In death, her face slackened and she looked serene, beautiful even. She was the epitome of somebody who had died peacefully in their sleep. Charlotte came back in with her eyebrows raised, questioning if everything was alright. I stood and caressed my palm over Nan's forehead and down over her eyes, closing them for the last time. 'She's gone, Charlotte.'

She picked up Nan's wrist, then after a few seconds she placed it gently down on the covers. 'I'm so sorry, Tara.' She pulled the sheet up towards Nan's face, but I stopped her.

'Not yet. I want to look at her for a while.'

I couldn't have held back the sobs even if I'd wanted to. 'I feel terrible lying to her on her death bed.' My words came out on shuddering breaths, like a hysterical toddler who'd been crying for too long.

Charlotte was firm but gentle. 'You didn't lie to her, Tara. You did the kindest thing possible. You gave her permission to pass on knowing Violet had come back to her. You gave her the greatest gift of all. You gave her peace, so try not to beat yourself up about it.' She squeezed my shoulder firmly. 'I'll be back in a little while.'

To say my emotions were in turmoil would be a gross understatement. Even though it was inevitable, Nan's death devasted me, but together with the revelation that George was my father, it was just too much to take in. My poor mother had been molested by her own step-father and had then spent her life protecting both me and Nan from the truth.

The stabbing pain in my chest confirmed my heart was broken. If you could have opened me up and prised my ribs apart, I swear you would've seen a crack right down the middle. My cherished Nan had gone and I had no idea what I was going to do without her.

45

1978

Violet crouched down in the sweltering heat, her fingers teasing out the stubborn weeds which had invaded the vegetable patch. Having no wardrobe of her own, she was dressed simply in a makeshift dress that one of the more talented monks had run up for her from an old habit. Still, the cloth was too thick and scratchy for the blistering August temperature. She'd been at Monasterio de Justina for almost two months and it was beginning to feel like home. Perched on a horseshoe bend in the Rio Duraton, protected on three sides by staggering limestone cliffs and guarded from above by the ever-circling peregrine falcons and griffon vultures, it was a place of safety that she'd never truly had before. She thought about her mother, that shadowy figure who was just beyond the reaches of her consciousness, and unexpectedly her throat thickened and she was forced to swallow several times to quell the tears. She stood up as she heard Br Isidore calling to her from across the walled vegetable garden. He was carrying a tray of homemade lemonade, which on a day like today tasted like nectar. She took a glass and downed the contents in one. 'Thank you, Br Isidore, I needed that.'

He looked at the vegetable beds, the soil weed-free and turned over. 'You must be tired, Violet. Come, have a rest over here in the shade.'

He led her to the wooden bench under the shelter of a pistachio tree. 'I need to work, Br Isidore. I need to pay my way. You and the others have been so kind to me, so patient.' She smiled. 'Even Br Florian.'

He took a sip of his own drink before turning to her. 'It is our pleasure, Violet.' He hesitated before continuing in what was obviously a forced casual tone. 'Um . . . have you thought about when you'll be ready to return?'

'To England?'

'You say that's where you're from, no?'

She closed her eyes, willing the details to come. 'I think so. I speak the language, so it would make sense. Everything's just so sketchy and blurred. It's like I'm looking through a steamed-up window. If only I could take my sleeve and wipe away the mist then everything would be so much clearer.'

She reached up to a low-hanging branch and plucked off a cluster of pistachios, their rosy hulls still protecting the nuts inside.

'They won't be ready for another month or so.'

'Oh, right, I didn't know.' She threw the bunch on the ground. There was so much she didn't know. 'Do you ever miss your home, Br Isidore?'

It was so long before he spoke again that Violet was convinced he hadn't heard her question. 'I miss my *Mama's* cooking, that is for sure.'

'What about other family? Brothers and sisters?'

He shook his head, his voice flat. 'No brothers or sisters.'

'What about girlfriends?'

'No girlfriend either.'

She held up her hand. 'I'm sorry, Br Isidore, it's none of my business. Forgive me, I shouldn't interrogate you like that. It's just that you're . . .'

'I'm what?'

She stood to leave. 'Nothing, ignore me. I need to press on. Thanks for the lemonade.'

She had more to say, much more, but the time wasn't right. A monk's day was governed by the Liturgy of the Hours, the set of prayers which marked the canonical hours of each day. The bell would ring for Vespers shortly, followed by Compline, and only then would Br Isidore be able to retire for the night, observing the Great Silence until mass the following morning. Fortunately only unnecessary conversation was forbidden and what she had to say was crucial. She hadn't been completely honest with Br Isidore. She had remembered something.

He was kneeling at the side of his bunk when she peered through the small square window on his door. His hood was down to reveal his shaven head, the stubble darkening his scalp indicating that another shave was surely due. She hesitated before knocking, not wanting to disturb him during prayer. She wasn't sure of the time, but the sun was low in the sky and she estimated it had about another hour to go before it dropped behind the hillside. She loved the balmy evenings out here in the mountains. Animals that had more sense than to venture out under the savage sun took advantage of the cooler temperatures and she'd witnessed pine martens, foxes and even wolves creep out from their hiding places. Even the annoying cicadas with their constant clicking and chirping made her smile.

She watched Br Isidore get to his feet and go over to his washstand. He poured the water from a jug into a ceramic bowl, swirling the contents with his fingers. Using both hands, he sloshed the water over his face. She knew it would be stone cold by now. The only way they had of heating it was in a metal water butt which was left out in the sun all day.

She tapped on the door as Br Isidore dried his face. '*Sí*?'

'I'm sorry to bother you,' she whispered. 'I know you're not supposed to talk but . . .' stopping to glance behind, she took an uninvited step over the threshold and closed the door behind her, '. . . can you just listen?'

'Violet, I will always have time to listen to you. What is it?'

'May I?' She indicated his bunk. 'I don't want to get you into any trouble.'

'This is my private cell, Violet. What happens in here is my . . . my . . .' He shrugged. 'I'm sorry, I don't know this word.'

'Your business?'

'*Si, exactamente.*'

He crossed over to the door and pulled the little hessian curtain across the window, before sitting down next to her on his bunk. 'Now, tell me what is giving you concern.'

'I . . . I've remembered something. Well, I don't think I'd actually forgotten it but rather . . . suppressed it, I suppose.'

He nodded his encouragement. 'In your own time.'

'I can remember my bedroom at home. The wallpaper . . . it was a pale blue and white and had big green ferns all over it.' She closed her eyes and clasped her hands on her lap, her voice sounding like a clairvoyant describing a vision. 'There was a single bed with a wooden headboard. On the wall above there was a painting of the Virgin Mary. There was a dressing table with a mirror, which had hinges so you could look at the back of your head if you wanted to. The bed had a crocheted rug on it, lots of brightly coloured squares stitched together and edged with a fringe. I used to sniff the fringe, let it tickle my nose and top lip. It brought me comfort after . . .'

She stood up quickly and ran over to the bowl, retching

into the water. Her neck was wet with perspiration, her face and neck flushed.

'Violet?'

She breathed in deeply through her nose and held her breath until the room began to spin. 'I'm alright, Br Isidore.' Wiping her face on the towel, she sat down again, her fingers fiddling with the hem of her dress. 'The first time it happened, I could hear him out on the landing, shuffling and grunting like one of those wild boars out there. He waited until I'd turned out the light and then he opened the door, peeled back my covers and slipped into bed with me. There was hardly any room and he pressed his body up against mine, his rancid breath in my face, his rough hands under my nightie.'

'Oh, Violet.'

'Shush, I'm fine, I need to do this.

'I was too shocked to scream and in any case my mother was out. He wasn't that stupid. But I was paralysed with fear and confusion. I just couldn't understand why he was doing this to me. Afterwards, I threatened to tell my mother but he said she wouldn't believe me and if I did tell then Poppy would pay the consequences.'

'Poppy?'

'My . . . my little dog.'

Br Isidore balled his fists.

'I didn't believe anybody could be that cruel and I told him I was going to tell my mother as soon as she got back from the bingo.'

'Bingo?'

'It's a game . . . it's not important. Anyway, he stormed out of the room and slammed the door. I just lay there hardly daring to move in case he came back. I was desperate to have a bath, to rid myself of his smell, the feel of his greasy hands on my skin and the stickiness between my thighs. I heard the back door slam shut and breathed a sigh of relief. He'd gone out somewhere, leaving me free to get myself cleaned up. I heard it then and my blood turned to ice. I hardly dared to look but at the second whimper I threw back the curtains. He was standing in the yard, his leather belt in his hands, Poppy tied up against the wall. Her little body trembled, her trusting eyes pleading with him to let her go. I couldn't stand it for one second longer. I opened the window and begged him to leave her alone. He looked up, a manic grin on his face. "You know what not to do, Violet," he said.'

Br Isidore took her in his arms, rocking her gently as he smoothed her hair. '*Es horripilante*, Violet, *absolutamente horripilante. Ese caballero* he was your *papa*, no?' In his rage his English had deserted him and she could feel him shaking beneath his robe.

Violet nodded. 'Well, step-father, but he was the only father I had. He'd brought me up as his own.'

'You were just a *niña*. How old?'

Violet screwed up her eyes and pinched the bridge of her nose. 'About eight, I think.'

'And you never tell your *mama*?'

She brushed his arm away. 'You make it sound as though it was my fault, Br Isidore. And that was what he made me think too.'

'No . . . I'm sorry. It was not your fault, none of it. You were just a *niña*; he was supposed to be the caring adult. How did it end though, Violet? Did you tell your *mama*?'

'No, I couldn't. I was too afraid. He said she wouldn't believe me, said he would hurt Poppy and I knew he was capable of that. He said even if my mum did believe me and called the police then he would be arrested and sent to prison and then we wouldn't survive without his wage and I would have to go into care and . . . and . . . it would be all my fault.'

'No, no, no, Violet. Don't ever think that.' He took her shoulders and made her look at him. 'Listen to me. You were an innocent *niña*, you were the . . . how do you say . . . *victima* and the blame lies solely with him.'

She carried on as though she hadn't heard him. 'Then one day I'd had enough. His night-time visits had become so regular that I was expecting them and if for any reason he didn't come in to my room, then I worried that I'd upset him in some way and he was angry with me. I was scared what he would do next. Scared that it would be worse than what he was already doing to me.' She covered her face with her hands, unable to witness the incredulity in Br Isidore's eyes. 'You see,' she said eventually. 'I'd become desensitised to it all. I'd got used to it . . . accepted it as normal behaviour.' She stood up and crossed the room, peeling back the curtain from the small window in the door. 'I knew there was a whole world out there that I was missing out on. I knew nobody else was going to help me to see it.' She injected a note of defiance into her voice. 'That's when I decided to run away.' She took a deep breath and tilted her chin upwards. 'And that's exactly what I did, Br Isidore. When I was fourteen, I ran away.'

'Where do you go to, Violet?'

She frowned at him, her expression disbelieving as she cast her arm about the room. 'What do you mean, where to? Here, of course. I ran away to Spain.'

He rose from the bed and opened the drawer in his desk, carefully lifting out the locket. 'Violet, I know you don't remember but I'm absolutely certain that this necklace belongs to you. I found it in the exact same spot where I found you. It cannot belong to anybody else. You know how isolated we are up here. The chances of someone else dropping a necklace in the same place, well . . . well . . . it is just too . . . I'm sorry, I can't think of any English words to tell you.'

She reached out and took the locket, running her fingers over the inscription as she read it out loud. 'Happy thirtieth birthday. Love Tara. Fourth of June 1978.' She looked at Br Isidore. 'You really believe this is mine? That I'm thirty years old?'

He nodded. 'Yes, I do believe that, Violet Skye. And somehow we need to find out where you've been for the last sixteen years.'

She held the locket in her fist, shaking her head. 'No, Br Isidore, no, I just can't. I'm never going back.'

46

2018

Dylan stood up and walked shakily over to the lectern. He looked so handsome in his suit and thin black tie, his hair combed into a neat style rather than being left to its own devices. The paper in his hand quivered and my heart ached for him. I could tell he was nervous but when I'd asked him if he'd deliver the eulogy, he hadn't hesitated, not for one millisecond. Before speaking, he took a sip of water and I silently praised the person who had had the foresight to place it there. He looked at me and smiled. I lifted my chin and sat up a little straighter. He could do this. Ralph clutched my hand and for a brief moment it was just the three of us again.

Dylan's voice was loud and confident. 'Beryl Ann Dobbs,' he began. 'Never have anybody's initials spelled out a more inappropriate word.' He took a deep breath. 'Because my nan was as far from BAD as it's possible to be. She may have been my great-grandmother but to me, my mum, my dad and all my mates for that matter, she was simply Nan. As a kid my favourite place in the whole world was Nan's house.' He stopped and winked at me. 'Sorry, Mum.' There was a murmur of laughter from the congregation. 'The cupboards were always full of stuff which was forbidden at home: biscuits, pop, and where most people would have a fruit bowl, there was a permanent tin of Quality Street on the sideboard. Whilst Mum and Dad were at work, she'd look after me during the school holidays. She gave me sweets, lollies, took me to bingo, taught me how to play Brag, always for money naturally.' He stopped again and wagged his finger at the congregation, doing a passable impression of Nan. "Never bet more than you can afford to lose, our Dylan" was her mantra. There was many a night where she fleeced me for all my spends. Next morning though, it would all be back in the old tobacco tin where I kept my pocket money.' He glanced at the coffin, smiling. 'She made ice cream floats, baked me my favourite chocolate and banana cake and when I was fourteen she introduced me to cider, allowing me just one glass one particular scorching afternoon.' He grimaced in my direction. 'Again, sorry, Mum.' More laughter. I joined in even though Dylan was making me out to be worse than a boarding school dormitory mistress. I was only looking out for his teeth for heaven's sake. 'We were both like naughty schoolchildren,' Dylan continued. 'I had a good excuse of course, I was a schoolchild, but Nan was supposed to be the responsible adult. We were always up to something. I lost track of the number of times she said "Don't tell your Mum, Dylan."

'She didn't have the easiest of lives but I know she was grateful for every single day. And I also know life got better for her when my own mum, Tara, went to live with her in 1978.'

I glanced over at the framed photo of Nan, propped up on an easel beside the coffin. It was a black and white photo taken around the time I moved in. She wasn't looking directly at the camera but off to the left somewhere, her head thrown back in laughter, the obligatory cigarette between her fingers and a long curl of smoke drifting in front of her face. It captured perfectly the essence of who she was.

'It can't have been easy,' continued Dylan, 'suddenly having a teenager come to live with you but it takes . . . took . . . a lot to daunt our Nan. She rose to the challenge and I think it kept her young. Even when she turned ninety she still had more energy than people half her age.' He paused for another sip of water. 'I feel immensely privileged to have had her in my life. She was courageous, playful, inspirational, tenacious and the stalwart of our family. You knew exactly where you were with her. She called a spade a shovel and she did not suffer fools. She spoke her mind but was never cruel or unkind. She was from an age that had never heard of political correctness but she was never mean and never intended to cause offence, although some of the stuff she came out with would make even the Duke of Edinburgh blush.' There was more laughter and Dylan had to swallow hard before continuing. 'But she wouldn't want us to be sad today. As she was fond of saying, "I've outstayed me welcome on this Earth, every day's a bonus now."' His gaze rested on the coffin. 'Well, I'm sorry, Nan, you can't have everything your own way because we are sad.' He stopped and pulled a tissue out of his pocket. 'In fact, we're absolutely heartbroken.' His voice finally cracked then and I couldn't sit by and watch for a second longer. I was on my feet and by Dylan's side in an instant.

I wrapped my arms around him and felt him go limp as he bent to rest his head on my shoulder. 'I'm so proud of you, son,' I managed. 'And Nan would be too.'

Me, Dylan and Ralph were the first ones out of the crematorium. We stood in a row ready to greet the rest of the mourners as they filed out. Considering Nan was ninety-one, there was a good turn-out. She would've been happy with it. Sandra came out first, dabbing at her eyes and looking elegant in a black woollen dress, a string of pearls at her throat. She'd been a punk when I first met her all those years ago and we didn't get off to a great start. When I looked out of Nan's window and saw her standing in the queue at the ice cream van, I thought we could never be friends. I'd never seen so many piercings on one face. Nan thought I should give her a chance though. 'I know it looks as though she fell face down into a box of fishing tackle,' she said, 'but she's a nice kid really.' Naturally, me punching her in the face didn't exactly help us forge a close bond, but after

I smashed up the headmistress's office, she found a grudging respect for me and against the odds we became friends.

I was still smiling at the memory as Sandra gave me a hug. 'I'm really sorry, Tara.'

'Thanks for coming, Sandra. I appreciate it. It's a hell of a long way from Bute.'

It was hard to think of something original to say to everyone, so I alternated between 'thanks for coming' and 'nice to see you again'.

I was genuinely choked when Charlotte appeared in front of me. The girl worked at an end-of-life hospice. She could go to half a dozen funerals a week if she had time. 'Charlotte, oh, Charlotte. I'm so touched you came. Nan was so fond of you.'

'And I of her. There's no way I'd have missed my chance to pay my final respects. I'm just sorry I didn't know her when she was well. She sounds like a formidable lady.'

Tom filed out last and it was a joy to see him too. 'Tom! You came.'

'I wouldn't have missed it for the world.' He seemed to realise he'd said this as though it was something he was looking forward to. 'What I mean is, I wanted to come.'

'Well, I'm glad you're here.' I turned to Ralph. 'Ralph, this is Tom Marshall. He's a . . . um . . . an old friend.' They shook hands politely. 'And this is my son, Dylan.'

'So I gather,' said Tom. 'That was some eulogy you gave there. Beryl would've been very proud of you.'

Dylan muttered his thanks and stared at his feet, clearly embarrassed by all the attention he was garnering.

It was only at the wake afterwards that I got to sit and have a proper chat with Tom. He was trying to cut into a Scotch egg with just his fork. 'Use your fingers,' I said. 'You know you want to.'

He smiled, picked it up and took a bite. He chewed it quickly and swallowed. 'I'm really sorry you didn't have a chance to find Violet before Beryl died.'

I hesitated, wondering whether to tell him that Nan had thought I was Violet. I decided against it. That was just between me, Nan and Charlotte and that's the way it was going to stay. 'Mmm, so am I,' I replied.

'You'll still go, though, won't you? To Spain, I mean?'

'Absolutely. It's even more important that I find her now.'

He raised his eyebrows. 'Oh?'

I brushed him off, not wishing to tell him about George just yet. 'I'll get Christmas out of the way and then go.'

He nodded over to where Ralph was chatting to Moira. 'Will he go with you?'

'Oh, God, no.' I guffawed. 'I'm not making that mistake again.'

Tom popped the rest of the Scotch egg into his mouth and tried to hide a smile, a knowing look in his eyes.

'What?' I said.

He wiped a napkin across his mouth. 'The offer's still open if you'd like me to go with you.'

I stared into his face, searching for traces of the teenager I was so in love with. He was long gone of course but as I gazed at him something stirred deep inside my rib cage. 'Thanks, Tom, I think I'd really like that.'

'Excellent, can I get you a drink from the bar?'

'Please,' I said. 'A pint of cider.'

He returned with the drink and I carried it over to where Dylan was standing chatting up a pretty waitress. I shook my head and smiled. Dear Lord, did he ever have a day off? 'Here,' I said, holding up the cider. 'This is from your nan.'

47

I hadn't exactly planned to spend Christmas at home. I'd honestly thought Dylan and I would be at St Jude's, making the best of it at Nan's bedside, trying not to think about the fact it would be her last. Home from Newcastle for the Christmas holidays, Dylan had complained that the house was not looking its usual festive best and I was inclined to agree. I should have made more of an effort but I just couldn't muster up any enthusiasm. I wrestled the artificial tree down from the loft and prised open its stiff branches. The fairy lights I had diligently packed away in a neat coil the previous year had somehow become an entangled mess entirely of their own volition.

I heard the front door open, followed by a set of keys being put down on the glass table in the hall.

'In here,' I called. 'You're just in time to help, Dylan.'

'Erm . . . it's me.'

I stood up, a string of fairy lights hanging over my arms. 'Ralph! For God's sake, how many times? You can't keep letting yourself in to my house whenever you feel like it.' I laid the lights across the back of the sofa and held out my palm. 'Give.'

'What?'

'I want that key back, now.'

'It's on my key ring in the hall.'

'Well,' I said, exasperated. 'Go and get it then.'

He slumped down on the sofa and started fishing through the box of decorations. 'I will, in a minute.' He held up a multi-coloured paper chain, somewhat crushed but nevertheless precious. 'Our Dylan made this in Reception. His first Christmas in school.'

I sat down next to him, smiling at the memory. 'He was so chuffed with it, wasn't he? Came running into the playground with it and promptly tripped over and tore it in half.'

'Bless him,' Ralph said, picking up a snow globe. He shook it and Prague Castle was temporarily obscured by a blizzard. 'Do you remember our first trip away together? Czechoslovakia as was.'

I took the snow globe and set it on the table. 'Yes, Ralph, of course I do.'

He picked up the globe again. 'Can I keep this?'

I grabbed it back, fully aware we were acting like two kids in the playground. 'No, you bloody well can't have it.' I clutched it to my chest. 'Did you want something, Ralph?'

He shuffled round to face me. 'I've been thinking.'

'Oh, God, you haven't, have you?'

He ignored my tone and carried on regardless. 'Why don't we spend Christmas together?'

I resisted the urge to belly-laugh. 'What? The three of us, me, you and Dylan?'

He opened his mouth to speak but the words seemed lodged somewhere he was unable to reach. 'Erm . . . no,' he managed eventually. 'I meant all of us. You, me, Dylan, Susie and the girls.'

My first thought was to dismiss this preposterous suggestion with an imperious wave of my hand. Then I thought about Susie wrestling with the turkey, her perspiring face crimson as the twins tugged on her apron, mithering for her attention, Ralph desperately trying to distract them, whilst I sat back sipping my champagne and chomping on a metaphorical cigar. On a perverse level, maybe there was some fun to be had.

Ralph obviously took my silence as a sign I wasn't keen. Then he had to go and spoil it. 'We're a blended family now, Tara, it would be natural for us to spend Christmas together.'

A blended family?

'No, Ralph.' I stood up and grabbed his arm. 'What would be natural would be for me to haul you off this sofa and throw you out onto the street.'

He frowned, no doubt wondering what on earth he'd said to warrant this outburst.

'We are not a blended family, you simpleton. You upped and left me for your pregnant secretary. There's no blending here.'

Ralph swept his hand through his hair, leaving it

standing on end, nutty-professor style. 'When are you ever going to let that drop?'

'Let that . . . let that drop?' I was so angry I didn't trust myself to say any more. 'Get out!'

'Come on, Tara, don't be like that. I was only . . .'

'Get out . . . get out . . . get out,' I screamed.

He was still protesting as I propelled him down the hallway. 'We could come here, I'm sure Susie could be of some help, set the table maybe, nothing too culinary, she's not the best in that department and I could . . .'

'Ralph,' I commanded as I picked up his keys. 'Shut up and take my key off that key ring immediately.'

He mumbled something about him being my next of kin and if anything was to happen to me then he should really have access to my place. I ignored his inane witterings, took the key and bundled him onto the doorstep. 'Oh, and another thing.' I paused for dramatic effect. 'I want a divorce.'

Dylan had graced me with his presence for tea and then gone off out again on some mercy mission to his friend Callum, who had been dumped by his girlfriend because she'd decided she would rather be with her steroid-enhanced personal trainer. 'He needs me, Mum,' he'd protested.

I needed him too but of course I didn't voice this. The day before I'd said goodbye to my beloved Nan, and tired as I was, I could've used the company.

I rested my feet in the hearth, watching the sparks rise off the new log I had just chucked into the wood burner. I closed my eyes, the tiredness crushing. Tears seeped out from beneath my eyelids as I remembered Nan. I hadn't wanted to leave Manchester and move to Lytham, but the truth is Nan saved me. I might have had to go into care had she not been there for me and who knows how I would've have turned out.

The doorbell rang but I ignored it. I wasn't expecting anybody and I certainly was in no mood for a debate with the Jehovah's Witnesses, even though they were usually so cordial and only had my best interests at heart. After the second ring, I reluctantly heaved myself off the chair. Tom was standing on the step, an apologetic smile on his face, a bottle of red wine in his hands. 'I thought you could use some company.'

I half-laughed, half-cried as I held the door open. 'How perceptive. Go through to the kitchen.'

'How are you?' he asked, easing the cork out of the bottle.

'I think my mood is best described as melancholy.'

He poured out two glasses and handed one to me. 'I've . . . um . . . been doing a bit of research. After the funeral yesterday, I couldn't stop thinking about Beryl and Violet and those days . . . and us . . . and well, I Googled that monastery.' He gave a small shrug. 'I hope you don't mind.'

'Of course not.' I gestured towards the fireside chairs.

'Come and sit down and tell me what you've found out.'

He settled himself into the chair, Ralph's chair as I still thought of it. 'It's still there, the monastery, home to around twenty monks, who keep themselves to themselves mostly, but they do produce soap and such like, oh and beer, would you believe? It all goes towards supporting the monastery. It's not exactly a commercial operation but over the last ten years they've welcomed visitors, although it's still relatively inaccessible to all but the most determined of tourists. The goods are sold in their gift shop and also in the nearby village of . . . erm . . . Bear with me a sec.' He pulled a piece of paper out of his inside pocket and put his reading glasses on. 'Here it is, yes . . . the closest village is called San Sedeza, which is in the province of Segovia.'

I'd already found out this information for myself ahead of my visit with Ralph, but I was touched he'd taken the trouble to look it up. 'Thanks, Tom. That's really kind of you.'

'I've also done some more digging around on the subject of memory loss. Br Isidore mentioned a brain injury resulting in some sort of amnesia in the letter and there's loads of stuff on the internet about that.'

He'd got my attention and I leaned forward, swirling the wine around the glass. 'Go on.'

He looked at his notes again. 'There are two types of amnesia, anterograde, where a person is unable to store and retain new memories, and retrograde, where a person cannot recall memories which happened prior to the injury. Well, I think Violet could have been suffering from retrograde amnesia.'

'I'm not sure that's right though, Tom. Br Isidore said she could remember things . . . disturbing things . . . from her childhood.' I took a huge swig of wine. 'She's referring to the abuse from George.' The wine left a bitter taste in my mouth.

Tom shrank back into his seat. 'Abuse from George?'

'Her own step-father. Nan told me on her deathbed that George is my father, although Nan had no idea at the time.'

'God, how awful, Tara.' He shook his head. 'I'm so sorry.'

The wine had mellowed me somewhat and I didn't feel like dwelling on the subject. 'Can we not talk about it just now? Tell me more about this amnesia thing.'

Tom nodded. 'If you're sure.' He consulted his notes again. 'There's something called Ribot's Law.'

'What on earth is that?'

'Ribot's Law targets the most recent memories first.' He rubbed his temple. 'You see, the neural pathways of newer memories are destroyed before older memories because the older memories have been strengthened by years of retrieval. So, in this scenario it is typical for people to lose decades' worth of memories from before the injury yet hang on to memories from childhood and adolescence.'

'Sounds grim.' I couldn't bear to think that my mother had only been left with such terrible memories. 'How could she function though, not being able to remember anything?'

'Retrograde amnesia is about forgetting events rather than facts, episodic memory it's called. However, sufferers retain semantic memory and are still able to make new memories.'

My head was spinning with it all and I held my glass out, even though I knew it wasn't going to help. 'I need more wine, Tom.'

He returned with the bottle and, after filling my glass, set it down in the hearth before continuing. 'Semantic memory refers to facts, general word knowledge, how to talk and what have you.'

He noticed my puzzled expression. 'I'll try to explain. Semantic memory contains information on what a rabbit is, for example. Episodic memory might contain information of a particular rabbit, meaning if you and Violet had had a rabbit, then she wouldn't be able to remember it, but she would still know what a rabbit is.'

In spite of the wine I began to realise the implications. 'And she'd understand the concept of a daughter but wouldn't remember she had one.'

Tom leaned back and slapped his thigh. 'Exactly! You've got it.'

I could feel the tears begin to build but knew I could not afford to let them escape. Once that particular dam burst there was no telling when it would stop. 'Are you still up for coming with me? To Spain, I mean.'

He raised his glass. 'Try stopping me.'

If I could have I would have jumped on a plane there and then. 'When can you go?'

He pulled out his phone and opened up his calendar. He scrolled away, blowing out his cheeks and giving an almost imperceptible shake of his head.

'I can go alone if it's difficult, Tom.'

'Don't be silly, Tara. I'm going with you and that's that. Beginning of Feb OK?'

I was hoping to go sooner, but didn't relish the thought of going alone. I'd waited forty years, what was another few weeks? 'Yes, that'd be great, Tom, if you're sure.'

'Absolutely. I'm away with the girls first week of January and then there's a couple of work things I'll have to move around, but yes, I'm sure, beginning of Feb will be fine.'

Christmas came and went exactly as I had expected. Despite Ralph trying to muscle in on my plans, the day passed quietly and without fuss. I relented and bought Dylan a stocking which he was delighted with, even though it was full of novelty stuff which would probably never see the light of day again. After lunch, we played Brag and toasted Nan with a couple of Snowballs. It was her favourite Christmas tipple and she would scoop round the glass with her finger, ensuring that she didn't waste a single drop.

New Year's Eve was a different kettle of fish. I've always hated it at the best of times, but losing Nan and the prospect of finding my mother again had put me in a reflective mood which ensured I was not particularly good company. Naturally, Dylan had a party to go to and off he went with my blessing. No way was I going to project my misery onto him. I was planning on having an early night, oblivious to the vacuous frivolities of this most tiresome of celebrations.

My phone buzzed and a text message from Tom flashed up.

Happy New Year! Fingers crossed it's a good 'un. What are you up to?

Damn. Although I hate New Year's Eve, what's even worse is admitting it and then having to confess I've nowhere to go. Why is there always so much pressure to say you're doing something exciting? I decided to stay true to myself and tapped out my reply.

Nothing much. Quiet night in.

His reply was instant.

I'm on my way! Xx

And just like that, my spirits lifted.

48

2019

Everything was laid out on the spare bed ready to be put into the suitcase. I'm usually a meticulous planner when it comes to travelling but I'd made the wholly incorrect assumption that it would be hot in Spain, even in February. Tom had put me right, pointing out that due to the elevation of San Sedeza, the average daytime temperature would be around thirty-five degrees Fahrenheit. It was actually forecast to be warmer in Manchester.

I took the mink coat out of the wardrobe and squashed it to my face. Despite the passage of time, it still smelled of Alf's hardware shop but instead of provoking the usual tears, this time my heart swelled with hope that I might just be able to give it to my mother at last.

I heard a tapping on the back door and frowned. Nobody used that entrance except for me and Dylan. I opened the bedroom window and looked down. As soon as I saw the familiar shape, I thought about pretending to be out. Bloody Ralph. Who the hell did he think he was?

He knocked again, more loudly, this time shouting my name as well. 'Tara, I know you're in there. Your car's in the drive and you never walk anywhere. Let me in. It's urgent.'

I ran downstairs, convinced something had happened to Dylan. I opened the door a crack. 'Is it Dylan?'

He frowned as though he had forgotten who Dylan was. 'No, let me in.'

I put my weight behind the door. 'Why, what do you want?'

'I can't talk out here on the step.' He cast a glance over the fence. 'You know what Nosy Nellie next door's like.'

'Whisper it then, because you are not coming in.' I impressed myself with my forceful stance.

'I've got nowhere else to go.'

Oh God, no.

I opened the door a fraction more and noticed a pull-along suitcase by his side. 'Don't tell me Susie's thrown you out.'

He shook his head. 'No, she hasn't.'

Thank Christ for that. My shoulders slumped with relief. 'Well can you get to the point then because I've got a lot to do. I'm going away tomorrow.'

'I've left her, Tara.' He managed a small smile and held his arm out wide. 'I'm back.'

In that moment I fully understood the expression *lost for words*. My brain could not come up with anything coherent enough to convey my utter disbelief at this incredible turn of events. I wanted to laugh, cry, slam the door in his stupid face, anything to block out the absurdity of his words.

'I . . . I . . . I mean . . . what?'

He put his foot over the threshold. 'It's cold out here, Tara, let me in.'

'Good one, Ralph. Now bugger off. You're on your own.'

'I've told you, I've nowhere to go.'

His pathetic tone annoyed me further. 'There's a Travelodge down the road, or you could go and sleep on that fancy couch in your office. I'm sure Mrs Blue Rinse will fetch your breakfast.' Breathing hard, but proud of myself, I slammed the door.

He pressed his face up against the glass. 'I'm still Dylan's dad, you know.'

I closed my eyes as I counted to ten, my fist covering my mouth. Then I could hold it in no more. 'You, you are not fit to be anybody's dad. It's a pity you didn't think about your paternal responsibilities when you were shagging Susie, or Anita, or Ruth or whatever the others were called. Don't make me laugh, Ralph, you are a pathetic excuse for a father and my only regret is I've lumbered Dylan with such a sorry waste of space. You make me sick, now go away and don't come back.'

I ran upstairs and threw myself on my bed, burying my face in the pillow to muffle my frustrated screams. I wasn't upset, there were no tears, just an immense rage that I had to unleash. I balled my fists and let my pillow have it.

49

The next morning I was much calmer, the only hangover from the day before being a sore throat. It was all out of my system though. I couldn't imagine why I had clung on to my marital status for so long. I was kidding nobody, least of all myself. I was going to be a divorcee and move on with my life. And it felt good.

Now I was free to focus on the search for my mother. I'd sorted through all my old photographs; the few that my mother and I had, some from school and some from Nan's collection from Lytham. The early photos were really hard to look through. The three of them, Nan, George and Mum when she was little. In one of them George has her on his shoulders, her chubby little legs wrapped round his ears. She's eating an ice cream cone which is smudged all over her mouth, but she's laughing and so is George as he holds onto her ankles. It actually made me feel physically sick to look at him, knowing what was to come, knowing that he was my father. I selected a few good pictures of Mum and Nan together in Lytham. I obviously wasn't taking any of *him* to Spain with me. There was a lovely one of me, Mum and Alf, standing outside his shop, arms around each other, squinting into the sunshine. Along with the photos, I had packed the locket and Br Isidore's letter, plus the article from the *Evening News* which Scotty Hamilton had kindly given to me. And of course, the mink coat. If we did find my mother, then these things could just be the key to unlocking her memory.

Tom turned out to be a most delightful travelling companion. Perhaps he was trying too hard, but unlike Ralph he didn't just plug himself into his iPhone during the flight and order one too many gin and tonics. Tom talked to me and more importantly listened to me. I told him I'd asked Ralph for a divorce and how liberating it felt. We talked about his late wife, Penny, and about his girls and I told him more about our Dylan. We chatted about the days ahead and how I would feel if my search proved to be fruitless. A question I was unable to answer.

Tom had already sorted out a rental car which we collected at Madrid airport and had mapped out a route to Segovia, where we were to spend the first night. All I had to do was sit back and admire the scenery, reflecting on the fact that I might just be on the same soil as my mother for the first time in over forty years.

Our hotel, situated just off the main plaza, was perfect for a romantic weekend which of course this wasn't. I could hardly forget the real purpose of our visit.

Tom held the door open for me. 'After you.' He took my case and followed me inside.

'*Buena noches*,' greeted the young man at reception. 'Is Mr Marshall and Mrs Richards, *si*?'

'*Si*.' Tom nodded. 'We have a reservation for two rooms.'

I surprised myself at the disappointment I felt in that moment.

After checking in, Tom carried my case up the winding staircase and handed me the key to my room. Not a key card, but a satisfying chunky brass key, that weighed the same as a house brick.

'Next door to each other,' he smiled. 'Shall we just freshen up and meet downstairs, then we can grab a quick drink before we head out to dinner?'

'Sounds good, say half an hour?'

'Perfect,' he replied before disappearing into his room.

I heaved my case onto the bed and opened it up, frantically scrabbling round for my toilet bag. I looked at myself in the dressing table mirror and came to the conclusion that half an hour was not nearly long enough.

Somehow, I managed it though. A quick shower, a fresh coat of foundation, some lipstick and a trusty clip to pin up my flat hair. I came out of my room on a cloud of hairspray just as Tom was locking his door. He looked me up and down. 'You always did scrub up well.'

We ate at a restaurant on the lively Plaza Mayor. Even

though it was gone ten, the square was buzzing with life. Entwined courting couples sat sipping their foaming glasses of beer, huddled under rugs to ward off the descending chill. Little kids played on the bandstand in the middle, oblivious to the dropping temperatures as they tore up and down the steps, the illuminated Gothic cathedral providing a stunning backdrop. It was a 'happening' place as our Dylan would say. Everybody seemed to stay up late in Spain and this was way past my usual bedtime but sleep was the last thing on my mind.

The waiter delivered our seafood paella in a pan the size of a satellite dish. Tom moved his reading glasses and mobile phone out of the way to accommodate it. The phone vibrated in his hand and he took a cursory look at the screen before biting his bottom lip and switching it off.

'Who was that?' It was none of my business but I couldn't help myself.

Evidently though he felt the need to explain. 'It's just this . . . um . . . woman I've been talking to.'

I sat up a little straighter but tried to sound casual. 'Talking to . . . you mean like a counsellor or something?'

'Good God, no.' He took a sip of his drink, obviously stalling for time. 'Talking to as in . . . you know, trying to arrange a meeting.'

'A meeting?'

He laughed. 'Bloody hell, Tara, do I have to spell it out?' He speared a prawn with his fork.

I shook my head. 'Yes, I think you do.'

The waiter appeared and topped up our glasses, respectfully nodding as he stood with one hand behind his back. 'The paella is good?'

'*Si*,' Tom answered. '*Si, es bueno.*'

'I didn't know you spoke Spanish,' I said when the waiter had gone.

'I wouldn't say that I spoke Spanish but it's nice to try and have a go. I think they appreciate the effort, don't you?'

I thought about Ralph, the absolute epitome of the idiot abroad. If somebody didn't understand what he was saying, he just spoke louder and introduced all kinds of ludicrous actions. I remember once we were in a particularly rural part of Greece and he wanted milk for his coffee. The perplexed waiter could only watch openmouthed as Ralph mimed milking a cow.

I shook my head to clear the memory. Soon Ralph would be history. 'Anyway, this meeting?'

Tom looked as though he'd hoped I'd forgotten. 'Oh . . . that . . . . well, after Penny died, I honestly thought I wouldn't find anybody else. In fact, I didn't want anyone. I know it sounds soppy and a cliché but she really was my soul-mate. Nobody could measure up to her, so what was the point in even trying?'

I swallowed hard, wishing I hadn't probed. 'Well, yes, obviously and she was the mother of your girls.'

'Exactly! How could anybody even come close?'

I ran my finger around my glass, producing an irritating whine which at least helped to fill the awkward silence.

'But . . .' continued Tom. 'Two years is a long time to be on your own, so I . . . joined an online dating website . . . with the girls' blessing of course.'

'Oh, OK . . . but . . .' I couldn't imagine anybody like him needing the services of a matchmaking website. He was the most popular lad in school and the best-looking by far. I could never understand what he saw in me. 'And, erm . . . this . . . woman. You've met her?'

He shook his head. 'Not in person. She lives about thirty miles from me. We've emailed and spoken on the phone a few times, Skyped once. It's just a case of getting our diaries together and seeing if we can make it work.'

'What's she called?'

'Geraldine . . . or Gerry, as she prefers.'

'So, it'd be Tom and Gerry then?'

He spluttered on his drink, laughing. 'I'd never thought about that.' He shook his head. 'Trust you.'

Not for the first time in my life, I was insanely jealous of another woman who had Tom's attention. I closed my eyes and thought about our first date to the ice rink when he'd danced with his cousin and I'd accused him of fancying her. I was mortified back then and I was determined I wouldn't make the same mistake again so I bit my tongue. 'That's nice,' was all I could manage.

He gave a slight shrug and held my gaze. 'Well, I don't think I'll be following it up now.'

The awkward silence was back. 'So, tell me more about your company. What is it you make again?'

'Valves.'

'Valves?'

'Yes. Ball valves, needle valves, double block and bleed valves.' He noticed my puzzled expression. 'For the oil, gas and petrochemical industries.'

'Oh, right.' I shovelled in a forkful of rice.

He laughed. 'It's usually a conversation stopper but I enjoy it. It's a good business and has provided me with a comfortable life style. I can afford to take a bit of a back seat. Get someone in to take care of the day-to-day things. Hence the reason I can afford to go away whenever necessary.'

'That's lucky for me then.'

He prised a stubborn mussel out of its shell and popped it into his mouth, followed by a good slug of wine. He looked at me from under his eyelashes, the whites of his eyes contrasting with his tanned skin. A grain of rice had stuck to his chin and I wanted to lean forward and wipe it away with my napkin but the gesture seemed too intimate. All of a sudden, I felt ridiculously nervous. I couldn't think of anything to say about valves, so I changed the subject. 'How was your holiday with the girls? Caribbean, wasn't it?'

'Turks and Caicos. It was perfect. So nice to spend time with them.'

'And how lovely that they still want to go on holiday with their father.'

'Ha, as long as I'm paying, they'll go anywhere with me.'

'Hmm . . . our Dylan's the same. Bless 'em, eh?'

It was gone midnight by the time we walked back to our hotel.

'Well, here we are,' Tom said, as he pushed open the door. We'd only walked across the plaza but my nose and cheeks were freezing. I headed towards the log fire in the hearth and held my palms out towards the flames.

'Here, let me,' Tom said. He took hold of my hands and rubbed them vigorously until I could feel the warmth returning.

'Better?'

I nodded, smiling. 'Better.'

He held out his arm, indicating the staircase. 'Shall we?'

'I suppose we should. Early start tomorrow.'

We stopped on the landing outside our bedrooms and he turned my body to face his, his hands planted firmly on my shoulders. 'Whatever happens, Tara, whatever we discover, I want you to know that I'm here right by your side. And if we don't find Violet tomorrow or even the next day, then it doesn't mean that we'll never find her. I promise you we won't give up until we have some answers, OK?'

His tone was gentle, so tender and caring that I could

feel myself welling up. 'That means a lot, Tom, thank you.'

He flicked me under my chin. 'Hey, come on. We go way back, us two.' He paused and looked me directly in the eye. 'We loved each other, remember?'

I'd never hated the use of the past tense more. 'Yes, Tom, we did. We loved each other.'

50

The medieval hill-top village of San Sedeza was quite simply breathtaking. We had to park the car in a tree-shaded car park at the bottom of the hill and walk the rest of the way, dragging our suitcases along the rough track until we passed through an archway in the wall which surrounded the town. The village was a ramshackle labyrinth of secret alleyways and cobbled streets, the ancient houses leaning in so much it looked as though a stiff breeze would bring the lot crashing down. The sky was deceptively clear and blue because in reality the early morning air was frigid. I pulled the mink coat tight across my body and turned up the collar. 'Wow, it's like a film set,' I marvelled. 'Absolutely stunning.'

After a great deal of searching alleyways, doubling back on ourselves several times, only to end up back where we started, we located the *parador* where we were to spend the next few nights. We were way too early to check in so we dumped our cases behind the tiny reception desk, strolled into the main plaza and decided to grab a coffee and a pastry before setting off for the monastery. I knew I was procrastinating because until somebody told me otherwise, I could hang onto the hope that my mother was still alive, somewhere.

The bakery, or *panadería* as it said over the shop window, was laden with a saliva-inducing display of warm bread and cakes: *pan blanco, pan rustico,* almond cake and apple tarts. I stood and inhaled the hot, buttery fumes, feeling the tickle of icing sugar at the back of my throat.

'I can feel my arteries closing up,' said Tom as he gazed at the jumble of sugar-frosted *churros*.

A young girl appeared from the back, wiping her hands down her apron. '*Buenos dias. En que puedo servirle?*'

I looked helplessly at Tom.

'Erm, *dos espresso, por favor, y dos . . .*' he pointed to the glass display, 'those things there.'

'*Leche frita, dos.*' She took two of the fritters, slid them onto a plate and dusted them with a puff of cinnamon.

We sat at a table in the window overlooking the plaza, the early morning sun slanting across the cobbles. An old stork's nest rested atop the bell tower and a nondescript black dog lay with its paws around a bone, licking off every last scrap of meat.

'Bit different from the old caff we used to go in, eh, Tara?'

My mind was elsewhere, wondering if my mother had ever walked around these cobbled streets. San Sedeza was the closest village to the monastery and the only village for miles around, so it was a possibility but by no means a given. Across the square a door opened and a woman came out, her red skirt swishing about her ankles, a white gypsy blouse tucked into her narrow waistband. Her hair was jet black and fell in waves around her face. There was no doubt about it. It was her. I jumped up from my seat and fled from the *panadería*.

'Mum,' I called as I got closer. 'Mum, it's me, Tara.' In my haste, I tripped over a kerb and almost crashed head-long straight into her. She held her arm towards me, a flash of concern across her face. '*Cuidado. Estas bien?*'

As soon as I heard her voice, I realised my mistake. 'I'm sorry, please . . . I just . . .'

I felt Tom's hands on my shoulders. 'Tara?' He took hold of my hand and guided me across the plaza and back into the sanctuary of the *panadería*.

I dabbed at my eyes with a napkin, feeling utterly stupid. 'I'm sorry, Tom. I'm so desperate to find her that my mind must be playing tricks.' I attempted a laugh. 'That woman must only be about forty.' I pushed the fritter away. 'Here, Tom. You'll have to eat it. I feel sick.'

I felt my mobile phone vibrating in my pocket. 'Who's this now?' I said irritably.

'Might be Dylan?' suggested Tom.

'Not unless he's run out of money . . . again.'

I looked at the screen, my finger hesitating over the button for a second. My face must have betrayed my shock because Tom half-stood and touched my arm. 'Who is it?'

'It's that private detective bloke, Scotty Hamilton.' I

wasn't ready for this and briefly toyed with the idea of letting it go to voicemail but Tom stopped me.

'Answer it then.'

The signal was not great and I missed a few words but I was able to get the gist of it. I thanked Scotty and ended the call.

'Well?' asked Tom

I took a swig of my coffee, my trembling hands barely able to hold the cup. My heart was beating faster than was good for me and I fought to keep the memory of Larry Valentine from spoiling my cautiously optimistic mood.

'Scotty's not found Larry, but he has found a relative of his. His sister-in-law, Carol Valentine. She was married to Larry's brother, Martin.'

'And has this Carol heard from Larry?'

'Nope. She says neither she nor Martin ever heard from Larry again; however, it transpires that Carol was the woman who spent the night at Larry's the day before Mum and he left on holiday. Do you remember the lady who really owned Larry's house telling us about the unmade bed and the lipstick on the glasses?'

'Yes, I remember. So Larry was in bed with his own sister-in-law?'

'It would appear so. Remember what he was like that morning? He was so late picking Mum up and she was frantic, worried he'd had a crash or something, and all the time he was in bed with his brother's wife.'

'Seems Larry had an awful lot of secrets. You were on to him straight away though, weren't you, Tara? You had the measure of him, you knew something wasn't quite right.'

'Believe me, Tom, I wish I had been proved wrong.' I stared out of the window at the now-deserted plaza. I hated thinking about that morning. The last time I ever saw my mother, I was as ticked off as any other fifteen-year-old who had thought she was off on holiday, only to find out that the invitation hadn't extended that far. We hadn't parted on bad terms though, Mum and me. I'd handed over the birthday present and wished her well. And I'd meant it. Hadn't I? I was sure I had. I genuinely thought she deserved some happiness. I tipped my head back and inhaled a deep breath. 'Shall we head off, Tom?'

He pushed up his sleeve and looked at his watch. 'Aye, we do really need to get moving. We've a bit of a drive and then a good couple of hours on foot to the monastery.' He pulled some euros out of his wallet and approached the counter.

The young girl took the money. '*Gracias*. You want . . . erm . . . take out? I can make for you?'

I patted my rucksack. 'No thank you. We've already packed something.'

Tom was eyeing up the almond tarts. 'We could take a couple of these, Tara. We've a long day ahead.'

Before I could say anything, she'd wrapped up two tarts and was asking if we needed anything else.

'These'll be grand, thank you,' Tom replied, stuffing them into the rucksack.

We left the *panadería* and made our way down the hill.

'What else did Scotty say then?' Tom asked.

'There's not much else to tell really. Carol wasn't surprised that she never heard from Larry again because she expressly told him he had to move on with his life. Carol was Larry's girlfriend but she left him and married his brother instead. He was devastated apparently.'

'Oh heck, poor Larry.'

I stopped and pinched Tom's arm. 'Oww, what was that for?'

'Poor Larry?'

He rubbed his arm theatrically. 'Sorry, I wasn't thinking.'

'Larry abandoned my mum on the mountainside, just left her there all alone. If Br Isidore hadn't found her she would have died and Larry would've as good as killed her.'

'We don't know that Larry left her.'

'Tom!' I was beginning to lose patience with this sudden apparent support of Larry. 'Where is he then? Where's the car? Where's his body?'

I stormed ahead, not waiting for an answer.

'Tara, wait, I'm sorry. I didn't mean anything by it.'

He caught up with me. 'I'm sorry,' he said again. 'I was just trying not to jump to conclusions, that's all.'

'I know,' I relented. 'And you're right, there's so much we don't know yet. I feel like I'm standing on the edge of a precipice ready to jump but not knowing whether I'll fly or crash into the rocks below. My nerves are shot but I shouldn't take it out on you, Tom.'

He aimed the car key at the door and the indicators flashed. 'Let's go and see what we can find out then.' He held the car door open for me. 'You ready?'

I slid into the passenger seat and stared at the winding road ahead. Who knew what we would find at the end of it. I looked up at Tom. 'Yes, Tom, I am. I'm ready.'

When you'd been married for as long as Ralph and I had, it was acceptable to drive long distances without speaking a word to each other. It didn't seem awkward or unnatural and it wasn't necessary to say something just for the sake of it. Tom and I drove along in a silence that was far from comfortable. The radio was playing but the cacophony of castanets and maracas was a little hard on the ears and difficult to tune out. I wasn't so much annoyed as slightly perturbed that he'd shown some sympathy for Larry. We had already proved that the man was a liar and now it appeared he was a cheat as well. I didn't waste one second feeling sorry for him.

Tom turned off the radio and rubbed his ear. 'Well, that was . . . um . . . different. Shall I see if there's anything else on?'

I looked out of the window at the fields rushing by, catching the occasional glimpse of cattle or goats grazing on the barren grasslands. 'No, it's fine, Tom. I just need a little peace and quiet to prepare myself for what's next.'

He didn't look at me, preferring to keep his eyes on the winding road ahead. He reached across and laid his palm on my leg. 'I understand.'

I covered his hand with my own, applying enough pressure to let him know that I didn't want him to remove it.

The road continued to climb and wind for several miles, until I felt quite bilious. I'm not the best traveller. In this regard, as in so many others, I take after my mother.

51

The track to the *monasterio* could only be undertaken on foot. Fortunately, there had been plenty of warning signs to slow down because the tiny rudimentary car park was situated at the tip of a particularly nasty hairpin bend. Tom brought the car to a stop in front of a rustic post and rail fence, the only thing separating us from the edge of the precipitous gorge.

We climbed out and peered over the edge, a cool but gentle breeze ruffling the trees on the opposite bank.

'Wow,' said Tom. 'That makes me feel quite giddy.'

I stared at the glittering river deep down in the canyon. 'It's spectacular, isn't it?'

Tom jostled the rucksack onto his back and took out a map, holding it at arm's length as he struggled to read.

I removed my reading glasses from the top of my head. 'Here.'

'Thanks,' he said, positioning them on his face. 'That's better.'

He studied the map, his finger tracing the outline of the river. 'It's quite straightforward really. We just follow

the river for about five miles. Can't go wrong. Shall we?'
He held out his hand to me.

And because it felt like the most natural thing in the world, I took hold of it.

The terrain was gently undulating rather than hilly but the stones underfoot were loose and the post and rail fence which surrounded the car park did not extend the length of the track.

'It must be somewhere along this path that Br Isidore found Violet, I guess.'

Tom was right. I stopped and looked around. 'How on earth did she get here by herself? It makes no sense. It's so isolated and she couldn't drive. Who knows how far she'd crawled?'

I quickened my pace, all at once desperate to reach the *monasterio*, to finally have the answer for which I'd been searching for forty years.

Heads down, careful not to stumble, we ploughed on until round the next bend, the *monasterio* came into view. We both stopped and gazed at the sandy-coloured walls clinging to the cliffs. It was situated on a peninsula in the river, surrounded on three sides by water, almost an island, completely cut off from civilisation. I couldn't imagine a more isolated place to live.

Tom pulled at my arm. 'Almost there, come on.'

We stopped at the even narrower track which led onto the peninsula, steep drops either side of us now.

'I . . . can't breathe, Tom. Can we just sit for a minute?'

My heart had begun to palpitate. It might've been the altitude, the exercise or perhaps just too much caffeine. Or the thought of seeing my mother again. Or finding out she was no longer alive. Suddenly I wasn't ready for the answers.

Tom sat down next to me. 'I know it's difficult, Tara. But surely knowing is better than not knowing.'

I leaned my head on his shoulder. 'I can do it, Tom. I just need to gather myself.'

As we edged closer to the gates of the *monasterio*, I could barely put one foot in front of the other, my mouth was dry and my throat felt as though it had closed up. The huge wooden door with its giant black hinges was firmly closed. Tom tried to turn the ring but it wouldn't budge.

'Let's go round the side,' he suggested.

We skirted round the crumbling walls until we came across another door, much smaller this time and slightly ajar. Tom pushed it open and I followed him into a small courtyard, with a covered well in the middle, the metal bucket swinging gently in the breeze.

'*Hola*,' shouted Tom.

'Over there,' I said, shushing him. 'There's the shop.'

'Brilliant,' he replied, making his way in the direction of my finger.

I yanked him back. 'Wait. What if . . . what if . . . my mother works in there?'

He frowned. 'Something tells me it's not going to be

that simple, unless you really believe in fairy tale endings. But if she is, then that's a good thing, surely?'

'Oh, I don't know, Tom. I'm not prepared for this. I don't think I can do it.'

'Do you want me to go in first?'

I nodded miserably, finding it hard to articulate my feelings. I sat on the edge of the well and watched as Tom disappeared into the shop.

Five minutes he was in there. I had bitten off four fingernails as I'd rocked back and forth, my whole body clenched as tight as a boxer's fist. I couldn't imagine what was taking so long. It seemed pretty simple to me. Either my mother was in there or she wasn't. Eventually, Tom appeared and walked towards me. I tried to interpret his body language as he came closer. A purposeful stride, a spring in his step, a slightly creased forehead but the hint of a smile on his lips.

I jumped up as he approached. 'Well, what took so long?'

'I've only been five minutes.'

'Sorry, I'm just . . . go on then, tell me.' I closed my eyes and waited.

'I talked to a young monk in there, although his English is primary school level so most of what he said was in Spanish. From what I can gather, he's only been here two years himself so he doesn't know anything about Violet or even Br Isidore for that matter, but he said if we come back in an hour we can speak to one of the other monks, a Br Florian. At least I think that's what he said.' He tossed his head towards the shop. 'It was a little difficult to interpret his hand gestures but Br Florian is either fifty years old or else he's been here fifty years. I'm not sure what he was trying to tell me. Anyway, after much stabbing at my watch, I'm pretty sure he meant for us to wait around an hour.'

'Oh my God, Tom. This could be it then. If he has been here fifty years then he's bound to know Mum.'

'I think there's a very good chance, Tara.'

He gazed up at the clear sky, at the huge birds soaring in pairs, chattering to each other. 'Now we just have to tread water for an hour.'

52

Br Florian was a tall man, broad-shouldered with a calm demeanour. He seemed to glide along as though beneath his robe he'd been fitted with castors. His English was passable although his heavy accent made him sound like he was speaking with a throat full of catarrh whenever he tried to pronounce his aitches. With his shaven head, it was difficult to tell how old he was but I guessed at around seventy. He ushered us into his office, dusty wood panels on one side, a floor-to-ceiling bookcase on the other. It smelled of a second-hand bookshop, cracked leather and stale ink.

Br Florian indicated two wooden chairs, stern and upright, not designed with comfort in mind. 'Please take a seat.'

He sat opposite us behind his desk, some sort of leather-bound ledger open in front of him. He closed the book and moved it to one side, which allowed him to clasp his hands together on the desk. 'You have a long journey, no?'

'You could say that,' said Tom, casting a nervous glance at me.

Br Florian smiled and nodded slowly. 'Erm . . . often, I . . . mmm . . . I think about this day. I think will I live to see it?'

I leaned forward, my pulse quickening. 'You mean . . . you've been expecting me?'

'I pray many times for it.'

'Did you know my mother?'

'I did, *si*. It was not me that find her. That was Br Isidore.'

'But you knew her? I mean, she was here for how long?'

'They leave here in 1981.'

'They?' asked Tom. 'Who's they?'

I jumped in before Br Florian could answer. 'Violet and Br Isidore, they left here together?'

I reached into my rucksack and pulled Br Isidore's letter out of the front pocket. 'This letter is dated 16 May, 1981. Br Isidore was about to take his solemn vows.'

Br Florian steepled his fingers and rocked back in his chair, shaking his head gravely. 'He could not do it. He left Monasterio de Justina after he return from England. And he take Violet with him.'

My mouth opened and closed. So many words wanted to come tumbling out, but I wasn't sure I could get them in the correct order.

Tom came to my rescue. 'Do you know where they went?'

Br Florian opened his desk drawer and lifted out a battered Bible. I had never seen a Bible that had been thumbed through as much as this one evidently had. From between the yellowing pages, he pulled out an envelope. 'This Bible, it belong to Br Isidore. He give to me before he left and I keep this in here to . . . erm . . .' He tapped the side of his head. 'So I know it is here.' He began to slide the envelope across the desk but before it could reach me I'd already made out the single word written on the front, the copperplate script ornate and reverent. Just one word. My name, Tara.

By the time we arrived back at the *parador* in the village, the sky was navy, one or two stars visible just above the horizon. Our cases had been taken to our room, just one room this time, with twin beds.

'Is this OK?' asked Tom. 'It's all they have.'

'It's perfect,' I replied, unlacing my walking shoes and flopping down on the bed.

I took out the note Br Isidore had left for me and read it again. Nothing profound, nothing sentimental this time, just facts. An address where he could be found should I ever pitch up at the monastery.

Tom closed the shutters on the window. 'We're getting closer, Tara. I've got a good feeling about this.'

I felt the same way but didn't want to jinx it by voicing my optimism. 'Let's see what tomorrow brings.' I patted the bed. 'Come here.'

He sat down next to me and I turned to face him. 'In case I haven't already said so, I'm glad you're here with me. I can't think of anybody else I would rather have by my side.'

And just so he was in no doubt, I leaned in and kissed him on the cheek.

53

I slept fitfully that night. I could hear Tom in the next bed, snoring softly, nothing like Ralph's pneumatic grunting. I actually found it quite soothing. I certainly had no desire to clamp a pillow over Tom's face. The hours crawled by, my head full of memories I hadn't allowed myself to think about for years. In the months after she vanished, I used to tell myself that by climbing into Larry's car that fateful morning, she had chosen him over me. It made it easier to cope with her loss if I convinced myself that she hadn't loved me enough, petulant fifteen-year-old that I was. For a short time, it worked. My grief and despair would be replaced by anger and a satisfying sense of karma. She'd abandoned her daughter and paid a heavy price. She'd got what she deserved by choosing a flaky, detestable man she barely knew over her own flesh and blood. Deep down though, I never believed this. My mum hadn't chosen him or abandoned me. I'd insisted she went even though I knew she didn't want to go without me. I've lost count of the number of times I wished I'd thrown a strop that morning, begged her not to leave me.

Neither of us could sleep long and by six o'clock we were both dressed and ready to go. The address we had been given was only a short walk away, no more than half an hour. Turning up on Br Isidore's doorstep after all these years was going to be shock enough, without dragging him out of bed. No, I'd waited this long. I could get through another few hours.

More pastries at the *panadería*, more coffee (as if I wasn't hyped up enough already), a walk around the half-asleep village, watching as the market stalls were laid out and covered with a rainbow of fruit and veg. Somehow, barely noticing, we managed to kill two hours. Tom held out the mink coat for me and I eased myself into it. I turned up the collar, the familiar smells from a lifetime ago almost reducing me to tears. 'Let's go,' I sniffed.

Br Isidore's homestead began with a wooden five-bar gate, leading to a deeply rutted track. Either side were paddocks, horses dotted around, their breath visible in the cool morning air as they nibbled on the grass. With every step my pace slowed but my heart quickened.

We could see the farmhouse with its low terracotta-coloured roof tiles and its window boxes, empty at this time of year but no doubt full of colour in the spring. It was rustic and quaint and all the things you might expect from a humble Spanish home in the middle of nowhere. There was a small garden to the left, the lawn there greener, as though it was tended to and not left for nature to take its course. At first, I thought there was a naked scarecrow standing guard but as we approached I could see it was a wooden cross with a small bush growing round the base. Obviously a grave. I shuddered as though someone had just walked over my own.

Tom nodded towards the cross. 'A grave,' he said needlessly.

I looked at him, not daring to voice my thoughts. Could it be my mother's grave? Would she have really been buried out here on unconsecrated ground? Had she come to love this place so much, it was her dying wish? I couldn't bear to think of her in the ground all alone, without other dead people for company.

We drew level with the cross and leaned over the fence. A name had been written across it, the white paint somewhat flaky but still legible.

'Diablo,' read Tom. 'Must be a dog or something.'

I blew out my cheeks, annoyed that my imagination had got the better of me.

The hinge on the gate made a shrill grating noise as Tom pushed it open just wide enough for us to squeeze through. A large hay barn stood on the left, the door ajar, a thin white cat displaying contortionist skills as it licked the tip of its hind leg.

'There's someone in the barn,' whispered Tom.

We stood and listened to the sound of metal clanking against metal, rhythmic and purposeful. Bang, bang, bang.

The horse gave a slight flick of its head as it saw Tom and me in the doorway. The man leaning over the anvil had his back to us. It was hard to know where to begin without startling him. This didn't look like a place that was used to casual visitors, especially at this hour.

Tom did the old clearing his throat thing. 'Ahem . . . excuse me.'

The man turned around, a glowing red horseshoe clamped between some long pliers.

'*Si, puedo ayudarte?*'

'Erm . . . *habla usted Ingles?*' asked Tom.

He dipped the horseshoe into a vat of water, the steam rising and hissing in front of his face. 'Yes, I speak English. Can I help?'

'Well, the thing is . . .' Tom began. 'We . . .'

I could stand it no longer and took a step forward, my voice stronger than I felt. 'Are you Br Isidore?' I held up the letter he'd written to me, as though I was a policeman with a warrant for his arrest.

He looked from me to Tom and back again, his mouth a perfect 'O'. He took off his hat and clutched it to his chest, leaning against the flanks of the horse to steady himself. He glanced at the letter, then stretched out his hand until it grazed my cheek. 'Is it really you?'

Incapable of speech, I pressed my lips together and nodded.

'Oh, Tara,' he said, as he stepped forward and took

hold of both my hands. 'You are really her? You know Violet?'

I fought to keep my voice steady. 'Yes . . . yes, I do. She's my mother.'

54

Br Isidore led us to the kitchen, all the while shaking his head, muttering something in Spanish that neither Tom nor I understood. I wasn't exactly sure who he was talking to but we both nodded politely as he took off his scuffed leather apron and asked us to make ourselves comfortable at the table. I took off the mink and slipped it over the back of my chair. I'm not sure why but I was expecting an old man. He was no spring chicken obviously, but he was lean and muscular, his face lined but still handsome in a craggy sort of way.

I clenched my teeth, holding back the one question I wanted to know the answer to, but hardly daring to ask it all the same. As Br Isidore pulled up a chair, I couldn't keep it in one second longer. 'Is my mother still alive?'

Br Isidore smiled and nodded his head vigorously. '*Sí, sí*, she is. I cannot believe this. You are Violet's daughter.'

I slumped back in my chair as the breath left my body. Even though I was sitting down, I could feel my legs shaking and knew for certain they would be incapable of holding me up. 'Where . . . where is she?'

Br Isidore glanced at the clock over the fireplace. 'Gone to town, she'll be back in a while.'

'Does she live here with you, Br Isidore?' Tom asked.

He nodded. 'Violet, she is my wife and I haven't used the name Br Isidore for thirty-seven years. My name is Leonardo Perez, but please call me Leo.'

I had so many unanswered questions buzzing round my head that it was difficult to know where to begin. 'I . . . I . . . what happened to her, why did she never come home?' I flicked a tear off my cheek. 'She had a daughter. Why did she never come back to me?' In spite of myself, I could hear the anger creeping into my voice.

Leo spoke softly and I wondered if this was a hangover from his days as a monk. 'You received my letter, or else you would not be here, so let me tell you my story. It's better you know the facts, I think, before your mother returns. Can you be patient, Tara? I promise to tell you everything.'

'Thank you . . . um . . . Leo. I want to know. Please take your time.'

He stood up, reached into a cupboard and pulled out three glasses and a bottle of brandy. My eyes flicked to the clock on the wall. We'd barely digested breakfast but who was I to judge?

Leo poured out three glasses and took a swig of his own, wincing as the liquor hit the back of his throat. 'I've been through this scenario so many times in my head and now that it is here I hardly know where to begin.'

His English was more than passable, although he tended to elongate all the 'i' sounds, *eet* instead of *it*, and he definitely had a problem with 'th'. Still, it was better than our Spanish.

'We're in no rush,' offered Tom.

'Thank you.' Leo drained his glass and refilled it. He gestured around the kitchen with his arm. 'This is my family home. I was born here in 1953 and my *mama* and *papa*, we had a holiday business. People came from all around Europe, especially England. I had to learn the language, I took extra lessons. Our economy was failing under Franco and so he reluctantly encouraged tourism to boost the growth. Our business, it was successful.' He gave a small laugh. 'We were never going to be, how you say, millionaires . . . but it was good.' He paused and stared into his drink. 'I was almost seventeen years old when my younger brother Mateo was born. The name means Gift from God. My *mama* and *papa* adored him and for me he was my little *camarada*, my best friend. I called him Little One.'

Leo pushed his fingers into his hair. 'Forgive me, this is difficult to talk about but it is where the story begins. It was the spring of 1978, the year I would turn twenty-five. Mateo was seven, soon to be eight. On the night it happened, I had been drinking.' He glanced at the bottle of brandy on the breakfast table. 'Not a lot, one or two beers, that is all. There was an argument between me and my fiancée, Gabriela. It was early evening, the sun was still up and Mateo was out in the garden with the butterfly

415

net I had made for him. He saw me come out of the house and called over to me, *Leo, look what I've got.* I could see by the flash of colour he had caught a Mazarine blue but I ignored him and got into the car. I saw his little face in the mirror but I didn't stop. I slammed the car into gear and jammed my foot on the accelerator.'

Leo pushed his chair back and reached for a framed photo on the mantelpiece. A little boy, grinning at the camera, his dark eyes shining from beneath long lashes, a front tooth missing. Leo ran his thumb over the image before continuing. 'In that moment of anger, I made a terrible mistake, one that will haunt me to my dying day.' He looked up at Tom and me, his voice wavering. 'I put the car into reverse.'

I gasped and clapped my hand over my mouth. Leo's obvious distress was hard to witness. We were complete strangers to him and yet here he was, allowing us access to his innermost demons. My hand shook as I picked up my glass of brandy, suddenly realising why it was there and grateful for it too. I took a calming sip. 'What happened, Leo?'

He shook his head, as he stroked his fingers over the photo. 'It's the terrible screaming I remember most. Gabriela had followed me out of the house and seen it all. The car lurching backwards and smashing into my little brother. The screaming brought my *mama* and *papa* running from the rear garden but I could not move. It was like I was made of stone, my hands stuck to the

416

steering wheel. The blood-chilling wail of pain my *mama* made when she saw the broken body of her cherished little boy, well . . . even today it wakes me from my sleep.' He returned the photograph to the mantelpiece and stared out of the window, but even from the back I could tell how difficult it was for him to relate this tragic tale.

'Mateo was declared dead at the hospital and a part of me died along with him. I vowed there and then that I would spend the rest of my life trying to atone for what I had done. I returned to the house to collect a few belongings. There wasn't much, nothing mattered anymore. The butterfly net was still on the ground and when I picked it up I noticed the butterfly was trapped inside. I carefully opened up the net and set it free, following the flutter of its bright blue wings as it rose into the sky. *Fly high, Little One*, I whispered.'

The tears were sliding down my cheeks as Leo turned around to face us. 'The butterfly,' I said.

Leo nodded. 'That's right.'

I picked up Br Isidore's letter, reading again how the Mazarine blue had landed nearby and led him along the path to where Violet was lying. Serendipity surely, rather than intervention from beyond the grave, but now wasn't the time to say so.

'Can I look at that again?' Leo held out his hand and I passed him the letter he had written thirty-seven years ago.

'I did not know what else to do. Violet could not

417

remember where she was from and what memories she did have were all bad ones. She was insistent that she did not want to return to England but I knew that someone was missing her.'

I opened the box and took out the locket. 'Because of this?'

'Exactly. I always hoped that you would be traced and given the key to the safe deposit box but after so many years, I admit I had given up on the hope.'

'Mum's name is Violet Dobbs, not Violet Skye. That's why it took so long.'

Leo sat down in the chair. 'Really, is that so? I've never heard that name before.'

Tom leaned in and asked the question that was in my mind but wouldn't quite reach my lips. 'What can Violet remember exactly?'

Leo lowered his voice, his fingers curling into fists. 'Bad things, Tom. Bad things. Her step-father, he abused her. At fourteen years old she ran away. After that, she remembers nothing.' He rubbed the side of his head. 'Here, she had a bad injury, I think.'

'It's true,' I added solemnly. 'Her step-father did abuse her and it resulted in a pregnancy.'

Leo looked directly at me, the realisation evident in his bewildered face. 'You?'

'I've only just found this out myself. From Nan, my grandmother. And for the record,' I added, a little too harshly, 'Nan had no idea.'

Leo held his head in his hands. 'Tragedies, everywhere.'

'Did Violet know you had travelled to England in search of her past?' Tom asked.

'No, I did not tell her, ever. She always insisted that the necklace did not belong to her. She did not know the name, Tara. And as I said, her only memories, they were bad ones.' He stabbed at the table with his finger to emphasise his point. 'Very bad ones.'

I looked at Leo's letter again, scanning down to the end. 'So, let me see if I've got this right. You went to London in 1981 because you were going to take your solemn vows and it was your last chance to find out where Violet had come from but you didn't tell her what you were doing?'

'That's right. I don't know why all she could remember was the bad things. She can't remember having a daughter, I know that.'

'Ribot's Law,' said Tom.

Leo frowned. 'Who?'

'It happens in cases of retrograde amnesia. More recent memories are destroyed before older ones. It can happen after a traumatic brain injury. I read about this woman in America who fell over in a supermarket, slipped on a rogue tomato, she did. She suffered a brain injury and lost twenty years of her life. She can't even remember giving birth and she has three children.' He shrugged his shoulders, almost apologetically. 'I've been doing some research.'

'Thanks, Tom.' I looked at Br Isidore. It was difficult to think of him as anything else. Ever since I had received his letter I'd had this image of a bald man, with a ring of hair just above his ears, wearing a long brown robe tied with a length of rope.

'Br Isidore,' I began. 'Sorry, I mean Leo. You didn't take your solemn vows though?'

'I couldn't do it, Tara. Violet had been at the *monasterio* three years by that time. We had grown close. I loved her in a way it was not permitted for a monk to love someone, if you know what I mean by this.' A flush of embarrassment coloured his olive skin. 'I was looking to God to forgive me, to save me, but Violet was the one to do it. She made me realise that I needed to forgive myself. Mateo's death was a tragic accident.'

'You came back here?' I asked.

'No, no, it was not possible. Too many memories and I thought my parents would not want me, and Gabriela, the girl I had left behind, she was here. I couldn't just disappear from her life and return three years later with another fiancée. No, we headed south and I found work as a blacksmith and Violet used to sing in a restaurant for the tourists. She has a beautiful singing voice.'

Tom and I exchanged knowing looks as we both remembered, and for the first time in days, a tiny puff of hope inflated my heart, just a little.

Leo carried on with his story as he poked at the fire. 'We came back here after my *mama* and *papa* passed away.

420

We carried on with the business, made a success of it. We are still full all summer. Violet is a fantastic hostess.'

'Did you have any children?' asked Tom.

I shot him a look. It had never occurred to me that I might have half-siblings somewhere.

Leo went over to the window and peered out. Seemingly satisfied that the coast was clear, he rejoined us at the table. 'Yes, we have a daughter, Sonia.'

'How lovely,' said Tom. 'Did you hear that, Tara, you have a sister.'

'Yes, I heard, Tom. I'm sitting right here.'

My immediate reaction was one of shock, which swiftly turned to jealousy and then anger. This Sonia had taken my place in my mother's affections. I was Violet's daughter, not her. I knew I was being unreasonable, so I steeled myself and tried to sound nonchalant. 'How old is she?' I did an admirable job of keeping my voice light and casually interested.

'Thirty-five. She lives in Madrid, works as a teacher.' Leo rested his hands under his chin. 'I'm going to tell you something now that I've never told a living soul.'

Usually when someone says this, my interest is piqued and I lean forward in anticipation of a scoop on the latest gossip. Not this time. I slid down in my chair, not sure I could cope with any more revelations.

'At the hospital,' Leo said, 'after Sonia was born, the doctor came to see me. He placed a hand on my shoulder and I thought he was going to tell me some terrible news.

421

I leaned against the wall, bracing myself. His voice was quiet but there was no mistaking what he said. "This is not your wife's first baby."'

'What?' I almost shouted. Tom laid a calming hand on my arm but I shrugged it off. 'Do you mean to tell me that all this time you've known Violet had a daughter?'

Leo looked alarmed and held up his palms. 'I knew she'd had a baby, I didn't know whether it was a boy or a girl, or even if the baby survived.'

'Why didn't you tell her? Don't you think she had a right to know?'

'I thought it would have been cruel. Imagine being told you'd had a baby but you could not remember anything about it.'

I stood up and slammed my hands on the table. 'My God, I . . .'

'Tara . . .' said Tom. 'Try to . . .'

I swivelled round to stare at him. 'Please don't say "calm down".'

'I wasn't going to. I was just going to say try to see it from Leo's point of view before you say something you might regret.'

'It is alright, Tom,' said Leo. 'I understand how this must feel for Tara. She has every right to be angry. She lost the most wonderful *mama* anybody could ever hope to have.'

I knew that, of course. I didn't need to hear it from Leo. Everything my mother had ever done was for my benefit. Even before I was born, she took action to make sure I would never know that I'd been a product of the abuse from her step-father. She made up stories about my real father being a boy she had truly loved, and spent the few years we had together protecting me from the truth. She worked hard to ensure that I wouldn't have to go without too much, often singing in seedy clubs where men would think nothing of pawing at her or making lurid suggestions. I know she hated every minute of it. Even when she met Larry, she was thinking it would lead to a better life for me eventually. I'd missed out on a lifetime of her joyful zest for life, her instinct to protect me, her wisdom and above all, her absolute unwavering love for me.

Leo had his head in his hands as I walked round and placed an arm across his shoulder. 'I'm sorry, Leo. I know you did what you thought was best for my mother. Please forgive me.'

He didn't say anything but reached up and took my hand. I understood.

We sat in silence for a minute or two, each of us alone with our thoughts, only the ticking of the clock marking time. The hinge on the gate outside gave its piercing whine and Leo looked up at me. He forced himself to smile. 'Your mother is back.'

55

Leo left the kitchen and hurried out into the yard to intercept my mother. I wanted to run after him but Tom held me back. 'Let him tell her, Tara. He knows her better than we do.'

'But it's not fair. She . . . she's my mum.' I realised I'd reverted back to sulky-teenager mode. 'Oh, ignore me, Tom. You're right.' I desperately wanted to peer out of the window but I'd got lead boots on. 'Take a look, Tom. What's happening?'

He looked out. 'I can't see anything. Leo is standing in front of her. All I can see is a basket of fruit and veg hooked over her arm. He's talking to her though.' He ducked down. 'And pointing over here.' He straightened up again. 'Oh, hang on, they're walking away, he's holding her hand, the basket has been left on the ground.'

I managed to stand and join Tom over at the window, catching my first glimpse of my mother in forty years. She was not as slim as I remembered and her dark hair was now silver and cut so that the soft waves finished just above her collar. We watched as they disappeared into the barn.

'What are they doing, Tom?'

'It was never going to be a quick conversation, Tara. Leo has a lot of explaining to do. We'll just have to wait it out.'

'I feel sick, Tom. What if she can't remember me? What if she thinks I'm an imposter after her money or something?'

He managed a laugh. 'After her money? Take a look around.'

He was right, of course. I was being ridiculous. 'Pass me that brandy, will you, Tom?'

He gave me a look that was just about the right side of judgemental. 'You sure?'

'Yes, give it here.' I swiped the glass but as soon as I smelled the brandy, I recoiled and set it back down on the table. 'Perhaps you're right.'

He peered out of the window again. 'Right, Tara.' He turned to face me. 'They're coming back. Are you ready for this?'

I closed my eyes and drew a long breath. 'How do I look?' I smeared my fingers under my eyes and fluffed my fingers through my hair.

Tom cocked his head and regarded me closely. 'Like Violet's daughter.'

The door opened and Leo guided my mother over the threshold.

'Violet,' he said, gesturing towards me. 'This is Tara . . . your daughter.'

As I stared at her, mute and no doubt open-mouthed,

the years rolled back. She may have been seventy years old but her iridescent beauty had not been diminished. Her skin was darker than I remembered and there may have been some subtle erosion of her once-sharp cheek-bones, but her eyes were bright and still framed by expertly crafted eyebrows. Her lips were stained ruby red and matched her long woollen cardigan. I immediately thought of Nan, and the regret I felt that she had not lived to see this day almost overwhelmed me. I felt Tom's reassuring arm across my back.

'Hello, Mum,' I whispered.

She pulled her cardigan tight across her body, her voice quivering. 'Hello.'

We all stood looking at our feet, nobody sure what to say next. The uncomfortable silence dragged on and I wondered who would be the first to crack.

It was Tom. 'You look well, Violet.'

A bit lame, but it was better than anything I could come up with.

'I . . . um . . . thank you.' She turned to Leo. '*Creo que sera major que me sirvas un brandy.*'

Leo took hold of her hand. '*Ven y toma asiento.*'

She was an older version of the person I remembered. There was no mistaking it was her but hearing her speaking in Spanish made her sound even more of a stranger. Although I had gathered she'd asked for a brandy and Leo had asked her to sit down, I was fervently hoping they'd switch to English.

We all took our places at the table and I decided to take the proverbial bull by the horns. 'Do you remember me, Mum?'

She stared at me, her eyes narrowing as she studied my face. 'No,' she said eventually. 'No, I'm sorry but I don't.'

'How can you not remember me?' My tone was incredulous rather than angry.

'Perhaps it would help if you tried to fill in the blanks, Tara.' Tom's calm voice was just what this little gathering needed.

I hardly knew where to begin but decided to leave out any mention of Lytham and Nan at this stage. I took out the photo of me, Mum and Alf standing outside his shop and pushed it across the table. She picked it up and stared at it before passing it over to Leo. I realised then that she had not seen a photo of her younger self for forty years. 'That's me,' she said, laying the photo down.

Buoyed on by her acceptance, I produced Exhibit B, the article from the *Evening News*. I read the headline out loud to her. 'The Skye's The Limit.'

She took the newspaper cutting and leaned into Leo so they could read it together. 'The Amethyst Lounge,' she whispered. 'I . . . can . . .' She rubbed her temples as I held my breath waiting for her to continue. She shook her head. 'I'm sorry.'

I pointed to the cutting. 'This is where you met Larry.'

She frowned. 'Who's Larry?'

427

'Larry,' I said louder, as though raising my voice would make all the difference.

Tom shot me a look. 'Tara . . .'

I understood and forced myself to speak calmly and quietly. 'Larry is the one who took you on holiday to Spain. All three of us were supposed to be going but he turned up in the wrong car and I stayed behind because I was obviously not part of his plan.'

'I don't remember.' She grasped Leo's arm. 'I don't remember any of this. Why is this woman here in my kitchen saying these things?'

'I just told you, Violet,' explained Leo patiently. 'I wrote to her, left the letter and the locket in a place of safety, should she ever be found. And now she has been found and she has come here to see you.'

Violet sighed but whether it was weariness or irritation, I could not tell. 'Where is this locket then?'

I nudged the box over to her and watched as she took the necklace out and held it in her fingers. She turned it over, read the inscription then prised it open with her thumbs. I could see her gazing at my young face, her eyebrows drawn together. 'This is you?'

'Yes. This is the present I gave you for your thirtieth birthday. You took it with you on holiday with Larry.'

'Alf helped her pay for it,' said Tom. 'He was so fond of you, Violet.'

'Alf? Who's Alf?'

I pointed to the photograph again. 'That's him. Standing

outside his hardware store. We lived with him in the flat above. He took us in when we were desperate, Mum. You must remember?' My voice had risen a couple of octaves.

'Tara,' warned Tom.

I remembered the mink coat. The sense of smell has an extraordinary power to evoke memories. I still have my primary school satchel and whenever I smell it, I am immediately transported back to my first day in the class-room. It had been raining and I'd stood helplessly in the cloakroom, unable to find my peg, my damp gaberdine heavy on my tiny frame. A boy with bright red hair, pale skin and a weeping cold sore on his lip stood in front of me and for reasons known only to himself, kissed me on the mouth. I was distraught. I was convinced he'd got some sort of lurgy that he'd passed on to me. I burst into tears and ran out into the playground. Oh, yes, one sniff of that satchel brings it all back in glorious tech-nicolour.

I eased the mink coat off the back of my chair. 'This is the coat that Alf lent you for your first gig at The Amethyst Lounge. It belonged to his late wife. He insisted you wore it.' I closed my eyes and pressed it to my nose. I was back in the shop, surrounded by firelighters, paraffin and paint stripper. I could picture Alf, half-way up a stepladder, arranging bottles of turpentine on a shelf. My heart ached for him, for me, for my mother and everything we had lost. I felt Tom touch my elbow.

'Are you alright, Tara?'

I sniffed loudly and raised my chin. 'I'm fine.' I held the coat out to my mother.

Slowly she rose from her chair and came towards me. 'Can I put it on?'

I eased her into the coat and she took a step backwards.

'You look *sensacional*, Violet,' said Leo, wiping his eyes. '*Maravillosa*.'

'Alf wanted you to have it,' I said. 'On his death bed, he made me promise to make sure you got the mink.' I choked out the next sentence. 'They were his final words.'

Violet lifted up her arm and buried her face in the crook of her elbow, inhaling the long-forgotten smell. She closed her eyes and swayed gently. Leo was on his feet. 'Violet?'

She shrugged him off, fled the kitchen and bolted upstairs.

56

It was at least an hour before Leo returned to the kitchen. I could tell by his pink eyes that he'd been crying. 'You can go up now, Tara.'

'Really, she said that?'

He nodded. 'Be gentle, Tara.'

With a solemn nod of my head, I picked up the locket and climbed the stairs. I pushed open the bedroom door to find her sitting on the bed, hands clasped in her lap.

'How are you feeling?' I asked, for want of anything more useful to say.

She touched her forehead. 'Confused, dis . . . dis . . .'

'Discombobulated?' I supplied, sitting down next to her.

She tilted her head and looked at me quizzically. 'Yes, that's right, although it's a long time since I've heard that word.'

I picked up her hand and spread her fingers. Starting with her thumb, I counted off the syllables. 'Dis–com–bob–u–lay–ted.' Having run out of fingers, I clapped my hands for the final syllable. Do you remember?'

'I . . . don't know, maybe.'

My heart quickened. Progress. At least it wasn't a 'no'.

'I know this is all a big shock to you, Mum. I can't imagine what it must feel like.'

'I've had a good life, Tara. I'm happy now. Leo is the love of my life and we have our beautiful daughter, Sonia.'

I bristled at the mention of her name. I couldn't help myself. 'I'm glad, Mum. I really am. I've dreamed up all sorts of scenarios over the years so to find that you're alive and happy is more than I could have dared to hope.'

'And you?'

I thought of Nan then and my promise to her. 'I did OK. After you left, I had to go and live with Nan in Lytham.'

I held my breath, waiting for her reaction. She flinched and clamped her hand over her mouth.

'It's alright, Mum. I know about George.'

'Tara, please don't say his name.'

'I know that you spent your life protecting me from the truth. Making up stories about how my real father had gone off to Mongolia with his parents to trap fur.'

She managed a small laugh. 'Did I say that?'

It was so frustrating. She recalled who George was immediately.

'What was the last thing you remember?'

'Leaving a house somewhere with my suitcase in the middle of the night. The next clear memory I have after that is waking up on the edge of a cliff, my head threatening to explode.'

432

'And no memory of me at all?'

'Tara, don't you think if I could've remembered, I would have been on that first ferry back home?'

I realised I was asking too much. I was that desperate for her to remember me that I was pushing too hard. 'You remember Nan though? Your mother, I mean?'

'Vaguely.' She gazed off into the distance, her eyes wide and glassy as marbles.

I squeezed her hand as tight as I could. 'Nan had no inkling at all about what George was doing to you, Mum.'

Parallel tears ran down her face. 'I hope she didn't.'

I felt around in my pocket, pulled out a crumpled tissue and waited whilst she blotted her cheeks. 'Nan would've believed you, Mum. I can absolutely promise you that. She was devastated when George confessed on his death bed. She felt she'd failed you, abandoned you when you needed her most.'

'I can't remember what I was thinking when I ran away. There's so much I don't remember. Sixteen years of memories were wiped away like chalk from a blackboard.'

I hung my head, unable to imagine what that must feel like. 'Honestly, I could not have had a better mum. I want you to know that. You and me were a little unit. We only had each other but it was enough. We survived because we loved each other and you were always trying to make things better for me. And when I went to live with Nan, I could see where you got it from.'

She stroked the sleeve of the mink coat. 'She sounds

like a wonderful person, Tara. I'm grateful that she gave you a good home, a happy life. It sickens me that my memories of *him* are clearer than my memories of her.'

I decided to have a go at lifting the mood. This was supposed to be a celebration, yet all we were doing was dwelling on the hideous parts of Violet's past.

'You have a grandson,' I said brightly. 'His name's Dylan, he's eighteen years old and he's studying to be a doctor. How about that?'

'A grandson? Well now that is . . . wonderful. Sonia doesn't have any children yet.'

I mentally chalked up a point to myself. 'I'd love for you to meet him.'

She swivelled round. 'Is he here?'

'No, no, he's back in England. You'll have to come and visit, you and Leo, you could come and stay and we could . . .'

She laughed. The same throaty sound that had filled my childhood. 'Steady on, Baby Girl, we've . . .'

I clutched her arm, making her jump. 'What . . . what did you just call me?'

She wafted her hand in front of her face. 'Oh, sorry, I don't know what I was thinking.'

'That was . . . that was . . . I mean, you used to call me that . . . Baby Girl. Even when I was a teenager you sometimes used it in spite of me asking you not to.' My words were coming out in a rush, tripping over each other in their eagerness to be heard. 'It was the last thing you ever said to me when you left with Larry. "I'll miss you, Baby Girl.'"

She turned towards me, scrutinising my face as if she would be required to recall every detail later. She reached out and smoothed her palm over my cheek, tears standing in her eyes. 'Baby Girl,' she whispered. 'Yes, I remember.'

Epilogue

The first stone hits his window with little more than a tap. Outside their voices are high and fearful, as they dare each other to knock on the door. He'll give it a few more minutes before opening it and letting them have what they want. He's resigned to the fact that it will always be like this, no matter how much he moves around.

He throws another chunk of wood into the fire, thinking about the choice he made which ultimately led him to this ramshackle house he's forced to call home. He could have stayed in that night and watched the new glorious colour television whilst drinking his boss's whisky. Or he could've gone down to the local snooker club and simply blended in with the locals. But no, he'd been distracted by the poster outside The Amethyst Lounge.

He coughs as the room fills with smoke. The chimney must be blocked again. His mind wanders back to the night that changed everything. He'd noticed she was being harassed, trying to fend off the unwelcome advances of some creep who had just bought her a drink. He'd gone to her aid, like the gentleman she thought he was. He had never meant for her to fall for him. He was living a lie and their relationship could never have been anything more than a casual dalliance. Carol was the one he was meant to be with.

He pulls the rug over his shoulders and nestles into it. He's cold but can't afford another log on the fire just yet. He gazes down at his hands, the fingers stained with nicotine, his long nails harbouring dirt underneath. The diamond signet ring has long gone, the Rolex too and the cash he'd taken from the safe. The only things he'd walked away with on that dreadful night.

He remembers the car going over the edge. He can still feel the air whooshing past his face and the feeling of weightlessness as the car seemed to float before settling on a ledge halfway down the cliff. It was almost dark, the smell of petrol hung ominously in the air and he knew he needed to get away. Violet wasn't in the passenger seat. He'd definitely checked. He was sure he had. But he was confused, disorientated and he'd panicked. It hadn't taken much of a push to send the car the rest of the way down to the river. The flash blinded him and the ferocious heat singed his face but he saw it disappear under the water, the flames doused, steam rising into the air. In spite of his own agony, he'd looked for her, calling out her name, even though his burned throat struggled to emit more than a croak. He spent hours looking, crucial hours he could have spent getting medical attention for himself. She must have still been in the car as he'd pushed it off the ledge. He had as good as killed her. He was too much of a coward to return to England and face the consequences of his actions. He would no doubt be looking at a stretch in prison for stealing the car, money and jewellery from his boss. He couldn't face going back to Tara and telling her what he'd done to her mother. He'd had no choice but to disappear.

He often wonders if he made the right choice. By now he would have paid the price for his crimes and been free to move on. Spain may be a vast country but there's really no place to hide. The tormentors always find him in the end. He's an easy target.

He runs his finger down his cheek and onto his neck where the scar tissue is thickest.

Another stone hits the window, this time with such force a crack appears. They will never leave him alone. As he opens the door, two boys cling to each other, their faces alive with excitement and just a little fear. He whips off his hood and watches as they both scream, tripping over each other in their haste to get away. Now they've found him, he knows they will be back and there will be more of them next time.

Only two days pass before another mob of boys creeps towards the hut under cover of darkness. The beams from their torches sweep across the grimy window and they realise to their disappointment that the monster has gone. All that remains is a dirty rug and dying embers in the grate.

As always, Larry Valentine has left nothing to chance.

Acknowledgements

There are many people involved in bringing a book to publication and I am indebted to the hard-working, inspirational team at Headline: Mari Evans, Jen Doyle, Viviane Basset, Vicky Abbott, Becky Bader, Frances Doyle, Hannah Cawse, Becky Hunter, Rhea Kurien and the Headline Rights team. Special thanks go to my talented and patient editor, Sherise Hobbs, whose insights and suggestions make for a better book. Thanks also to my agent, Anne Williams, for her guidance and expertise.

I am also grateful to Sonia Murillo Álvarez at La Academia in Cheadle, Cheshire, who kindly read the manuscript and corrected my Spanish. Any remaining errors are my own.

Thanks to my husband, Rob, who once again has supported me throughout the whole process, especially as my driver, photographer and translator during my research trip to Spain, and to Mum and Dad for continuing to tell everybody they ever meet that their daughter is an author.

Finally, to the readers who take the trouble to contact me directly, thank you. You brighten my days and keep me going. I want you to know I really appreciate it.

Author's Note

The inspiration for this novel came as the result of a family cycling holiday in 2017. Our trip began in the historic city of Segovia, about an hour's drive from Madrid. Although we only had to cycle around fifty kilometres each day, the terrain was punishing and the June heat relentless. Our accommodation each night was pre-booked and our luggage moved on for us. We were given helmets, water bottles and a map and then left to our own devices.

Each town or village we stayed in had its own charm and personal welcome but it was the tiny medieval town of Pedraza which impressed us the most. The town stands at an elevation of 1,073m in the Segovian foothills. We had to dismount our bikes and push them up the short but steep hill to enter the town through an archway in the walls. At the heart of the town is the main square or Plaza Mayor and it really was like walking onto a film set. I was so inspired by the place that I decided it would be a wonderful setting for a book.

The next day's cycling took us into Las Hoces del Rio Duraton National Park. The vertiginous limestone cliffs rise a hundred and fifty metres above the river which has carved out the deep canyon for centuries.

We consulted our maps and we were told we could make a ten-kilometre detour to visit the Hermitage of San Frutos, which stands on a peninsula in the river. After much moaning from the kids, aged 23 and 19, my husband and I got our way and off we set along a winding track made of nothing more than rubble.

After securing our bikes to the rickety fence, we then had to walk another couple of kilometres to the hermitage itself. The area is home to the largest colony of griffon vultures in Europe. The hermitage is no longer inhabited but it was here around the year 680 that Saint Frutos did penance with his brother and sister, Valentin and Engracia. The setting is spectacular and further fuelled my imagination. As we sat under the shade of a tree, enjoying our packed lunch whilst marvelling at the winding river below, I had no idea then that the Hermitage of San Frutos would become the Monasterio de Justina or that Pedraza would become San Sedeza.

Photographs © Robert Hughes

447

The Inspiration for
The Amethyst Lounge

Although The Amethyst Lounge is a fictional place, readers from Manchester and the surrounding area may recognise it as The Golden Garter in Wythenshawe.

The building is now home to Gala Bingo but in its heyday The Garter, as it was affectionately known, was the place to go for the ultimate night out.

The Golden Garter opened its doors for the first time on 7 October 1968, when none other than Bruce Forsyth topped the bill. Customers could enjoy a three-course meal, which would set you back fifteen shillings, (or seventy-five pence), whilst being entertained in the plush surroundings. The waiting staff all wore green and gold striped waistcoats as they catered for up to 1,400 guests. Anybody who was anybody, and plenty who had yet to make it, graced the stage at The Garter, including Dusty Springfield, Norman Wisdom, Eartha Kitt, Lulu, Bob Monkhouse, Tommy Cooper, Olivia Newton John and The Bee Gees. The final show took place on 27 December 1982 with a performance from The Fortunes.

For a longer trip down Memory Lane, visit www.thegoldengarter.co.uk or www.wythenshawe.btck.co.uk.